Three Italian husbands—tall, dark and about to marry!

Claimed by the Italian

Three powerful, passionate romances from three classic Modern authors, Diana Hamilton, Christina Hollis & Kathryn Ross.

D1637644

Claimed by the Italian

DIANA HAMILTON
CHRISTINA HOLLIS
KATHRYN ROSS

First published in Great Britain 2012
by Mills & Boon, an imprint of Harlequin (UK) Limited,
Eton House, 18-24 Paradise Road, Richmond, Surrey TW9 1SR

CLAIMED BY THE ITALIAN
© by Harlequin Enterprises II B.V./S.à.r.l 2012

Virgin: Wedded at the Italian's Convenience, *Count Giovanni's Virgin* and *The Italian's Unwilling Wife* were first published in Great Britain by Harlequin (UK) Limited in separate, single volumes.

Virgin: Wedded at the Italian's Convenience © Diana Hamilton 2008
Count Giovanni's Virgin © Christina Hollis 2007
The Italian's Unwilling Wife © Kathryn Ross 2008

ISBN: 978 0 263 89684 8
ebook ISBN: 978 1 408 97046 1

05-0412

Printed and bound in Spain
by Blackprint CPI, Barcelona

VIRGIN: WEDDED AT THE ITALIAN'S CONVENIENCE

BY
DIANA HAMILTON

Diana Hamilton is a true romantic, and fell in love with her husband at first sight. They still live in the fairytale Tudor house where they raised their three children. Now the idyll is shared with eight rescued cats and a puppy. But, despite an often chaotic lifestyle, ever since she learned to read and write Diana has had her nose in a book—either reading or writing one—and plans to go on doing just that for a very long time to come.

CHAPTER ONE

WITH a convulsive shiver Lily Frome wriggled her skinny frame deeper into the swamping fabric of her old dufflecoat. Saturday morning the High Street of the tiny market town was usually thronged with shoppers, but today the bitter late March wind and icy flurries of rain had kept all but the most hardy at home.

Even those who had gritted their teeth and popped to the shops for essentials scurried past her, heads downbent, studiously ignoring the bright yellow collecting tin adorned with the 'Life Begins' smiley face logo. Usually as generous as they could afford to be, because the small local charity was well known and approved of, today the good citizens of Market Hallow obviously weren't turned on by the idea of stopping for a chat or fumbling in purses for the odd twenty pence piece—at least not in this inclement weather.

Ramming her woolly hat lower on her head, her generous mouth downturned, Lily was about to give up and head home to the cottage she shared with Great-

Aunt Edith and report failure when the sight of a tall man emerging from the narrow doorway that led up a flight of twisty stairs to the local solicitor's office above the chemist's. He was about to head in the opposite direction, turning up the collar of his expensive-looking dark grey overcoat as he began to stride away.

She'd never seen him before, and Lily knew pretty much everyone in the area, but he looked well heeled— at least from what she could see of his impressive back view he did. Her wide, optimistic smile forming naturally, she sprinted after him, ready to spell out the charity's aims and efforts, and neatly inserted herself in front of him, avoiding an undignified head-on collision by the skin of her teeth, waving the collecting tin and leaving the explanations until she'd got her breath back.

But, staring up at six feet plus of devastating masculine beauty, she felt that by some freak of nature her lungs and breath would for evermore be strangers. He was the most fantastically handsome man she had ever seen or was ever likely to. Slightly wind-rumpled and rain-spangled dark-as-midnight hair above a pair of penetrating golden eyes had what she could only describe as a totally mesmeric effect.

It was so strange to find herself completely tongue-tied. It had never happened before. Great-Aunt Edith always said she would be able to talk her way out of a prison cell, should she ever be so unfortunate as to find herself locked up in one.

Her smile wobbled and faded. Transfixed, she could

only stare, her water-clear grey eyes sliding to his wide, sensual mouth as he spoke. His voice was very slightly accented, making her skin prickle and shivers take up what felt like permanent residence in her spine.

'You appear to be young and relatively fit,' he opined flatly. 'I suggest you try working for a living.'

Sidestepping her after that quelling put-down, his hands in the pockets of his overcoat, he walked away. Behind her, Lily heard someone say, 'I heard that! Want me to go and give him a slapping?'

'Meg!' The spell broken, her wits returning, Lily swung round to face her old schoolfriend. At almost six foot—towering a good ten inches above Lily's slight frame—Meg was a big girl in all directions. No one messed with her—especially when she was wearing an expression that promised retribution!

Her cheeks dimpling, Lily giggled. 'Forget it. He obviously thought I was a beggar.' A rueful glance at her worn old dufflecoat, shabby cord trousers and unlovely trainers confirmed that totally understandable conjecture. 'All I lack is a cardboard box and a dog on a piece of string!'

'All you lack,' Meg asserted witheringly, 'is some sense! Twenty-three years old, bright as a button, and still working for next to nothing!'

For nothing, these days, Lily silently corrected her friend's assessment of her financial situation. 'It's worth it,' she stated without hesitation. She might not have the most glamorous or financially rewarding job in the world, but it made up for that in spades in the satisfaction stakes.

'Oh, yeah?' Unconvinced, Meg took her arm in a grip only an all-in wrestler could hope to escape from. 'Come on. Coffee. My treat.'

Five minutes later Lily had put the bad-tempered stranger and the weird effect he'd had on her out of her mind. She soaked in the welcome warmth of Ye Olde Copper Kettle at one of its tiny tables, cluttered with doilies, a menu penned in glorious copperplate, and a vase of unconvincing artificial tulips. She placed the collecting tin with its smiley face on the edge of the table and removed her sodden woolly hat, revealing flattened, dead straight caramel-coloured hair. Her triangular face lit up as the stout elderly waitress advanced with a burdened tray, and she sprang to her feet to help unload cups, sugar bowl, coffee pot and cream jug, asking, 'How's your grandson?'

'On the mend, thanks. Out of hospital. His dad said that if he so much as *looks* at another motorbike he'll skin him alive!'

'Teach him to treat country lanes like a racetrack,' Meg put in dourly, earning a sniff from the waitress, who otherwise ignored her, smiling at Lily, nudging the collecting tin a fraction away from the edge of the table.

'Not good collecting weather! This place has been like a morgue all morning. But I'll be at your jumble sale next week if I can get time off.'

Lily's piquant face fell as she watched the older woman

depart. The twice-yearly jumble sale, held to raise funds for Life Begins, looked like being a washout. She voiced her concern to Meg. 'This is a small town, and there's only so often you can recycle unwanted clothes, books and knick-knacks. So far donations have been poor—mostly stuff that everyone's seen and left behind before.'

'I might be able to help you there.' Meg poured coffee into the dainty china cups. 'You know Felton Hall's just been sold?'

'So?' Lily took a sip of the excellent coffee. The Hall, situated a couple of miles further on from her great-aunt's cottage, had been on the market since old Colonel Masters had died, six months earlier. It was the first she'd heard of the sale, but Meg ought to know, working as she did for a branch of a nationwide estate agents based in the nearest large town. 'How does that help me?'

'Depends if you've got the bottle to get up there before the house clearance people get their feet over the threshold.' Meg grinned, vigorously stirring four spoonsful of sugar into her cup. 'The contents were sold along with the property. The Colonel's only son works in the City—probably owns a penthouse apartment, all functional minimalism, as befits a high-flying bachelor—so he had no interest in his dad's heavy old-fashioned stuff. And the new owner will want rid of it. So if you smile sweetly you might get your hands on some half-decent bits and bobs for that jumble sale. Worst-case scenario is they shut the door in your face!'

* * *

Paolo Venini parked the Lexus in front of the latest addition to his personal property portfolio and eyed the Georgian façade of Felton Hall with satisfaction. Situated on ten acres of scenic, nicely wooded countryside, it was ideal for the ultra-exclusive country house hotel he had in mind.

All he had to do to start the ball rolling was get the county preservation people on side. The initial meeting was scheduled for tomorrow afternoon. It should go his way. He had minutely detailed plans for the interior conversion to hand, drawn up by the best listed building architect in the country. Only he wouldn't be around to head the meeting himself.

His sensual mouth compressed he let himself in through the imposing main door. He was edgy. Not a state of mind he allowed, as a rule. His adored mother was the only living soul who could breach his iron control, and late last night her doctor had phoned to tell him that she had collapsed. Hospitalised, she was undergoing tests, and he would be kept closely informed. The moment his PA from his central London office arrived he'd head back to Florence to be with his frail parent.

Never lacking for life's luxuries, nevertheless she'd had a rough ride. Losing her husband, father of her two sons, ten years ago had left her bereft. Losing her eldest son and her daughter-in-law Rosa in a tragic road accident a year ago had almost finished her. Antonio had been thirty-six, two years Paolo's senior. Eschewing the family merchant bank, he'd been a brilliant lawyer with a glittering career in front of him—and what had made it even worse was the fact that Rosa had been eight weeks pregnant with the grandchild his mother had longed for.

Madre's talk—once she'd got over the initial shock of the tragedy—was now centred around Paolo's need to marry and provide an heir. Her desire to see him married. His duty to provide her with grandchildren to carry on the name and inherit the vast family estates.

Much as he aimed to please her, giving her his attention, his care, his filial love, it was a duty he had no wish to fulfil. Been there, done that. One embarrassingly disastrous engagement, from which he'd emerged with egg on his face, and one marriage that had lasted a mere ten months. One month of blinkered honeymoon bliss followed by nine of increasingly bitter disillusionment.

He would like to give his parent what she wanted, see her sad eyes light with happiness, watch the smile he knew the news of his imminent marriage would bring, but everything in him rebelled against going down that road again.

Unconsciously his frown deepened, lines slashing between the golden glitter of his eyes as he entered the vast kitchen regions, searching for the makings of a scratch lunch. Penny Fleming should have been here by now. He'd phoned his London PA first thing, instructing her to set out for Felton Hall immediately, having packed enough for a few days. He couldn't leave until he knew she was here and fully briefed about tomorrow's meeting.

Aware that an ear-blistering tirade was building on the tip of his tongue, ready to be launched at Miss Fleming's head the moment she crossed the threshold, he scotched the idea of lunch and took a carton of orange juice from the haphazardly stocked fridge. After he'd left the solicitor's this morning he should have hit the shops for something more appealing than the pack of dodgy-looking tomatoes and a lump of pale, plastic-wrapped cheese that looked as unappetising as it undoubtedly was, which he'd misguidedly purchased from a service station on the drive up here yesterday evening.

Well, Penny Fleming would just have to shop for her own needs—if she ever got her butt up here! He slammed the fridge door closed with a force which would have sent the thing through the wall in a house less solidly built, then expelled a long breath.

Edginess brought about by his frail parent's collapse, his need to be with her, his frustration at having to hang around, had already made him even more cutting then was usual when that beggar had jumped in front of him. He'd have to make an effort not to read the full riot act to his PA when she finally turned up.

Trouble was, his temper was never sweetened by delay, by less than immediate and superhuman effort in those he employed, or by fools and layabouts!

* * *

It was worth a try. As Meg had said, the new owner could only shut the door in her face!

Easing the ancient Mini out onto the lane, Lily waved to her Great-Aunt Edith, who was watching from the window, and set off down the tangle of narrow country lanes for Felton Hall.

Concern for her elderly relative wiped the cheery smile from her face as she steered into the first bend. Many years ago Edith had started the charity—just a small local concern—organising bring and buys, jumble sales, writing begging letters to local bigwigs, setting out her aims. She had relied on volunteers—especially Alice Dunstan, who had meticulously kept their accounts. Now Alice had left the area, which meant the accounts were in a mess and funds were dismally low. The people carrier—bought second hand, courtesy of a legacy from a well-wisher—was due for a major service and MOT, and the Mini was clapped out. The insurance bill was due—they couldn't operate without that—and she simply didn't know where the money was coming from.

And, worse than that, for the first time in her eighty years Edith had admitted she was feeling her age. The indefatigable spirit was fading. She was even talking of being forced into closing the operation down.

Lily set her jaw. Not if she could help it! She owed her great-aunt everything. It was she who had taken her in after her mother had died when her father, claiming that he couldn't cope with a fractious eighteen-month-old, had handed her over to his departed wife's only living relative and done a bunk, never to be heard of again. The old lady who had legally adopted her, given her love and a happy, secure, if rather old-fashioned childhood was owed her very best efforts.

If the Hall offered rich pickings next Saturday's event would be a success, and the hurdle of the insurance bill could be jumped. Lily's natural optimism took over, and she put her foot down, but had to stamp on the brakes as she rounded the bend, sliding in the mud to avoid running into the back of a shiny new Ford that was all but blocking the narrow lane.

Clutching the wheel with white-knuckled hands, Lily watched the driver's door open. A smartly suited thirty-something woman emerged and hurried towards her, her beautifully made-up face a mixture of hope and anxiety.

Anxiety won as Lily wound down her window. 'Oh— I hoped—I've been here for ages. My boss will be waiting and he doesn't *do* waiting! Roadworks on the motorway, then I got lost—took the wrong turn out of Market Hallow—and then I got this wretched puncture! And, to cap it all, I left in such a hurry I forgot my mobile, so I can't let him know what's happening. He'll kill me!'

The poor woman looked on the verge of hysterics, and her boss—whoever he was—sounded foul! Hiding a grin, Lily scrambled out of her old car. This elegantly clad secretary-type had obviously hoped for a burly man to happen along. Her hopes must have taken a nosedive when she was confronted by a short skinny female!

'No worries.' Lily let her grin show. 'I'll soon get you going again.'

'Oh—are you sure?' she asked, not sounding too convinced.

'Open the boot,' Lily offered firmly. To save on garage bills she did most of the vehicle maintenance herself, and had gone to evening classes to learn how.

Ten minutes later the wheel had been replaced with the spare, and the front of her relatively smart belted raincoat was covered in mud—ditto her hands and best shoes.

The morning's driving rain had been replaced by a miserable drizzle, so she wasn't soaked to the skin as she had been earlier. But her hair was hanging in rats' tails and she must look as if she'd been mud-wrestling! And she'd been at such pains to smarten herself up for her encounter with the new owner of the Hall!

But it was worth it when she was on the receiving end of a huge grin of gratitude. 'I can't thank you enough! You've saved my life! All I can say is I hope someone comes to *your* rescue if you ever need it!'

Finding her slight shoulders grasped, and a kiss planted on both cheeks, Lily could only grin as the woman drove away, then returned to her own car to scrub as much of the mud as she could from her hands and shoes with the few tissues left in the box. But there was nothing she could do about the awful state of her raincoat.

Hopefully, her unlovely appearance wouldn't have the new owner slamming the door in her face. On the whole people were responsive to good causes. On which strengthening thought, she turned into the long, tree-lined driveway to Felton Hall, her spirits rising when she saw the stranded woman's car parked beside a top-of-the-range Lexus, then wobbling as she recalled how the distraught female had said things that made her boss sound like a monster!

But she wasn't going to back away now. She grasped the iron bell-pull and gave a decisive tug.

Having waved aside Penny Fleming's excuses, Paolo Venini had handed her the architect's folder and the other papers she needed to review before the next day's meeting. He had almost finished succinctly briefing her when the ancient doorbell clanged discordantly. 'See who that is and get rid of them!'

Pacing the book-lined study, he glanced at his watch. The bank's private jet was on standby. It would take him roughly an hour to reach the airport—less if he really put his foot down. What was keeping the woman? How long could it take to open a door and tell whoever was standing there to go away?

He had all the instincts of a high-achiever, and aggression in the face of tardiness and delay was one of them. It drew his dark brows down in a frown, which deepened as a conciliatory-looking Penny Fleming emerged from the doorway with that grubby beggar-girl in tow!

Exasperated, Paolo drew in a deep breath, about to tell his usually robotically efficient PA that unless she got her act together she would be fired, and to remember

that he didn't give that warning twice. But, no doubt to
forestall the expected verbal onslaught, she rushed in.

'This is Lily. She works for a local charity. Is there
anything she could take for a jumble sale?'

Madonna diavola! He was beset by fools! And the
creature he'd clearly mistaken for a beggar this morning
looked like a charity case herself!

But he was not an ungenerous man. He gave handsomely to many worthy causes.

He addressed the scrawny, mud-stained female.
'What is the charity?'

Lily swallowed. This was the drop-dead gorgeous
guy who had had such a weird effect on her this
morning. He might be fantastic to look at, but, boy, did
those eyes turn into shards of gold ice as he looked at
her! He probably had a heart of pure ice to match!

When Penny, as she'd named herself, had opened the
door and listened to her request with evident sympathy,
Lily's confidence had soared. Especially when Penny
informed her in a whisper that she believed her boss was
indeed unlikely to want to keep the contents of the
house, and one good turn deserved another so she'd see
what she could do.

Lily could see he was impatient. That sensual mouth
had compressed above a rock-solid jaw. He probably
didn't *do* patience either!

She answered belatedly, but as firmly as she could.
'My great-aunt started Life Begins ten years ago. I help.'
Encouraged by the way Penny gave her elbow a squeeze,

she ploughed on. 'We help old people locally. Practical stuff, like shopping, cleaning, helping them stay in their own homes if they fall outside the social security net, driving—'

'*Basta!* Enough.' He slashed through the increasingly confident spiel. She had amazing eyes. Clear. Innocent. Honest. And the quickest way to get back to serious matters was to just let her have what she wanted. 'Wait in the hall. When she is free, Miss Fleming will help you decide what's suitable.'

Dismissed from The Presence. Heartfelt words of thanks tripped from her widely smiling mouth as she backed out of the room. But he wasn't listening—was already turning to answer the phone that had begun to ring. Telling herself that she didn't care, didn't mind being got rid of as if she were a really insignificant and annoying irritant, Lily waited as directed. She had got what she'd come for. His permission to walk away with the sort of stuff that would persuade the punters to part with their hard-earned cash and put Life Begins in a slightly more viable financial position.

His eyes haunted, Paolo ended the call, ignored Penny Fleming's 'Are you all right, sir?' and strode from the study, his mind made up.

There was only one thing to do. As always, when presented with a problem, his agile brain came up with the solution at the speed of light.

The consultant's call had confirmed his worst fears—fears that gripped his heart in an icy fist. His mother didn't have long to live. That had been the underlying message he'd picked up from behind the medical jargon. He would make her last hours on this earth happy. It was the least he could do.

And that scruffy charity worker would be stupid to turn down a decent donation in return for helping him out.

CHAPTER TWO

HAD he changed his mind? Lily questioned uneasily as, with her elbow held in a grip of steel, she was as good as frogmarched back into the study.

Had he suddenly decided she was up to no good, intent on emptying his house and making off with the proceeds in the name of some fictitious charity?

She certainly felt uncomfortably like a criminal as he curtly dismissed his PA and commanded her to 'Sit!' as if he were training a disobedient dog.

Lily's face flushed scarlet. Who did he think he was? 'Now, look here—'

But one killing flash of those golden eyes silenced her, had her obeying, perching on the edge of the chair in front of the huge desk. As if satisfied by her compliance, he strode to the other side, but didn't sit. Just loomed.

He was looking at her as if she were some previously undiscovered life form. Lily squirmed.

'Are you trustworthy?'

Taken aback, Lily gaped. So she was right—he thought she was a conwoman!

'Well?'

Of all the nasty, ill-tempered, suspicious—! Affronted now, she lifted her pointed chin, her eyes cooling to glacial grey, and gave him a dignified reply. 'Of course I'm trustworthy. I'll only take what Penny says I may. And if you want to check my credentials—'

A slashing movement of one lean, long-fingered hand effectively silenced her again. 'Take what you like. This isn't about that. I want to know if, in return for a sizeable donation to your charity, you will allow me to use your name and keep silent about the transaction—now and in the future.'

Lily's eyes widened in astonishment, her soft mouth dropping open. 'Use my name?' Staring at the forceful set of his jaw, those mesmerisingly beautiful eyes, the harsh slant of his cheekbones and the way his sensual mouth was clamped in irritation, she could only imagine he'd either gone mad or was embroiled in some dodgy scheme or other.

Whichever, she wanted no part of it! 'What on earth for?' she demanded, unconsciously aping her great-aunt's stentorian tone—the tone used to great effect on the rare occasions when the forthright old lady was displeased.

One sable eyebrow rose in amazement that such imperious volume could issue from such a scrawny scrap of a thing. A disarming hint of a smile appeared, and two hands were expressively spread.

'I don't have time to go into detail. But last night my mother collapsed. Hospital tests reveal she has a brain tumour. The operation takes place the day after tomorrow. The prognosis isn't good. In fact, it couldn't be much worse,' he announced heavily, the glittering gold of his magnificent eyes now shadowed by thickly fringed black lashes, deep lines scored on either side of his handsome mouth.

Lily got to her feet, instinctively leaning towards him, her voice soft, her huge eyes brimming with sympathy, seeking his. 'Oh—poor you! You must be so worried! No wonder you're in such a bad mood,' she declared forgivingly. 'But it's amazing what surgeons can do these days. You mustn't give up hope! Really you mustn't!'

'Spare me the platitudes.' He shot her a look of brusque impatience. 'Let's cut to the chase.'

So he couldn't take sympathy, Lily decided. That figured. He probably couldn't give it, either. And that reminded her that she still didn't have a clue what he'd been on about when he'd offered a donation in return for the use of her name. She flopped down again. Why *her* name, for pity's sake?

'My mother's dearest wish is to see me married and producing an heir to the family wealth. That I show no signs of doing so is a source of deep distress to her and I regret that,' he supplied flatly, 'but for reasons which are none of your business marriage is a state I have no desire to enter. However, to make what might well be her last days happy I intend to tell her I've fallen in love and am engaged to a woman I met in England.'

For a long moment Lily couldn't believe her ears. 'You'd lie to your own mother! How immoral can you get?'

He shot her a look of withering contempt. 'It doesn't please me to do it, but it would please her. That, and only that, is the point.'

Those stunning features were riven with pain, and Lily's soft heart melted. 'I suppose I can see why you think a white lie's forgivable in the circumstances,' she offered falteringly, not quite sure she totally agreed. But the poor man was hurting. He clearly thought the world of his very ill mother, and the awful news had shaken him. He wasn't thinking straight, hence his crazy plan.

'Listen, have you considered the possibility that the operation might well be a success?' she asked softly, pointing out something she was sure couldn't have occurred to him. 'Then you'd have to tell more lies, say you'd broken the engagement. She'd want to know why—and she'd be even more upset.' She noted the ferocious frown line between his eyes, but continued understandingly, 'I expect you're in shock after that news, and that's stopping you from thinking logically.'

Paolo gritted his strong teeth. She was seriously irritating him. Obviously a creature with the attention span of a gad-fly—veering from bristling moral outrage to saccharine triteness in the flicker of her impressively long eyelashes.

When he put forward a proposition he expected the recipient to sit quietly, hear him out and reach a conclusion based on the facts as offered. Most typically *his* conclusion.

A slash of colour washed his strong cheekbones as he spelled out through gritted teeth, 'Without the operation she will die. Fact. With it, the chances of her pulling through are slim. Fact. She is seventy years old and not strong at the best of times,' he imparted grimly. 'My mind's made up. All you have to do is agree to my request.'

'I'm not comfortable with it,' Lily confided earnestly. 'If you really do intend to do this couldn't you invent a name? Any name?'

Resisting the impulse to pick her up and throw her out, he confessed austerely, 'I deal in facts and figures, not make-believe. A real woman's name I would remember. A name I made up might slip my memory in the grip of emotion.' Not something he was overjoyed to admit to even to himself, let alone this hugely annoying creature. He shot a dark look at his watch and demanded lethally, 'Well?'

Lily took a deep breath. He was clearly set on going through with it. Nothing she'd said had stood a chance of changing his mind. And it had touched her deeply when he'd made that remark about worrying he'd forget a made-up name if he got emotional. His conversations with his mother prior to her operation would be highly emotional for both of them.

Shrugging her slim shoulders resignedly, she gave in. 'OK. I agree.'

'And total secrecy?'

'Of course.' How could he ask that? 'It's not something I'd remotely want to have known!'

'And?' Irritated beyond endurance by her holier-than-thou attitude towards what was, after all, a kindness to a desperately ill woman, he grated. 'Your name? Lily *what*?'

'Oh!' Her face flamed. He must think she was an idiot! 'It's Frome. Lily Frome. Shouldn't you write that down?' she suggested, as he just stared at her, making her feel ridiculously squirmy inside.

'No need. As I told you, I never forget facts. How tall are you?'

'Why?'

'Because Madre will ask what you look like,' he grated through his teeth, as if talking to a child with the IQ of a snail.

'Five foot one and a half,' Lily muttered, as he withdrew a chequebook from one of the desk drawers and began to write.

He slid the cheque over the desktop, his eyes lifting as he enumerated, 'Big grey eyes, small nose...' he drew the line at voicing that, come to think of it, she had a totally luscious pink mouth. 'Hair the colour of—*caramella*.' He almost smiled before inborn practicality and self-possession kicked in. '*Arrivederci*, Lily Frome.' He extracted car keys from the pocket of his beautifully tailored suit trousers. 'I have a flight to catch. Miss Fleming's somewhere around. She will look after you.'

And he was gone. Leaving Lily staring at his cheque for five thousand pounds and wallowing in the sense of unreality which was swamping her, because the happenings of the last twenty minutes were totally weird.

Two weeks later, at just after ten o'clock, Lily gave her last passenger a cheery 'Goodnight!' after seeing her safely inside her home—one of a pair of former labourer's cottages—and clambered back into the people carrier, expelling a sigh of exhaustion.

It had been a long day, following a long night spent trying to put the accounts in order. She started the engine and set off through the dark lanes for home. The usual sort of day. Organising the two willing volunteers, visiting the housebound, doing chores they couldn't manage themselves, drinking tea and chatting, driving old Mr Jenkins to his doctor's appointment.

It was worth it, though. Even if ferrying eleven senior citizens with no transport of their own to the monthly whist drive in Market Hallow's sports centre and back to their homes again was time consuming, the pleasure the old people got from the outing, from socialising with friends over tea and biscuits, made every minute special. After all, one of the charity's main aims was to alleviate loneliness and isolation.

And thanks to Paolo Venini's generous cheque—plus the jumble sale, which had raised a record level of funds—they were managing to carry on. At least the financial crisis was over for the time being. But they would have to advertise for more volunteers in the parish magazine. She and their two part-time volunteers couldn't do everything.

Shelving that downbeat observation, she wondered how Paolo's mother was, if the operation had been a success, and immediately conjured up an image of his spectacular, totally unforgettable features. He often occupied her thoughts—which was natural, she excused herself. Without that strange encounter the charity would probably have folded.

And it was not, definitely not because she fancied him, as Penny Fleming had dryly commented when, driven by something more than mere nosiness, Lily had bombarded her with questions about her boss.

'Females have a habit of going weak at the knees around him,' Penny had cautioned. 'But there's no mileage in it. He's the take 'em and leave 'em type. With one broken engagement behind him he upped and married a French actress, but got rid of her before their first anniversary. I don't know the ins and outs, but my guess is he was bored. That's my opinion anyway, because no woman's lasted more than a few weeks since then. His dumped wife died of an overdose a couple of months later, poor thing. If you fancy him you're on a hiding to nothing, believe me!'

'I don't fancy him!' Chilled by that last revelation,

Lily had protested tartly. 'In any case, I'll never set eyes on him again!'

The obvious truth of that state of affairs had left her feeling oddly regretful—a feeling that stubbornly persisted. Which was why when, yawning widely, she finally let herself into the cottage and found Paolo Venini sitting with Great-Aunt Edith in front of the parlour fire, her heart felt as if it was exploding within her under-endowed breast.

'Miss Frome—' He rose to his feet, spectacular in a beautifully tailored pale grey suit, crisp white shirt and dark grey tie, the image of the highly successful merchant banker detailed on the internet. Handsome, powerful, charismatic. And heartless?

Her knees weakening shamefully, swamped by the effect he always seemed to have on her, she got out thinly, 'What are *you* doing here?' and received her great-aunt's curt rebuke.

'Manners, Lily. Manners! Our benefactor has introduced himself to me and has been waiting for you.' She heaved her solid tweed and twin-setted bulk out of the armchair. 'Signor Venini has a proposal which, in my firm opinion, is the generous answer to all Life Begin's future difficulties. Listen to what he has to say. It will mean changes.' She smiled at the tall Italian. 'But then nothing stays the same. Onward and forward—or stagnate!'

On which typical rallying cry the old lady excused herself and retired for the night, leaving Lily wondering what the strictly principled lady would say if she knew exactly *why* their 'benefactor' had made that hefty donation.

And his new proposal—whatever it was—would have heavy strings attached. Strings her upright great-aunt would have no knowledge of! If the hard-nosed banker gave he would undoubtedly want something in return.

'So?' Suspicion glinted in her eyes, and her slender frame was rigid—until he smiled. It was like a bolt of lightning, setting up a tidal wave of tingling reaction. His impossible sexiness, *sinful* sexiness, took her breath away, and made her deeply ashamed of reacting like all those other gullible females Penny had talked about.

'We shall sit,' he announced, with infuriatingly cool calm, looking incredibly exotic against the old-fashioned background of the shabby parlour with its Victorian clutter.

Sinking into the armchair her elderly relative had recently vacated—not because he'd told her to but because in his vicinity her legs felt disgracefully wobbly—she found her breath hard to catch, because his sheer presence seemed to suck all the air out of the room. His gaze held her mesmerised as he took the chair on the opposite side of the dying fire, leaning back, elbows on the arms, lean hands steepled in front of his handsome mouth, those golden eyes still smiling with speech-stealing warmth at her.

'Your great-aunt has quite the reputation,' he stated. 'A formidable woman with admirable charitable ethics, yes? Tirelessly working for the benefit of others over the years. She now deserves to rest. Yes, again?'

The softly accented flow of words reached a pause. He was obviously waiting for her response, her full agreement. Lily pressed her lips together. She would be a fool to trust a purring tiger!

Paolo lowered his hands, dropped them loosely between his knees and leaned forward. His slow smile was decidedly dangerous.

Lily's tension level racked up a few more notches. He didn't have the look of a recently bereaved loving son. Her suspicions hardened.

'Nothing to say? As I recall, on our previous encounter you were—to put it politely—remarkably chatty.'

Gabby, he had mentally named her. In less fraught circumstances he might even have found her chatter amusing. But now she was as animated as a stone, her small triangular face pale, dark smudges of fatigue beneath wary grey eyes, her slight body, clad in well-worn denims and a tired-looking fleece, tensely held. Her hair, scraped back in an unflattering ponytail, made her look younger than what he now knew to be her twenty-three years.

He gave her an encouraging smile, confident that, as always, he had reached the right decision and that, having done so, his strength of character and dominant will would prevail.

In receipt of another of those nerve-tingling smiles, Lily felt her mouth run dry, but she finally managed, 'Why are you here?'

'Of course—the proposal I put to your great-aunt,'

he slid in smoothly. 'You may not know it, but I, both personally and corporately, donate huge sums to worthwhile charities. Now, Life Begins is worthwhile, but it is seriously underfunded and understaffed. You stagger from one financial crisis to another, and your great-aunt is no longer young enough to do much. You rely on two part-time volunteers. The rest you somehow manage yourself—cleaning, shopping, driving the old and infirm to hospital appointments, organising outings. Need I go on?'

Lily's chin firmed. Penny must have told him all this stuff. In the short time that the older woman had been at Felton Hall they'd become very friendly, and she'd told her a lot about the charity.

'You've been talking to Penny,' she stated flatly.

Was he about to offer to make another donation? Her nerves skittered. What would he ask of her in return? Or was her tiredness making her paranoid? Perhaps he genuinely wanted to help and there would be no unpleasant strings—like making her agree to be part of a lie. He'd already said he donated generously to many worthwhile charities…

He agreed. 'Yes, I talked to Miss Fleming on my return to London a couple of days ago. Briefly. She was highly impressed with what you do. But in the interim I've been camping out at the Hall and making enquiries locally of my own.'

She began to relax and feel sorry that she'd misjudged him. Especially when he went on, 'You need proper funding to pay a reasonable salary to a locally based fundraiser and organiser whose job would include recruiting volunteers. And you need a small local office where this administrative work—which I would fund on an annual basis—would be done. Run properly, the charity could even begin to expand its area of operation. This is the proposal I put to your aunt. She couldn't have been more grateful.'

'It would be the answer to her prayers!' Lily confessed, forgiving him entirely for metaphorically twisting her arm when he'd offered that first donation.

It would be the answer to her own prayers, too. She loved the work, but hated the never-ending anxiety about funding and fitting everything in, the constant fear that they'd have to stop operations and let all those sweet oldies down.

'You're very generous,' Lily said fervently, her huge eyes glittering with emotion-fuelled moisture. Then she reminded herself that she should be generous, too, and make belated enquiries about his sick mother—even gently ask if he had spoken to her about his fake engagement or whether he'd thought better of it.

'Generosity has its price, unfortunately,' Paolo drawled levelly, getting to his feet.

Suddenly he wasn't comfortable about this, but needs must. He had always been protective of his mother—even more so since the death of Antonio and her visibly increasing frailty. And his mother's needs came before his own.

'Why am I not surprised?' Her heart sinking, Lily

curled her legs beneath her and shuffled back in the chair as far as she could go, distancing herself from his smothering, dominant presence. 'I might have known you operate on the maxim that there's no such thing as a free lunch—so what's your price?' she muttered disparagingly.

'Two weeks of your life,' he came back, smooth as silk. 'As I'd hoped, the news of my engagement gave my mother great happiness. Enough, indeed, to give her a new lease on life. She's made steady progress since the operation that her consultant warned had only a slight chance of success. I firmly believe that the news of my engagement enabled her to pull through. Now, naturally, she is insistent that she meet my fiancée.'

'And you want me to—' Appalled by what he was suggesting, Lily planted her feet on the floor and sprang to attention. 'No way! Look, I'm truly glad your mother's doing well, but I did warn you what could happen if you lied!' And then she wished she'd stayed scrunched up in the armchair, because he was suddenly close. Far too close. He was so beautiful he made her feel giddy. How unfair that such a prize specimen of Mediterranean manhood should be so devious. And have such an effect on her!

She was an adult—a grounded adult—not some silly teenager drooling over some unattainable pop star, for goodness' sake!

Viewing her flushed features, the over-bright eyes, Paolo responded wryly, 'You gave warning of an outcome that fills me with joy. I am not about to regret it. Now—'

His hands parted his suit jacket and slid into the side pockets of his elegant trousers, drawing Lily's fascinated attention to the sleek narrowness of his hips. She swallowed roughly and he continued, 'You know what I have proposed regarding the future well-being of Life Begins. In return I shall want you to spend a couple of days in London while I set the ball in motion. Then accompany me to Florence, where you will act the part of a newly engaged woman, satisfy my mother, and then return here.'

'Get one of your leggy model-types to do it!' Lily shot back at him, recalling with ire the serial simpering arm-candy blondes pictured clinging to him when she'd avidly scoured the internet for information about him, driven by a curiosity she hadn't been able to control.

His fascinatingly sexy mouth indented slightly, fabulous lashes lowering over the golden impact of his eyes. 'What a short memory you have,' he drawled, adding insult to injury when he added, 'No way does a leggy blonde fit the description of a vertically challenged toffee-head. I described Lily Frome, my brand-new fiancée, down to her small nose—remember?'

Outraged by his unflattering description of her, Lily fought to restrain the impulse to hit him. The words blistered her tongue as she got out, 'I won't do it! Go—and don't come back!' Adding, in case he wasn't fully on message, 'And take your funding offer with you—I won't be paid to act out a lie to a trusting old lady!'

'As you wish.' Paolo dipped his dark head just briefly, his strong features giving nothing away. He knew precisely when to press a point and when to stand back and wait until, inevitably, his will prevailed.

He walked towards the door, turned. 'If you're happy to disappoint your great-aunt and let down the people who rely on your help, so be it.' And he left her.

The now fuming bundle of scrawny womanhood needed time to cool down.

CHAPTER THREE

IT HAD taken only one restless night for her to reluctantly recognise that by turning down Paolo Venini's offer of funding because of her principles she was being pretty selfish. An uncomfortable reality that had made sleep impossible.

When she had arrived down for breakfast, drained and bleary-eyed, her great-aunt had clinched the matter by asking, with the eager chirpiness that had been missing for many months, 'So, what did you think of Signor Venini's proposal of funding? I told him that I, personally, was overwhelmed with gratitude, but that the final decision had to be yours, because of late I've been something of a passenger.'

'Nonsense! Without you, and the need you saw, Life Begins wouldn't even exist.'

Lily had been worried over her elderly relative's recent decline into a state of fretful anxiety. She'd tried to keep their financial problems from her, but the old lady was anything but a fool.

'And without *you* it would have ceased to exist,' Edith pointed out, forecasting, 'Even with all the hard work you put in it still wouldn't have been too long before we would have had to concede defeat—I may be ancient but I'm not senile!' Sitting at the breakfast table, she poured tea and unfolded her linen napkin briskly. 'Don't hover, child. Eat your toast. I hope you were properly grateful to Signor Venini—with him as a benefactor we can go from strength to strength. I haven't felt less troubled for many months. I feel ten years younger this morning.'

So that meant two old ladies had been given reinvigorating hope—Signora Venini and Great-Aunt Edith— and Life Begins would continue to help those unable to help themselves. All courtesy of Paolo Venini's blackmailing tactics!

Driving to the Hall, swallowing her pride along with her conscience, was the hardest thing Lily had ever had to do. But stay on the high moral ground, as everything in her prompted, and she'd be letting so many people down.

Opening the main door before she'd even had time to cut the engine—almost as if he'd been waiting for her— Paolo received her change of tune without the merest hint of surprise—as if he'd fully expected that, too—and only the very slightest dip of his sleek dark head informed her that he had actually registered her words.

'Come. There is much to be done.' Moving ahead of her, his stride long and loose, he led the way to the study. Dressed this morning in beautifully cut chinos and a midnight-blue cashmere sweater that hugged the impressive width of his shoulders and the narrowness of his waist like a second skin, he was super-spectacular, and—contrarily—made her wish she'd taken some trouble with her own appearance. Not rushed out barefaced, dressed in her badly fitting cords and shabby fleece that she usually wore when working.

Vastly annoyed with herself for that unwelcome and foolish thought, she sat herself down when his abrupt hand gesture indicated the seat in front of the desk. She was beneath his notice. If she was dressed in jewel-encrusted satin with a crown on her head he still wouldn't see her.

And why the heck should she *want* him to notice her? Stupid! He might be gorgeous to look at, but he was rotten inside. A man who would lie to his own mother, a blackmailer, a womaniser, with a chunk of ice where his heart was supposed to be. Any woman who fell in love with him was doomed to bitter heartbreak or worse—as proven by what had happened to the wife who had begun to bore him!

Seated, his hand near his cellphone, his tone was clipped as he told her, 'The previous owner's housekeeper and handyman husband occupied a spacious conversion in what used to be a stable block here. It will provide adequate living and office space for the fund-raiser/organiser I intend to put in place. I'm interviewing two possibles tomorrow.'

'You arranged that before you knew I'd agree to be

blackmailed?' Her face an outraged pink, Lily could have slapped him for his out-and-out arrogance—for the wealth and clout that ensured he could make things happen just because he wanted them to.

A slight upward drift of one strong ebony brow dismissed her outburst, and he continued blandly. 'You will give me the relevant details of your part-time volunteers—names, addresses, phone numbers—and I'll persuade them to work full-time while you're away. Make your diary available to me. I'll drop by and convince your great-aunt that you need a short break. A chauffeur will pick you up at five to drive you to my London apartment, where I will join you in two days' time—the night before we fly to Florence. I suggest you go home and pack.'

'Can't.'

Everything was happening at breakneck speed. Lily felt as if she were being dragged by wild horses over uncharted territory, so it came as a powerful relief to find herself able to put a stop to his dictatorial handling of the situation. She met his eyes, iced-over gold, then tilted her small pointed chin at a stubborn angle.

'I'm due at Maisie Watkins' house. She's recently had a hip replacement operation, so I walk her dog every morning and do a bit of cleaning for her. Then there's other stuff. I'll be working all day. There's absolutely no need for me to kick my heels in your London pad when I could be here doing something useful!' She almost added *So there!* but thought better of it, because he was looking at her as if she were an irritating fly that needed swatting.

'There's every need,' he countered grimly, penetrating eyes sweeping with barely veiled distaste over her scraped-back hair and down to her scruffy trainers.

'Madre is not simple-minded. She would never believe I plan to marry a scrubbed-faced child with the dress sense of a tramp,' he condemned toughly, determined not to be swayed by the momentary flash of hurt in those clear grey eyes, or the way her shoulders slumped, as if she were trying to hide herself in that awful thing she wore above a pair of trousers that wouldn't look out of place on a farm labourer.

'I don't mean to be unkind.' The words, softly spoken, came out of nowhere. Took him by surprise. He breathed in deeply, got himself back on track and continued with chilling bite. 'I do know what I'm doing— believe me. To that end I've arranged for a personal shopper to call for you at my London address at ten tomorrow morning. She has *carte blanche* to kit you out in the kind of clothes Madre will expect to see on the woman I've chosen to be my wife. Similarly, an appointment has been made for you with a top hairstylist.' He swept up the phone, dismissing her. 'Whatever else you have to do today, be ready to leave at five. You can see yourself out.' And he began to key in numbers.

So here she was, in the guestroom of Paolo's spacious London penthouse apartment, ears pinned back for the sound of his arrival, with her hair expertly styled into a sleek jaw-length bob, two horrendously expensive suit-cases packed with horrendously expensive designer gear which had been virtually forced on her at the side of the bed, and his jibe about her looking like a scrubbed-faced child with the dress sense of a tramp still rankling.

What woman would go out made-up to the nines and wearing her best gear to walk a big unruly dog, wash floors and clean windows and stuff? Or were the women who entered the rarefied atmosphere of his life always perfectly groomed, elegantly attired—looking decorative their only justification for taking up space on the planet? Probably!

Her heart jumped as her straining ears caught the sound of footfalls. He'd arrived.

It was a big apartment, all polished hardwood floors, stark white walls and the minimum of furniture. Leather and steel stuff, nothing in the way of softness. Not at all homey—like the man himself.

Her heart-rate quickened as she heard him draw closer. He was pausing outside her room now.

A tap on the door.

She resisted the impulse to scramble beneath the feather-light duvet and pretend to be asleep, because she wasn't a coward and he was only human.

She watched him enter. Formidably handsome, dressed in a dark grey business suit, he was every inch the incredibly wealthy banker—one of the world's movers and shakers. She had to remind herself he was also a heartless womaniser who only had to flick a finger to have the world's most beautiful females flocking, each and every one of them believing she could hold his interest for longer than the last, each and every one of them getting the elbow when coming up against his low boredom threshold. And his boredom was utterly inevitable according to Penny Fleming, who should know.

'*Madonna diavola!* Do you have to look like a terrified rabbit?' Broad shoulders rigid, he strode into the room. If his supposed future wife was going to look as if the devil himself had come to get her every time she saw him, then the deception that was necessary to his mother's continued good progress was dead in the water!

She'd wondered if he would notice her new hairstyle and comment. Of course he hadn't. All he'd noticed about her was her resemblance to a rabbit! 'You spook me!' she confessed on a mumble, pulling the edges of the swamping bathrobe she'd found in the *en suite* bathroom closer together.

'I? In what way?'

He looked genuinely puzzled, brows drawing together above those spectacular golden eyes, so she told him. 'You're like a steamroller squashing an ant. You want something. You get it. Never mind the objections of lesser beings! Feeling like an ant in your way is not fun.'

His expressive mouth twisted wryly. 'I see.'

Not used to tiptoeing around the finer feelings of his employees, because they were paid handsomely to perform their duties and were well used to jumping when he said jump, he had seen no reason to treat Lily Frome any differently.

She—or her charity—was being paid to act the part of his fiancée for a short while, which, logically, made her his employee. But her reaction to him told him he was going to have to tread more carefully in what he could now see was a delicate situation. He must get her on board or the deception would fall flat on its face.

'I'll have to take care to make a detour around any ant that gets in my way.'

His slow smile was pure magic. Lily shivered. She hated the way he could affect her but, annoyingly, she didn't seem able to do anything about it.

On the whole it was better for her equilibrium when he simply barked out his orders and dismissed her, she decided wretchedly. And when he asked, 'Have you eaten?' all she could do was dumbly shake her head.

'Good.' That heartbreaker smile flashed again. 'I've ordered takeaway.' He advanced, held out his hand. 'Come.'

Looking pointedly away from that outstretched hand, because the temptation to slide her own into its lean, strong warmth was really intense, Lily muttered, 'Not hungry,' just as her empty stomach gave a betraying growl of protest. 'And I'm not dressed,' she added for good measure.

Carefully holding onto his patience, Paolo countered, smooth as cream, 'Come as you are. It's not a party! Besides, we need to talk. We've an early start, so it's now or never, because I shall have to work on the flight out.'

He would think she was behaving ridiculously, Lily conceded. And she was. Ignoring his hand, she slid her legs out of the bed and made sure she was decently covered by the huge bathrobe. Lifting the skirts so she didn't trip over the trailing length, she followed him out of the room and gave herself a pep talk.

Theirs was a business arrangement—a shady business arrangement, she reminded herself forcefully. She'd agreed to go along with it despite her reservations, so it was time she started to behave like an adult around him. They would have to talk things over—she certainly needed to know if the part-timers had proven willing to take over her work while she was away—and she was going to have to make herself stop having these attacks of juvenile silliness every time she looked at him.

Trouble was, he had the sort of magnetic sex appeal she had never encountered before, and that, combined with his staggering male beauty, was potent stuff. But she could discount that. Of course she could. Hormones and lust. What she knew of his character was more than enough to put those two evils back in their boxes.

As they approached the glass-topped table in the dining area, a uniformed waiter appeared from the clinically sterile kitchen. Another followed, pushing a trolley, and the table was already laid with silverware and sparkling crystal.

Lily's eyes widened. This was Paolo's idea of a takeaway?

The sudden and hastily suppressed urge to giggle made her feel as if her lungs were about to burst. For her, a takeaway was a rare treat consisting of cod and chips in a warm, greasy package, or foil cartons of sweet and sour chicken and fried rice from the local Chinese restaurant.

This—giant prawns with a delicate lemon sauce, slices of meltingly tender venison on a bed of wild mushrooms, a syllabub to die for—was obviously a wealthy man's idea of a takeaway!

Too busy enjoying every mouthful, and reflecting on how the other half lived, Lily forgot the deceitful part she was expected to play during the coming two weeks for long enough to relax and ask, 'Why champagne?' She'd only tasted it once before, at a friend's wedding, and hadn't liked it. So this had to be something special because she'd already got through two glasses.

'To celebrate the start of—' He'd been about to say *Our hopefully brief association* but, recalling her rather thin skin, substituted 'Of our mutually satisfactory business arrangement.'

He was leaning back in his seat and his eyes were gleaming in an almost sultry way, she registered, with a strange and unwelcome inner flutter, coming straight back down to earth with a thump.

She put her champagne flute down on the table with a clatter. 'I don't feel like celebrating. Not when our so-called business arrangement is based on a whopping lie.'

'A white lie aimed to please a frail elderly lady,' he reminded her, careful not to snap, as was his inclination when his judgement was questioned. 'And you might be interested to hear that a certain Kate Johnson will be in place at the charity by the end of the month. She will take care of fundraising and day-to-day organisation. She has impeccable references, having worked as a fundraiser for a well-known charity based in Birmingham. Also, substantial funds have been placed in the charity's account,' he completed with cool precision.

The slightest dip of his head brought the waiter gliding forward to receive his instruction that coffee would be taken in the living room.

Squashed again, Lily recognised, as he escorted her through. The slightest hint of criticism flattened as he rolled over her with his reminders of what Life Begins would be gaining at his no doubt vast expense.

'May I suggest,' he drawled, as he watched with concealed amusement as she tried to perch on the edge of the slippery surface of the leather sofa and control the wayward swamping folds of the vastly over-large robe she was wearing, 'that for the next two weeks we pull together, not in different directions? As far as my mother is concerned we are engaged to be married. She will expect us to behave as lovers—and I hope you will try—but if you can't manage that you must act as if I am at the very least your friend and not your enemy.'

Lily's face flamed. Act as if they were lovers? The very thought made her heart beat so fast she was sure it

would leap out of her chest. He could take that preposterous suggestion and bury it deep in the nearest dustbin!

Thankfully, she was spared the need to give an immediate answer by the arrival of the coffee tray and
Paolo's final dismissal of the waiter.

Stealing a look at him from beneath tangled lashes, she
felt her tummy flip alarmingly. It was so unfair! Just look
at him—every inch the powerful alpha male, sophisticated, breathtakingly wealthy and staggeringly good to
look at. Sexy. In spades. She could have coped much better
if he'd been fat and bald with the sex appeal of a frog!

Clamorous warning bells had rung at the prospect of
even *pretending* to be his lover. For him it would be
tongue-in-cheek play-acting, but for her it would be too
dangerous to contemplate.

Even before the waiter had closed the door behind
him, she blurted, 'This scam you've dreamed up can't
work! For a start, friends don't trample on each other,
treat each other as if their opinions are worthless. So it
will be really difficult to pretend you're my friend!'

He'd taken a chair on the opposite side of the low
coffee table. He poured dark, hot coffee into small gold-
rimmed cups, his movements deft and economical, and
conceded, 'I see your point. However, now matters are
arranged, everything smoothly in place, it will be different—I promise.'

In all areas of his life, business and personal, he made
decisions and acted on them, allowing nothing to get in
his way. Using persuasion to counter an objecting voice

was unusual for him, but with so much at stake he had to grit his teeth, keep his temper, and *try*.

He smiled. The slow, sexy smile that dazzled her eyes and set her pulses racing.

'If you have an opinion, and it is valid, it will be listened to.'

Big of him! 'Does there always have to be a caveat?' She accepted the cup he offered. Whatever opinion she offered he was bound to say it wasn't valid!

'Scusi!' He flashed her a disarming grin and relaxed back in his chair. When she wasn't regarding him as the devil incarnate she could be amusing company. Come to think of it, he might enjoy moulding this stubborn, unremarkable scrap of female opposition to his will. Brilliant eyes assessed her thoroughly. Maybe she wasn't quite as unremarkable as he'd thought. 'The new hairstyle suits you perfectly. Pretty.'

He caught the surprise in those big grey eyes before she looked quickly away, her pale skin pinkening, and to his own amazement he found he felt ashamed of himself. He hadn't been treating her like a human being with feelings that could be hurt—or completely squashed, as she'd accused.

Her hands—delicate, fine-boned, small hands, he noted for the first time—were unsteady as she replaced her cup on its saucer. And, realising it was time to quit while he was ahead, he said gently, 'Goodnight, Lily. It's late and we have an early start. Sleep well.'

He watched with veiled satisfaction as she scrambled

to her feet and exited in swamping folds of out-of-control bathrobe.

Tread softly, a little gentle flattery, and the next two weeks would be sailed through with no problems at all.

CHAPTER FOUR

As SHE boarded the Venini private jet, with Paolo's hand lightly insistent on the small of her back—a reminder, as if she needed one, that it was now far too late to back out—Lily felt seriously light-headed. Partly nerves at the prospect of what lay ahead of her—her role in a distasteful deception—and partly, she had to be honest, because Paolo was being *nice* to her.

She'd gone to bed with his compliment about her new hairstyle throbbing in her ears and heating her skin, totally amazed that he had actually noticed something positive about her appearance.

She could have got over that, of course she could, but then the way his eyes had registered stunned approval when she'd presented herself early this morning, wearing the wickedly expensive cream-coloured linen suit and heeled sandals that she'd selected to travel in from the clothes that had been picked out for her, had really knocked her for six.

Especially when he'd moved right up to her and tilted

her chin, producing a clean white handkerchief and gently wiping away the scarlet lipstick she'd taken such pains to apply.

At the touch of his cool, lean fingers, the gentle movement of the fabric against her lips, every sane thought had flown right out of her head.

His eyes, veiled by thick dark lashes, had been intent on what he was doing, his beautiful mouth just slightly smiling, and every inch of her suddenly tense body had craved to move closer to the dominating male strength of his. She had nearly fainted with the urgent throbbing of every cell in her body when he'd run a finger softly over her parted lips and imparted, in a tone that was thicker and deeper than she had heard before, 'You have a lovely mouth. Soft and incredibly lush. Pink and inviting. It's a sin to cover it with screaming scarlet.'

'Inviting.' What did *that* mean? That he'd wanted to kiss her? Her heart had begun to pound and clatter; her breathing had grown ragged.

She'd gulped.

With a feeble effort, which he could have stayed with the tip of one finger, she had forced herself to twist away from the sheer temptation of him.

Of course he hadn't wanted to kiss her! As if! It was completely obvious what he'd been doing.

She could pinpoint exactly when he had started to treat her like a living, breathing female. Right after she'd told him she couldn't even begin to treat him as if he were a friend when all he did was trample on her.

Paolo Venini was turning on the charm solely in the hope of making her more compliant—she could see straight through him!

Even so, her tummy muscles clenched now as he leaned over and fastened her seat belt for her. She could see every pore of his olive-toned skin, the darkly shadowed jawline, the gleam of those brilliant eyes. She breathed in the mineral tang of the aftershave he used and felt giddy.

He was so dangerous!

But only if she allowed him to be, she reminded herself sternly. And she wouldn't! She could be strong enough to ignore all that overcharged sexual charisma.

As the plane taxied down the runway she consoled herself with that heartening thought, and when they were airborne, made haste to release her seat belt to stop him moving up close and doing it for her. When he half turned in his seat, angled towards her, she was as proud as if she had just won an Olympic medal when she managed casually, coolly, 'You said you wanted to work. Please go ahead. I'm not about to disturb you and hurl objections at you at this late stage.'

'I'm relieved to hear it.'

Warmth in his voice—a smile, even. Nerves prickling, Lily kept staring straight ahead. Looking at him always caused her problems.

Her profile was a delight. Long lashes veiling those big grey eyes, neat nose just slightly pinched around the nostrils, lush lips clamped together. A sign of her apprehension? Compassion stirred within him for the first time. She didn't like the situation he'd dragooned her into, and it was up to him to try to smooth the way for her.

There had been other firsts, too, he recognised in retrospect. Like noticing the flattering new hairstyle that framed her kittenish face. And then this morning he'd been actually stunned by a woman's appearance— something that had never happened before. Without the workmanlike trousers and shapeless tops the skinny kid had been revealed as a delightful pocket-sized Venus. The expertly tailored suit she had chosen to wear to travel in skimming small but perfectly formed breasts, emphasising a tiny, tiny waist and showing off the very female curve of her hips.

A glow of what could only be pride in his achievement coursed heatedly through his veins. *He* had brought about this startling transformation, and Madre would have no trouble believing that this was the woman he had chosen to be his wife.

Faint colour touching his slanting cheekbones, he reached into an inner pocket. Her head was turned away. She was staring out at the clouds. He touched her arm and she stiffened. Wary. Like a kitten who didn't know where the next kick was coming from.

His strong, dark features clenched. *Madre di Dio!* Had he, through the force of his character, treated her so badly? Things would have to change. His parent was strongly moralistic, sheltered, strictly reared, and she deplored what she called the laxness of the younger generation, but even she would expect a newly engaged couple to touch each other!

'Lily.' Her name, falling softly from his lips, gained her attention. She turned, her eyes wide. He took her hand and felt her tense. 'Wear this.' As he slid the ring onto her wedding finger Lily flinched, a shiver running right down her rigid spine and back up again as he imparted warmly, 'It has been passed down through generations of Venini brides. Madre will expect to see you wearing it.'

The diamond was simply huge, set in antique gold and surrounded by cabochon-cut sapphires. A fabulously expensive prop for a horribly cheap deception! Everything inside her rebelled afresh.

Firmly dismissing the frisson she'd experienced when the mind-bogglingly handsome and wickedly sexy Paolo Venini had placed the ring on her finger, she cast around for some objection he would go for—because her real one would cut no ice with a man who didn't appear to have a conscience and always thought he was right.

'It's much too big. I can't wear it. I'd only lose it, and it's got to be worth a fortune,' she got out as she attempted to remove the ring which symbolised their sham engagement.

His large, lean hands closed over hers. 'I'll have it made smaller.' Like the rest of her, her hands were tiny, her fingers long and slender. Amazingly, feeling them beneath his own much larger hands made him feel quite urgently protective.

'You can't do that,' Lily pointed out blithely, doing her utmost to ignore the way his skin burned against hers. 'I know you don't want to marry right now. But one day you will. And then you'll have to have it altered back again, to fit a bigger finger.'

Incisive golden eyes held hers, his sensual mouth curving as he countered teasingly. 'I would never marry a woman with fat fingers! Wear it for the time being. Once she has seen it on your finger I'll tell my mother it has to be altered. I know what I'm doing, believe me.'

He still held her hand. When she tried to pull away his grip merely tightened. Rivers of sensation racing through her made her feel weirdly distracted, and she struggled to focus before she finally managed earnestly, 'I don't think you do—know what you're doing. Not really. Think about it. How long can an engagement last? A couple of years? Ten? Some time you're going to have to tell her the whole thing's off. Then how will she feel? Really disappointed because her hopes of seeing you settled and giving her grandchildren have come to nothing!'

He withdrew his hand. Lily felt the coldness settle over him, and his features were bleak as he incised brittly, 'I would be overjoyed if I believed that Madre had two years left to her.' Turning away, he reached for the briefcase that held his work, completely dismissing her and the conversation.

But Lily, once her easily touched sympathies had been engaged, wasn't prepared to accept his dismissal.

The poor man was dreadfully worried about his mother, and despite the successful outcome of her operation he was still of the opinion that she wouldn't survive very long. Wriggling round in her seat to face him squarely, she said gently, 'You love your mother very much, don't you?'

'Naturally.' The word held a bite.

So the hard nut did have a soft centre. Prepared to explore the phenomenon, to understand him better and forgive his sin of coercion, she pressed, 'And you'd do anything to make her happy?'

'That is what this is all about.' Briefcase abandoned, he slewed round to face her, his eyes derisive. 'Don't tell me you'd forgotten? You can't imagine I'm going through this charade for the pleasure of your company!'

As soon as the words were out Paolo regretted them. She looked as if she had just received a slap in the face. But he had spoken the absolute truth, and if her feelings were hurt, tough. He was not in the habit of stepping softly around the feelings of employees who were being paid handsomely to do as he required—and Lily Frome and her charity were being paid far more handsomely than most.

With a slight shrug of wide, immaculately suited shoulders, Paolo lifted the briefcase again and settled down to work.

Apart from explaining that for the duration of her recuperation his mother was staying with her nurse and companion at the family villa in the hills beyond

Florence, Paolo remained silent as he drove a sleek Ferrari through the unspoiled Tuscan countryside.

She might as well be invisible, Lily decided, and told herself she didn't care. Being ignored was absolutely better than when he was being nice, because when he complimented her, smiled at her or took her hand she, to her shame, went all gooey inside, and promptly forgot what a manipulative creep he was. He might have a slightly redeeming soft spot where his parent was concerned, but beneath that stunning packaging he was mostly just bad-tempered, impatient, arrogant and devoid of conscience. He might have a brilliant brain when it came to business, but he was happy to ride roughshod over the feelings of those he considered to be his inferiors.

That assessment planted firmly in her mind, she told herself that she had to remember that Life Begins would benefit immensely from his funding. Her great-aunt would sleep easier, and she, when this was over, would work hard and try to forget the part she had played in the charity's salvation.

As for the next two weeks—well, she would get through it as best she could. And maybe, if she presented herself as the sort of woman Signora Venini wouldn't welcome into her family, the poor thing wouldn't be at all upset when her hateful son told her the engagement was off! She'd be mightily relieved!

She could pretend to be a complete bitch—cold, hard, only showing any animation when asking how much Paolo was worth—or she could be a complete boor—talking with her mouth full, shrieking with raucous laughter at nothing in particular, scratching herself and burping. Deciding which gave her a heady feeling of control, of paying him back for forcing her to do this.

She must have been grinning at the possible scenarios, because he gave her a sharp look that wiped the smile from her face as he said, 'We're here,' and swung the powerful car between two immense security gates that swung open at his approach.

The wide, curving drive was bordered by tall cypresses which banded the fine-gravelled surface with deep shadows, and Lily's amusing mental pictures vanished, leaving her feeling deeply apprehensive. This was serious, and she knew that there was no way she could attempt to act the part of this intimidating man's fiancée and change her character at the same time!

Her heart taking residence in her shoes, she watched as the immense white-stuccoed villa came into view. Large windows glittered in the afternoon sun, and giant stone urns filled with colourful flowers flanked the shallow flight of steps that led up to the main door.

One cue, the door opened, and a slim, white-jacketed servant hurried towards the car as it slid to a halt. Exiting, Paolo spoke in his own language. The only words Lily could pick out were references to his mother, as she sat in her seat like an overlooked package.

The imposing villa was completely intimidating. A

palace fit only for the rarefied and screamingly wealthy. How could she, an ordinary, dirt-poor charity worker, hope to even *pretend* to fit in? For the millionth time she wished she'd never agreed to this. Just gritted her teeth and struggled on as best she could.

When Paolo strode round to her side of the car, opened the door and extended his hand to help her out, all she wanted to do was screw herself down in her seat and refuse to budge.

His manufactured tender smile tightened. He must have seen the mutiny on her face, Lily recognised, and she released a pent-up breath, reluctantly accepting his assistance. After all, she had made a bargain with this devil in heart-throb's clothing, and she didn't go back on her word, so annoying him would get her nowhere.

'Mario will take your luggage up to your room.' His arm was around her small waist. 'I suggest you freshen up while I greet my mother. And try to remember that we're supposed to be head over heels in love with each other.'

A statement guaranteed to make her stomach turn over and set her knees trembling.

His strong arm around her was the only thing keeping her upright, Lily realised as he steered her towards the imposing entrance. Her legs had gone completely tottery, and a million butterflies were having a ball in her tummy. She could only manage a wavery smile as he introduced her to a smiling middle-aged lady.

'Agata is my housekeeper. She has excellent English. Apply to her for anything you need for your comfort.'

His smile broadened, the arm around her waist drawing her closer. Lily shuddered in reaction. 'She will show you to your room, *cara*. I will come for you in a short while.'

He was really getting into character, Lily grumbled to herself as she followed Agata's broad back up the wide sweeping staircase—even dredging up an endearment for the benefit of his housekeeper. Deception must come easily to him. In the play-acting stakes she would come a very poor second!

As the ornate staircase branched in two directions they veered left, and on the first landing Agata flung open the first door they came to. 'Your room, *signorina*. You like?'

How could she confess that the vast, opulent room intimidated her when those kindly dark eyes were smiling into her own?

'It's beautiful, Agata, thank you.'

Her luggage already stood at the foot of the enormous canopied bed. Spirited up by means of some discreet servants' staircase, she guessed, and could only widen her eyes in wonderment when the housekeeper stated comfortably, 'The English tea will be brought to you immediately. Donatella will unpack for you, and if there's anything else you require then you must please ring for me.' She left before Lily could gather her wits together to protest that she didn't want to be any trouble.

So this was how the other half lived, she thought uneasily as she edged gingerly over the thick-piled cream-coloured carpet towards the row of tall windows—louvred and ornately draped—that marched along the length of one ivory-coloured wall. Surrounded by luxury, good taste and the trappings of vast wealth, with servants to cater to one's every whim and no need to lift a finger.

The panoramic view over manicured gardens to the rolling Tuscan countryside was truly magnificent, and she was lost in admiration when a pretty Italian girl bearing a tea tray entered after a deferential knock.

'*Signorina…*' The girl placed the tray on a low table beside a silk-upholstered armchair, her brown eyes curious as they swept Lily's diminutive figure—no doubt checking out her probable future mistress, Lily realised, feeling decidedly queasy.

'Thank you,' she said, although tea was the last thing she wanted. Her stomach would reject anything she tried to put into it. But she sank obediently into the chair and poured the tea, her hand shaking. Someone had gone to the trouble to make it, and this poor girl had struggled up all those stairs with it, so she had to make an effort.

Nevertheless, the sight of the maid opening her suitcases was enough to get Lily to her feet again, protesting, 'Look—there's no need, really. I can do that myself. It's no trouble.'

But the maid obviously had no English. She just looked up anxiously, and Lily felt foolish and about two inches tall. The young Italian girl would take unpacking for guests as completely normal—part of what she was hired to do. Having a crazy foreigner gabbling at her in a language she didn't understand would make her feel as if she were doing something wrong. Lily was going to have to remember that she'd entered a world that was totally different from her own.

'Sorry.' Her face pink with embarrassment, Lily backed away limply. Desperate to escape without daubing more egg on her face, she headed for a door she'd noticed set between the vast wardrobe and an antique dressing table.

Confronted by an elegantly proportioned bathroom, complete with a huge marble bath, a shower unit, and enough fluffy towels to serve a rugby team, she kicked off her shoes, deciding that the shower would make the perfect hiding place. Just until she had got her head around the uncomfortable feeling that she was way out of her depth.

Carefully placing the unwanted and over-large engagement ring on the marble top of the vanity unit, she stripped off and scurried into the shower. She stayed there, pounded by hot water, wondering how long it would take Donatella to finish unpacking and remove herself, leaving her with the solitude she would need to get herself into the right frame of mind for the dreaded first meeting with the poor woman she was about to so cruelly dupe. She wondered nervously how she would cope when Paolo played his role, as promised, and treated her as if she were the love of his life. Go to pieces, probably! She'd never deceived anyone, and didn't know how she was going to do it.

'*Porca miseria!* No one takes a shower for an hour! Do you intend to boil yourself?'

Mortification followed shock as Lily peered through the steam at one clearly aggravated Italian male. His sharp suit jacket was soaked, where he'd flung open the glass door and reached in to cut off the flow of water, and his sharp tongue was in evidence as he ordered, 'Get dressed! My mother is anxious to greet you.' He reached for a huge towel and thrust it at her, faint colour flaring over his high cheekbones, his mouth clamped tight over his teeth.

Grabbing at the towel, Lily was suddenly and horribly aware of her nakedness, of the way his brilliant golden eyes had swept her from top to toe and then blanked. Wrapping herself up like a parcel, she watched him shed his wet jacket and walk away, collecting the ring from the vanity on his way back into the bedroom, stepping over her discarded clothing.

Overheated from the prolonged onslaught of hot water and deep embarrassment, Lily plucked up another towel and began to rub her hair dry. In her shock at his abrupt and totally unexpected arrival she'd just stood there, naked as the day she was born, like a transfixed rabbit. Did he think she'd been flaunting herself? Her skin crawled with utter humiliation.

No wonder he'd looked so blank! His preference lay with tall, leggy blondes with all the social graces. He wouldn't want the complication of the bog-standard hired help apparently coming on to him! In his mother's company he would expect her to act like a besotted bride-to-be, but in private he had no interest in her as a woman.

Her face flamed anew when she heard his incisive, 'Wear this. And make it snappy.'

Emerging from the folds of the towel, Lily saw him place a pale amethyst shift dress on the chair that stood just inside the door before he walked back out again. Lacy briefs and matching bra, too—part of the supply that had been bought for her back in London, so that she would look the part he had assigned her: high-maintenance bride-to-be, exactly what his parent would expect to see.

Her tummy squirming, she dressed in the garments he had taken it upon himself to select. Feeling the soft silky fabric of the exquisitely crafted dress touch her skin like a lover's caress made her shudder.

Everything was so wrong. She didn't feel like herself at all. These clothes weren't *her*. In fact, the amount that had been spent on her clothing for a mere fortnight would have kept a family of four for a year, she realised, appalled. Such a waste!'

Her mouth set in mutiny, she stalked into the bedroom, where he was waiting in unconcealed impatience, and announced, 'In future *I* choose what I wear. You might have paid for the stuff—and paid me to lie for you—but you don't own me!'

He shot her a look of exasperation. He was landed with an aggravating, argumentative pest with a body to set male pulses racing. Clueless, too. Left to her own devices she would smother those delectable curves in ugly swamping garments. She should be grateful at being given the sort of beautiful clothes that did credit to her hitherto hidden loveliness, not come at him shouting the odds.

At the memory of her earlier nakedness—which he had done his level best to blank—he felt unwanted heat crawl over his skin, and his voice was a rough undertone as he commanded, 'Come here.'

He swept a silver-backed hairbrush from the dressing table, and as she stubbornly refused to budge he strode over to her and began to stroke the tangles out of her still damp hair, the lean fingers of one hand firmly beneath her chin to stop her wriggling away.

'In future you may choose what to wear.' Her jawbone was so tenderly delicate, her skin so soft beneath the pads of his fingers, her hair like caramel silk. 'Today I hurried you—' He broke off, aware that he was doing something totally unprecedented, trying to placate an argumentative employee. Oddly, his voice was emerging like soft velvet. Clearing his throat roughly, he continued, 'My mother is so anxious to meet her future daughter-in-law. I can't bear to keep her waiting. I know how long women take to dress and fuss over their appearance.'

At the 'future daughter-in-law' falsehood Lily snapped out of the dizzy, intoxicating trance she'd fallen into the moment he'd touched her, stroked the brush through her hair, his magnificent body so close to hers. Stepping away from him, and drawing herself up to her full insignificant height, horrified by her weakness where he was concerned she reminded him, 'I am *nothing* like your usual vanity-obsessed lady-friends! So don't treat me as if I am!'

'Stop arguing.' Curbing impatience, Paolo slipped the fabulous ring back on her finger. There was a feisty glitter in those big grey eyes. Present her to his parent while she was in this mood and the whole thing would be over before it began. Trust him to pick a woman who couldn't hide her feelings!

He needed a purring kitten, not a spitting cat. There was only one thing to do. His hands going to her slim shoulders, he bent his dark head and kissed her.

CHAPTER FIVE

As HIS beautiful mouth took hers Lily was utterly swamped by the shattering emotion which crashed through her with the force of a hurricane. She had never experienced anything remotely like this before. It blew her mind.

Totally incapable of rational thought, she felt instinct take over, and her lips parted to give him better access to the sweetness within. Her entire body was shuddering helplessly as his arms slid from her shoulders to her tiny waist to hold her more closely, to meld her to his lean, powerful length.

She had been kissed before, but never like this—like fire and honey, every cell in her body singing in uncontrolled response as his tongue slid deeper in sensual exploration. Her mindless caressing fingers revelled in the feel of taut muscles beneath the fine fabric of his shirt, and her hands suddenly gripped his wide shoulders in wild reaction as she felt his hot, hard arousal against the quivering softness of her tummy.

Reduced to an unthinking mass of sensation, she raised her hips to press against him, moving with instinct-driven feverish urgency. She heard him groan as a long shudder raced through him, and when his hands slid down to her buttocks, pressing her even closer, the blood in her veins ignited and fierce desire pulsed insistently through her trembling body.

Lily hadn't known that such sensations could exist. Intoxicated, she slid her hands around his magnificent torso, fingers fumbling at the buttons of his shirt because she couldn't get close enough to him. He felt the same. She knew he did. Because his hands were moving restively over her silk-clad body with hungry heat, and then they were sliding the hem of her dress up around her thighs, and the part of her mind that was still amazingly capable of halfway rational thought registered that he was consumed by the same high-voltage passion that was thrumming through every cell of her body. And it was glorious!

Until with a driven groan Paolo lifted his head and held her away from him.

Struggling to retrieve her breath, shocked into immobility, Lily was held by the unfathomable depths of those shimmering golden eyes, partly screened by thickly dark lashes. She could drown in those eyes, she thought shakily, dazed, her tingling, sensitised body still in recovery from the emotional onslaught of his raw passion.

'We should go,' Paolo reminded her in a low, thickened murmur. His hand, not quite steady, reached out for hers, his eyes drawn to her enticing, incredibly responsive body, to her gleaming eyes and flushed cheeks.

He wasn't at all sure what had happened. He felt heat crawl over his skin and his driven admission, 'That was amazing,' pole-axed him—because he hadn't consciously meant to confide that opinion. He didn't know where it had come from. It had simply happened—as if they shared a bond, a passion that went soul-deep.

He pulled in a deep, ragged breath. Before this moment his comments had never, ever been unguarded, and he had always mildly despised those who spoke without thinking through the consequences of what they said.

Fortunately he had the belated good sense to put the shutters up and not voice his further opinion that if his frail parent hadn't been eagerly waiting for them their kiss would have ended up far, far differently. On that bed. And that would have been a disaster. He lived by his own set of rules, and one of them stated that female employees, no matter how attractive, were off-limits.

As it was, though, he had achieved his initial objective, he tried to console himself. Lily Frome looked the image of the blushing bride-to-be. Soft and pink, about to melt into his arms at the first opportunity. But that didn't give him the satisfaction he had thought it would, he recognised uneasily.

Thankfully, the walk down to the small salon on the ground floor gave him time to get his libido back under strict control. What had happened, he rationalised, had been due to base lust. He hadn't been with a woman for a long while, and seeing Lily Frome in all her delicate, promising nakedness had acted on his male libido like a flame on petrol.

Given the circumstances, his initial decision to kiss her, nothing more, had been logical—a means to an end. The outcome, the loss of control on his part—and on hers?—was regrettable. But entirely normal given his months of celibacy.

Thankfully his voice emerged sounding reassuringly normal, too, as he paused before an ornately carved fruitwood door and advised, 'Just be yourself and you will delight her.'

Lily at last came down to earth with a bump, her befuddled mind clearing at the speed of light. Was he being sarcastic? Of course he was—what else? 'Being herself' meant being a dead ordinary, nose-to-the-grindstone, unsophisticated simple girl. In short, the type of woman he wouldn't give a second glance. He knew that.

And yet... Memories of that kiss slammed back to scorch her brain. Vividly recalling the greedy way she'd responded, she blushed furiously and knew she was about to sink into a morass of super-heated suffocating shame.

But it hadn't been all one-way traffic, she told herself defensively.

He had kissed her as if he'd meant it. Passionately. She'd had little or no time for boyfriends in her busy life, but she wasn't stupid. She knew when a man was aroused. And he had been. So that had to mean he had wanted more than kisses.

Heat engulfed her entire body and her breathing shortened. She was horribly aware that he was now looking at her with shimmering, assessing eyes, and she hunched her shoulders, hoping the cringing posture would disguise the shameful way her breasts were peaking and tingling beneath the silk.

'Hold your head up,' he uttered scathingly, irked by the way she was looking—like a woman about to face a firing squad rather than the glowing bride-to-be of a few minutes earlier. Then, remembering he had to tread softly around her, he advised more gently, 'No one's going to eat you, *cara*! Leave most of the talking to me. And remember I'll be right beside you—holding your hand!'

That was meant to reassure her? Hollowly, Lily decided it didn't. Being around him always made her uneasy. Vulnerable. Far too aware of his dynamic sexual appeal. And now, after what had happened, she was fearfully aware of how easily he could cut through her flimsy resistance. Panic skittered through each and every nerve-ending.

She wasn't simple-minded. She knew he didn't even like her. She irritated him. Normally he wouldn't dream of coming on to her; she would be beneath his lofty notice. But, walking in on her nakedness, he had decided, Hey, she'd been bought and paid for, so why not enjoy the action for a couple of weeks? The trouble was, what had happened back in her room told her that she would probably do nothing to discourage him. She shuddered helplessly, hating what she'd discovered about herself.

Opening the door, Paolo dropped her hand and slid his arm around her waist, drawing her with him over the threshold into an elegant room, with white walls, white drapes, cream upholstery and crystal bowls of scented hothouse flowers on every available surface.

Seeing the frail white-haired lady seated at a circular table in the deep window embrasure, Lily felt her heart twist in her breast. She dragged in a deep breath and wished she could disappear in a puff of smoke. The situation was growing more scary with every moment that passed, and she felt truly dreadful over the part she was expected to play.

The radiance of Signora Venini's welcoming smile made her feel even worse, but as if he sensed it Paolo gave her waist a reassuring squeeze and strode forward, bent to give his parent a gentle hug and drop a kiss on the fragile skin of her pale cheek. 'Mamma, I'm so sorry you've been kept waiting. My fault entirely. When I'm with Lily I forget how time flies.'

He had dropped the more formal 'Madre', and Lily could scarcely believe the change in him. His voice so tender, his smile so gentle, his respect very obvious. Nothing like the man she had come to know: austerely impatient, critical, and often cold—a man who bowed to no one.

He obviously adored his mother and cared deeply for her. Against all her principles Lily could reluctantly understand where he was coming from. And sympathise. Or almost.

She still didn't think lying was right, but Paolo truly believed it best to pretend that his future with the woman of his choice was settled, in order to put his fragile mother's mind at ease.

Her heart was pattering against her ribs as the elderly lady extended a slim white hand. Her smile was warm but her voice was feeble as she said, 'Lily—how lovely to meet you at last. Come, sit with me. Paolo has told me so much about you.'

Paolo smiled his encouragement but Lily could see the strain behind it, and, despite her distaste for deceiving the fragile woman, it gave her the necessary impetus to move forward, sit on one of the vacant chairs around the table, smile and lie her socks off. 'And I'm happy to meet you, too,' she greeted her, because Paolo, now stationed directly behind her, his hands on her shoulders, was clearly desperately anxious for his surviving parent, and up close Lily could see why.

Signora Venini looked as if the slightest breeze would disintegrate her frail body. More than the recent scar that ran beneath the line of her snowy white hair—that would heal and eventually disappear—it was the lines of utter weariness, of sadness, etched on her once beautiful features that told a story of a woman who had been tired of living for a long while.

Lily's tender heart felt wrung out as she unconsciously covered the opulent family betrothal ring with the fingers of her other hand and blurted sincerely, the words tumbling out, 'You've been through a major operation, *signora*. You need plenty of rest, peace and quiet—not visitors!' And, despite the warning tightening of Paolo's fingers on her shoulders, she ploughed on, verbalising as much of the truth as she dared because she needed to be out of here. Needed to put as much distance between her and the man she now knew could make her act like a sex-starved trollop as soon as possible.

'I told Paolo that under the circumstances I didn't think the timing of this visit was at all sensible. It could easily have waited until you were feeling stronger.' She managed a smile which she hoped would come over as conspiratorial. 'But you will know how stubborn Paolo can be! Even so, I think it would be best if I left tomorrow, or the day after at the latest, and didn't intrude further on your recuperation period.'

Lily smiled softly, willing the older woman to agree, but her slim hopes were crushed when she got a decidedly firm, 'Nonsense! Getting to know my son's future wife will be the best tonic I could possibly have! The one bright spot in a year that has been so awful!'

Amazingly, the older woman's tawny eyes sparked now with lively determination. 'And for us to get to know each other time is needed, *si*? In fact I expect my son to persuade you to stay with us for much longer than the mere two weeks he promised me—we have a wedding to arrange!'

* * *

'You've got to put a stop to this!' Lily hissed frantically half an hour later when Carla, Paolo's mother's friendly but firm companion, appeared to chivvy the reluctant older woman away for a rest before dinner.

'Silenzio!' An inescapable hand shot out to take her wrist. 'Keep your voice down,' he ordered in the same driven undertone. 'You will be heard. Come.'

Her legs feeling like jelly, her heart pounding fit to suffocate her, Lily was led by one very determined male out of the room, across the marble-slabbed hall, down two corridors and out of a side door to a massive paved terrace, with loungers set to catch the evening sunlight at one side and a long teak table and benches set beneath a vine-covered arbour at the other.

Ignoring the choice of seating, Paolo led her down a shallow flight of stone steps to the garden—a maze of box-bordered paths, sentinel cypress trees and an abundance of roses in leaf and promising bud.

Only when she tripped did he slow his pace, an arm going round her to steady her. 'We sit. And we talk with sense.'

Registering from that slight slip in his usually impeccable English that he was almost as disturbed as she by the afternoon's events, Lily sat—was glad to—as he brought her to a carved marble bench seat beside an antique stone fountain.

Confident that he would be as horrified as she by his mother's excited wedding plans, she started, 'There has to be a way to put her off! You got us into this mess—

now get us out of it! I did my best—told her I had a charity to run and couldn't commit to anything else for ages. But she didn't listen!'

'Total waste of breath,' he incised without hesitation. 'Mamma knows I've stepped in. When I become involved things happen and happen smoothly. That being so, she would know that *because* everything is in hand your absence would be of little or no consequence,' he insulted blandly.

Fit to spit bricks, Lily glared at him. Arrogant brute! 'Then put your so-superior brain in gear and think of something!'

Anger lit her big grey eyes. But something else sparked within those luminous depths. Fright?

Settling beside her, Paolo draped an arm along the back of the seat. Deliberately relaxing his body. Two of them indulging in hysterics would get them precisely nowhere.

'I admit I didn't expect her to launch straight into immediate wedding plans with such gusto,' he confessed, his lips curving in appreciation of the stony glare she gave him—until her scathing response set a slow burn of discomfited heat running over his cheekbones.

'No, you expected her to be gasping her last and whispering about how happy she was, going to her maker knowing that you were settling down to marriage!'

The moment the words were out Lily regretted them—hated herself for even thinking them, never mind flinging them at him.

Her soft heart ruling her head, she offered softly,

'I'm sorry. That was a horrible thing to say.' She reached for his hand, clenched on his knee, and curled slim fingers around it. 'Of course you've been worried about your mum. When someone we love is ill we can't help it—can't help dwelling on the worst-case scenario, praying it won't happen but desperately afraid it will. It's quite natural.'

His hand was still a fist beneath her cool fingers. Affronted dignity was written on his stunning features. Mindful that she was probably irritating the hell out of him, she added uncertainly, 'I wish I had a mum to worry about.'

Paolo's shuttered eyes switched to find hers. Warmth curled around his heart, squeezed it. Lily Frome. Those huge eyes were drenched with the softness of sympathy, lush lips quivering slightly. In spite of her diminutive size she had a big heart, was so unused to hurting anyone she was swift to apologise when she felt she had.

And he had variously bullied, insulted and ridden roughshod over her. She didn't deserve that. He had kissed her, and yet he knew next to nothing about her. That was an insult in itself.

Uncurling his fist, he laced his fingers between hers. 'What happened to her?'

Taken aback, Lily blinked. Her soft mouth parted, then clamped shut again. Something really weird happened to her when he was being nice to her. She tried to analyse it and couldn't.

He prompted gently, 'Well?'

'I—' Lily was floundering. It was the look in his eyes that did it. The golden gleam was assessing, yet kind, warm. His hard male mouth had softened. As if she were a human being with feelings instead of an employee paid to do as she was told—an automaton that he could switch on and then switch off and put back in the cupboard and forget about when the task was completed to his satisfaction. It was unnerving.

'She died,' she got out. 'When I was a baby. I don't remember her.' She smiled shakily, her eyes meeting his at last. 'I do have a few photographs, though. She was really pretty.'

'Then you must take after her.' His fingers tightened on hers. 'And your father?'

He thought she was pretty? She sucked her lower lip between her teeth. His hand, laced with hers, felt so good. Too good. She wished it didn't. Wished she had the strength of mind to snatch her hand away. But she hadn't.

Lily lifted her slender shoulders in a tiny shrug. 'He left. He handed me over to my mother's aunt. There were no other relatives.'

'How often do you see him? Hear from him?'

Her chin lifted at his suddenly grim tone. 'Never. OK? Though, to be fair to him, my parents married young. Too young. They were still in their teens when I was born. I guess he couldn't cope with the demands of a baby. I must have been a mistake. I expect he thought he and Mum would have years of married life together before they had to settle down to be parents.

He would have seen letting Great-Aunt Edith adopt me as the best thing for me.'

Dio! Paolo's eyes widened in perplexity. How could a man hand over a tiny scrap of his own flesh and blood and walk away? Yet she was making excuses for the inexcusable! Did she always turn the other cheek? Look for the good where others could see only bad? If so, she was unique in his experience!

He was looking at her as if she were from another planet, Lily registered, confused. She moistened her dry lips, parted them to stress that her lack of parents had nothing to do with the knotty problem they were facing, then promptly forgot what she'd been about to tell him when he leaned forward, sliding his arms around her as he kissed her.

Tender this time. Achingly tender. Amazingly beautiful. And her head was spinning, her heart hurting, when he broke the kiss, held her head into his shoulder and murmured softly, 'I've given you a hard time. It is my turn to apologize, *cara*. It won't happen again.'

Where had that come from? Never apologise, never explain—what had happened to the code he lived by?

Shaken with the depth of what he was feeling—compassion, admiration, disgust with his earlier unfeeling treatment of her, whatever—he turned his head to touch his lips to the so-vulnerable spot below her ear.

'Trust me. I got us into this mess, just as you said, and I'll get us out of it.' He could feel her heart beating beneath her perfect breasts. Nameless emotion claimed him and his voice was dark and husky as he told her, 'In the meantime relax, enjoy being here.'

He almost added *with me*, but stopped himself in time.

CHAPTER SIX

SHE was becoming addicted to him, Lily admitted with agitation. Really addicted to him. When he was with her, by her side, in the same room, meeting up with his mother for lunch or dinner, she couldn't take her eyes off him, and when he turned his beautifully shaped head, caught her moony eyes on him and gave her that lazy, sexy smile of his, she just about went to pieces.

Did he know that? Know that he only had to smile at her, casually touch her hand in passing, rest his hand lightly on her shoulder, to make her breathing quicken, her heart leap, her body sting and burn with sexual tension?

She had the terrifying feeling that she was falling in love with him, and she so didn't want to! Why, in full knowledge of what she was looking at, would she want to buy a one-way ticket to a place called Misery?

She could tell herself with cold, stark truth that this new display of tender togetherness he'd displayed during the couple of days they'd been here was just an act, but it didn't make the slightest bit of difference.

And as for kissing her—well, she'd worked that out too. Without any trouble whatsoever. Both times he kissed her had been when she'd displayed serious misgivings or signs of mutiny. In that first instance, her deep reluctance to meet his mother, and in the second her hysterics over his mother's insistence on making plans for a wedding that wasn't going to happen.

He was manipulating her, but knowing that didn't make a scrap of difference either. And that made her the worst kind of fool—her own worst enemy.

Her cheeks pink with annoyance—at herself, mostly—she swiftly tucked her shirt into the waistband of the classic cream-coloured linen skirt she'd selected from the abundance of fabulous garments Donatella had unpacked for her, ran a comb through her gleaming jaw-length fall of hair, and added just a touch of gloss to her lips. Looking in the mirror, she smiled wryly at the understated high-maintenance reflection she saw there, and set off to obey Carla's summons, issued from the house phone near her bedside five minutes earlier.

Signora Venini was taking her morning airing on the terrace and would be pleased if Signorina Lily would join her.

It would be the first time she'd been alone with Paolo's mother, and the prospect made her feel even more nervous. Without his presence as a buffer who knew what she might let slip by unguarded word or look? Especially if the older woman brought up the scream-inducing subject of wedding arrangements. She just wasn't used to pretending to be what she wasn't. Living a lie.

Paolo, as he'd informed her last night, would be spending most of the day in Florence on business. He'd invited her to go with him—to hit the shops, do the tourist thing until he was ready to return. She'd refused flatly, wanting time alone to get her head straight, talk herself out of what she was beginning to feel for him, put in some hard work on her sense of self-preservation.

Now she wished she'd accepted his invitation, if only to avoid the coming *tête-à-tête* and the pitfalls it was sure to present.

Reaching the doors to the terrace, Lily allowed herself a moment to let the soft light and gentle warmth of the Tuscan spring wash over her, and hopefully begin to relax her, starting slightly when a cheerful, *'Buongiorno*, Lily!' hit her ears.

'Signora,' Lily responded feebly, her feet carrying her with a reluctance she hoped didn't show towards the table beneath the vine-covered loggia, where the old lady sat in the dappled shade.

'Sit with me. And do you think you could manage to call me Fiora? Less formal, *si*?' Her smile was pure charm. Lily now knew where Paolo had got it from. When it suited him! '"Mamma" we will save until the happy day when you are my daughter-in-law.'

Knowing that day would never dawn, Lily felt slightly sick as she forced herself forward and sank into a chair on the opposite side of the table.

How she hated deceiving this nice old lady! Part of her was strongly urging her to come clean, confess all, put her conscience to rest and weather the storm that would erupt from Paolo's direction. But then Fiora said, 'How pretty you look—my cynical son has followed his heart and at last chosen well. A lovely young thing in possession of a loving and gentle heart, instead of a glossy model with a calculating machine where her heart should be! You are going to make him very happy!'

All Lily could manage was a painted on smile that covered the sinking conviction that there was no way she could tell Paolo's mother the truth—because not only would it shatter the old lady's obvious happiness, it would cause a deep rift between mother and son, and she couldn't bring herself to be responsible for that.

Thankfully, Agata arrived with a tray of coffee, and while Fiora was pouring from the elegant silver pot she confided, 'The nurse my son hired has departed—such a bossy creature! I told Paolo that as I felt so much better she was not needed.'

'And he agreed?' He was so protective of his mother, so anxious for her well-being, that Lily couldn't keep the note of sheer astonishment out of her voice.

'Not without argument!' The hazel eyes lit with laughter, and Lily reflected that Paolo's mother did look better. There was colour in her cheeks and strength in her voice now, and the faint bruising around her eyes had disappeared. 'He had to agree that the news of his wedding has given me a new lease of life!' She reached out a hand to cover Lily's, where it lay on the sun-warmed wood of the tabletop, and confided soberly, 'My husband's death ten years ago was a terrible blow. Sergio and I were very dear to each other. But I had my two handsome sons to live for. The hope of grandchildren.'

She sighed, withdrew her hand and laid it with the other in her lavender silk lap. 'Then, just over a year ago, my son Antonio and his pregnant wife died in a car accident. Another dreadful blow. And Paolo, to my sorrow, seemed quite determined never to marry again.' She shrugged her thin shoulders. 'In a way I could understand his reluctance. He couldn't trust his emotions, you see. Twice they'd let him down very badly. But of course he will have told you all this.'

With effort, Lily nodded, cringing inside. Another lie! Paolo wouldn't confide in her, tell her anything personal. She was a mere employee, fit for carrying out his orders and nothing more. She could tell Fiora that it hadn't been his emotions that had let him down because he didn't have any—not real ones—except in respect of his adored mother. It was all down to a low boredom threshold, as Penny Fleming had explained. But she'd hold her tongue and let the old lady keep her fond illusions.

'Apart from a mother's natural wish to see her son happy and settled, I knew that if Paolo didn't marry the ancient bloodline my Sergio was rightly so proud of would die out, and that was another great sadness to me. But—' a smile broke through the miasma of sad memories '—he has found you, lost his heart and found a happy future. So, after a long and painful year I can look forward to the future with a sense of joy I had never expected to know again.'

It was the first Lily had heard of the tragedy, and Fiora's year of hopeless depression. At last she could fully understand why Paolo, on hearing of his mother's possibly fatal illness, had decided to lie. He would have been at his wits' end, and must have seen announcing a fake engagement as the only way to give his adored mother a measure of happiness.

But fully empathising with him now didn't make the deception any easier. It made it harder.

She was relieved when Fiora's companion appeared, to chivvy the older woman into taking her morning rest.

'To get your strength back you must rest often,' Carla stated with a sideways smile for Lily, holding out a hand to help the older woman to her feet.

'Lily and I were having an important conversation,' Fiora objected with hauteur, waving aside the proffered hand. 'And I can walk unaided! Leave us—I am not in the least tired.'

'That is because you have behaved sensibly up to now and rested, as your consultant said you should,' Carla countered levelly, and Lily hid a smile, wondering who would win this contest of wills. Her money was on Fiora!

She would have lost it, she recognised sickly, when Carla delivered the power punch. 'You will need all your strength to plan for and attend the wedding you're so excited about. Tire yourself and you will be fit for nothing!'

Fiora rose to her feet promptly at that remark, admitting, 'For once you are quite right.' The smile she gave Lily was pure mischief. 'I will see you and Paolo at dinner this evening. I have something exciting to tell you both.' And she allowed herself to be led away, grumbling, 'Remember, Carla, that if you get to be too bossy you will go the way of the nurse!'

Her companion's comfortable grin showed she knew the threat was hot air and bluster and certainly not meant.

As soon as the other two had entered the imposing villa Lily leapt to her feet, too wired to sit still one moment longer. Why was Paolo absent when she really needed him?

Her hands clenched into fists at her sides, she paced over to the stone balustrade and stared unseeingly out at the view over thickly wooded hillsides and fertile valleys. In her opinion Paolo was far too laid-back about the situation he had catapulted them into.

She had to make him understand that he must somehow put an end to talk of imminent wedding bells! *Now*. Right now! Before they found themselves even deeper enmeshed in Fiora's plans!

She had tried on the occasion of her first meeting with his mother. Stressing her need to be home, working, because it was all hands on deck as far as the charity went.

To no avail.

So it was up to him. And since he wasn't around, and she felt she'd go stir-crazy if she thought about it for one more moment, she'd have to do something to take her mind off it.

Turning on the heels of her supple leather courts, she headed smartly for the villa, slipping up to her room, settling on the side of the bed and picking up the phone. The nerve-racking situation made her feel as if she was fighting her way through dense clouds, no map to give her directions, and the best person to help her feel grounded again was her great-aunt.

Edith picked up on the second ring, her customary no-nonsense, 'Yes, who is this?' bringing the first real smile to Lily's lips for days.

'Me, Aunt. How are you coping alone?' Suddenly she could see a possible way out. 'Short-handed, it must be difficult. Did you find someone to exercise Maisie's dog?' If she could get her great-aunt to admit that in her absence the charity couldn't meet its obligations she'd have the perfect excuse to cut her stay in Italy short.

'Don't fuss, child! We are coping beautifully. Kate Johnson is in place. She came early. And as soon as she'd settled into her accommodation at Felton Hall she started to organise the volunteers. She's found two—got the vicar to plead for help after his sermon— and is advertising for more in the local paper. She even managed to get Life Begins a good write-up. I can't think why we didn't think to do that ourselves! It takes a well-paid professional to get things right. Even at this early stage everything is looking far more hopeful. I would have thought that young man of yours would have told you all this. He's in daily touch by telephone. He's obviously taking his involvement very seriously.'

'Young man of yours'? She couldn't mean Paolo, could she? How absurd? Lily fell into a glum silence, her escape route well and truly blocked. She was glad for the charity's sake, of course she was, but it didn't help her situation. Which, she admitted uncomfortably, was really selfish of her.

'You still there?' The volume of the question made Lily flinch and squawk an affirmative, holding the receiver away from her ear as her great-aunt boomed on, 'So no need to fuss! Now, are you having a lovely time?' Thankfully not waiting for an answer, she continued, 'When our new partner suggested he give you a holiday in Italy, mentioning that his mother had recently been ill and could do with some young company, and that you looked very tired, I realised I had been neglecting your welfare. You've been working far too hard for too long…'

Lily mentally shut out the unnecessarily loud one-sided conversation. So *that* was how he had persuaded Edith to agree, without questioning his motives, to allow her to go to Italy without any fuss. She had often wondered. But she should have known he could charm the birds out of the trees when he had to. When Paolo Venini wanted something he got it. One way or another.

Cutting into a pause for breath at the other end of

the line, she said, 'Look after yourself, Aunt. And I'll see you soon.'

At least she devoutly hoped so.

Paolo swung the car onto the long curving drive up to the villa. He was running late. He would be hard-pressed to shower and change before dinner, taken at the earlier hour of seven as a concession to his mother's recuperation. His meetings had run on for longer than he'd expected, and for some reason he'd been anxious to get home, so he hadn't been his usual incisive self. His mind had been elsewhere.

Because he wanted to see Lily? Be with her? The thought flickered briefly, unwelcomely, across his mind. Of course not! Or if he did then it would only be to check things out, reassure himself that she hadn't, without his presence, his guidance, done or said something to give the game away.

His strong jaw tightened. He gave thanks hourly for his mother's recovery. That it had been hugely helped along by his fictitious engagement gave him pause. But he hadn't expected her to jump on the wedding band wagon with such spritely agility! Only yesterday she had been pestering him to seek an appointment with the priest, fix a date for as soon as possible after her final appointment with her surgeon.

When he told her, as he would have to, that there was to be a lengthy postponement she would be disappointed. He knew that. But she would understand the importance of a sudden—invented—crisis. A need for him to travel to his headquarters in New York, Madrid, London or wherever. His need to clear business before he could settle down to married life. She had been married to the head of a world-renowned mercantile bank for long enough to know that the sound running of the business came before personal considerations. Another bending of the truth. Distasteful but necessary.

Removing Lily, whom she had confessed happily that she'd taken to her heart, would pose a different problem. The excuse that she was needed back in England to work with the charity wouldn't wash because his mother knew he had intervened and thus made Lily redundant.

But he had the problem solved. Her great-aunt was elderly. Needed her. His mother would understand that—understand that depriving an old lady of the company and care of the great-niece she had adopted as a small baby, loved as if she were her own child, would be unkind. Thus, the engagement would stretch and stretch, until some time in the future he could say that long engagements didn't work and the wedding was off.

Hopefully by that time his mother would be much stronger, more able to handle the disappointment. There would be recriminations coming his way, but his shoulders were broad. That his thinking was devious, to put it mildly, was in no way a pleasure to him. Normally direct, he found deceit left a bad taste in his mouth. But in this case the ends—his beloved mother's return to good health—justified the means.

He would have to explain all this to Lily. His jaw relaxed. Put her out of her misery! Though, to do her credit, she had acted the part he'd assigned her more convincingly than he'd expected.

Her role as a woman who was deeply in love couldn't be faulted. Nothing personal—she knew the financial viability of her charity depended on her co-operation— but the way she looked at him, her eyes dreamy, her cheeks flushing with pleasure when he smiled at her, silver lights sparkling in the clear depths of her eyes was completely convincing. And when he touched her, took her hand, slipped an arm around her tiny waist to draw her forward to join the conversation between himself and Mamma, he would hear the catch of her breath, watch as the pulse-beat at the base of her slender neck quickened and see those lush lips part. He was hard put to see a flaw in her performance. She had a totally unexpected acting ability.

Such kissable lips, too, as he'd discovered. Had her response been play-acting, too? Somehow he didn't think so. Unconsciously, a softly sensual smile curved his long mouth. Who would have believed that the muddy scrap of his initial acquaintance could have been transformed into such a delicate, bewitching beauty?

Sexily responsive, too. Heat rolled through him and his body surged at the memory, and, unbidden, the aching need to hold her again, take that generous mouth, and take things further, much further, gripped him with driven savagery.

Basta! Enough! Braking the powerful car in a shower of gravel, he exited, shutting the door with enough force to shatter the silence. Having sex with Lily Frome, no matter how irritatingly tempting the prospect seemed, was a road he was *not* going to travel! Quite apart from the fact that she was temporarily his employee, and therefore strictly out of bounds, she was not his type.

His type. A heavy frown scored his forehead. Tall, blonde, leggy, polished. He'd been briefly engaged to one and almost as briefly married to another. That was before he'd learned the hard way that commitment was for fools. And now the blondes—when he could be bothered—were still tall, eye-worthy, polished and clued-up, taking a casual, sophisticated affair in their leggy stride. Cool, knowing the rules of the game.

Ergo, Lily Frome was *not* his type! She was tiny. But perfectly formed. She had hair the colour of a toffee apple. She was sweet, caring, not afraid to answer back, open and honest, so disturbed by what he had as good as coerced her into doing that she probably had nightmares every time she went to bed.

Went to bed— He strode into the villa by a side door, slipped up to the first storey by the staff staircase, to avoid meeting anyone, and tried to push the connection between Lily and bed right out of his mind. Mention a casual affair to her and she'd run a mile. Screaming!

Or hit him with the nearest heavy object!

And he, for one, wouldn't blame her. She was gorgeous, warm-hearted, intrinsically good, and she deserved far, far better than that. She deserved someone who would love her, value and treasure her.

Lily knew she was running around like a headless chicken. A naked headless chicken!

She'd put off having a shower and changing for dinner in the hope of waylaying Paolo on his return. Because she'd known she would explode if she didn't corner him and make him do something about his poor deluded mother and her talk of weddings!

But half an hour before the appointed time for the formal dinner *en famille* that Fiora enjoyed so much he still hadn't arrived. Giving up hope, she'd sprinted into the shower and out again in record time, then scuttled around, pulling on fresh underwear, plucking something in a lovely smoky blue colour out of the wardrobe and dragging it on—only to find that though the front of the dress was modest enough it left most of her back bare down to her waist, leaving her bra straps exposed. And the skirt was as bad—it sort of clipped her bottom before flaring down to her ankles, showing a glaringly obvious panty line.

Muttering something that would have had her great-aunt telling her to wash her mouth out with soap and water, she stripped off to her skin, started to pull the dress on again, then threw it onto the bed, diving for the well-stocked cupboard and throwing garments out, looking for something that wouldn't show all her underwear.

* * *

'Lily…' The words that would have had him asking how her day had gone flew out of his head. If there'd been problems then suddenly they weren't important. He'd walked into her room unannounced, as if he had the right. To find her naked, flushed. Bewildered?

His breath caught. A hard tight knot in his chest. He should apologise, retreat.

He found himself moving forward instead, closing the door behind him. Tugged towards her as if he had no will of his own. She was exquisite. A surge of sexual need swamped him. He stopped breathing.

She should be backing away. Angry. But she wasn't.

Her tiny bare feet seemed rooted to the carpet. Did she feel, as he did, that this was meant? Fated? That there was nothing either of them could do about it? Always in charge of his own destiny, this was a first for him.

Closer. His eyes found hers and held. Her clear wide gaze made his heart turn over. Her soft lips were parted in unconscious invitation. The delicate pink crests of her perfect creamy breasts peaked in betrayal. Did she burn for him as he burned for her?

One touch of his hand, his unsteady hand, his skin against her skin and there would be no turning back. As he knew his own name he knew that. Her slender body was a siren call. Irresistible.

He dragged a breath into his oxygen-starved lungs. Lily was an innocent. Not his type, not the usual blonde sophisticate who saw good sex as a fair exchange for a few weeks of his attention, fancy restaurants, weekends in Paris, St Tropez, Rome, taking a parting gift of some costly jewel or other with no regrets.

The feeling that he would die before harming Lily, hurting her, overwhelmed him.

Turning, he reached for the control he'd almost lost during the handful of minutes that had passed since he'd walked in on her, reached for a robe flung carelessly over the back of a chair and enclosed her in it as she looked up at him in a way that turned his insides to water.

The backs of his fingers drifted over the warm skin that covered her delicate collarbone as he closed the fabric, and it was almost his undoing. His voice was thicker, more brusque than he'd intended, as he stepped away, putting much needed distance between them, and gave his belated apology, 'Forgive me. Walking in without your invitation to enter was crass.' He gave a cursory glance at his wristwatch. 'Dinner in five minutes. Mamma will be waiting.' And he left before he could succumb to the heartbreaking confusion in her beautiful eyes.

CHAPTER SEVEN

'I HAVE a lovely surprise for you!'

Fiora had waited until the sea bass had been served by the now silently departing Donatella, and Lily noted with a sinking feeling that her eyes were sparking with excitement.

'We are to have an engagement party on Friday!' she announced. 'The first social gathering we have hosted in over a year! This afternoon I have arranged everything on the telephone.'

'Have you, now?' Carla, exotic in a deep scarlet flowing gown that suited her ample figure, patrician features and glossy black hair put in repressively. 'While my back was turned?'

'Exactly.'

'And you don't think you should have waited until you are strong enough to cope with such excitement and busyness?'

'Mamma?' Paolo echoed the companion's question, and for the first time since entering the dining room Lily looked directly at him, willing him to veto his mother's insane idea.

In his white dinner jacket he looked exactly what he was—sophisticated, urbane, perfectly at home in his exquisite surroundings. White on white. White walls, long windows where gauzy white drapes fluttered, tall white candles on the table drawing gleaming reflections from the antique silverware, Venetian glass and sparkling china. White blooms in a creamy porcelain bowl gracing the centre of the table.

Lily's lashes swiftly screened her tortured eyes. Watching him idly toy with the stem of his wine glass, relaxed, his sensual mouth softening even as he raised one strongly marked eyebrow in the direction of his mother, she felt as if someone had kicked her in the stomach.

She didn't think she would ever, ever be able to face him alone again! A raging blush burned her face. The way she'd just stood there, for the second time caught as naked as a newborn, stunned, immobile, watching the slow drift of his golden eyes as he moved towards her, trapped by a fierce sexual tension. It must have seemed to him that she was blatantly inviting him to touch her, make love to her!

Which was exactly what she had been doing, she recognised with searingly painful honesty. She had wanted him so very desperately that her normal sense of modesty and self-respect had departed without a single trace!

But he couldn't have made his lack of interest any

plainer. Apologising for his intrusion and covering her up with that robe. And leaving. A definite *thanks, but no thanks*! She had never felt so humiliated, so deeply ashamed of herself in her life!

It had taken more courage than she had imagined she possessed to pull on the most sober garment she could find and appear for dinner. Now, she belatedly wished she had taken the coward's way out—pleaded a headache and buried herself deep beneath the bedclothes, refusing to come out until this nightmare had gone away.

'Don't fuss, Paolo!' Fiora forked a little of the delicious fish. 'It is to be a small affair only—to mark your betrothal, as is proper. Just your cousins—I know you have no time for them, but I want to show Lily off to what little remains of our family.' She laid down her cutlery after clearing her plate, welcome evidence of her returning appetite. 'As for the extra work—what are staff for? It will give me great pleasure to sit back and simply direct operations!'

Once again Lily steeled herself to raise her eyes in Paolo's direction, swallowing shakily as the impact of his lean male beauty hit her. Tightening her soft pink mouth as her heart clattered against her ribs, she waited for him to put a halt to it all—rule out any idea of an engagement party. After all, he was king of the roost. This was his home, his fake engagement.

But all he said was, 'Then, provided you don't overtire yourself, we will humour you, Mamma.'

Paolo heard Lily's rush of indrawn breath, saw her

slender white shoulders—revealed by the black silk slip dress she was wearing—stiffen, before they sagged as she slipped a little lower in her chair, as if she were trying to hide herself under the table.

Poor sweet Lily! An iron band tightened around his heart. He'd put her through one ordeal after another. He would make amends, he vowed silently. He would make things right if it was the last thing he did.

She had looked strained and subdued since she'd joined them. Because of what had happened—almost happened—back in her bedroom?

His body hardened intolerably as mental images flooded his brain.

He felt he had shown quite remarkable restraint in the circumstances. He had been driven wild by need, yet he had done the honourable thing and backed off. Surely she would understand that by doing that and not following his primal instincts it showed he had grown to respect her, admire her and care for her? That he had put her physical and emotional well-being before his own desire to possess her enticingly sexy body?

When she understood that he had respected her innocence, not taken advantage of what she had undoubtedly unknowingly offered, she would begin to respect him too. Would grow to like him and forget how he had manipulated her into a situation he knew she felt deeply uncomfortable about. For some reason it was vitally important.

What was it about Lily Frome that brought out the male protective instinct in him? The need to look good in her eyes? Until now he had never cared how other people saw him.

His brooding golden gaze rested on her, and his heart squeezed painfully inside his chest. That dress made her look so fragile, threw the pallor of her skin into prominence. She looked achingly delicate. Fragile and breakable.

He didn't want to break her. He wanted to—

Muttering his excuses, he left the table and went to take a long cold shower.

'Lily said she wanted some fresh air,' Fiora said in answer to Paolo's question, not raising her eyes from the lists she was writing, rapidly covering the sheets of paper, underlining some items several times, starring or circling others.

To-do, or Have-done lists for the coming party, he guessed, helping himself to a much-needed cup of un-sweetened dark coffee from the pot on her breakfast tray.

His night had been passed in deep thought. His body and mind had thrown up a problem. But, as always, having looked at the problem from all possible angles, he had found the answer.

All he had to do was persuade Lily to reach the same conclusion.

Since his ill-fated disaster of a marriage, and before that his farcical engagement, he had cynically distrusted his judgement where women were concerned. He had found, and subsequently taken it as read, that women would bend over backwards in their haste to fall in with his slightest suggestion because of what was in it for them—being seen with one of Europe's most eligible unattached men in all the right places, being pampered for as long as his interest lasted, and finally departing from his life in receipt of a handsome pay-off.

But he wasn't thinking about his usual type here; he was thinking about Lily. And she was so very different. Which was why—

His brow furrowed as Fiora laid aside a sheet of paper, which from where he was standing looked decidedly covered in hieroglyphics, and remarked with a touch of rebuke, 'The dear girl looked pale and strained. I hope you haven't done something to upset her.'

'Of course not.'

The words stung like acid in his mouth. He'd done nothing *but* upset her since he'd as good as blackmailed her into playing a part she found demeaning and distasteful! He shifted his feet uncomfortably. He wasn't used to being in the wrong. He didn't like it.

'Good. Mind you don't.' The glance his mother gave him was admonitory. 'She is a lovely young woman in all respects, and nothing at all like those dreadful painted harpies you kept getting yourself photographed with—much to my despair!'

Paolo stuffed his hands into the pockets of his off-white chinos. 'Don't nag, Mamma.'

'I am your mother. I shall nag if I wish.'

His long mouth twitched. 'The days of the harpies

are over, I assure you.' Had been for quite some time now. He had discovered that casual affairs were not only a bore, they left him deeply unsatisfied.

'I should think so, too! While you're here I would like your permission to ask my dressmaker to attend. Primarily to create Lily's wedding gown, but I'd also like him to run up something for me—the mother of the groom must look her best.'

His golden eyes lit with laughter. She was priceless. Her 'dressmaker' was one of the most talented and internationally sought-after designers in Italy.

'As you wish, Mamma.' He stooped to drop a kiss on her forehead, anxious now to be off and begin to put his plans into operation, but she caught his hand, holding him, her eyes fond, and gazing up at the son who inspired frustration, exasperation, and above all absolute devotion in the maternal heart.

'As you know, I see that surgeon person in three weeks' time. I would like you to arrange the marriage for as soon as possible after that.'

He raised her hand to his lips, serious now, his eyes darkening. 'Only if you have a clean bill of health and the doctor gives you the go-ahead. Not even my desire for the wedding will allow me to let you overtire yourself.'

'I'll waltz through the consultation—you'll see!' Her smile was radiant. 'And waltz at your wedding! Now, run along—go to your fiancée.'

But finding Lily was no longer his most pressing priority. Things were moving at breakneck speed. What had started off as a deception to make what he had genuinely believed to be his mother's last few days happy had turned into something quite different.

Strong white teeth showed in an unrepentant grin as he strode into his study. There were things to arrange before he set about persuading his pretend fiancée to become his real one and agree to be his wife.

Kill two birds with one stone. Assure Mamma's happiness, her peace of mind, her interest in a bright future, give her the prospect of grandchildren, and at the same time assuage his now deeply felt need to care for Lily, protect her, make love to her, make her his own.

The idea of marrying again didn't seem as distasteful as it had done. Lily would be a wife he could trust, honest and straightforward—except when he coerced her into betraying her principles. His mouth tightened.

He knew he wanted her permanently in his life. And what he wanted he always got.

Didn't he?

His mouth set, he lifted the receiver and began, rapid-fire, to punch in numbers.

Feeling light-headed, Lily sat on the herb-strewn grass, drew her legs up, looped her arms around them and dropped her head down onto her knees.

She'd risen early, creeping through the villa like a thief, intent on avoiding Paolo because being anywhere near him with the memory of the way she'd behaved last evening still raw between them was out of the question.

But her conscience had pricked her when she'd met Carla, taking a breakfast tray into Fiora's room. Paolo's mother had shown her nothing but warmth and kindness since her arrival. She was a lovely lady, and would only worry when her absence was discovered—an absence Lily was determined would last for several hours.

So, worrying the elderly lady being the last thing she wanted to do, she'd poked her head around the door in Carla's wake and said, as brightly as she could, 'Fiora, *buongiorno*!' Paolo's mother had been already up and dressed, bright-eyed and bushy-tailed, a huge notepad on her lap. 'As it's such a lovely morning I thought I'd explore the gardens and maybe grab an hour or two of sunbathing.' And she'd headed off as quickly as she could.

The beautiful gardens were extensive, with many secluded areas where she could sit in solitude. And even though she was sure Paolo wouldn't set out to look for her—his abrupt departure from the dining room last night instead of spending the remainder of the evening with her and his mother, as had been his custom, told her that he'd found that bedroom scene deeply distasteful and would want as little to do with her as possible during the remainder of her stay here—she needed to get right away from the villa's immediate environs for the few hours she desperately needed.

And so when she'd found a wooden door in the high stone perimeter wall she'd pushed it open and found herself out on the open hillside, where she'd sunk down on the grass and scrunched up in a bundle of exhausting emotions, knowing she would need far more than a few hours to get her silly self sorted.

She'd fallen in love with Paolo Venini.

She'd done her best to convince herself that what she felt was nothing more serious than a normal female reaction to a powerfully charismatic and sexy male. Lust. Something that would thankfully and quite rapidly fade when she was no longer constantly in his presence, when all the contact with him she had would be his promised regular and long-distance funding of the charity organiser he'd set in place back in England. A case of out of sight, out of mind.

But he would never be out of her mind. That was the stark, unpalatable truth of it. He would always have a place in her heart, and her heart would ache for him. And her body would cringe with shame whenever she remembered how she'd stood before him, naked and needy.

He had turned his back on her and walked away. After pointedly draping a robe around her, demonstrating his uninterest. And why *wouldn't* he walk away? she asked herself brutally. He could grit his teeth and act a part when they were in his mother's company, for the sake of the deception he had instigated, and he might be highly sexed—one only had to look at the succession of busty blonde bimbos who passed through his life—but skinny, unsophisticated nobodies would leave him cold.

She was just someone he'd paid to play a part. Someone he would never have noticed if he hadn't had a brainstorm and decided to manufacture a fiancée to ease his mother's mind, back when it had seemed unlikely she would survive her operation, let alone recover from it. She had to remember that. It would help her recovery from the illness of falling in love. Someone, somewhere had likened it to an illness, hadn't they?

About to get to her feet and walk off some of her pent-up emotions, Lily tensed, her breath solidifying in her lungs, her pulse going haywire.

She sensed his presence even before he spoke, and her mouth ran dry.

'Lily, are you hiding?'

Deny it? Pretend that bedroom scene hadn't happened? Or face it out? A split second to make up her mind.

She lifted her head. Watched the effortlessly graceful way he sank to the ground beside her and mentally cursed his raw sexual magnetism. But she drew on some reserve of courage and gave him the truth, her small features tight. 'Yes. Hiding. I'm embarrassed about what happened before dinner yesterday, OK? And, if you're wondering, I don't normally make no attempt to cover up when a man walks in on me in my birthday suit. Right?'

And, having said her piece, she quickly changed the subject. 'And I'm mad as blazes at you because you didn't put a stop to that engagement party nonsense when I'm sure you could have done!' She saw him smile and turned her head away sharply, biting down on her soft lower lip, because that smile of his was enough to turn the sanest woman into a gibbering wreck.

'And you have much experience of men surprising you in a state of nakedness?' His voice was as rich and dark as chocolate.

Lily's skin quivered. 'No, of course not!' Why didn't he just drop it? Was he cruel enough to be getting a kick out of embarrassing her?

'I thought not. You are truly an innocent.'

He was sitting so close she could feel his purr of amusement. Or was it more like satisfaction?

Either way, it was one more strike against her! He wouldn't rate lack of experience highly, much less fall in love with an 'innocent' as he had named her. That meant she just had to stop living in cloud-cuckoo land, moping and pining and wishing he would catch the same illness she had come down with! He didn't even fall in love with the type of woman he bedded—cool, blonde, sexy and knowing. He just used them, grew bored, and tossed them aside! So what chance would *she* have?

He might laugh at what he would have seen as an attempt to entice him, so it was up to her to show him she had a mind of her own and wasn't to be sidetracked or poked fun at!

'Don't change the subject.'

'And that is?' he asked, with provocative smoothness, stretching out his long muscular legs, angling his body into hers so that she wanted to move away, right away, but couldn't make herself.

Hot colour scorched her cheekbones. What was the matter with her? She craved his nearness like an addict craved a fix. She knew how bad it was for her, but she couldn't make herself get up and put distance between them. She was a hopeless case where he was concerned!

Furious with herself, she grumped at him. 'That awful engagement party your mother's busy organising! You must stop her before even more people get drawn into our shameful lies!'

'Ah, that.' He touched the side of her face with the backs of his fingers, then withdrew his hand and reached into a pocket to produce a small velvet-covered box.

Her skin still burning from his touch, Lily could only stare transfixed as he slid the dazzling ring onto her wedding finger. 'A perfect fit now. I told you I'd get it altered.'

The smugness in his voice fired her to blazing anger. 'I could slap you!' she hissed, scrambling round so that she was on her knees, facing him. 'I *told* you not to mess with the family heirloom when it's only going to be a stage prop—you stupid, arrogant—'

'My refreshing Lily!' Almost lazily he reached forward, hands on her shoulders, pulling her down to his level, one of his legs pinioning hers. 'You are the first woman to remind me that I am not perfect! The only woman apart from Mamma who has the spirit to argue with me—I like that.' He dropped the lightest of kisses onto the end of her nose. 'I like it very much. It reminds me that I am human.'

His nearness, the heat of his body against hers, the scent of his skin, were desperately tantalising, and made her tremble. She loved him so much, and she hated herself for loving him. She just knew that her resolve to keep him firmly at arm's length was rapidly dwindling, like mist in the heat of the sun, even though she also knew that he was doing what he'd done before. Distracting her to take her mind off her objections to a fake engagement party that he wasn't going to veto because this further descent into deceit didn't bother him.

Her body stiffening, where before it had been weakly melding with his, she fisted her hands against his chest and pushed. 'I'm warning you—if that fake party goes ahead, I won't be there!'

'Neither will I, *cara.*'

Her smooth brow furrowed at that, her hot words swallowed. Was he going to put a stop to it after all? It seemed like it. Gradually her fists unfurled, her palms lying against his chest where she could feel the steady beat of his heart, the heat of his skin beneath the soft fabric of his collarless shirt.

Brilliant golden eyes searched hers. Her breasts felt heavy and her skin tingled as a shameful heat coiled deep inside her, intensifying as one of his hands slid down her body to rest against the curve of her hip.

She tensed. Did he know what he was doing to her? Did he care? Probably not! She was just some fluttery female he could bend to his will with the effortless expenditure of just a little of that overwhelming sexual appeal of his! And yet—

'What do you mean?' With a determined effort to get

out of the danger zone she wriggled away, but he simply placed a strong lean hand on the small of her back and hauled her back again. Her breath was expelled in a gasp at the close contact with his powerful body, and her words were little more than a ragged whisper when she pressed on, with difficulty, 'You said you wouldn't be at the party, either.'

Hoisting himself up on one elbow, his eyes gleaming between their fringing of thick dark lashes, he smiled at her before lowering his proud head to take her lush pink mouth with his, stroking with a sensuality that made her whimper and quiver before he imparted, 'We won't attend a fake engagement party, my Lily. I want it to be a real one.' And, as her eyes widened in bewilderment, he said. 'I'm asking you to marry me.'

CHAPTER EIGHT

LILY stared at him in shock. She opened her mouth to speak but no words came out.

Paolo simply smiled with sheer male complacency as he gently threaded his fingers through her silky-soft hair and positioned her to meet his exact requirements. He lowered his dark head and murmured against the moist softness of her lush pink mouth, 'You will be my bride, Lily,' with all the innate self-assurance of the alpha male who always got what he demanded, and for whom pleading or even merely asking nicely was foreign to his dynamic nature.

That type of arrogant domination shouldn't turn her bones to water and her skin to fire, make her ache to submit, but it did. And, much as she deplored it, there was nothing she could do about it.

With helpless resignation she was excruciatingly aware of the coil of stinging heat deep in the pit of her stomach, the insistently urgent straining of her breasts beneath the thin cotton top she was wearing—aware, to her everlasting shame, that Paolo Venini only had to touch her and she was aroused to such a peak of sexual excitement, of loving and longing, that she forgot everything—who she was, who he was, her common sense and self-respect, everything she valued about herself.

Desperate to get the word *no* beyond the tight constriction of her throat, all she managed was a quivering moan of instinctive response as he parted her lips with his and began a totally erotic assault on her senses. His tongue plunged into the inner yielding sweetness with raw masculine urgency and his hands slipped beneath the soft fabric of her top, his groan of satisfaction telling her befuddled brain that the discovery she was braless did more than merely please him.

As deft hands pushed her top up, exposing her straining pink-crested breasts to his simmering gaze, Lily made a furious effort to pull herself together, fighting the need to surrender to this man she loved more than she'd thought possible.

Squirming away from him, shaking, her face flushed and troubled, she managed, 'This is madness!'

At that a slow smile softened his sculpted features, and his golden eyes, hazed over with the smoke of desire, crinkled at the corners as he breathed, 'If this is madness, then I like it. I like it more than I can say, *cara*! I can't get enough of it!'

And he closed her to him again, and this time his kiss was filled with fiery passion, robbing her of breath and sanity. Only when they came up for long-denied air could

Lily get out on a shaky gasp, 'Why would you want to marry when you've already told me you hate the idea?'

She pushed self-protectively away from him, privately thanking her guardian angel for allowing her that much strength of mind. And he let her. He had to have some ulterior motive for that insane proposal. She hadn't a clue what it was, knew only that it had to be cruel, because she was already hurting.

'Don't tell me you've fallen in love with me!' she managed unevenly.

And she despised herself for what he must see as the pall of disappointment that covered her expressive features as he took one of her hands and countered, 'What is falling in love? Just a sanitising phrase to make the basic urge of lust seem more acceptable.' He trapped her hand with lean bronzed fingers. 'I freely admit to lust—you turn me on, you make me burn, you touch me on a deeper level than any woman has ever done, *cara mia*. I know you too are desperate for our lovemaking, the way you respond tells me this, but I also know you are not mistress material. You are sweet and innocent, and I would not demean you by asking you to share my bed without marriage.'

There was unhidden male appreciation in his warm golden gaze now. 'Therefore, I have changed my mind about marriage. It would not be such a bad thing.'

With one fluid movement he reached for her again and tumbled her back onto the herb-scented grass, that tormenting hand slipping beneath her top to explore her

unbearably sensitised breasts, sending a fireball of eroti-
cism scorching through her.

His wickedly sensual mouth was a whisper away
from her trembling lips as he murmured urgently,
'Marriage. Think of it, my Lily. Being able to enjoy your
delightful body, giving you pleasure with an easy conscience, caring for you, pleasing Mamma instead of
having to present her with a broken engagement at some
time in the future.' His hand was now sliding down to
the soft curve of her tummy, making her weak with
longing—until he asked on a thickened growl, 'What
could be more convenient?'

Convenient!

For him!

Give Fiora what she wanted, make her happy. Allow
him to slake his self-admitted lust until she bored him
as, with his track record, she surely must.

And what about me? she wanted to howl, but didn't.
No point in letting him see how deeply he could hurt her.
Allowing him to guess that she'd fallen in love with him.
Adding several more cubic metres to that already
massive ego of his!

His insulting proposal was all about doing his duty by
his mother and slaking his newly discovered lust for
someone he had termed an innocent. The way he'd talked
about bedding her with an easy conscience made her pretty
darn sure he'd never had sex with a virgin before.

And how did he know she was a virgin—an 'innocent'?
Was it that obvious? Was she that gauche?

Well, the novelty of bedding a virgin would soon wear off, Lily knew. Tears stung at the backs of her eyes. He had a low boredom threshold. She knew that, too. He would tire of her, as he'd tired of his first wife, and she'd be shuffled off, hidden away, forgotten. Broken?

Not even the short-lived ecstasy of being his novel new wife would compensate for that sort of hurt.

But not for anything would she let him guess at the emotions that were threatening to pull her apart. Give him the smallest hint of how she really felt about him and he'd move in for the kill! And, knowing how weak she was where he was concerned, she'd make a very willing victim!

Taking a deep breath, she called on every last scrap of her will-power and told him, more or less levelly, 'I won't marry you, Paolo. I'm flattered. I think. But it's not going to happen.'

Steeling herself for another determined assault on her senses, she was left bewildered and perhaps, she thought, with more than a little self-disgust, disappointed as he slowly released her.

He was on his feet with enviable ease, his hands thrust deep into the pockets of his cargo pants, his smile frighteningly assured. 'Then, *cara*, I have two more days before the party to change your mind. Don't stay out in the sun too long. Even at this time of year delicate skins can burn.'

Somehow Lily managed to avoid Paolo until dinner that evening. Cook had excelled herself, with lobster in a light sauce followed by caramelised grapes, but she was barely able to swallow more than a mouthful of each.

Forcing herself to keep up with Fiora's lively chatter on the dreaded subject of the coming engagement party was the only way she could deflect attention from her lack of appetite. Inside she was wound up tight, fit to blow at any moment.

As for Paolo—well, she didn't dare look at him. But she felt him watching her, and from his occasional lazy comments she knew he understood how she was struggling to avoid his gaze, and was mightily amused by it.

Because—

Because he knew as well as she did that he only had to exert a fraction of the sexual magnetism he possessed in spades to have her helpless, completely in his power, agreeing to anything he demanded of her—even a marriage she knew would end in bitter failure.

And it scared her silly!

She wanted him—wanted to be his wife more than she'd ever wanted anything before. The offer was there, but she couldn't take it.

With the evidence of one broken engagement, one short-lived marriage and countless casual affairs behind him, she would be committing emotional suicide if she gave in to temptation. If he loved her she would be the happiest woman on the planet. But he didn't. He'd said as much. And she wasn't prepared to have her heart broken.

She wasn't that recklessly stupid, was she?

Diving into a tiny gap in the on-going conversation

around the table, Lily asked in a thin, tight voice she didn't recognise as her own, 'Fiora, could you spare Carla for a short while tomorrow morning? I need to go into Florence—without Paolo. I'd like to buy him a betrothal gift!' She forced a smile to hide her dismay at yet another miserable lie, her heart rattling. 'If she could drive me in, I could find my own way back.'

She held her breath, fully expecting him to offer to drive her himself. He'd know the betrothal gift was pure fabrication and smell a rat. Know she was avoiding his company at all costs because she was terrified of his stated intention to make her change her mind about accepting his proposal before the guests arrived for the wretched party.

But all he said was, 'Mario shall drive you, *cara*. Just tell him what time you wish to return and he will come for you. Spend all day exploring our beautiful city, if that is what you want. But as for a betrothal gift—all I need is your sweet self, you know that. However, if it pleases you to choose something, a small gift to mark the occasion, then I, of course, will be delighted.'

Louse! What was he playing at? He would know that her sudden desire to go into town was an avoiding tactic. That she didn't trust herself when faced with his devastating brand of 'persuasion'. She might love him, but she would never understand him in a million years!

She did look at him then, and the perfection of his features took her breath away. The slow, sexy smile he gave her worked its usual havoc. Her breath catching, she excused herself, pleading a slight headache, and headed for the sanctuary of her room, locking the door behind her. Just in case.

Florence was an assault on Lily's already reeling senses. So much beauty, so much style, it was difficult to take in—especially as she felt in need of an enormous ball of string in order to find herself back in the square where Mario had dropped her off and had promised to collect her at five in the afternoon.

Footsore, but slightly easier in her mind after time alone, without the fear that Paolo might find her and work that special magic that could make her resolve melt like ice on a summer's day, Lily made it back to the meeting place with half an hour to spare. Tables outside a trattoria provided an excuse to sit in the shade, and the espresso she ordered was more than welcome.

Dismissing the occasional feeling that she was being followed as paranoia, she knew what she had to do.

Just this evening and tomorrow to make sure she didn't give Paolo the opportunity to use all his formidable powers of persuasion, and then hopefully the arrival of his mother's guests on the following day would severely limit their time alone together.

And so she'd be at the fake engagement so-called celebration. She couldn't carry out her earlier stated intention to boycott it because that would upset Fiora, and she didn't want to do that, but after that she'd be off. She would have to manufacture some urgently pressing reason for an immediate return to England. She didn't know what, but she'd think of something.

'*Signorina*—you are ready?'

Blinking, Lily glanced at the slim young man in dark trousers and immaculate white shirt. Mario. Exactly on time. Suspicion solidified into certainty.

She rose, collected her bag. 'Have you been following me, Mario?'

'*Certamente*. The *signor* instructed it.' He grinned widely, lifting narrow shoulders. 'You are precious to him. No harm must come to you.'

Fuming, Lily stalked across the *piazza* to where the gleaming car was waiting, Mario trailing in her wake. So much for her hours of freedom! In spite of what Mario thought, this was *not* about caring, anxiety for her well-being. It was all about Paolo's control. She had become his property, she realised with a sinking feeling. Followed. Watched. And no doubt he would demand a detailed report of what she'd been doing, she thought with ire.

But it wasn't Mario's fault. He had only done what he'd been told to do by the all-powerful Paolo Venini. So she was able to keep up a light-hearted conversation as they journeyed back through the Tuscan countryside, her mind working on another level as she formulated exactly what she would say on the subject of people with nasty suspicious minds who put minders on the tail of other people!

More than ever convinced that her only option was to return to England as soon as she'd done her duty by

Fiora and been put on show at the wretched party, she decided, with deep reluctance, that she would have to compound her sins and lie again. Say Great-Aunt Edith was ill and really needed her.

It was utterly distasteful, but it was the only thing she could think of that Fiora would understand. She would be disappointed that her visit was to be cut short, the plans for the wedding put on hold for a while, but she would understand and sympathise with the need.

And it would be up to Paolo to confess that the wedding was off at a time of his choosing!

The high she experienced at having thought herself out of the mess lasted until the car drew to a well-bred halt in front of the villa.

Then crumbled into hopelessness as she saw Paolo, looking heart-stoppingly gorgeous in slim-fitting denims and a white T-shirt, emerge from the open doorway, an all too healthy Great-Aunt Edith smiling fit to split her face at his side.

Her last escape route had been well and truly blocked by that dramatically handsome grinning devil!

CHAPTER NINE

IT WAS almost as if he'd read her mind even before she'd worked out her escape strategy, Lily thought, near to hysterics as she advanced on suddenly shaky legs towards the now broadly grinning pair, asking baldly, 'How did *you* get here?'

'What a welcome, child!'

To her astonishment Lily found herself crushed against her great-aunt's stout bosom in a rare show of open affection. 'By private jet and helicopter! Just imagine—I felt like royalty! Paolo arranged everything!'

'We couldn't celebrate our engagement without her,' came his unwelcome cool assertion.

Extricating herself from the bear-hug, Lily shot him a look of loathing. He gave her back a smile of simmering amusement, shot through with the satisfaction of a male who made things happen to get what he wanted.

No wonder he hadn't raised any objections over her awayday—he'd just put one of his staff on her tail and set about finalising the arrangements for the transportation of her elderly relative, in doing so making sure she, Lily, was put into an even more difficult situation! Ruthless and manipulative wasn't in it!

'I've been so excited since dear Paolo phoned with the news of your engagement!' Edith exclaimed warmly. 'And I don't think I've slept a wink since he invited me to come here and stay for the wedding!'

Oh, yes, he had her thoroughly outmanoeuvred.

'Why don't we go round to the terrace? Agata will provide us with cold drinks,' Paolo slid in, velvet-smooth. 'Mamma is resting before dinner. She might believe she is one hundred per cent fit, but she is still frail,' he added, with a detectable note of warning aimed at her, Lily realised with helpless rage.

He had no need to remind her of Fiora's delicate health, Lily thought darkly. She had grown genuinely fond of his mother, and if it hadn't been for her own un-willingness to distress her unduly she would have left Italy the moment she'd acknowledged she'd done the unthinkable and fallen in love with a man who was so wrong for her—valid excuse or not!

Fiora's continuing recovery from her life-threatening illness was his strongest bargaining tool. And now he'd brought her great-aunt in on the act, giving him another. She could kill the manipulating devil!

Her eyes boring into his broad back as they walked round to the side of the immense villa, she barely registered Edith's, 'I hope I didn't tire her. We had such a long and interesting chat after I arrived. Forgive me if I kept her too long.'

Arrested by the anxious note, Paolo turned, his smile warmly sincere as he swiftly reassured her. 'You are Lily's family, Edith—and Mamma prizes family relationships above all. Her retirement had nothing to do with your more than welcome presence, I promise. Carla, her companion, and I always insist that she rests each afternoon. Meeting you, having you here, makes her happy. And happiness is the best medicine, yes?'

Another none too subtle warning for her, Lily fulminated as they passed beneath the long pergola, festooned and dripping with wistaria, and headed for the steps that led up to the broad terrace.

As soon as she got her great-aunt on her own she would have to confess that the engagement—as far as she was concerned—was a total sham. Explain what had led up to this sorry situation. She wasn't looking forward to it. There was no one more upright and straightforward than her relative, and she would rightly deplore the deceit and make no bones about saying so!

But the opportunity was lost when Paolo left them to go in search of the housekeeper. Edith immediately turned to her, her eyes over-bright with emotion, and declared, 'I can't tell you how happy your news has made me, child! Such a weight off my mind! I must confess that I have worried about your future well-being for some time now. No—hear me out,' she demanded, as Lily opened her mouth to protest. 'I won't be around for ever, and who knows what has become of your feckless father. I hated to think of you being left alone in the world.'

She gravitated to a table in the shade and ordered, with just a hint of her old asperity, 'Sit. Don't hover, child. I *have* worried about you,' she stressed. 'Working all hours for little reward save that of knowing you were helping people who needed it. No opportunity or time to meet a suitable young man or embark on a financially rewarding career. I blamed myself for being so bound up in Life Begins and not giving a thought to your future. Not doing nearly enough for you.'

'Don't talk like that!' Lily cried emotionally. 'You'll be around for ages yet! And you did *everything* for me,' she protested with vehemence, distressed at what she was hearing, adding with heartfelt sympathy, 'It can't have been easy.' At a time when most women would have been thinking of slowing down, taking things a little easier, Edith had taken in a baby that had been as good as abandoned. 'You gave me family, a feeling of belonging, a happy and secure childhood.'

'It was never difficult, child. Never!' Edith's eyes grew moist with rare sentiment. 'And now I need no longer worry. News of your forthcoming wedding has taken a huge weight off my shoulders, believe me! Such a strong, caring man—so much wealth…' She waved an expressive hand at their surroundings. 'Mind you, were he as poor as a church mouse I would still heartily approve. Whatever his financial situation he would

make any woman a fine husband. As it is, his generosity means that we can safely leave the future of Life
Begins in capable hands, so that's one more anxiety
laid to rest.'

Paolo didn't rejoin them. Agata, bringing iced fresh
orange juice, imparted that the *signor* sent his regrets.
He had work to do and would see them at dinner.

Leaving her great-aunt in her room, exclaiming over
the amenities and deciding which of her two dresses was
more suitable for the coming dinner, Lily set out to look
for him. Fit to spit tacks. What right had he to go behind
her back and bring her unsuspecting great-aunt into this
mess of his?

He was good at humiliating her—wasn't he just?
She'd thought she'd been so clever—avoiding him
and his threatened 'persuasion'—but all the time he'd
had all the aces up his sleeve, had been laughing at
her. No wonder he'd allowed her to go out of her way
to avoid him!

Marching straight into the room he used as a study,
she found him standing by the tall window using his
cellphone. Shifting from foot to foot, she waited until
he had finished the call, refusing to let herself be impressed by his dark male magnificence, her eyes still
spitting sparks of rage when he turned to her and smiled.

'How dare you?' She launched straight in, practically bouncing up and down in her need to go over there
and slap him.

'*Cara?*' One perfectly shaped dark eyebrow arched in a query Lily found totally exasperating.

'You *know* what I'm talking about!' Bright spots of anger flared on her cheeks. 'You *know* what you've done. Now there'll be two old ladies to disappoint instead of one! Have you any idea—? Do you know what she said to me? She said knowing my future's secure—huh!—has taken a huge load off her mind!'

Eyes glittering, she was almost incoherent with rage that he had put her in this dreadful situation. 'You use people like pawns to get what you want. You never consider their feelings,' she accused wildly.

With difficulty Paolo stopped himself from grinning from ear to ear. Little Lily Frome was a bewitching delight. A small bundle of hissing fury!

It took courage to stand there and bad-mouth him, he acknowledged with renewed admiration. Used as he was to everyone—especially the bed partners who were now definitely history—treating him as if he were some kind of god, bending over backwards to please him, feeding him servile flattery, Lily in confrontational mood made him feel fully, vitally alive for the first time in years.

'I do what needs to be done. Haven't you heard the saying that the end justifies the means?'

As Lily watched him move towards her she felt stifled. The air locked in her lungs. Her small hands fisted. 'The end'—he meant marriage.

To her!

Not because he loved her. As if! But because it would

be convenient. Not wanting to disappoint his mother because he adored her, and after the tragedy that had taken his brother, his sister-in-law and their unborn child, he would do anything to make her remaining years contented. And, hey, bedding a virgin would be a novel experience. He could teach her everything he knew about sexual pleasure. Until he grew bored!

Thanks, but no thanks! She might love him, warts and all, and lust after him until it became a burning ache she could barely contain, but she had too much self-respect to allow herself to accept his insulting proposal.

And he was now close. Too close. Even so, she found the will to jerk her chin up at a defiant angle and meet his eyes.

Big mistake!

The smouldering mesmeric quality, the glittering golden lights, made her feel light-headed. He always had that effect on her, she mourned in silent self-contempt. And when he took one of her hands and uncurled her fingers she could do nothing to stop him.

Stroking her palm with one lean finger, he cracked down on the urgency of his desire to carry her over to the couch, strip her, reveal again the tantalising all-woman nakedness that had already been open to his avid view. To slide eager, questing hands over every de-lightful curve and hollow of her small but exquisitely proportioned body, discover the secret heart of her femininity and pleasure her until she was begging for release. To make her his.

But she was to be his wife. He was determined on that. And as his future wife she commanded his respect. Thrusting aside the erotic fantasies, promising himself that they would be played out in full on their wedding night, he said thickly, 'No one needs to be disappointed, *cara mia*. Our marriage will make everyone happy.'

Such rampant sex appeal was dangerous. She felt hot, restless, her breasts tight, the nipples pushing against the thin camisole top she was wearing beneath an elegant linen suit, and her mind had been reduced to a fuzzy blank—apart from the tiny voice that was urging her to give in, do anything he wanted her to do, admit she loved him. Then the realisation that he was manipulating her again brought her to her senses as effectively as if he'd tossed a bucket of icy water over her.

Snatching back her hand, she took a step away, a pulse beating furiously at her temples. He was working on her soft nature. Clever enough to understand that she would hate hurting anyone she loved. He knew how fond she and Fiora were of each other. Knew she cared deeply for her great-aunt, valued all she'd done for her, the sacrifices she'd made when she'd adopted her, brought her up as if she were her own child.

Well, she'd show him she wasn't as soft as he obviously thought she was. Her chin high, she got out, 'You forgot me when you listed the people who would find happiness through our marriage. Or was I supposed to be included in "everyone"?'

Scorn for his methods, when all he had to do was say

he loved her and mean it, which she knew would never happen, gave her the strength to walk out, telling him, 'I *won't* marry you. I'll leave you to break the bad news in your own time and carry the results on your own conscience—if you have one!'

Lily gazed at her reflection with no enthusiasm. She was wearing the smoky blue backless designer gown—minus underwear—hoping it would make her feel more like a grown woman with a mind of her own rather than a doll in the hands of an expert puppet-master.

It wasn't working. Her mind, what was left of it, was being jerked every which way. Her adamant decision to reject Paolo's proposal out of hand was wavering, then veering back on track again, until something else happened to swing it right back in the other direction.

The latest being the shattering conversation she'd had with her great-aunt a couple of hours ago.

'I want to talk to you.' The old lady's whisper had been loud enough to singe her ears. 'It's not necessary, but I'd like your agreement.'

Wondering what Edith was on about, Lily had found herself in the small salon that overlooked the gardens at the rear of the villa, the door closed firmly behind them, the old lady peering round to make sure they were alone. 'You know Fiora and her companion plan to move back to her home in Florence immediately following the wedding? Well, what do you think of this?' She'd pulled in a big breath, then added on a rush, 'I'm invited to move here to Italy—make my home in Florence with them! Such a lovely city, I believe. I've always wanted to see it, but never could afford the time or the pennies to do it!'

Speechless at that heart-sinking announcement, Lily could only stare into her beloved great-aunt's glowing eyes.

'Cat got your tongue?'

'I—' Struggling to get her head around this latest development, Lily didn't know where to start. 'What about your cottage—the charity?' But she knew what the answer would be.

It came as expected. 'The charity's fine—more part-time volunteers than ever, splendid fundraising activities planned, Paolo's support. And as for the cottage—it goes to you in my will. But married to Paolo you won't need it. So I shall sell it and pay my way in Florence with the proceeds.'

Her heart some miles beneath her feet, Lily said, 'So you've made your mind up?'

'As good as. Fiora and I get on like a house on fire. I wouldn't consider the move if we didn't. Apparently her apartment is enormous, fully staffed. And we'd be company for each other. Carla's splendid, but Fiora says she often longs for someone nearer her own age to talk with. And of course I'd be near to you—not that I'd be forever visiting and being a nuisance, but I'd be near.'

And, as if Lily's wide-eyed stare was not the enthusiastic reception she'd expected, the old lady had added confidently, 'Paolo's opinion has been sought. He thinks it's a splendid idea!'

I just bet he does! Lily thought now, heartily sick of everything being 'splendid', and turning from the mirror. Outmanoeuvred again! If she persisted in her refusal to marry Paolo those happy plans would bite the dust.

Great-Aunt Edith had a strong, unshakable sense of duty. She would no more go ahead with her plans to move to Florence, sell the cottage to fund her life here and in the process see her, Lily, homeless or living in a bedsit, than sprout wings and fly. They would move back to England and take up the life they had left.

Could she be selfish enough to deny the old lady the luxury and ease she deserved in her declining years?

Edith had never married. A teacher for many years, she had founded the small local charity and adopted her great-niece on her retirement from full-time employment at the age of sixty, having worked hard all her life with precious few of life's small luxuries. Didn't she deserve something much better now?

And, to make everything so much worse, Paolo had been so warm, so attentive—respectful, even—during the last couple of days. The perfect Italian fiancé. On the one hand it had made her fall more deeply in love with him, and on the other it made her feel decidedly murderous!

Looking forward to this evening's engagement party with as much pleasure as she would if faced with an appointment with her dentist for root canal work, she heaved a heartfelt sigh and slipped her feet into high-heeled mules.

The guests would be waiting for the happy couple to put in an appearance. Her stomach gave a violent lurch. Apparently a handful of Paolo's closest friends had been invited and, ominously, the village priest. And the cousins, of course. Three males and a female. They'd arrived an hour ago, but she'd only had time to smile wanly, register the males with sharp suits and indolent attitudes, and a striking Latin beauty who looked bored, before they'd been shown to their respective rooms.

On reflection, she thought she could sympathise with Paolo for having little time for them, but grumbled at herself for being uncharitable enough to condemn on first sight a bunch of people who were probably perfectly nice.

Nervously twisting the heavy ring on her finger, she straightened her spine. She couldn't hide in her room any longer. Time to face them and take part in this distasteful charade. Try to stop going over and over the uncomfortable facts that in refusing to marry Paolo she would distress her great-aunt, casting a pall of disappointment over her remaining years—not to forget Fiora, who would be one very unhappy lady.

As if her anguished thoughts, centred on the impossible male who was the author of all her present troubles, had conjured him up, Paolo entered the room.

Lily's progress towards the door skidded to a halt. In his white dinner jacket he was breathtakingly handsome, his hard male mouth softened into that sensual smile that always took her wits and scattered them.

Covering the space between them in a couple of fluid strides, his eyes holding her, entrapping her, he took her hand and lifted it to his lips, confidence oozing from every pore as he commented, 'You look spectacular, *cara mia*. A future bride any man would be proud to claim.' He held her hand against his broad chest, tugging her closer with a gentleness that almost defeated her, making her deplore the weakness that urged her to lean into him, to cling and never let go. But then he claimed, 'Not too long ago you accused me of considering everyone's happiness but yours—'

Which gave her the strength of mind to counter, 'And considering only your convenience—'

'Let me speak.' His voice lowered to a spine-weakening husky promise. 'I could make you happy. I will make you happy,' he stressed in amendment, and Lily sucked in a shaky breath, hypnotised by his golden eyes, by the lean, olive-toned male beauty of his unforgettable features, horrified by her internal admission that, yes, he could make her happy.

Ecstatically happy.

For about a week.

Until she bored him. And she was left broken, like his first wife.

Denying herself the relief of flinging her head back and wailing like a baby deprived of its most treasured plaything, she pushed out, 'We don't want to keep the guests waiting, do we?' and headed for the door. She paused just long enough to take a deep breath and make sure her voice emerged sounding as if she were in control. Of herself. Of everything. 'You may be king fish in the pond you swim in, but I will not be forced or emotionally blackmailed into doing something I know would be wrong for me—something I don't want to do.'

Then was undone as his arm snaked around her narrow waist, his warm breath feathering her ear as he whispered, 'But you *do* want to do it, my sweet Lily. And if I had the time I would prove it to you now.'

Her face flaming, Lily leant against him, needing his support because her legs had gone hollow, her whole body weakened by the shameful hunger he could awake in her effortlessly. Miserably aware, as they went down to greet the guests, that she was fighting a battle on two fronts.

With him. And, more terrifyingly, with herself.

CHAPTER TEN

PAOLO leant against the frame of the open French windows, one hand in the pocket of his narrowly cut black trousers, the collar of his dress shirt undone, the shimmering gold of his eyes partly veiled by an enviably thick fringe of black lashes.

Watching her.

Lily's delicate loveliness drew every eye in the room, and the dress she was wearing made him so hot for her he couldn't wait for this tedious party to be over and he could take a long cold shower.

Overturning his long-held rejection of the idea of re-marriage had been the right thing to do, he congratulated himself, his eyes following her as she and the wife of one of his oldest friends moved out of the way of a couple who were dancing to music pounding out from the state-of-the-art stereo system. Cousin Orfeo's idea, he supposed, suppressing vague irritation. Fortunately the grand salon had been largely cleared, and could accommodate those of the guests who chose to indulge in the pointless activity.

With ease he dismissed his notoriously workshy, playboy cousin, and returned his mind to a far more pleasant subject.

Marriage to Lily, who didn't treat him with tedious simpering deference, who didn't have a greedy eye on the main chance, as proved beyond all doubt by her rejection of his proposal when every other woman he knew would have tied herself in knots to accept such an offer, was the obvious step to take. It would be of indisputable benefit to all concerned, an entirely logical step. And logic—not emotional muddle—was how he liked to live his life.

He would no longer have to endure the constant feeling of guilt because his former refusal to settle down and sire an heir and a spare was causing his mother a great deal of grief—even more so since Antonio's death.

He would have a wife and companion he could trust implicitly, and in return Lily would have status, his care and fidelity, his children.

A band tightened about his heart at that entirely novel prospect. And the hope that their first child would be a girl, small and delicately formed, with those huge silvery grey eyes just like Lily's, hit him like a thunderclap.

Unused to bracketing himself and children together, he found the picture pretty startling. He shifted his feet and decided that he liked the idea. At least, he amended, with Lily as the mother of his children he liked the idea.

His eyes narrowed. She was being approached now by his cousin Renata. Lazy, like the rest of the clan, offspring of his father's unlamented, light-fingered brother, and believing the world owed her a living. Greedy, bitchy.

Still watching, he twitched his long mouth. Lily didn't know it, but her over-emphasised refusal to be his wife was soon to be turned on its head. Everything was in place. The arrival of her relative, planned and executed with precision, had set the scene. The unlooked-for but fortuitous liking the two senior ladies had quickly formed for each other, and their consequent decision to share the apartment in Florence, had been the icing on the cake, the last nail in the coffin of Lily's resistance— proof, if he needed it, that the gods were on his side.

Tomorrow he would take Lily to his villa in the hills above Amalfi. Alone with him, she wouldn't be able to hold out, resist his powers of persuasion. He had been around long enough to know when a woman was sexually attracted to him, and she was. He'd read the signs. Her days of digging her heels in were numbered! And to his dying day he wouldn't let her regret it.

He had done his duty as a host, circulating, receiving congratulations on his betrothal, had danced attendance on his mother and Edith. In a moment he would claim his Lily, make sure he mentioned the visit to Amalfi in front of his mother and Edith, certain that she wouldn't make a scene and refuse to go anywhere with him, because he knew that she was already beating herself up over the prospect of having to sorely disappoint the two women some time in the near future.

Which worked to his advantage, but made him

deeply uncomfortable. When it came right down to it he didn't like himself for playing on her caring nature, for manipulating her. But it would be for the best in the long run. Her life with him would be happy, and she would want for nothing. He would make sure of that.

A sudden scowl darkened his eyes. Lily, turning white-faced away from Renata, had brushed against his cousin Orfeo, who promptly swept her unresisting body into his arms and into a clumsy parody of a foxtrot.

His stubby fingers were splayed over the unblemished creamy skin of her back, sliding down her delicate spine and dipping beneath the barrier of fabric. His oiled-looking head pressed against hers as he whispered something.

Murderous rage surged through Paolo. How dared that oily creep paw *his* woman?

He strode forward.

She was hating every second of this. The congratulations, the curious looks veiled with sycophantic smiles, the whole wretched lying charade she'd got herself caught up in. And, worst of all, the radiantly happy smiles of Fiora and her great-aunt as they sat chatting together at a table in an alcove.

Worst of all, that was, until Paolo's cousin Renata slid up to her, a glass of red wine clutched in long white fingers, almost wearing a dress of sequinned scarlet.

'Nice work!' she said. 'You've nailed the wealthiest man in Italy—probably in the whole of Europe. It won't last, of course, but think of the big fat settlement you'll get when he decides marriage bores him!' She gave a tinkling laugh as brittle as breaking glass. 'Dear Paolo the heartbreaker. He has the attention span of a gnat when it comes to the female sex—fact, I'm afraid. He can't help it! His first wife got the elbow after only a few months. She overdosed, you know, only a few months after they broke up. Some say it was deliberate.' She shrugged, as if disassociating herself from the slander. 'For your sake, let's hope you're made of sterner stuff!'

Refusing to dignify that piece of malicious spite with a response, Lily turned away, feeling sick at what the other woman had implied. To her huge annoyance she found herself swept into the centre of the room by another of Paolo's cousins.

Dancing was the very last thing she wanted to do. She wanted to escape the noise, the pointed questions and speculative looks, the pervasive scent of the banks of flowers that seemed to be everywhere. Switch her mind off and stop fretting over this horrible situation. Just for a little while. Just until she found the strength she'd need to tell her great-aunt and Fiora the truth.

And the wretched man was actually *pawing* her! The crudities he was murmuring in her ear disgusted her, and as she tried to pull away his hot, heavy hand slid down to her waist and hauled her into him. The aftershave he must have drenched himself in made her feel as if she were about to throw up.

'Beat it, Orfeo!'

Never had Lily been so glad to see Paolo. Her anger with him for putting her in such an unenviable situation vanished like mist in the sunlight.

She felt weak with love, totally debilitated with longing, her mind—what was left of it—in so much turmoil she felt as if her brain had been boiled!

She wanted so much to be with him, accept his proposal. But she knew she couldn't. Mustn't.

Her knees shook as he slipped an arm around her shoulders, and, trying to stiffen her already tottery resolve, she took a moment to remind herself that given what she knew about him—what appeared to be general knowledge—marrying him would be self-destructive madness.

Yet Paolo Venini looked as if he would tear the younger man into pieces, limb from limb. Outrage had darkened his eyes to blazing ice. Looking up into his hard, rivetingly handsome features, she felt her eyes well with feeble tears.

'Don't let that lowlife upset you, *cara mia*,' he urged as the younger man sloped away, tugging at his tie in red-faced humiliation. 'If he comes within a hundred miles of you again I will kill him! Him or any man who shows you disrespect!'

Her soft mouth wobbled into a smile. Almost she could believe him. But did that mean he was jealous? He had his faults, but she had never numbered possessiveness among them. Where his women were concerned his *modus operandi* seemed to be to take what he wanted for as long as his interest lasted, then throw the current female aside and forget her. Move on. Not really the actions of a man with a possessive streak.

Paolo dropped his protective arm and curved a hand around her waist. 'Come with me, *bella mia*. We will escape together.' Time enough later to take her to sit with Fiora and Edith and mention the trip to Amalfi. Right now Lily was looking stressed, and she needed to unwind. That—her well-being—was his first priority. 'No one will miss us, and if they do they will understand the need of a newly betrothed couple to be alone together, to take time out for a few minutes.'

A danger light flashed its warning, but Lily recklessly ignored it as he guided her through the open French windows. As the cooler, soft night air enfolded them Lily leant into the strength of his lean, toned body. Needed to.

This was what she needed, she decided, on a rush of relief at having left the party behind, as he led her down a grassy path, the sound of music, chatter and laughter thankfully receding.

Tonight had been a nightmare. Her emotions all over the place. With him at her side as he'd introduced her to the guests she'd felt wired to the point of detonation, stingingly aware of every breath he took, every movement he made. When he'd left her to circulate on her own she'd felt bereft. Weak. The self-protective need to resist him fading to nothing.

Such had been her emotionally muddled state that she'd actually been on the point of searching the room to find him and tell him she *would* marry him. Partly for

Fiora's and Great-Aunt Edith's sake, but mostly, she knew, because she couldn't bear the thought of never seeing him again. Then that dreadful woman had come up to her and spilt out her spite. Spite that had a firm basis in fact, reminding her that Paolo would never love her, just use her to ease his conscience where his mother was concerned. She didn't know how she could love a man like that. But, for her sins, she did.

She bit down hard on her lower lip, annoyed with herself. Her brain was hurting. She didn't want to think of any of it, wanted just to close her mind and enjoy this brief period of silent tranquillity.

'You are quiet, my Lily.' His voice was like a caress, setting tiny shivers to sensitise her skin.

'I've switched my mind off,' she confessed.

She registered his amused, 'Ah—that I can understand!' just loving being this close to him. Strangely, she felt unthreatened now. He had rescued her from that pawing idiot back there, whisked her away from all those curious stares, from his friends and family probably trying to work out how plain, ordinary her had snared a guy who was so anti-marriage it was legend. Did they all think, as that creepy cousin of his had crudely suggested, that she was so fantastic in bed that he had to hang on to her? The very thought made her go hot all over.

All she wanted to do was not think of any of it, make a renewed effort to empty her stubborn mind of all those knotty problems and enjoy the silence and the solitude.

He was matching his pace to hers, not talking, his arm around her waist, thankfully keeping his mouth shut on the subject of marriage—because right now she was sure she couldn't handle it.

His hand resting on the curve of her hip felt so right. The air was full of the gentle scent of the flowers and wild herbs of the hillside, the moonlight gleaming on the stands of silvery eucalyptus, turning the night to the sort of soft magic that talking would destroy.

Determined that nothing would come between her and this so desperately needed period of tranquillity, she didn't protest, didn't even think of trying to when, at the end of a path she hadn't explored before, they came across a summerhouse festooned in climbing roses in early bud.

'We will sit a while.' Leading her to a wide padded bench seat that ran along the full length of the far wall, he eased her down, laid a hand against the side of her face, turning her head so that he could see her eyes in the dim silvery light. 'I didn't see you relax with a drink in your hand all evening. Would you like me to phone through to the house and have someone bring us champagne?'

Instinctively nuzzling into his hand, she let a smile thread her voice as she said, 'Such decadence! Thank you, but no. I don't need to have alcohol to relax.' She didn't add that being with him here, like this, was intoxicating enough. She'd been arguing with him ever since they'd met and she was tired of it. Just for a few moments—until they returned to the villa and normal battle-ready positions were resumed—she wanted to sink into this feeling of real closeness.

For some reason her answer seemed to please him. She felt him smile. Now, how could that be? Could she really be that closely attuned to him? she pondered, with a little shiver of awe.

'You are cold?' His voice had a strange rough edge as he turned her head towards him. Moonlight bathed them with a faint silvery glow, casting his features into harsh relief, all planes and angles, but his eyes were soft—what she could see of them before he dipped his head and used his sensual mouth to close one pale eyelid and then the other, his lips drifting down to lay a feather-light kiss on one corner of her mouth.

Without understanding how it happened, only that it had to, Lily's lips parted as she sought his teasing mouth. She loved his kisses, and taking one tonight couldn't be wrong—could it?

He laced his long fingers in her hair as he took her soft pink lips in a kiss that knocked out her senses, promised heaven, made her feel fully alive and yet weak with hunger for him all at the same time.

Her hands came up to cling to his broad shoulders for support, her peaking breasts pressed against the cool fabric of his shirt, and she felt him stiffen, a tremor racing through his perfectly honed body as he lifted his mouth from hers.

A tiny mew of frustration escaped her. She felt like a starving orphan, deprived of warmth and succour.

Greedily, she tugged at his shoulders, reclaimed his mouth, and submitted to a surge of white-hot pleasure as with a groan Paolo took her swollen lips again and plundered the moist interior with explicit thrusts of his tongue.

Suddenly, for Lily, it wasn't enough—not nearly enough.

Heat flamed deep in her pelvis as her restive hands moved from his shoulders to the sides of his face and down, thrusting at the parted sides of his white dinner jacket. Furiously her fumbling fingers worked at the buttons of his shirt, desperate to touch his skin, explore the warmth, the strength of his superb male body.

It wouldn't end with just touching. Lily knew that. But her sense of self-respect, of morality, was vanquished by the sheer power of his erotic hold over her senses. And as he lifted his mouth from hers, removing his jacket with a muffled oath, then caught her to him, burying his face in her hair as he tried to deal with the fastener at the back of the halter strap, his fingers were unsteady.

He was always so in control, but he was losing control now, Lily thought, a wave of tenderness washing over her. Just for tonight his needs came first, and she lifted her hands to release the stubborn clasp. She heard the heady sound of his indrawn breath as the silky fabric slid away to expose the pink-crested peaks of her breasts to his desire-hazed eyes.

'Ah—*bella, bella*! How I want you!' His voice was hoarse as he eased slowly away, putting space between them. 'But my sweet Lily blossom—'

Reckless, fizzing need had her twining her slim arms around his neck, sliding forward and stopping his words as her mouth took his with helpless greed.

In the time it took to take a breath Lily felt him relax. The tension that had taken hold, tautening his powerful body, drained out of him, and now he was kissing her with totally erotic expertise. Her fingers worked with frustrated energy to release the buttons of his shirt, parting the fabric to splay her hands against the hard muscles of his chest, and she was hot with longing as he eased her back against the cushions and took one rosy nipple into his mouth, then moved to the other.

Her head arched back on her slender neck as hot, exquisite sensation flooded every nerve-ending, and he gave a deep groan of male appreciation as she helped him remove her dress with eager, scrabbling hands.

The dress disposed of, Paolo stood and removed the barrier of his clothes with haste, standing before her with the moonlight gleaming on the olive-toned skin that sheathed his male magnificence.

A feverish knot was tightening deep inside her, and with a shaky whimper she held pale, slender arms out to him. As he came to her she knew that her life had been leading up to this one moment of sublime intimacy with the man she loved. Just this one time—a time that would live for ever in her memory. To be treasured. And maybe the memory would surface sometimes for him, making him smile a little as he looked back and remembered…

* * *

'You are everything I ever dreamed of and more,' Paolo murmured with husky sincerity as he slid her shoes onto her dainty feet while dawn rose over the Tuscan hills. He reached for her hands and drew her to her feet. 'You understand *amata mia*, there can be no question now of our not marrying.' He bent his head to place a gentle kiss between her wide, hazy eyes. 'I used no protection. You might be pregnant.'

He felt her shiver. His brows drew together. Surely that was not distaste at the thought of bearing his child? It couldn't be that, could it? Not after the utter perfection of what they'd shared!

Then logic kicked in, and his smile was soft with relief. The dawn air was cold. *She* was cold. He draped his jacket around her shoulders for protection, and slipped a proprietorial arm around her waist as they walked out into the garden.

He hadn't meant it to happen, had meant to show respect and wait until their wedding night. But how could he regret one second of last night?

Worldly-wise, some would say cynical, he had never believed in the fanciful notion of falling in love. But it had happened! His heart swelled until he thought it might burst out of his chest, and his arm tightened around her waist as her pace slowed to a standstill.

Dio mio! How could he not have realised? He'd been growing more in love with her all the time—and his proposal, his manipulations, had had nothing to do with pleasing Mamma, but with pleasing himself! And the first solid indication to enter his thick head had been the violent feelings of white-hot outraged jealousy he'd experienced when he'd seen Orfeo paw her!

Awe at the strength and depth of his feelings for his sweet Lily, for the generous gift of her virginity, made his voice husky as he curved her against the length of his body. 'I was going to take you to Amalfi for a few days— I have a fully staffed villa there. But I've shelved that plan until later, after we're married,' he husked against her hair. 'All my time will be taken with wedding arrangements, making sure it happens as soon as humanly possible.'

Suddenly his hands went to her narrow shoulders, easing her away again. Her melting, exquisitely soft responsiveness had changed to marble-statue rigidity. A cold knot formed inside him. For the first time in his life he felt unsure. He hated the feeling!

'Nothing to say?' His voice sounded harder than he'd expected. He hated himself for that, too!

Lily pulled in a shaky breath. His mention of a possible pregnancy had literally stunned her. His Italian genes would not let him walk away from a child he had sired, and as for letting her raise the child alone, having only visiting rights—well, as far as this macho Italian male was concerned that would be unthinkable, too.

She felt herself shrink within the comforting folds of his white dinner jacket, and her mouth felt as if it were formed out of rock as she asked thinly, 'And if I'm not pregnant?'

Paolo grinned, relief flooding his bloodstream. Was

that all she was worrying about? True, with hindsight he could see that his initial proposal of marriage hadn't been very flattering. All that stuff about pleasing Mamma, when in reality, with patience and the passage of time, he could have handled the flattening of his mother's hopes,

But Lily hadn't known that at the time—hadn't known that he could do whatever he set his mind to. And that included easing himself out of an engagement that had started off as a white lie without causing undue distress to his parent. Maybe now she was suffering from the misapprehension that, having tasted the delights of her body, he had lost interest—he savagely cursed his former reputation—and perhaps would only insist on marriage if an unplanned pregnancy were involved.

'No difference,' he assured her. 'We marry!' And he swept her effortlessly into his arms and carried her back to the villa—rather, Lily thought dazedly, like a warrior bringing home the spoils of war.

He was looking mightily pleased with himself, too, she noted, his midnight hair rumpled, a smile curving that shockingly sensual mouth, golden eyes gleaming with life. He simply took her breath away every time she looked at him. And last night—she would never forget it. Never regret having known such unbelievable ecstasy.

Her eyes filmed with moisture as she remembered that first time, the first of many, when he had come to the barrier—the barrier of her tiny cry of pain—and had stilled, gently withdrawn. She had arched her pelvis, pulsating with frantic need, begging him, 'Don't stop. Don't!'

She would never blame herself for her self-admitted shamelessly wanton behaviour. Never. It had been so beautiful. Limply, she wondered if she could be blamed for taking the next step.

Marrying him only to face heartbreak when the inevitable happened and he moved on, when her novelty value wore off and he sought the delights of some simpering blonde bimbo, satisfied that the woman he'd married to please his mother would be content to stay in the background.

Was that what had happened in his first marriage? Had his wife discovered an infidelity and left him? Had she, as Renata had implied, preferred to overdose rather than face life as a spurned wife?

Dared she risk it?

Could she bear to see her great-aunt and Fiora so bitterly disappointed if she didn't?

Could she face turning down the man she loved to distraction?

CHAPTER ELEVEN

LEAVING the tiny church in the centre of the village that nestled in the valley below the villa, clinging to Paolo's arm, Lily felt totally unreal.

The ceremony had passed like a dream sequence. Her exquisite dress of hand-embroidered ivory silk, the fabulous diamond-encrusted tiara that Fiora had insisted she wear—another family heirloom, apparently—the beautiful bouquet, all seemed to belong squarely in a fairytale rather than to her.

And the tall, incredibly handsome and sexy guy at her side—would he ever truly belong to her?

Stop it, she chided herself. It might not seem real, but you're not dreaming this. It *is* your wedding day and nothing must spoil it!

And she smiled for the photographer.

Her turmoil over whether or not she dared accept his proposal had been brought to an abrupt halt when Paolo had carried her back into the villa in the early morning after the engagement party.

Great-Aunt Edith had been waiting with a face like thunder, her hair coming adrift from its usual tight bun, her stout body enveloped in the sturdy dressing gown she'd had for years.

'And where do you think *you've* been all night?' she'd asked, the stentorian tone pitched at full volume. 'Carla and I insisted Fiora retired to bed hours ago, though the poor dear was fretting. You both disappeared without a word to anyone. Explain yourselves!' she'd demanded, for all the world as if they were naughty children and not adults, one of them a financial legend in the banking world!

Paolo had grinned with a marked lack of repentance, unfazed by one indignant old lady, and remarked smoothly, 'I'm sorry you've been inconvenienced. There really was no need.'

Lily shuddered. Great-Aunt Edith had the strict moral values of a strait-laced Victorian spinster, and what other explanation could there be for a man and a woman creeping in at dawn in such a state of dishevelment!

Carla, hovering at the old lady's elbow, a cup and saucer balanced in one hand, attempted to pour oil on troubled waters by remarking lightly, 'Nothing to get in a state about—what do newly engaged young couples do? I did tell you not to worry.' But that only provided another reason for a trumpeting snort of distaste.

Her back rigid, Edith turned away, waved aside the proffered cup of tea and, with Carla following in her wake, making vague clucking noises, departed.

Lily, wondering why her relative hadn't vented her moral outrage by booming *anticipating marriage!* had collapsed in giggles against Paolo's broad shoulder, and that had been the moment when she'd given in to fate and announced, 'That's done it! We'll have to marry now—otherwise she'll brand me as a fallen woman and make my life a misery!'

Only half joking, she'd realised, as he'd held her even closer and kissed her until she felt her head would spin off her shoulders, that what she'd said was as good an excuse as any for letting her heart rule her head.

During the weeks since then she had seen little of Paolo. The need to tie up business loose ends had kept him either in the Florence head office, or jetting off to meetings in various capital cities, or catching up on arrangements for the forthcoming wedding.

Busy herself with endless fittings, being prodded, tweaked about and told to stand up straight by the flamboyant much-lauded designer Fiora favoured, being consulted over her choice of flowers by the earnest wedding organiser Paolo had engaged, discussing her great-aunt's plans for the sale of her cottage and the transfer of what she called her 'bits and bobs' to Florence, relieved that she'd been forgiven for her bad behaviour, she had still had time to miss him terribly.

She'd also discovered, with a huge and completely unexpected sense of deep disappointment, that she wasn't pregnant.

'You are so beautiful,' Paolo breathed now, as he

handed her into the rear of the limousine that was to take them back to the villa for the small wedding feast, taking both her hands in his as he joined her.

His eyes gleamed like molten gold. She was his now, for all time, and his task of teaching her to love him as he loved her was only just beginning.

'It's the dress,' Lily offered confidingly, knowing he was only saying that to please her, because without fancy trappings she was just ordinary, but loving him for trying to make her feel special.

'Wrong.' The look he gave her sent a gigantic surge of heated sexual awareness through her, bringing back X-rated memories of the night they'd spent together to make her whole body quiver and burn. And when he husked, 'Your naked body is more stunningly beautiful than anything you could possibly wear,' she went bright pink and launched herself at him.

She simply couldn't stop herself, and almost collapsed with sensual overload as he took her willing mouth and kissed her with a devouring hunger that made her vow, there and then, that she would do her utmost, in every possible way, to make sure that she never bored him, never even came close.

Her legs still wobbly from the effect of the sizzling kisses they'd shared on the drive back to the villa, Lily entered the marble-paved, flower-decked hall of the opulent house that was to be her home, walking on air. He might not love her—and she had to be adult about it and accept that he had married her because he'd found it convenient—but it was up to her to wipe his rakish past from her memory and work on making herself *so* convenient he would never think of straying.

The wedding party was small, and security men were discreetly stationed on the driveway. Others patrolled the perimeter on the very slight off-chance that the paparazzi had got wind of a ceremony that had been left deliberately low-key, and Lily, listening to the best man toast the bride and groom, decided that nothing could or would go wrong on her wedding day.

Great-Aunt Edith was beaming beneath the brim of her formidable hat. Lily was glad her much loved relative had chosen to make her home with Fiora. She would have missed her, worried about her being on her own, had she returned to England. And Fiora looked fit as a fiddle, having got the thumbs-up from her consultant, not at all over-tired by the excitement of the wedding.

Her tummy churning with a longing to be alone with her drop-dead handsome new husband, Lily barely touched the delicious food provided by the team of caterers, but drank more than she should of the vintage champagne. She reflected in a rose-tinted glow that even Paolo's cousins seemed to be behaving themselves, and that Renata, dressed down in a plain suit of brown satin, her abundant black hair coiled neatly at the back of her head, must have deliberately chosen not to upstage the bride. Which was really nice of her, because she was stunning and could so easily have done so.

The meal over at last, Lily bestowed a vibrant smile

on her husband, swallowing a giggle because he looked as if he had just taken an icy shower. Cool wasn't in it! She got to her feet, brushing aside the hand he lifted to restrain her, and imparted in a loud whisper, 'Your mother and my great-aunt are getting ready to leave. I'll see them on their way while you chircu—circulate round the rest.' Then she floated away, quite amazed that for once it was she who was dishing out the orders instead of the other way round!

'You're tipsy, child!' Edith accused her as Lily helped her into the car that was to transport them to the Florence apartment.

'It is a very special occasion,' Fiora offered soothingly, 'and I know she doesn't make a habit of it. I believe black coffee helps,' she advised, and Carla, seated in front beside the driver, gave her opinion.

'It's all the excitement.'

Lily, waving violently, even after the car had disappeared, agreed with that.

Excitement at the thrilling prospect of being alone with her fantastically gorgeous brand-new husband had stopped her eating, and whenever she'd lifted her glass for a sip or two of the ice-cold liquid she'd found it topped up to the brim again by one of the over-attentive waiters, with the result that, yes, she did feel a bit floaty.

Forcing herself to walk in a straight line, she headed back inside the villa, determined to make for the kitchen regions and drink gallons of water. But before she could make it there she found her arms taken by Renata, who swung her round and marched her into the empty room that had been Fiora's sitting room during her stay here.

Astonished to find herself hi-jacked, Lily sank unresistingly onto the sofa Renata steered her to, her mouth dropping open as she struggled to find something sensible to say when the other woman sank down gracefully beside her and said, 'Everyone's about to leave, but there's something I want to show you before I go.'

She reached for her slim suede handbag and Lily beamed. Perhaps Paolo's cousin felt bad about the things she'd said on the night of the engagement party and was trying to make friends. If that was the case she'd meet her halfway, because she hated to think there'd be ill-feeling between her and any member of the family she'd married into.

'Oh, lovely—what is it?' she asked, and glanced at the glossy photograph that was placed in her hands, trying not to betray her complete incomprehension.

The studio portrait portrayed a staggeringly beautiful young woman. Perfect bone structure, long blonde hair, and what Lily could only describe as really sexy come-to-bed dark brown eyes.

'Solange,' Renata provided. 'Paolo's first wife. She was my best friend.'

'Oh.' Lily didn't know what to say. She passed the photograph back, fighting the urge to rub her fingers on the velvet upholstery of the sofa and rid herself of contamination. That would not only be childish, but insulting too. She knew Paolo had been married before, and didn't like talking about it, so she hadn't ever asked what his first wife had been like. Why the drama queen reaction now, on discovering that she had been so lovely?

'She was French. They met in Paris. She had everything—sophistication, breeding, the natural ability to be the life and soul of every gathering, a promising career on the stage—but she gave it all up when they married.'

Lily shivered. It was far from cold in here, but the look of malice she now detected in the other woman's eyes chilled her. She was beginning to get a thumping headache, but was determined not to throw a wobbly, betray her vulnerability, so she said stiffly, 'As she was your friend you must miss her, and I'm sorry. But my husband's failed marriage has nothing to do with me.'

She would have left the room, but Renata purred, 'Oh, but it has. I'm trying to warn you, you see, do you a favour. I thought you should know what Solange was like. If such a woman couldn't hold his interest for more than a few months, what hope have *you*?'

Lily got awkwardly to her feet. Her legs felt peculiar, as if they didn't belong to her, but she wanted to get out of here, away from this woman who was blatantly doing her level best to poison her marriage before it had properly begun—preying on doubts and fears she already had, did she but know it!

'Wait! There is something else you should see.'

Her heart lurched. Lily's feet refused to move another step. A horrible feeling of nervous tension kept her glued to the spot as Renata came towards her, unfolding a sheet of newsprint.

'An English tabloid—dated one week ago. Look at it.'

Shaking hands accepted the sheet of paper. Lily didn't want to look at it, but couldn't stop herself. Her heart seemed to stop beating. Her entire body felt as if it had closed down as she recognised Paolo exiting one of London's most fashionable and screamingly expensive restaurants.

Caught by the camera flashlight, he was shown with his arm protectively around a leggy blonde who seemed to be trying to climb inside his Savile Row suit. The slick heading asked 'Latest Love for Billionaire Banker?'

Feeling sick with betrayal, Lily thrust the newsprint back at Renata, heard her purr, 'He always goes for blondes—I expect they went back to his hotel, or on to a club and then back…'

Lily walked out, avoiding Paolo and the departing guests by using the staff service staircase. She made it to her room, headed straight into the *en suite* bathroom and was violently sick.

Five minutes later, ashen-faced, she was stone-cold sober. One week before their marriage and fidelity had had no meaning for him.

For the first time Lily gave heartfelt thanks that she wasn't expecting his child.

There would be no children. This marriage was going nowhere. But wallow in her misery she would not. She was tougher than that. She had agreed to marry him knowing his reasons, with her eyes fully open to his faults. That she had let her love for him delude her into thinking that they could grow together, have a stable, happy marriage and create a family, was regrettable— a lesson learned the hard way.

She was sitting on the window seat when he entered the room, already removing his tie. His eyes dazzled her, and he was wearing that heartbreaker smile, and she wondered painfully if she would ever get over the effect he had on her. She wished she'd had time to get out of her wedding dress. But at least she was in control. Totally.

Paolo tossed his jacket over the back of a chair, his mouth quirking as he asked, 'Feeling better now? The champagne went to your head, I think.'

He was advancing. All six foot plus of tall, dark dangerously handsome masculinity.

Her mouth went dry. She looked away. Had to.

'Have I told you how beautiful you are? I want to make love to you. But making love to a drunken woman is the last thing on this earth I would want to do.'

In that he sounded deadly serious. With a fleeting feeling of shame she recalled how she had slurred her words, floated tipsily from the table. If she didn't know what she did she would be apologising for that lapse right now, vowing that it had never happened before and wouldn't happen again.

But she *did* know.

Lily looked at him then, straight into those incredible golden eyes, and watched them go cold as she told him,

'You got what you wanted. A convenient marriage. Fiora's peace of mind. An undemanding wife who will stay in the background, at least for the time being. But I won't sleep with you.'

CHAPTER TWELVE

PAOLO gave her a look of savage condemnation. *'Madonna diavola!* What are you talking about?'

'You heard.' Lily was holding onto her control as if she were clinging to a lifebelt in a raging sea. His leanly handsome face was pale beneath his olive-toned skin, tension lines bracketing his grim mouth. He looked in shock.

Swallowing roughly, she told herself not to give in to the aching need to go to him that claimed every part of her tense body. To hold him, plead a sudden brainstorm or something, beg him to forget what she'd said.

Stoically, she reminded herself of all she had learned. 'The convenient marriage you wanted will stay where it belongs. On paper. I won't share your bed.'

His hard jawline lifted and his eyes narrowed on a fierce demand. 'Why?'

Tell him the truth. Ask what happened between him and Solange. Ask what he was doing with that blonde in London a week ago and listen to his lying explanation. Or maybe he'd tell it as it was, remind her that he didn't love her, didn't believe in it, and regarded himself free to have affairs.

As neither scenario held any appeal whatsoever, she told him the first lie that popped into her head. 'I did what you wanted—got you out of the hole you'd dug for yourself. In return, and until you decide to go for an annulment, I'm owed. I'll live in the lap of luxury, have anything I want. No more getting up at the crack of dawn to wet-nurse a bunch of old people. No more looking at lovely clothes in shop windows and knowing I could never afford them. No more—'

'*Basta!*' he commanded icily, his features like granite. 'I thought you were different from all the others. I regret my mistake.'

Swinging sharply on his heels, his proud, dark head high, he walked from the room.

With that chilling condemnation piercing her heart, Lily burst into uncontrollable tears.

'And where is that son of mine today?' Fiora wanted to know as she dispensed coffee in the lovely high-ceilinged sitting room with its entrancing view over the rooftops of the ancient city to the blue-hazed hills beyond.

'Milan,' Lily answered, a shade too hesitantly—because when he'd given her his itinerary it had been bitten out, as if he begrudged the expenditure of breath wasted in talking to her at all. Relieved to see her hands weren't shaking as she accepted the delicate china cup and saucer, she tacked on, 'For a few days.'

Sitting forward in her wing chair, her head tipped to one side, Fiora said quietly, 'I hope Paolo's not neglecting you.'

'From what he said, I thought you were to honeymoon in Amalfi,' Edith put in, sounding puzzled. 'And I'm sure he told me he intended to pick up his yacht in Cannes to give you a cruise of a lifetime.'

'Life happens,' Lily responded, as airily as she could. 'Business stuff. You'll know all about that.' She directed a stiff smile at her mother-in-law. As the wife of a prominent banker herself, she'd understand that such men always put work before anything else, but all she got was, 'I must speak to him. I have his mobile number. Solange always complained that he was a workaholic.'

Lily's heart squeezed painfully. This was her chance to learn something about his first marriage. She had to take it. 'It was sad—what happened to her—wasn't it?' she prompted.

The sudden rush of adrenalin ebbed away as Fiora merely commented, 'Of course. We shall never know what happened in that marriage. Paolo never speaks of it, and I respect his wishes far too much to ask. It is in the past. He has you now, and a wonderful future to look forward to. Now—' she changed the subject adroitly '—you will stay to lunch?'

'Thank you, but, no.' Lily glanced at her watch. 'I

asked Mario to collect me. I only dropped by to see how the two of you were getting along.'

'Famously!' Edith beamed. 'Like a house on fire! Fiora is trying to teach me Italian—with scant success!—and this morning I heard that my estate agent has received a firm offer for the cottage.'

'When the money comes through I shall take her shopping for some new clothes. She may protest all she likes, but one is never too old to be introduced to Italian style,' Fiora pronounced, busying herself with pouring more coffee. 'I thought via Tornabuoni—I have offered funds, but your dear great-aunt is too stubborn to hear of it! Tomorrow we plan to visit the Boboli Gardens— and, before you start to fuss, I shall take it very easy!'

And so the final half hour of her visit passed without any more awkward questions, any more mention of Fiora contacting her son on the subject of the non-existent honeymoon—or any useful revelations as to the reasons behind the break-up of Paolo's first marriage.

When the car turned into the long driveway Lily said, 'Drop me off here, Mario. I'll walk up to the villa.'

She felt so restless. The feeling had been burning her up ever since her wedding day. Walking quickly to use some of the pent-up nervous energy that made sitting still a torment, she wished, quite uselessly, that she hadn't lied to Paolo about the reasons behind her refusal to make their marriage a real one.

She'd lied to save her pride—believing that it was the only thing left of any value at all to her, hating the thought of coming over as a jealous wife and offering him a big fat clue to the true state of her feelings for him. She was unwilling to let him know she was a world-class idiot, who had self-destructively fallen in love with a man who cynically admitted he didn't know the meaning of the word and who treated women as if they were of as much long-term value as yesterday's newspaper.

So she'd lied. She wished she hadn't.

She'd had little opportunity or encouragement to tell him the truth, though. She'd seen him a scant handful of times since that day. He'd been polite, chillingly so, and so remote. The time they actually spent together was as brief as he could make it, killing dead any hopes she might have had of opening up a meaningful conversation, of making him stay around long enough to listen. It wouldn't make their marriage any more viable, but at least he'd know she wasn't the idle gold-digger she'd made herself out to be.

As she rounded the final bend, perspiring from the heat of the sun and the pace she'd set, she slowed down, frowned. She didn't know who the red sports car in the drive belonged to, but she wasn't in the mood for visitors.

Entering the immense, cool-tiled main hall, she was met by Agata, her kindly features clouded with unease.

'Signorina Renata is here, waiting for you, *signora*. She is in the small salon. She instructed me to bring her a bottle of the *signor*'s best Meursault, and the last time I looked in the bottle was nearly empty.'

Anger rose in a hot tide, but Lily managed to give

a smile of sorts and thank the housekeeper. Renata Venini was the last person she wanted to see. And the small salon was her favourite room, smaller and less grand than the other rooms in the palatial villa. She often sat there herself, finding a peace of sorts for a short while, surrounded by the flowers she'd picked and arranged as something to occupy her long empty day. She hated to think of that wretched woman sullying her space.

Telling herself to cool it, that it was unfair to blame the bearer of bad news, that the other woman had only been telling the truth, Lily pushed open the door and stepped over the threshold.

'So you arrive at last!' Renata was lounging on a cream-upholstered chaise, an empty glass and a bottle containing a few dregs on the table at her side. 'I must say I was surprised to learn you were still here.'

'Really?' Lily wasn't going to give an inch until she knew why Paolo's cousin was really here. She just hoped, desperately, that it wasn't to give her more evidence of his womanising.

Renata yawned, closely examining her scarlet-tipped fingernails as if for flaws, obviously unimpressed by Lily's attempt at cool. 'Absolutely. Do you know—' she leant over and poured the last of the wine into her glass '—this used to be Solange's favourite room? For the view of the fountain and the roses—so pretty.'

One more thing spoiled for her! Grinding her teeth to stop herself from telling the other woman to sling her hook, Lily had to literally force herself to remain calm. 'Why are you here?'

'Friendly visit. As I told you, I wanted to know if you were still here, or if you'd done the sensible thing and returned to wherever it is you came from. And how *is* dear cousin Paolo?'

There was nothing friendly about this woman where Lily was concerned. She might have been telling the truth, but it had been done with malice and spite. 'He is well.'

'You know that for sure?' A trill of laughter. 'How can you when he's never here? Oh, don't look so surprised! I have no spy among your servants. They are all too loyal to his lordship to tell me anything. But did you know that one of your under-gardeners is having an operation for something or other?'

Lily, standing firmly where she was, just inside the door, said nothing. Old Carlo Barzini was recovering from a gall bladder operation. She had had fruit and a cured ham delivered to their house in the village, but she wasn't about to enlighten Renata, who wouldn't be interested in any case.

'His simple-minded son—Beppe, I think he is called—doesn't understand this tribal loyalty,' Renata went on. 'He tells me my cousin has hardly been seen here since the wedding.' She emptied her glass and heaved herself upright. 'Up to his old tricks. Keep little wifey locked up at home and swan about earning lots more money to spend on whatever leggy blonde happens to be flavour of the month.'

'I think you should go.' Lily was breaking up inside, but she wasn't going to show it.

'I'm sure you do. However, I am too tired to drive, so I'll find a nice comfy bed and rest awhile. This is Venini property, after all. And I am a Venini by birth, not by borrowed name.' She headed none too steadily for the door, brushing past Lily, rigid with rage. 'Oh, and warn the housekeeper that I may be staying on for dinner.'

Underwhelmed by that prospect, Lily screwed her eyes shut to stop herself crying, and swallowed the painful lump in her throat. Spinning on her heels, she sped out of the house. Renata had touched a raw nerve when she'd said that stuff about 'little wifey' being locked up at home.

She felt like a prisoner. If she wanted to go anywhere Mario drove her. If she wandered through the extensive grounds one of the gardeners always seemed to be around.

Fuming now, she stood on the gravelled forecourt. She had to escape—just for a little while. To be on her own and think. Things couldn't go on the way they were.

Could she pin Paolo down long enough to ask him to go for an immediate annulment? Telling him that she wanted nothing from him would at least take away the bad taste left by the way she'd lied about enjoying the wealth he had to offer.

And surely the break-up wouldn't affect Fiora and Edith? She'd seen for herself how comfortable they were with each other, had listened to their plans for future outings and spending sprees.

As for her—what she'd do, how she'd manage when she got back to England—well, she'd think of something.

Stress made her muscles tight, her breathing painfully difficult, and hot tears stung behind her eyes. But she wasn't going to cry. All this was her own fault. No one else was to blame. She'd had plenty of warning about what he was like, but she'd ignored it. He'd told her he didn't love her, didn't *do* love, that their marriage would be 'convenient', and she'd ignored that too!

After one night of ecstatically beautiful sex, and discovering her love for him, she'd decided that the marriage would work, that he would stay faithful to her. Well, she'd been wrong.

Keyed up to the point of explosion, she determined to get away from the environs of the beautiful villa that had come to feel like a prison—even if she found an army of Paolo's staff trailing after her. Then she noticed for the first time that Renata had left her keys in the ignition of her scarlet sports car.

The fleeting thought that the other woman wouldn't be needing it until she'd slept off the effects of the wine she'd drunk was all it took before she was in the driving seat, gunning the engine, and speeding down the drive.

The Ferrari scorched to a halt. Paolo exited, his long legs carrying him at speed towards the main door of the villa that seemed to be sleeping peacefully in the late-afternoon sun.

When Fiora had called his mobile that morning he'd

known something had to be very wrong. She never phoned him while he was working except in an emergency. The last time it had happened had been when she'd begged him to come home because Antonio had been involved in that dreadful accident.

Superficially she'd been asking why he and Lily weren't on their planned honeymoon. He'd neglected to tell her that there was no point in a honeymoon if the bride wouldn't have anything to do with the groom, and fobbed her off waiting for the real reason for her call.

'Lily came on a short visit this morning. She's only just left. There's something wrong, and you must forget you run a banking empire and do something about it. She's lost weight. Edith and I both noticed it. And her eyes are so sad. All those sunny smiles are missing. She didn't say so, but we are both sure she is unhappy. You may be a powerful man, my son, but you are also a husband who is making a very big mistake in leaving his new bride alone to pine.'

His strong face clenched, he'd ended the call, made his apologies, and strode out of the meeting he'd been chairing.

A big mistake. Since his marriage to Solange he'd made sure he never made mistakes, but his gut feeling told him he had this time. Weight loss and sad eyes didn't gel with the type of woman who admitted she'd married a man solely for what she could get out of him.

She wasn't in the suite of rooms she'd used since he'd first manipulated her into coming here.

The way she'd destroyed their marriage before it had begun had shocked him, hurt his pride, hurt his heart—the heart that had finally learned how to love. So, rather than display his shocking vulnerability where she was concerned, he'd removed himself.

He should have stuck around, found out what had turned his sweet Lily into an avaricious monster, discovered if she'd been telling the truth or using that preposterous statement to cover something else. Instead he'd buried himself in work—always his refuge.

Grinding his teeth, he clattered down the stairs to summon his staff and ask them for his wife's whereabouts. Then he noticed the empty bottle and solitary glass through the open doorway to the small salon.

His blood ran cold, then scaldingly hot. Lily rarely drank, and never to excess. But she'd been tipsy on champagne on their wedding day. His darkly handsome features tightened. Had she got a taste for the stuff? Hence the solitary glass and empty bottle?

A movement on the periphery of his vision galvanised him. The main door still stood open, as he'd left it, and Beppe was trundling a wheelbarrow across the forecourt. Not the most reliable source of information, but as everyone else seemed to have disappeared he'd do.

Two minutes later he was back behind the wheel of the Ferrari. Yes, Beppe had seen the *signora*. She had driven a car away very fast. No, Mario had not been with her.

Paolo's heart was beating despite the iron band that seemed to be squeezing it to pulp. No point in going to see which car was missing from the many vehicles garaged in the old stable block. With that much wine inside her she wasn't fit to ride a tricycle!

When he discovered who had allowed her to have the ignition keys, he would kill the idiot!

That he had no idea where she'd been heading didn't matter a damn. He would find her. He had to.

Ferocious tension held him as he sent the powerful car hurtling round bends, up a steep gradient that led to a spectacular viewpoint, much loved by visitors to the area. Cresting the rise, he saw her leaning against the safety barrier. In the same moment he recognised his cousin's poky sports model.

Out of the Ferrari in no time, covering the distance to where she was in two seconds flat, he took her arm, pulled her round to face him and lashed out, '*Madre di Dio!* What do you think you're doing?'

Her heart thumping against her ribcage with shock, Lily was speechless for several seconds as she stared, wide-eyed, into his tautly grim features. She'd heard a car screech to a standstill and cursed whoever it was who had come to spoil her solitude just when she was getting things sorted out in her head.

Pulling herself together with an effort, she narrowed her eyes at him and said, 'And hello to you, too!'

He dealt her a chilling glance. 'This is not the time for sarcasm. With the amount of alcohol you have in your blood *anything* could have happened!'

Her face bone-white, eyes wide with incomprehension, Lily searched his unforgiving features and wondered just what it was about this arrogant, bullying, congenitally unfaithful man that made her love him so very much. She must have had a common-sense bypass, she decided mournfully. Then she remembered what he'd said, and said hotly, 'I have *not* been drinking. Why assume I have?'

Very much on her high horse, she snatched her arm away from his grasp and rubbed the tender spot where his fingers had dug into her flesh.

'On the evidence of a single glass and an empty wine bottle,' he returned heavily. He expelled what felt like solidified air from his lungs. 'When Beppe told me you'd taken off behind the wheel of a car—' Dark colour flooded his fantastic cheekbones as he admitted, 'I was worried.'

Lily's soft mouth tightened as the penny dropped. He must have called in at the villa, seen the empty wine bottle and decided she'd gone joy-riding in a drunken stupor.

Pulling herself up to her negligible height, she put him straight. 'I didn't drink that stuff. Renata did. She was there when I got back from visiting in Florence. She's crawled into some bed or other to sleep it off. I took her car because I wanted to go some place to think—away from my keepers!'

There was relief in his roughened tone as he frowned down at her. 'Renata and over-indulgence adds up. What is *she* doing here?'

Determined not to answer that right now, Lily said

thinly, 'We need to talk about the future. We can't go on like this.'

'Not here.' The need to straighten stuff out and not hide his head and his breaking heart in his work was what had brought him back, shattering all speed records. He paced to his cousin's car, locked it and pocketed the keys, explaining tersely, at Lily's gabbled objection, 'Someone can drive her here to collect it when she's sobered up. Right now, I don't trust you out of my sight.'

His profile was so grim as he drove them back through the twilight that Lily didn't dare bring up the vexed subject of their marriage and the annulment thereof. She was still biting her tongue to stop the rapidly piling up words from spilling out when, with a hand firmly on the small of her back, he propelled her into the now brightly lit great hall, bawling for Agata and informing the astonished woman that she was to hold dinner until he informed her they were ready. Should Signorina Renata surface she was to wait in the staff quarters until he could deal with her. No interruptions were to be permitted, on pain of instant dismissal.

'You are such a bully!' Lily condemned breathily as he ushered her into the small salon and closed the door with pointed firmness behind them.

'Only when my patience has reached its outer limits,' he came back. The scowl he wore now was pretty fierce, but he didn't scare her. She'd stood up to him in the past. She could do it again.

But first she needed a moment to gather her thoughts.

The concise sentence that encapsulated her need for a speedy annulment, the advancement of enough funds to buy an air ticket back to England, had somehow flown out of her head, and she needed to sound businesslike, not babble.

Walking to the window, she gazed out. The fountain was always lit up as night fell, and the beds of roses that surrounded the stone basin were gorgeous. She would miss this lovely house when she was gone.

And she would mourn for what she and Paolo could have had.

'Come here, Lily.' The instruction was softly couched. A tremor shook her slight frame. She turned slowly, reluctant, now it had come right down to it, to face the final death knell of their marriage.

But she had never been short of courage, had she?

Watching her, standing so straight, Paolo felt as if he were coming apart. Fiora was right. She had lost weight, and she looked terminally tired. Somehow he had messed up—big-time. It was up to him to get to the bottom of this. He wanted to go to her, take her hand, lead her to the sofa he had parked himself on, but knew he couldn't. She clearly didn't want him touching her.

'Right.' He cut to the chase, getting to his feet but not moving closer. 'You married me, and yet you deliberately set out to destroy our marriage by refusing to share my bed. It occurs to me that is grounds for an annulment, which would mean you wouldn't be entitled to anything. And yet you claim to have married me solely for a lavish lifestyle,' he expounded with clinical precision. 'It doesn't make sense.'

In a shocking state of agitation, Lily twisted her hands together, happy that he'd seen through her stupid lie, yet feeling a dreadful fool for having told it in the first place.

'It was a pathetic lie,' she admitted. 'I really don't want anything from you—you've already done masses for the charity—'

'Then why did you say it?' he demanded, with no patience whatsoever. 'You had to have a reason, and nattering on about what I've put into Life Begins isn't doing it for me!'

Her troubled face crumpled. She couldn't bear this. In a rush to get it over with, she blurted, 'It's my fault! I shouldn't have agreed to marry you. Not knowing what I did.'

'That being?'

His voice sounded as if it had been filtered through ice. Telling herself not to be faint-hearted, Lily launched in. 'This is going to sound really dreadful. And I don't suppose you can help yourself.' In a pause for breath she was sure she could hear his teeth grinding, so she pushed rapidly on. 'You get bored with women very easily. Even when you're engaged or married to them. And you can't resist blondes and playing away with them. I knew all this stuff, but when I went and fell in love with you I thought I could make you like me enough to stay faithful.'

Realising she'd let the cat out of the bag, Lily fell into

an appalled silence. Paolo was staring at her as if he couldn't believe his ears and she couldn't blame him—because he wouldn't want to hear what he would classify as sentimental twaddle.

'What?'

He was advancing towards her. Slowly. If she hadn't known better she would have said his state was trance-like. But macho Italian males didn't do trances.

'I—er—well, actually it was a piece in a London paper. A photo taken of you coming out of a fancy restaurant with some blonde glued to you. A week before our wedding!'

Much to her horror, her eyes welled with tears. She was coming over as such a wimp!

'Say that again, *mi amore*.' He took both her hands.

Flustered, Lily repeated, 'A week before our wedding.' She wondered if he was checking dates to verify which blonde in particular he'd been seeing, and wished he wasn't touching her because that made life so very difficult.

'No.' Wired as he was, he had to take this calmly. 'What you said about falling in love with me.'

Her face flushed with embarrassment. He really was something else! Going for her weak spot, gloating! Disregarding what she'd said about that blonde as if his two-timing behaviour was something she had no right to mention!

But there was no wriggling out of it. Not when those golden eyes seemed to be reaching right into her soul.

Swallowing thickly, she bit the bullet. 'I'll be the first to admit it was stupid, but I really fell for you. It sort of grew on me, and I knew if we had a normal marriage I'd get so hurt I wouldn't be able to stand it.'

His fingers tightened on her hands as he drew her closer to him. And he said unevenly, 'I will never hurt you, *cara*. I love you far too much!'

'You don't have to say that,' Lily mumbled disconsolately, then decided she was being pretty dumb—because why would he say that if he didn't mean it? Unless, of course, he was thinking about the effect the sudden break-up would have on his mother? 'You don't *do* love,' she reminded him, trying not to notice the fizz of excitement that claimed her at the contact with his lean, sexy body.

'True.' His lips were on her hair. 'Until I met you. Like you, it sort of grew on me.' His mouth had moved to the lobe of her ear. 'I was in love with you long before I recognised the condition—not having had the experience before.'

Her heart was singing. His lips trailed down the side of her neck. She was rapidly reaching the point where she'd believe anything he said. Wrenching her head away from the indescribably sweet temptation of his lips, she said, with a shake in her voice, 'That's not true! You were engaged once. You must have thought you loved her. And then you got married. You must have felt something for her—you never mention her. And what about that blonde you were with that night?'

'Ah.' His grin was unashamedly rueful. 'We have to go through the serious stuff before I get to kiss my wife. Pity. I was enjoying myself for the first time since you banned me from your bed!'

Forgiving him, because she'd been feeling just the same, she allowed him to lead her to one of the twin sofas, biting on the corner of her mouth as she registered that he was looking decidedly serious now.

'Since when have you started reading that brand of gutter press?'

Silence. Lily bit down harder. As it was, Paolo didn't rate his cousins. She didn't want to give him cause to despise them.

'Tell me, Lily,' he asked gently. 'Someone must have shown you the piece. Was it Renata? I can't think of anyone else capable of such spite.' When she nodded uncomfortably, he said soberly, 'She holds a grudge because of what happened with my first wife. She introduced me to Solange. She was her closest friend and on/off bed partner—although I didn't get to know that until much later. I'm certain that Renata thought she'd get her hands on some of the family wealth through Solange. Any chance of that vanished when I ended the marriage.'

'Why did you?' Lily sat up very straight. Suddenly she knew she could believe him implicitly. He'd already been very open on a subject even his own mother said he never talked about.

'I made an error of judgement. For the second time in my life.' His fine eyes darkened. 'Believe me, it's tough to have to admit that. The first was when I got engaged to Maria. I was nineteen, she was six years older, with a modelling career that I guess, with hindsight, was going downhill. She was glamorous; I was flattered. Cocky, if you like! My parents disapproved, but I thought a mixture of flattery and rampaging hormones was love. I soon discovered it wasn't, and the only thing that hurt was my pride when I overheard her telling a friend that she'd landed a meal ticket for life.'

'Oh, my!' Lily's eyes widened until they almost filled her face. 'Poor you—you must have been shattered,' she breathed, unable to imagine anyone wanting to marry him for his money when he had so much else to offer.

'Not so you'd notice.' He grinned at her, then sobered. 'It made me wary, and no bad thing. Then, years later, when I was introduced to Solange, I'd reached a point in my life when I thought it was time to settle down long-term, start a family. I made a list of pros and cons, and the pros outweighed the cons.'

'How very businesslike!'

A dark eyebrow rose. 'I was still being wary, remember? To cut a long story short, she said she was madly in love with me. Said she wanted my children, the whole bag. She was beautiful, classy, witty. Suitable. We were married after a very short engagement. On honeymoon I discovered that she was an alcoholic and a drug addict—something she'd cleverly hidden from me. I tried to get her to admit she needed help, but whenever I mentioned it she threw a screaming tantrum, flounced out, and usually ended up at some wild party, returning some time the next day, barely able to stand, vowing it would never happen again. But it always did. In the end I lost patience—told her to get help for her addiction or say goodbye to our marriage. Frankly, by that stage I was beyond caring. I sometimes think I should have tried harder. If I'd really loved her I would have tied her up and delivered her bodily to a clinic with the knowledge and experience to deal with such things. But I didn't love her.'

Lily took his hand, hating to see him blaming himself for something he hadn't been able to control. His fingers tightened around hers as he went on flatly, 'She chose to walk out and went to Renata. It was then I discovered they'd been having a sexual relationship for years. I washed my hands of her. Her lifestyle was out of control, and soon she died—an accidental overdose.'

Lily wrapped her arms around him. He must have had a horrible time. No wonder he'd bawled her out earlier. He must have thought she'd taken to the bottle, that history was repeating itself.

'Well, I love you to bits,' she vowed. 'And I don't drink more than the odd glass socially, and I don't want your money, and you're stuck with me—'

'Aren't you forgetting something?' He tilted her chin and brushed his mouth lightly over her luscious lips. 'The identity of the blonde I wined and dined?'

Coming back down to earth with a bump, Lily tilted her head consideringly. He'd said he loved her, and she believed him, so 'Tell me her name and I'll go and kill her!' She giggled.

'That would be a pity. She's an excellent head of futures. I was running on a tight schedule—planning to take my wife on an extended honeymoon—and dinner was the only slot I could find in my diary. A working dinner. My days of indulging in short-term, no-strings soulless affairs with bimbos are over—have been for some time. And there were never as many as the tabloids credited me with. I've fallen madly, irrevocably in love with a real woman, and right now I want to take her to bed and get this marriage up and running. Agreed?'

'Not very romantically put—but, yes, I agree.' She gave him a tender smile and he gave her a wicked one back.

'Romantic I can do. Later.' And he marched her into the hall where Agata was hovering, looking at a loss.

'Is Renata about?'

'*Si, signor.* In the kitchen. She has eaten, but is growing—' she sought suitably tame words '—a little annoyed.'

'Good.' He tossed the car keys over. 'Give her these and ask Mario if he will drive her home. She can collect her car tomorrow, when she's sober. It is parked on the side of the road by the viewpoint, a couple of kilometres away. Mario will know where I mean.'

At that he gave Lily the sort of smile that had always made her fizzle and melt, swept her up in his arms and headed for the stairs.

Later he was very romantic indeed. Lily decided she'd never have anything to complain about for the rest of her life, and made a staunch vow that he wouldn't, either.

COUNT GIOVANNI'S
VIRGIN

BY
CHRISTINA HOLLIS

Christina Hollis was born in Somerset, and now lives in the idyllic Wye valley. She was born reading, and her childhood dream was to become a writer. This was realised when she became a successful journalist and lecturer in organic horticulture. Then she gave it all up to become a full-time mother of two and to run half an acre of productive country garden. Writing Mills & Boon® romances is another ambition realised. It fills most of her time, between complicated rural school runs. The rest of her life is divided between garden and kitchen, either growing fruit and vegetables or cooking with them. Her daughter's cat always closely supervises everything she does around the home, from typing to picking strawberries!

To Martyn, who makes all things possible.

CHAPTER ONE

KATIE had expected Tuscany to be hot and dusty. She had not expected it to be so beautiful, and perfumed with the scent of herbs basking under a hard blue sky.

'You will be expected to hit the ground running, Miss Carter. Signor Amato rarely makes allowances for anyone— especially not an interior designer!' Plump, neatly suited Eduardo leaned forward and tapped on the glass separating them from the limousine's chauffeur. He issued a curt order in Italian and then settled back into the cream leather seat beside her. 'Signor Amato must visit his city office later this morning and he is attending a dinner given by an Australian delegation this evening. His day operates to the second. As his right-hand man at the Villa Antico, I must ensure that we reach there on time.'

'I'm sorry my flight was cancelled. I was supposed to land yesterday.' Katie's fingers gripped her briefcase. Of all the days to get caught up in a security alert. This dream job was really important to her. Giovanni Amato had a reputation as the world's most reclusive billionaire. When the Marchesa di San Marco's personal recommendation had secured Katie the job of restyling his ancestral home north of Florence, she had hardly been able to believe her luck. Everything had been

planned down to the last detail. She had arranged to stay overnight in Milan, to make sure she was fresh for this morning
meeting. Then all her arrangements had collapsed like a house
of cards. Instead of being cool, calm and collected, Katie was
stiff and overtired after a night spent in the airport. Her palms
were suspiciously damp and her heart was racing, too. This was
not how she was supposed to arrive on her first day in heaven.

Working in a place like this will be no hardship at all, she
thought as they sped through rolling countryside dotted with
pretty little stone and tile villages. Eventually the sleek black
Amato limousine turned in at an enormous pair of wrought
iron gates. The chauffeur lowered his window and checked
in to security. Obediently the gates slid open. Then the car set
off down a long avenue of lime trees. Katie gasped as a classic
Tuscan villa loomed into view. It was only slightly smaller
than Windsor Castle.

An intense young man in Armani emerged from the house
as the car drew up. He opened Katie's door before the vehicle
stopped, breaking into its air-conditioned comfort. The heat
enveloped Katie like a thermal blanket.

'My goodness, what lovely weather,' she began, but Antico
staff were not chosen for their small talk.

'Signor Amato will see you in the White Office, Miss Carter,'
the butler said to Katie, then turned to Eduardo. 'She is late.'

'Show me the way and I'll run,' said Katie.

Giovanni Amato was standing with his back to the door.
Windows stretched from floor to ceiling in his cathedral-like
office and silhouetted his tall, muscular frame. From that first
moment, Katie knew he would be a force to be reckoned with.
A commanding figure in beautifully cut linen trousers and a
crisp white shirt, he made a gesture of acknowledgement as

she entered the room. Then he went back to pouring a flow of eloquent Italian into the tiny mobile at his ear. Katie had to wait until he finished his call before she got her first proper look at him.

'I hope I did not disturb you, Signor Amato,' she said as he turned, then stopped. He had a face that men could fear but women could not resist. One look into those intense grey eyes and she might have been lost—but for his expression. Momentarily it looked as though he had the weight of the world on his shoulders. And then the handsome, regular features broke into a practised smile.

'Not at all—it's Miss Carter, isn't it? I'm pleasantly surprised to meet you. The contractors Mima usually recommends are tough Neapolitans!' he said in perfect English. Raising one hand, he ran fingers through his thick dark hair. There was no need. It was cut short enough to remain tidy without attention, but that did not stop him. He flexed his shoulders, and the cut of his shirt hinted at powerful muscles beneath. Then, stretching his left arm with lazy elegance he inspected the silver Rolex on his wrist.

'I was told you would be late, but five minutes? That is nothing.' He smiled again and for a moment there was an air of devilment about him. 'Sometimes my staff worry too much, but I am not about to criticise them. When they are working well, my days run smoothly. That is all I ask.'

Katie was speechless. He was absolutely charming and his easy manner continued as he walked around his work-station and perched on the edge, facing her.

'A desk puts up such a barrier between people, don't you think?' Reaching behind him, he picked up a china *Viola* mug, tasted the contents and pulled a face. 'Cold cappuccino retains all of its caffeine but none of its pleasure. Excuse me while I ring for a replacement.'

Katie looked around the spacious office as he rang down to his kitchens. The Villa Antico's faded splendour was obvious here. All Giovanni Amato's high-tech equipment had been plonked in the centre of a gracious room full of peeling paintwork and threadbare carpets.

'The kitchens have bad news, I am afraid, Miss Carter. I am supposed to leave in ten minutes for a meeting in Milan and my super-efficient PA suggests we don't linger over coffee.' He laughed, shaking his head.

'Er…yes—ok…' Katie floundered. This man was as serious as he was good-looking. There was clearly a time limit to this audience with him. 'Right, well, I'm Katie Carter…'

'I know. You come with the highest recommendations from my friend the Marchesa di San Marco. I don't know how much she has told you, but I inherited this place from my father a while ago. When he was in residence it was allowed to decline into the pitiful condition you see all around you. Now I have decided it is time for the Villa Antico to rise again. I want to restore the high standards of the past, so all traces of its most recent occupancy are to be swept away. With no time to restyle it myself, I need a specialist. All my staff here work to the highest standards. Contractors are expected to have the same attitude.' He was lost in thought for a moment and then his lips flickered a spark of amusement at her. 'Do you know, I've just realised that in some small way I envy you, Miss Carter. Here you are—a self-made woman, Mima tells me, who has fought her way up from nowhere. You are responsible only for yourself. It makes me wonder how far I could have taken Amato International if I had started from scratch. Family loyalty and tradition are my driving forces, and there's no doubt I have the killer instinct necessary to protect the old firm, but what are the qualities you needed to start from nothing, I wonder?'

He gazed at her appreciatively for some moments, a half smile playing around his lips. Katie could only guess how devastating its full power might be, but his expression soon became serious again.

'The fact is that I need a base where I can retire from public life, Miss Carter. I don't intend to entertain here—that takes place on my yacht or in one of my city apartments. But when Mima visited, she was so full of the wonders you had worked at her Villa Adriatica she thought you would be good for this old place. I have never yet disappointed a lady and I was not about to begin with Mima. So here you are.' He spread his hands in a gesture of welcome.

Katie said nothing. She knew that clients always had strong ideas about what they wanted. She expected such a success-ful, busy man to have a list of requirements. She waited for him to reel them off. Instead, his smile remained immovable. He could have the most beautiful eyes in the world, Katie thought, if it wasn't for one thing. They were dove-grey, long-lashed and perfect—but there was a hint of something dark behind them. What was it, she wondered—pain? Suspicion? The way he shifted slightly when he mentioned his father hinted at some sort of friction in his past. There were secrets beneath all that easy, designer-dressed efficiency. Katie could sense it.

Their exchange was interrupted by the arrival of Eduardo, with a message that it was time to leave. Launching himself from the table edge, Giovanni pulled his jacket from its hanger in a cupboard and slung it over his shoulder.

'I am due in Milan, Miss Carter. Do you know the Amato building? They serve the most *excellent* refreshments there.' He turned to his PA. 'The young lady and I will continue our meeting on the flight, Eduardo. As we go downstairs we will be passing one of the first areas for improvement, Miss Carter.

It has not been redecorated for at least thirty years, to my certain knowledge.'

He held the door open for her and they passed from the office into a warren of halls and wood-panelled passages. Katie was awestruck at the size and splendour of the place. It would take her a lifetime to find her way about. She was booked to be here for only thirty days. At the end of the long passageway, Giovanni seized the polished brass handles of a pair of double doors. As he opened them, a gust of warm air hit them. It was perfumed with beeswax polish. Katie followed him into a vast room. Shafts of sunlight from tall windows fell across ancient floorboards that centuries of polishing had given a rich golden glow.

'When you need to find this place again, it is called the Smoking Gallery,' he said, answering one of her questions before she could ask it.

'Then you are a smoker, Signor Amato?'

He chuckled. 'No. My great-grandfather saw some interesting architecture while visiting England a century ago. When he returned, he ordered his men to recreate some chimneys of the type he had seen there. Unfortunately, because they do not draw smoke upwards from the fire, it always blows back down.'

He walked over to a great black marble fireplace on one side of the room. Positioning one foot carefully on the fender, he pointed up at the chimney-breast. Ancient wooden panels hung there, illustrating the Amato family tree. It was decorated with brightly coloured coats of arms and ancestral flags and descended from the ceiling like a many-fingered stalactite. Names were picked out in gold leaf. Beside each one was either a shield or a banner, enamelled with the appropriate family colours.

This man had history. Katie wondered what it was. She glanced at him and was about to speak, but found his face bleak and pained. This look was replaced almost instantly with his usual charming smile. Despite that, Katie was alarmed. She looked back at the panelling to try and see what had made his expression slip.

His family tree was nothing but facts and figures. A huge span of Amato history was laid out before her. It trickled down to end on one side with the single golden name Giovanni Francisco Salvatore Amato. Her magnificent surroundings nudged Katie into a conclusion. This man had no wife and no offspring—yet. That must be what concerns him, she thought. There might be advantages in being born a commoner, like her, after all. Giovanni Amato must shoulder the sole responsibility of continuing his grand family line.

Katie soon discovered it was dangerous to make any assumptions about her new employer. They were not couriered to the city by private jet. Instead, a helicopter stood on the estate's private airfield, ready to go. After helping her in, he swung himself into the pilot's seat and clipped on a headset.

'I'm surprised billionaires don't make business come to them, rather than the other way around,' Katie managed to say, despite her initial terror. He did not reply immediately, but they lifted off smoothly enough. Then he steered the machine around to give her a swallow's eye view of the Villa Antico.

'There are two reasons why I do this, Miss Carter.' He hovered, reversed, and then worked a dignified slalom around his rooftops. The helicopter was so low, Katie could have looked right down inside its barley sugar chimneys—if she had not been clinging to her seat and fighting to keep her nerve.

'The first reason is that, no matter how good the satellite link, nothing replaces a handshake. People like to meet me in person. And who am I to deny them that pleasure?' With the twitch of an eyebrow, he shot a playful look straight at her heart. It scored a direct hit. The effect was obvious, but Katie knew she had to hide it. Women must turn to jelly before him all the time, and she never followed the herd.

He side-slipped the helicopter speedily to the north-west.

'Does that gasp mean you want me to slow down, Miss Carter?' With a reassuring smile he checked and levelled the machine. 'Don't worry. I've never lost a passenger yet.'

Relieved, Katie released her death-grip on the upholstery.

'You said there were *two* reasons, Signor Amato.'

He looked at her with a grin of pure relish.

'Oh, yes…' Making an impossibly tight turn, he dropped the helicopter again to sweep a down-draught along his venerable avenue of lime trees. 'The second reason is that I enjoy it, Miss Carter.'

Katie soon overcame her initial fear of helicopter travel. In time, she even managed to glance out sideways. Looking down was still too much of a challenge. She wondered what her mother would make of this. Poor mousy little Katie, who hated any sort of fuss, had grown up to travel in a billionaire's private helicopter!

Her wonder increased as they drew near Milan. Instead of cypress trees, city skyscrapers rose above a layer of wispy cloud.

'See that? It is the headquarters of Amato International.' Giovanni pointed out a building. As they flew closer, Katie saw a white H on its roof. She gripped her seat, nervous again as Giovanni dropped in towards it.

'It began as a local concern, centuries ago,' he told her when they had landed safely. 'Then my family was approached by merchants who were looking for investment. Things improved rapidly after that. Early in the last century, car makers had to decide how to fuel their engines. Investors were faced with a similar choice.'

'Amato International chose to support petrol?' Katie said and her host laughed in agreement. His family must have been blessed with good luck a million times over the generations, Katie thought as she followed him into the executive lift. She wondered if he appreciated it. Despite his affable nature, she guessed that Signor Giovanni Amato kept his real thoughts well and truly hidden.

They travelled to the executive suite in a lift lined with mirrored glass. Katie found it hard to know where to look—or rather, she knew exactly where to look but tried to resist. Giovanni Amato was reflected all around her. If she kept her eyes to the front, it was impossible to avoid his acute stare. His tall figure flanked her on either side—one real, one reflected. Looking up was no escape from his presence either, although it was not so nerve racking.

They stepped out of the lift into ankle-deep carpet. Katie automatically priced the wall-to-wall luxury at not less than one hundred euros per square metre. The fact that she did such a thing brought her up short. Perhaps work really was invading her whole life if she had started putting a cost on her surroundings.

Katie had seen for herself that family life and work did not mix. Her past made her determined to lead a quiet life. Work was the thing. She could please people simply by doing something that she loved. That was her recipe for a happy life so far and it was making her very successful. She had started a Saturday job in her local fabric shop at the age of fourteen. It had been intended as a few hours' escape from home each week, but from the moment she had walked in on her first day

Katie had been in paradise. Colours and textures entranced her. From rich ruby velvets to star-spangled chiffons, the fabric shop had provided a release from the dull reality of keeping house. Katie's dream of a career in interior design had led to a college course. Then she had set up her own consultancy business. Now here she was, working with some of the richest and most influential people in the world. Even now she could hardly believe her luck!

Such a privilege had its price. Katie had a reputation for complete discretion. She said nothing, no matter what. She had seen and heard things that would make her a fortune many times over if she revealed them to the press. But, in Katie's opinion, money was not everything. She knew what she was worth and charged no more and no less than that. When it came to giving service and satisfaction to a client, she was streets ahead. Her favourite quotation was, 'It's never crowded when you go the extra mile.' Word soon spread. She had been able to take on assistants to share the workload. Yet Katie still did all the most important things alone. She had seen what happened when you got too closely involved with other people.

She was not going to let anyone ruin *her* life.

The executive lounge was wall-to-wall excess. Garish modern art jostled for attention around the red-painted walls. One side of the room was entirely made of glass. Like an eagle's nest it gave the executives of Amato International a regal view of the city, far below. There were a lot of puzzled looks and the odd smirk as Katie walked nervously into the office with Giovanni Amato. Instinctively she kept a step or two behind him and tried to be invisible. He was having none of it. Putting a protective hand to her shoulder, he drew her forward and made a direct announcement to the leering of paunchy officials.

'Gentlemen, Miss Carter is head of a firm of contractors. They will be refurbishing my Villa Antico, so she needs to get an idea of my tastes. I may have many skills, but I lack the time to discover if decorating is one of them. I have brought her here to use you, and these offices, as some examples of what I do *not* need in my private life,' he teased them affably, and they responded to him with laughter.

'Miss Carter will be working closely with me over the next month and needs to get a taste of my methods and working conditions.' He continued, 'To save time, I have brought her here to meet the secretaries.'

The executives of Amato International were still grinning, but now they looked good-natured, not feral. In their world, women were either slaves or honorary men. Katie let Giovanni lead her past them, grateful she was wearing practical working clothes. Her black trouser suit was severe almost to the point of being funereal, but she still had to run an off-putting gamut of appreciative stares from the other executives.

Giovanni Amato did not share his male executives' hobby of ogling. Katie decided it was probably because he knew how it felt to be openly admired. When he led her into a large anteroom staffed by personal assistants and secretaries, there was a flurry of excitement. Every woman in the place stopped to look at him. He seemed not to notice, cheerfully introducing Katie as his new contractor and then going back to join his colleagues. She was left to field a thousand questions. All the girls were desperate to know what it was like inside the Villa Antico. Some had attended a staff party held in its grounds during the previous summer, but none had entered the actual buildings. Katie explained that so far she had only seen the White Office.

'Be sure to let us know what the bedrooms are like, won't

you?' winked Signora Gabo. She was a greying, matronly type—but it hadn't stopped her blushing and giggling with the rest of them when Giovanni Amato had walked in. 'Every A-list woman from the glossy magazines wants an invitation to his house, but nobody seems to be having much luck.'

Felicia, a thin girl peering through curtains of long blonde hair extensions, nodded sagely. 'All the society hostesses are trying to get in on the act. I've heard him talking to my boss Guido about it—everyone wants to introduce the world's most eligible bachelor to the love of his life. He's getting a bit tired of it, he says. The trouble is, there are so few women of quality for him to choose from. Of course, a man like that can't marry just anybody.'

'Why not?' Katie's innocence met with peals of laughter.

'Because he's a count, that's why! Though he doesn't use his title when he's working. The girl Gorgeous Giovanni marries will come from one of the titled houses of Europe, I expect—although going by that poem made up by a newspaper columnist to describe some of them, he'd be better off choosing one of us: "Four feet two, eyes of blue, twenty stone and not a clue…"'

'That's a terrible thing to write!' Katie gasped, but she had to suppress a guilty giggle. 'Didn't anybody complain?'

'No—mind you, I doubt if many of them can read.' Signora Gabo looked over the top of her glasses as she tapped sheets of paper into a neat pile. 'That isn't what aristocratic women are for, Katie.'

'He wants a titled virgin with an IQ larger than her bust, apparently,' Felicia chipped in. 'We all want him to get married soon. There's nothing like a wedding!' She sighed, and everyone else joined in. 'But it doesn't look as though we're going to be in luck. He trawls through shoals of celeb-

rity women who all think they might become his next
Contessa, but he's always careful not to linger too long over
any one girl.'

Signora Gabo shook her head. 'He works too hard for that.
Hanging on to an inheritance is difficult. He makes it look
easy, but only because he puts his good family name before
everything else. We have his father, the old count, to thank for
making him like that. Signor Giovanni has to increase the
value of what can be passed on to his heirs, and that takes a
lot of doing,' she finished with a wise nod.

'He won't have anyone to leave it to if he doesn't father a
child himself,' Katie replied.

She could not wait to get back to the villa and start planning
her work. Going to Milan with Giovanni had given her plenty
of time to discover his dislikes and priorities. It had also shown
her the pace at which he worked, and the pressure. When they
left Milan behind and headed back to the Villa Antico, his relief
was visible. Katie almost felt relaxed about the return flight.

'I had a useful time at your office, Signor Amato. Although
I did find your fellow executives a bit overwhelming.'

'They are good men, but their brains are in their trousers
when it comes to beautiful women.'

Katie blushed at the compliment and found it almost impossible to look at him.

There were no acrobatics on the way home. Giovanni set
his helicopter down in its circle with pinpoint accuracy. Then
he went to help her from the cockpit. This time Katie hesitated before taking his hand. If he noticed anything at all, it
was the delay. He reached out to support her wrist with a firm,
sure grip. Katie felt her stomach contract, but she was irresis-
tibly drawn out of her seat.

In desperation she tried to keep focused on her work.

'This trip was extremely valuable in getting a taste of your working conditions, Signor Amato. But it was rather taken up by talking to your staff.'

'And lunch.' He slipped her a wicked glance. 'I gather the girls showed you the best trattoria in Milan?'

Katie blushed again, conscious of the way his life revolved around his working day. 'We were all back exactly on time, Signor. I wonder—would it be possible for me to attend Amato International again at some point and perhaps take a look around the rest of your office block?'

'Why not come straight out and say that you'd like a contract to rework *all* my property, Miss Carter?' An enigmatic smile hovered around his lips. 'You have a lot of ambition for one so young, no?'

Katie coloured again, but this time she kept her nerve. 'Yes. I can't deny that the idea was in the back of my mind. But nothing more than that.'

'Good thinking—having an eye to the future is invaluable in business,' he agreed, to Katie's relief. They were crossing a stretch of grass that separated his airstrip from the villa. He stopped and reached up to pull off his tie and unfasten the top two buttons of his shirt. A tantalising glimpse of dark hair became visible, below his throat. It made Katie wonder what else his austere white shirt was hiding. Amazed at such an unusual thought, she sucked in a breath of wonder. Then she heard a soft laugh and looked up.

'My, my, Miss Carter, that is a blush as chaste as any Contessa. The Marchesa di San Marco never told me you had noble blood in your veins when she recommended your work. I hope you aren't one of her grasping relatives, down on their luck.'

It was spoken lightly, but it still brought Katie up short. She could hardly believe anyone could make such an accusation in so offhand a manner. Fighting off gold-diggers was one thing, but Giovanni Amato should not be allowed to get away with insulting his workers.

'I am nobody's grasping relative! I got this job on my own merits,' she responded fiercely. She would show him—he would have to come down off his high horse when he discovered what a good worker she was.

'And so I should hope,' Giovanni replied with satisfaction. 'I don't have the time to supervise your every movement while you are here.'

'I would not let you.' Katie tilted her chin and looked him straight in the eyes, then wished she hadn't. He *was* gorgeous. There was no other word for it.

'Excellent. I'm glad we agree,' he said evenly. And, with a gesture for her to follow, he strolled off towards his house.

CHAPTER TWO

'THIS is Signor Amato's itinerary for the next thirty days.' Eduardo handed Katie a piece of heavy cream paper that bore the Amato crest. 'Business appointments are in red, social ones in green, and engagements combining the two are cross-hatched. The timing of your month here was chosen because he will be based at the Villa Antico, rather than travelling between his other properties here in Italy and abroad. You will be able to experience Signor Amato's taste for yourself and, of course, talk to him about his personal preferences.'

'My goodness,' Katie murmured as she studied a closely typed timetable. It covered the current month in detail, but the previous and following weeks also crowded in at the top and bottom of his busy schedule in note form. 'The Hamptons, Manhattan, a yacht, Nice… Does the man never spend more than a couple of nights in any of these places?'

'No.' Eduardo looked thoughtful and then reached out a neatly manicured hand for the paper she held. 'I understand from Signor Amato that you are to be allowed full access to the villa, in which case now might be an ideal moment to make a study of the White Bedroom. Signor Amato is guest of honour at a dinner this evening. If you begin now, Miss Carter, you will have some time in which to work upstairs, undisturbed.'

'Oh, but I couldn't possibly go to Signor Amato's suite now. He'll be getting ready to go out.'

Eduardo laughed, his prosperous jowls shimmering. 'I do not mean you should work on his personal suite, Miss Carter. You would be dealing with separate rooms. They were used, until the old Count's death, for—' he looked up, searching for what to say among the carved fruit and flowers that decorated the ceiling of his office '—something that Signor Amato would rather have wiped from the record as soon as possible, shall we say?'

Katie's imagination went into overdrive, but she was too discreet to ask for more details. This impressed Giovanni's assistant, who soon lost his initial suspicion of her. He led her through the marble halls quite cheerfully, but was surprised when she wanted to be shown her own suite first. 'I shan't be a minute, Eduardo, but I need to collect a toolbox... Wow!' she gasped as he showed her into a large salon.

On closer inspection it was as faded and shabby as the rest of the house, but Katie's first impression was of glamour, space and light. It was a world away from her small city flat. All the huge windows had been thrown open to air her suite, and filmy net curtains billowed in a sweetly scented breeze coming in from the gardens. Work forgotten, Katie wandered through her spacious temporary home. She gasped at the marble, gold and mirrors of her bathroom and marvelled at the size of her dressing room. She had brought the minimum amount of luggage and her first thought was that it would be lost in the echoing vastness of cupboards and racks when she came to unpack. Then she opened a closet door and found that her things had already been put away, and the suitcases stored on their own stands. Katie decided that if this was how the other half lived, she could get used to it quite easily. She made a mental note to thank whoever had dealt with her things later, but for now there was work to be done.

'I offer a complete interior design service, Eduardo,' she said as he queried the kit she had picked up from her room. 'There is no point in covering up infested timber or unsafe structure. Naturally, mine is only an initial survey. I employ a qualified structural engineer to provide the definitive report. But as a first move I like to find out what is going on for myself.' She did not tell Eduardo the real reason for her curiosity. Before she'd teamed up with Marcus, her tame surveyor, several sub-contractors had tried to take advantage of her. They'd thought a young woman would neither know nor care if they skimped on their work. Katie had taught them otherwise. She was not willing to compromise. Everyone employed by Carter Interiors had to give one hundred per cent all the time—and no excuses. That included her, too.

Eduardo carried an enormous keyring. It jangled under the weight of the crudest ironware Katie had seen. Some of the keys must have dated back to a time when the first parts of the ancient villa had been built. After a dizzying number of right and left turns, they entered a strangely silent corridor. All sounds of domestic staff going about their work died away. A strip of Indian carpet laid on the polished boards muffled sound. Faded flock wallpaper covered the walls. The ceiling must have been three metres high and the corridor a couple of metres wide at least, but after the great open spaces of the rest of the villa it felt almost cramped. Its chocolate-brown paintwork and burnt sienna wall-covering only added to the feeling of being enclosed. Katie had to fight the impulse to duck her head. They passed several gleaming panelled doors. Then Eduardo stopped at one and inserted a well-worn brass key in its lock. The door opened. The room beyond was white—white walls, white paintwork and white muslin curtains. In its centre stood an enormous white circular bed, the size of a Roman arena.

'Here we are, Miss Carter. What do you think? Seductive, eh?' Eduardo could not hide the sarcasm in his voice.

'It's extremely…bright, isn't it?'

'Not at night, Miss Carter. I can assure you of that.'

'That beautiful old fireplace over there—does it still work?'

'Sadly no, miss. This salon is immediately above the Smoking Gallery. The rooms share a chimney.'

'That is a pity.' Katie frowned. She was already making a note to contact an expert in open fires. Something had to be done to make this room more welcoming. The place must be made less clinical and more of a—Katie flinched at the word—boudoir. It was the last effect she wanted to create for a truly masculine man like Giovanni Amato, but there might be a middle way. If there were, she would find it.

'Thank you, Eduardo,' she said as the PA moved to leave. 'Will it be all right if I visit the gallery below, later?'

'You are to be given free access to the villa, Miss Carter. Signor Amato is not expected to return from his evening out until the early hours. Although I expect you will be finished long before then.'

It only felt like ten minutes later when Eduardo returned with a silver tray bearing coffee and treats.

'Signor Amato has just left for dinner, miss. He suggested that you might like some refreshments. And what are your own arrangements this evening?'

'Am I supposed to be going out, too?'

'It is not obligatory, miss.' Eduardo smiled. 'You may order dinner to be served in your room, in the dining hall or, if you would prefer to send out for a pizza, we can do that for you.'

Katie hoped her face did not show how impressed she was. Staying here was sheer luxury—and she was being paid for it, too!

'What is on your menu this evening, Eduardo?' she asked politely.

His expression became almost patronising. 'Anything you desire, Miss Carter.'

Katie gasped at that. The kitchens were probably geared up to serve teeny-tiny portions of exotic food and she suddenly realised she was starving. There was another problem, too. Katie did not want to take advantage of her situation by choosing anything overly expensive. On the other hand, ordering a great pile of the bread and cheese she loved might offend her client's highly trained staff.

'In that case, I think a little chicken and salad will do nicely.' She smiled, hoping her meal would come with a slab of focaccia.

'Thank you, Miss Carter. And where would you like to eat it?'

'In my room, I think, Eduardo,' Katie decided. 'And whenever it is ready will be fine by me.'

Confusion ran over Eduardo's face. 'No, Miss Carter, that is not how this house works. We serve at the times and in the places you specify.'

Katie sat back on her heels. In other grand households she had always eaten with the staff. No one, neither Katie nor her clients, had thought to suggest anything else.

'I shall be working here for about another hour, Eduardo. When I have finished, there's something I want to check in the Smoking Gallery and then I shall retire to my suite, thank you.'

When Eduardo left, Katie allowed herself a small smile. There are advantages to being employed by a pampered single man, she thought.

She investigated the hospitality tray Eduardo had brought. Six handmade biscuits sat on a china plate. The one thing worse than being served a tiny dinner would be leaving some of it because I've filled up on biscotti, Katie thought. After eating two, she left the others untouched, but it was with deep regret. Then, on impulse, she popped a couple into her pocket—just in case dinner turned out to be fashionable rather than filling.

By the time she carried her toolbox down to the Smoking Gallery it was already dusk. The door was still unlocked, so she went straight in.

A bat flickered through the enormous room, disappearing up into the shadows. Katie shivered, relieved that it would only take her a few moments to check her client's armorial colours. She ran over to the fireplace. Its tall mantelpiece meant that Giovanni Amato's entry was almost too high for her to see through the gloom. Taking out her pocket torch, she played it across the painted panels to pick out his name. The beam soon fixed on the name she was looking for, but as it did Katie noticed something else. She moved her light slightly to the right. There was some discoloration in the wood that had not shown up when it had been bathed in sunlight earlier in the day. The more she looked, the more Katie saw.

Giovanni Amato's name was picked out in gold leaf, like all the others. The difference was in the surface upon which it had been written.

She stared. This family tree had been carefully altered, with her client's sole name replacing two linked entries.

* * *

Katie could not sleep that night. Her mind was racing, and there were several reasons. The sheer majesty of this beautiful place was almost overwhelming. Her rooms—which Eduardo dismissed as 'the small guest suite'—were large, beautiful and airy. It was difficult to stop wandering around their threadbare luxury. Her mind was forever running over ideas for the places she had surveyed today, but every so often her thoughts returned to the mystery of the amended family tree. What, or rather who, had been covered up and replaced by Giovanni Amato's name?

For a long time she lay in bed, staring up at the shadowy sweet chestnut beams criss-crossing her ceiling. Then she must have fallen asleep, for suddenly she was catapulted awake by a sound from outside. Dragging on her dressing gown, she dashed to the elegant French windows of her bedroom. Opening them let in a cacophony of birdsong—and the rhythmic beat of a swimmer. Katie stepped out onto her balcony. The Tuscan dawn engulfed her, almost as though she had plunged into a pool herself. The early morning was still. Its air was cool, thin and bubbling with birds. Below her, a rectangle of water glowed with lights set below its surface. Long, lean lines ran through it with a glass-cutter's accuracy. Giovanni Amato was making them.

Katie took a step forward. She put her hands on the ironwork balustrade. It was cold with condensation, but she hardly noticed. The sight below absorbed her whole attention. The swimming pool must be twenty metres long. Time and again Giovanni's lithe naked body vanished in a perfect turn at each end. Katie watched, transfixed. To the east clouds split with sunshine, like a ripe fig. Had he only just returned from that private dinner? She went on watching, mesmerised by him and the thought of his punishing work schedule.

According to the list Eduardo had given her, Giovanni break-fasted at six o'clock each morning. Then he retired to work in his home office.

'Good morning, Miss Carter.'

She jumped. He had flipped out of his latest turn and was leaning back against the side of the pool. Arms outstretched along the poolside, water swirled around the rippling image of his golden body. Katie clapped her hands over her face.

'Oh, my goodness! I am so sorry, Signor Amato.'

She heard a turbulence of water and then a full-throated chuckle.

'You can uncover your eyes now, Miss Carter.'

His voice, rich with amusement, came from directly below her. She dropped her hands and looked down. He had secured a snowy white towel around his waist and was using a second one to rub his head and upper body dry. As she had suspected, he rippled with muscles. As he worked the towel, biceps and triceps flexed in a way that was impossible to ignore. Tossing it aside, he ran his fingers through the tousled thatch of his thick dark hair. Then he planted his hands on his hips and looked up at her.

'I always like to put in a hundred lengths or so before breakfast.'

'Oh, then you haven't just returned from your evening out?'

He gave an eloquent shrug. 'No—I got back a few hours ago. Sleep is not something that troubles me much.'

'I didn't have much trouble with it myself last night.' Katie gave a sigh, but it was not on account of her sleepless night. She had never seen anything like Giovanni's muscular torso. His sleek, sun-bronzed body was perfectly accentuated by a dark pelt of body hair. It shaded his chest and ran in a narrow line down his flat, toned belly. Katie tingled with nervous excitement. Until now, the only place she had seen a naked man was on TV. Now Giovanni Amato was live and loveable, right in front of her. How would it feel to run her hands over that perfect aristocratic form? The sight of him aroused her and the novelty of this new sensation increased its effect. Katie's home life and money worries did not leave much time for distractions. Temptation had always passed her by. Now she was looking straight at it.

Her eyes reached his face. Did he know what she was thinking? His expression was not giving anything away.

'I'm sorry to hear that. Did something keep you awake, Miss Carter?'

Katie's mind dragged itself away from his body and back to thoughts of the wall panel in the Smoking Gallery.

'Yes,' she said, and then thought better of bringing the subject up straight away. 'I was so full of ideas for your…White Bedroom,' she said carefully. 'I found it hard to drop off.'

'Then we must discuss your thoughts. I am eager to get that place cleaned up as soon as possible. Breakfast will be coffee and rolls. Is that OK for you?'

'It sounds wonderful.' Katie nodded.

'Good—we'll meet in the dining hall, then, in ten minutes.'

With that, he disappeared into a vine-covered pool house. Katie continued to watch for a minute or two, transfixed by what she had seen. Giovanni's body was as honed as his mind. Yet again she caught herself wondering how it would feel, and blushed.

Twenty minutes of increasingly frantic search later, Katie was desperate for a glimpse of Giovanni Amato's fully clothed body, let alone anything more interesting. She could not find the dining hall. Eventually she heard the creak of floorboards in a distant cross-passage and ran towards it. Pink-faced and panting, she caught sight of a figure just as it disappeared around a corner.

'Excuse me! I'm looking for the dining hall.'

In the silence that followed, Katie had a terrifying image of wandering the passages for the rest of her life, slowly starving to death... Then she felt a rush of relief as a young butler answered her call. 'You won't find either of them up *here*, Miss Carter.' He stared at her, mystified. 'In any case, do you mean the summer dining hall or the winter dining hall?'

Katie almost screamed with frustration, but it wasn't the boy's fault that she was lost. 'I need to be in the room where Signor Amato is taking breakfast,' she said as reasonably as panic would allow.

'Ah, that is the summer dining hall. Go back along this corridor, take the second on the right and go down two flights to the Lesser Entrance. You'll see a door in the far corner. Beyond that is the rear corridor: go straight along it and into the kitchen block. From there, the third green door to your left opens straight into the summer dining room.'

'Isn't there a short cut?' she asked desperately.

He looked her up and down. Katie's smart business suit was clearly giving him pause for thought.

'Only for those willing to take the staff lift.'

'Oh, I don't mind that. Thank you!' Katie gasped, and he led her to a hidden utility area.

Half a lifetime later she burst into a huge, echoing room of chandeliers and gilded mirrors.

'Ah, Miss Carter.' Giovanni dropped his copy of *La Repubblica* to watch her hurry to the table. 'Where is the fire? Coffee is on offer, although I feel I should recommend tea to calm your nerves.'

'I—I got lost.' Pulling back a Regency-striped chair, she took her place at the polished mahogany dining table. Giovanni had his elbows on the arms of his carver. His fingers were loosely laced before him. He made no move to show her where the drinks were, so she stood up again. In doing so, she almost collided with a butler. He had arrived silently at her elbow, teapot in hand.

'This is such an enormous house. I went around and around in circles.'

'As an interiors expert, perhaps you should not be telling me that.' Giovanni tried not to laugh, but failed. 'We shall get you a map, Miss Carter.'

His scrutiny continued as she settled herself. It was direct, but there was a certain amount of warmth behind it. Katie found it impossible to look away, despite the unsettling effect he was having on her. It was unusual enough to take breakfast with an employer, but this one seemed genuinely interested in what she did for a living. It was a concern she wanted to foster, not spoil. Now she was smouldering like embers with the shame of messing up right at the beginning of her first full day. It was not a good start.

'I can only offer you my apologies, Signor Amato. It will not happen again.'

He made a sound that Katie took to be approval, but then stood up with obvious regret. 'I intended to discuss your initial plans as we ate. Unfortunately, I am due a conference call, which must be taken in my office. I'm sorry we missed this opportunity, but perhaps we can talk when I finish my own work this evening? But now I must go. Enjoy yourself. *Ciao!*'

As he left, Katie kept her head down over her cup of

Darjeeling. She was not about to head for the buffet table while there was the smallest risk she might cannon into him. That would be the *end*.

The trill of a mobile phone spoiled her plan. She heard him stop right behind her, swear softly, then answer it.

Katie sipped her tea. She was starving. How much longer would it be before she could get up from her seat without the risk of making a fool of herself in front of him? The huge dining room was so quiet it was impossible not to be aware of the stream of muffled words pouring from his phone. Eventually, Giovanni interrupted them with such honeyed thanks that Katie could not help but look around at him. The amusement she saw in his eyes made her shiver. His expression came alive and danced with her heart. She was sorry when the call ended and his expression changed. He snapped his mobile shut and popped it into his pocket again.

'I may not need to delay your beauty sleep this evening after all, Miss Carter.' He laughed and with alarm Katie felt the warm glow of his personality reach out and envelope her again. 'The fact is, I was due to be entertained by a client later today. Unfortunately my host has had to drop out. As lunch reservations at Il Ritiro are highly prized, he has kindly offered me his booking. How would you feel about coming, too? It will give me the perfect opportunity to show you some of our famous hospitality, and study your plans at the same time.'

Before Katie could reply, Giovanni was summoned to the expected conference call in his office. She let out her breath in a long sigh of relief. She had been scared that being late for breakfast might be a sacking offence. Instead, all she had lost was some time alone with him, and now she was being offered a luxury lunch to make up for it. She could have hugged herself. How lucky could one woman be?

CHAPTER THREE

KATIE worked in the Smoking Gallery all morning. While she was there, a sketch map of the Villa Antico was delivered to her. It was accompanied by a request from Giovanni that she should be at the front doors by midday. An expansive hand had added the words 'To help you find the way' and signed it with the single word 'Amato.' Determined not to be late a second time, she set the alarm on her mobile. She loved her work so much it was easy to lose track of time.

The great house was silent as she went to keep their appointment. Her own suite was bright and sunny, but a cool breeze rippled around the villa's marble halls and chestnut panelled corridors. Katie knew that it took a small army to keep the place neat and tidy. She had met most of them, and liked them. They all got on together. It was such a pity their happy group couldn't dispel the unloved feeling of this old place.

It was exactly one minute to twelve when Katie arrived at the front doors. She did not get a chance to try her strength on the great iron ring of its handle. A butler arrived as she was putting out her hand and opened the door for her. Stepping back smartly, he let in a gust of warm, herb-scented air. The courtyard faced north. Some of the large gravelled area immediately outside the house was in deep shade, but beyond its shadows the stones glowed with sun.

Giovanni was precisely on time. His Ferrari swung around from the rear of some outbuildings and stopped right beside her. Getting out of the driver's seat, he made his way around to open the passenger door. Although his smile was only formal, Katie's heart still flipped. Her usual severe black working uniform had been replaced with dark linen trousers and a pale yellow blouse and she wore strappy leather wedges to keep her feet cool, but he had the power to make it all feel hot and constricting. She had to remind herself that this was nothing more than another business meeting for a busy Italian count. It felt a lot more enticing to her.

'You look lovely, Miss Carter. It is a pleasure to see you looking a little more relaxed.' His lips twitched in a teasing smile. 'Now you are dressed to enjoy our climate.'

Katie's eyes widened. His remarks were so personal. She hadn't thought he would take much notice of what she wore, let alone expect such a compliment. In agitation she fumbled with her case of designs and, as she did so, dropped her sunglasses. While she struggled to keep hold of her slippery files, Giovanni bent and retrieved them.

'Versace?' He smiled. 'Somebody has obviously been paying you too much, Miss Carter.'

Katie cursed her clumsiness. Giovanni Amato was good-looking enough already. Now he was adding a roguish smile to his charm, which released a strange fluttering feeling within her. This was not what she wanted to experience during a business lunch. She liked things to be kept strictly impersonal, and had to throw off his gaze before answering. 'I receive what I am worth, Signor Amato.'

She heard him chuckle as he dropped into the driving seat

beside her. It was such an evocative sound that a warm rush of anticipation instantly flooded through her. She quashed it almost as swiftly. Working for this man should be exciting enough. She could do without the added surge of attraction she felt for him. Opening the car window, she tried to cool down by thinking of other things.

'You should make the air-conditioning work for you, Miss Carter,' he said as the Ferrari sped up through the hills like a bead of mercury.

'I like the perfume of this countryside.'

'It is the vines. At this time of year they are growing so quickly you can see them move.' He was smiling as he drove, resting one hand on the steering wheel, the other on the gear lever. Katie could not answer. She was trying to concentrate on the view and hoped his typically Italian driving would not send them plunging down into the river far below.

'What is the matter?'

He was looking at her, not at the narrow twisting road. Katie could not suppress a tiny noise of alarm.

'Miss Carter?'

'It's nothing. Nothing,' she strained through pursed lips.

Suddenly they were whipping around a corner at such speed she squealed like a rabbit.

'There *is* something wrong.'

Katie was almost speechless with fright. 'No—no, only…why do you drive so fast, Signor Amato?'

'Fast?' He sounded puzzled and looked down to check the dials on his dashboard. 'Oh…I should have remembered from our trip to Milan that you like to take things steadily, Miss Carter.'

He eased off the accelerator. Their speed dropped smoothly away and Katie let out her breath in a relieved stream.

'I take my driving for granted, having travelled these roads so often and for so long. It's funny that no one else has ever mentioned it to me, though.' He shot her a curious glance. Katie recognised it from their first encounter in his office. He had been fascinated then by the qualities she needed to succeed. She knew that criticising a client's skills should not be among them.

'Perhaps you would have been happier if we had come out on the company bicycles, Miss Carter?'

His words instantly punctured her worries and she laughed. '*You*? You're not telling me *you* can ride a bicycle?'

'Certainly! The Villa Antico and the countryside around it was my refuge when I was growing up. Of course, my great-uncle was in residence as count here, then.' He was now concentrating on the speedometer more than the scenery and Katie felt herself beginning to relax. Then he unconsciously turned up her thermostat again. 'I used to power up and down these hills on my trusty Tommasini. It was exhilarating.'

Katie remembered the sight of him naked in the pool. And then envisaged his strong thighs working hard as he cycled through the hills. She gave a self-conscious giggle and he laughed in return.

'That's better. You should loosen up more often, Miss Carter. Let a little of our southern warmth thaw your chilly northern efficiency.'

By the time he pulled up in the restaurant car park, Katie was almost at ease with his presence, although the thought of lunch with a billionaire was still pretty nerve-racking. She was glad when he retrieved her work from the back of the Ferrari and then opened the passenger door for her like any ordinary gentleman.

The restaurant had been created out of an ancient farm-house. Cultivating rich guests was easier than fighting with the thin, stony soil. Katie was enchanted. There could not have been a more perfect setting among the blue Tuscan hills. To complement the picture, some tables were set outside, beneath a rose and vine draped loggia.

The head waiter came out in person to greet them.

'Ah, Signor Amato—what a pleasure it is to see you here again so soon.' The waiter clapped his hands and passed a practised eye over the case in Katie's hands. 'Will you be re-quiring Internet access?'

'No, not today, thank you, Luigi,' Giovanni said, and they were shown to a table beneath the twining greenery. It had the best position by far, with a spectacular view of the valley below.

Their settings were laid as they approached. Two young waiters dressed in black uniforms with crisp white aprons worked at lighting speed. They set out silver cutlery and crystal-ware, which glittered in the dappled, dancing sunlight. A covered jug of mineral water clinking with ice completed the scene.

The head waiter pulled out a delicate ironwork chair for Katie. As she took her place he picked up the intricately folded napkin on her side plate. Flicking it out with a crack, he swept it across her lap. As she thanked him, one of the other waiters handed her a menu.

Studying the copperplate handwriting before her, Katie realised she was way out of her depth. Her Italian was not good enough to choose from this list. It gave her few clues about what to expect. What if she chose something she did not like? Keeping her mind on business when faced with this gorgeous client would be difficult enough. The embarrass-ment of making a wrong choice of food would be too much to bear. She stared at the descriptions, desperately trying to recognise more words or phrases.

'Are you ready to order, Miss Carter?'

To confess would make her feel a fool. Instead, she fastened on something else about the list that worried her. 'There are no prices on my menu, Signor Amato.'

'That is so you can select without being distracted by the cost,' he said airily. 'Does anything particularly catch your eye?'

Katie dithered. It was all probably wonderful—and expensive. Every working-class instinct was telling her to choose the cheapest thing, which was impossible without prices. Every fibre of her self-made being begged her to go for steak. At least she could translate that, but would it seem extravagant, compared to everything else? She kept trying to decipher other descriptions. What would her host think, when someone employed to make decisions about his home couldn't choose between items on a menu?

'Is there anything you would like me to translate for you, Miss Carter?' He had thrown her a lifeline, but before she could confess he started laughing. 'Although I'm afraid my descriptions might be hazy. The staff here have been trying to teach me the correct culinary terms for years, but I'm afraid all their signature dishes still look like stew to me.'

Relieved, Katie asked him to translate the small but impressive choice of local seasonal dishes for her. In the end, she narrowed her choice down to marinated pigeon or Valdichiana beef.

'Then…may I suggest the beef?' His words were slow, gauging her reaction. 'It is my particular favourite, but don't let that influence you in *any* way.'

Katie's response to his mischievous smile made him snap his menu shut and hand it to the waiter. His order included two steaks with vegetables and a single glass of Sassicaia. As her own menu was lifted from her hands, Katie suddenly thought of something, but decided to keep quiet. Giovanni picked up on it straight away.

'Why are you looking like that, Miss Carter? You aren't having second thoughts, are you?' he queried, pouring them each a glass of water.

'I was wondering why there weren't more vegetarian options.'

'Why? You aren't a vegetarian.' He chuckled.

The casual way he dismissed her query annoyed Katie. It was too much like her mother's refusal to take anyone else's feelings into account.

'How do you know I'm not?' she countered, but instantly regretted it. There was no place in Giovanni Amato's world for nut cutlets. Where he came from, it was all haute cuisine and fine wines, she realised. *That must be why Eduardo gave me the option of a takeaway pizza last night. The villa staff probably think I don't know any better.*

Giovanni stopped laughing and looked at her. It was a rare woman who answered him back, but today he chose to take it as a good sign. Several times that morning she had taken on the doe-eyed look women always got when he was being himself. At least Miss Katie Carter had some spirit. That would make it easier when it came to stifling any romantic ambitions she might have. His heart had been out of bounds for years and he had no intention of releasing it, although she was becoming a strong temptation…

'As your host, Miss Carter, I make it my business to find out these things. For example, I happen to know that you had chicken for dinner last night. It follows, surely, that you can have no objection to eating meat,' he finished evenly. 'Now, are you going to open your file so we can start work, or have you already written me off as hopelessly controlling and manipulative?'

Katie laughed, but he did not. Although his voice was light, dark clouds were gathering in his grey eyes. The physical longing that rippled through her each time she looked at him instantly melted into concern. He is hurting, Katie thought with sudden realisation. She squashed the thought almost immediately. It was ridiculous. This man was a count, a successful businessman *and* wealthy beyond the scope of her imagination. What did he have to look downcast about? As far as she knew, the only worry in his mind would be finding a sufficiently regal mother for his future son and heir.

Other men would kill for a problem like that.

'Yes, I think we'd better get on, don't you?' she said briskly. Work would protect her from dangerous fantasies about what might be going on inside his head. This was a business meeting, pure and simple, she told herself. The sort of thing he does a dozen times a day with a dozen different people. I'm nothing special.

Unzipping her case, she brought out the first page of sketches and ideas. Immediately his attention fastened on the papers in her hand.

'Ah, this must be my father's entertainment suite…I shall certainly be glad to see that go.' He took the sheet from her with long, strong fingers and studied her work intently.

'I have contacted an expert in London,' Katie explained, 'who thinks it may be possible to modify your chimneys so that the suite and the Smoking Gallery beneath it can have open fires again. Your city offices look so modern and industrial. I thought you would like to return home to a more intimate atmosphere. That is why the new paintwork and walls have been given natural tones of cream, pale apricot and terracotta. There is still white muslin at the windows, but the rooms have been given a warmer, more relaxed feel.'

'Yes,' he said, lost in thought as he took a sip of water. 'I want a complete change, and this is an excellent start. I suppose your cosy chats with the staff have informed you that the main reason for all that white was apparently practical?'

It was Katie's turn to query him with a glance. In response he replaced his glass, put his elbows on the table and gave her a provocative look. 'Then my staff are even more discreet that I thought. Allegedly, the White Bedroom makes it easier when playing Find the Lady in the dark, Miss Carter.'

Katie felt a furious blush rising all the way up from her breasts to her face. His eyes locked with hers. He threatened to smile. Using all her self-control, Katie managed not to look away. The thought of being alone in that stateroom, in the dark, with Giovanni Amato suddenly filled her whole being. With immense effort, she fought against her feelings of anticipation. What was happening to her? This was a job of work—the one thing in life that never let her down. She had no time for dreams—even if she was sitting opposite the world's most desirable man. He is just a client, she thought fiercely. Giovanni Amato is no different from any other man.

But he was. Those intense grey eyes drilled into her like diamonds. It was as though he could see right inside her mind.

Their antipasti arrived. It was bruschetta cut into tiny shapes, each with a different topping: a rasher of salami, red beads of sun-dried tomato or slivers of fig and prosciutto twisted into intricate curls.

'You seemed a little uneasy earlier on, Miss Carter,' he enquired as they ate.

'Uneasy? No, Signor, it was simply the novelty of these lovely surroundings. I don't usually have time for restaurant lunches or a social life. I always eat at home, with my dad,'

Katie said, beginning to relax. Shaded from the sun, their table was ideal. The warmth was wonderful and the food was even better. 'Work is my life, Signor Amato.'

Giovanni nodded in approval. 'It is a shame more women do not share your dedication,' he said as one of the waiters brought out a glass of red wine on a silver salver. 'That is for my guest, thank you, Carlo.'

'I assumed it was for you,' Katie said in amazement as the Sassicaia was placed beside her. The rich red liquid glowed like stained glass in the filtered sunlight.

'I *never* drink and drive, you will be glad to learn.' He treated her to a meaningful smile.

'It was very rude of me to criticize your driving,' Katie acknowledged. 'I'm sorry.'

He waved her apology away. 'Don't mention it. It has been five years since I let anything get in the way of common sense. It is never worth it.' His last words were dark with meaning. Katie glanced up. He was gazing into the middle distance, his lips a grim line. Once more his whole expression was pained. It was so unbearable Katie felt she had to bring him back to the present. Her glass of wine provided an excuse for her to stir and break his mood. He returned to reality when he saw her take a sip. Putting the glass down again, she touched the napkin to her lips.

'Then you agree with my initial colour scheme and ideas, Signor Amato?' she said once she had his attention again. 'Of course, you need only make final decisions when you have seen samples and fabric swatches.'

'Yes, go with those ideas. I can modify them later, if necessary.' He was back to business as quick as a flash.

'Initially, I wondered about using the colours of your family crest for decorating that room,' Katie began casually as their main course arrived. He looked pleased at the quality of his beef and she decided this might be the moment to bring up the mystery that had been puzzling her. Heart thundering, she picked up her knife and fork. 'I happened to go into the Smoking Gallery at dusk to check the details. The funniest thing showed up in my torch beam. There must be a flaw in the wood of the panelling. A patch of discoloration beneath your name makes it look as though—'

'It is a flaw, most certainly.' He cut through her words as easily as he sliced his steak. Katie might have believed him, but for one thing. He was not looking at her as he spoke. Giovanni Amato's direct stare when speaking was one of the most challenging things about him. Now he refused to even glance in her direction. Katie was intrigued, but she knew better than to press the point.

'In the end, Signor, I decided that red, blue and green weren't the world's most seductive colours.'

Katie noticed him smile at her words. When he raised his head those even white teeth flashed briefly.

'Did Eduardo tell you it was my father's favourite suite?'

'He hinted at it, although without giving details, thank goodness. Your mention of what went on in there confirmed my suspicions.'

Giovanni found her reaction highly amusing. 'And so you have designed a room in which you would like to be seduced?'

Katie's eyes flew to his. It might have been meant as a joke, but when he saw her expression he stopped laughing. For the longest second in recorded time they stared at each other. Her heart turned somersaults in the turbulence of his gaze. There was definitely something hidden behind his eyes, and a sudden mad impulse made her want to reach out and touch him. She resisted. Katie was beginning to learn that when it came to Giovanni Amato, some things should remain unspoken.

She always tried not to repeat her mistakes. Next morning she arrived in the great summer dining hall well before six a.m. Giovanni was already seated at the head of the table. Dressed in a formal dark suit and pale blue shirt, he was engrossed in the business section of *La Repubblica*. As the heels of her sandals clicked across the marble floor, he put down his paper.

'*Buon giorno,* Miss Carter.' He watched as she chose a place halfway down the twenty-seat table. Today the guarded look in his eyes had been replaced by curiosity.

Katie felt bound to say something. 'Thank you for inviting me to eat breakfast with you, Signor Amato.'

He laughed off the compliment. 'Nonsense, Miss Carter, it is nothing but common courtesy. You are a guest in my house.'

Katie smiled at the butler who had arrived magically at her side. 'Not exactly, Signor. I am employed here to do a job of work. That makes me a member of your staff.'

'I don't think so. My staff don't normally wear colours and styles like that.' He raised his eyebrows at her pink, close-fitting top.

'I know, I know.' Katie blushed, as amused as he was. 'It's the effect of all this sunshine. After what you said yesterday about my working clothes, I decided to choose something more exotic than my usual starchy white shirt. I didn't think anyone would notice such a small thing. Don't worry—I'll change straight after breakfast. This top doesn't really say "work" to me, either,' she added apologetically.

Giovanni found himself unexpectedly aroused. He wondered how long it would take to work up a physical immunity to her. If she had any more nipple-skimming

T-shirts like that one among her off-duty clothes, the answer was: quite a while. He shook out the pages of his newspaper again to distract himself from his thoughts of Katie Carter and that delicious little top.

But, as Katie was served with rolls and a cappuccino, he looked up and watched her smile in thanks. She turned and caught his gaze and an unexpected spark of tension simmered between them.

She was saved from the lingering intensity of his stare by the sound of her mobile.

'Oh…' She unclipped the handset from her belt but, before she could redirect the call, Giovanni stopped her.

'Answer it, Miss Carter. I know how it is—a missed call means missed business.'

Amazed at his tolerance, Katie took her call.

'Dad. Hi—listen, it's great to hear from you, but actually I'm in a meeting at the moment—' She stopped. Her host was gesturing at her.

'Family matters are more important than business, Miss Carter. Carry on with your conversation.'

'But I can always spare a few minutes for you, Dad.' She laughed with her father as he remembered the time difference. He had thought Katie would still be getting ready for work. Her laughter soon died when she realised why he had telephoned. Giovanni lowered his newspaper completely as he saw her frown.

'Is something the matter at home, Miss Carter?' he enquired as her call ended and she clipped the mobile back on to her belt.

'Yes—and no, Signor. My mother has announced that she wants to pay an extended visit to my father. The problem is…'

She hesitated. How could she tell this virtual stranger about the walking collection of character faults that had given birth to her? Oh, if only her father wasn't so gentle and forgiving! Katie could not bear to think of him being hurt again, as he surely would be. 'The problem is that my mother rarely contacts him without some…hidden agenda. My father had heart bypass surgery not long ago, and he shouldn't be expected to take her in. I know from painful experience that her return always means trouble.'

'Your father must develop enough backbone to resist her. His recent health problems may have helped. Facing disaster often causes men to stiffen their resolve—especially when it comes to women.' Giovanni flourished his newspaper and returned to studying his stocks.

Katie seethed. His family life might have been as bad as hers, but she was not about to have her father scorned as well as her mother. Dad *is* too soft for his own good and I *am* only a guest here, but I'm not going to let him get away with that, she thought angrily.

'How can you say that, Signor Amato?'

'My own experience does not lie, Miss Carter. Unless and until the good influence of motherhood takes over, women often deceive, flatter and scheme to get their own way,' he concluded in a low voice.

Katie shook her head slowly. For his character sketch to be accurate, her mother must have been a regular Jezebel before maternity hit her. Joyce Carter's fickle, flighty behaviour had made Katie the woman she was. When puzzled, Katie always asked herself what her mother would do in similar circumstances. Then she took care to do exactly the opposite.

'Not all women are alike, Signor. Some of us are hardworking, trustworthy and loyal.'

'Hmm…' he began, and then looked thoughtful. 'I must

admit your attitude to work impresses me. I have never known any other woman put in similar hours to mine.'

'Then you must be mixing with the wrong sort of girl, Signor.'

'Whereas you don't have time to mix with men at all?'

Giovanni's statement echoed what she had hinted the day before. Work gave her no time. She had admitted that. But still she met his retort with a cool gaze. 'I have never yet met a man who understands why I feel as I do about my work. But, unlike you, Signor, I would never write off fifty per cent of the human race without first giving them a chance.'

Two dark, impenetrable expressions met across the polished mahogany of the dining table. They each reached for their coffee in the same instant, and the moment was broken.

'Where will you be working today, Miss Carter?'

'I shall continue with the first floor suites, Signor. Would you like to be present when I begin on your rooms?'

He flicked another glance at her, but found that her words had been without flirtation. The blush that lowered her long dark lashes now was one of guilt at saying the wrong thing, not coquetry. He continued to look at her long after coming to that conclusion. Something stopped him looking away.

'No. I don't think that will be necessary, Miss Carter,' he said at last.

Katie finished her light breakfast quickly. She told herself she was keen to get on with her work. This was not entirely true. Part of her wanted to escape from Giovanni Amato. Whenever she was in his presence, her body simmered. Everything about him—the drift of his aftershave, his low, confidential tone, the clear golden skin—drew her eyes to him with an urgency that could not be denied.

Early that morning, she had woken seconds before the

splash that announced his dive into the pool. Incapable of resisting the lure, Katie had left her bed and gone to the French
windows. They had been left standing open all night. Katie
liked to think there was only a veil of white muslin between
her and the nightingales singing in the olive groves below.
This morning, though, her mind had been on other things.
She had not gone onto the balcony. Instead, she stayed
hidden in her room, looking out over the pool. Giovanni
Amato's naked body was perfectly illuminated by the under-
water lighting. She watched as he powered up and down,
sleek as a seal. When at last the pounding beat of his strokes
stopped and the water grew still, her heart sank. The glow
of excitement low in her stomach became an ache of longing
which had been tormenting her ever since. The only cure for
that was work—and work that avoided Giovanni Amato as
much as possible.

Keeping away from him was easier said than done. Katie
worked methodically through the first storey of the house.
After beginning with the old 'entertainment suite,' she thought
it logical to continue her work on the same floor. Unfortunately for her hormone levels, that eventually meant
entering Giovanni's office.

The White Office revolved around his enormous island of
a desk. With its banks of telephones, scanner, fax, computer
and modem links, it drew Katie's eyes almost as much as the
man behind the monolith. For nearly an hour she measured
and sketched, making notes and trying to avoid catching his
eye. In turn, he issued instructions down the phone, rattled
away at one keyboard or another and carefully ignored her.

When her survey was over, Katie tried to tell herself she
was glad. It was not true. The atmosphere of his office fizzed.

It was the excitement of seeing and hearing a man at the top of his game, directing multi-million dollar deals worldwide.

She took a while packing the toolbox with her tape measure, pencils and notebooks. During all that time he never spoke to her. In fact he only looked up to acknowledge his PA, when Eduardo entered the office.

'*Scusi*, Signor—Miss Carter.' Eduardo nodded towards Katie as she knelt on the floor surrounded by her work. 'The Princess Miadora's office rang. Sadly, she is indisposed and will not be able to attend your party this evening after all.'

Giovanni threw down his fountain pen and clasped his hands behind his head. 'Damn. That leaves you with a planning problem, then, doesn't it, Eduardo? Who is to sit with Signor Balzone and sweet-talk him into helping the project?'

'I was hoping you might suggest a suitable replacement, Signor.'

Katie heard her client sigh. He must have shaken his head, too, because, as she picked up her things and set off for the door, Eduardo began to reel off a list of names. Katie tried not to listen, but it was impossible not to—and wonder. The Amato contacts were so starry, his address book must glow in the dark.

'The Duchess?'

'No—she told me herself she was booked solid.'

'The Marchesa Chiara?'

'She is on her yacht, somewhere in the Indian Ocean.'

'Lady Carina Foakes?'

'She's in London for her son's birthday.'

'Mrs Delabole?'

'She is off prospecting in The Hamptons, along with Myra Haigh-Davies, Kiki Lipton and all the other trust-fund talent you have tried to foist on me over the years, Eduardo.'

As Katie reached the door there was a pause in the list of eligible females. With a twinge of disappointment she realised that was the last bit of gossip she would hear.

And then Eduardo followed her out of the White Office and caught up with her as she walked along the corridor to the next suite.

'May I trouble you for a moment, Miss Carter?'

'Of course you can, Eduardo. What is it?'

'Signor Amato was wondering…' the PA began, looking shifty. Then he giggled. 'All right—to be honest, *I* was wondering…do you have any engagements this evening, Miss Carter?'

Despite his grin, Eduardo looked a worried man. Katie could not bear to heighten his tension by inventing a social life for herself.

'Er… no. Why?'

'Signor Amato is hosting a party in aid of charity on his yacht tonight. I carefully crafted the guest list months in advance, as usual, but now we find ourselves one lady short. Signor Amato's guest of honour is a single man. He cannot possibly be left without a lady to escort into dinner. I was wondering…might you agree to make up the numbers?'

Katie considered this, but not for long. Anyone would be mad to turn down the chance of mingling with the rich and famous on a billionaire's yacht.

'All right,' she said cautiously, trying to ignore the fact that she must be their guest of last resort. 'Yes—I'll do it. Why not?'

The worry drained from Eduardo's face as he saw her enthusiasm increase. Then horrible reality doused Katie's dreams.

'Oh—I've just realised I'll have to say no after all, Eduardo.' She made a little moue of understanding as the PA's face fell again. 'It's a horrible excuse, but I really *don't* have anything to wear. I came here to work, not party, so there's nothing suitable in my luggage. We must be miles from the nearest dress shop, so it isn't as though I could nip out and buy something, even if I *liked* clothes shopping.'

Eduardo sympathised with her disappointment, but then stopped. Suddenly, he began looking Katie up and down as though calculating her size. Then he beamed. His smile became so wide his eyes almost disappeared behind his plump pink cheeks.

'Ah! I may be able to do something about that, Miss Carter. Come with me—but not a word to the Count.'

They walked along the second floor balcony. Dark, gloomy portraits glowered from every wall. Katie noticed some discreetly placed buckets beneath a glazed dome, high above. Something other than sunshine must stream down from those leaded lights when it rained. Eduardo pointed out Giovanni's private suite as they passed. Twenty metres further along the corridor, they stopped at an identical mahogany door and Eduardo unlocked it. With one touch to its highly polished brass handle, the door swung open.

Katie was ushered into a shadowy suite. The fragrance of beeswax polish that wafted through the rest of the villa had no escape from these shuttered, half forgotten rooms. It mingled with the memory of expensive perfumes and new things. Eduardo went over to the windows. Folding back the shutters, he let sunlight pour in. The suite was set out like Katie's own, but on a much grander scale, and its furniture was covered with dust-sheets. She got some idea of its character from glimpses of upholstery peeping out from beneath the covers. It was all very pink and gold—and fluffy. Her mind never far from her work, Katie decided this place would go down in her notes as the 'Pink Princess Suite'.

'Now, if you would care to follow me, Miss Carter.' Eduardo crossed the drawing room and went through a door into the bedroom beyond. Like the old 'entertainment suite,' this was almost completely white. Instead of being circular, the bed here was an empress-sized rectangle. Its dust-cover had slipped and Katie caught sight of a white silk headboard, deeply buttoned with large gold nuggets. She was almost lost for words. Her mind went straight back to the alteration that had been made to the Amato family tree. She had a dozen questions, but Eduardo's expression warned her not to pry.

'This is nice…' was the only comment she could think to make.

Eduardo said nothing. Katie waited for him to give her some clues about the room's most recent occupant. He did not. Instead, he moved into a dressing room half the size of Katie's own suite. Fitted cupboards took up one whole wall. They were painted in a high gloss white, with details picked out in gold. Uncovering a dressing table, he took a keypad from its drawer. Opening the white suede case, he revealed ranks of small gold keys, each marked with a white identifying tag.

'Now, Miss Carter, let us consider. It is early summer, so that means we should be looking in Range Two…' His finger hovered across the second leaf of the keypad. 'Hmm, for dinner on the yacht—a nautical theme, perhaps, so that means the blues and greens…' Running down the rows of tiny labels, he selected a key. Approaching one of the cupboard doors, he opened it.

Katie's eyes widened. Inside the closet hung more clothes than she had owned in her whole life. Each was stored in a clear protective cover. It was all filed in strict colour code, from palest sky-blue to midnight velvet.

'Which would you prefer—trousers and a top? That seems to be your style. You can mix and match from dozens of those.'

Katie could believe it.

'Or there are skirts—'

'I think it had better be a dress, Eduardo. I don't usually wear them, but this sounds like a formal affair.'

'When the Count throws a party, it always is.'

'Then it should be full-length,' Katie decided.

Eduardo looked more pleased by the minute. His smile gave Katie the courage to ask a question.

'Eduardo, why doesn't everyone refer to Signor Amato as 'The Count' when he is not at work?'

'Because he stopped using his official title altogether when—'

He brought himself up short, and began again.

'—The Count stopped using his title when it became obvious he would be the last of his line.'

That partly explained the alteration to the panel in the Smoking Gallery. It also set alarm bells ringing inside Katie's head.

'Wait a minute, Eduardo. Whose clothes *are* these?'

'They belonged to the late Contessa, Miss Carter. Signor Giovanni decreed that she should be erased from his life. That is why only his name appears on the Amato family tree now. It seemed too hasty a decision at the time, to me. His father was still alive then and living here as count…so I persuaded him to have everything transported here from Signor Giovanni's marital home in Milan. I did it in case he ever regretted destroying the Contessa's things completely. Up until now he has not, but you never know…' he added quickly, putting a finger to his lips. Katie did not need the warning. Eduardo's voice was firm enough to block any more questions heading in that direction, but her nerves sent her down another route.

'I can't possibly wear a dead woman's clothes!' she announced.

'Why not? The Contessa Lia has no more use for them.'

The reply shocked her.

'What in the world will Signor Amato say if I appear dressed as his wife? I suppose the Contessa Lia *was* his wife?'

Eduardo gave her an uncomfortable smile.

'She must have looked really lovely in all these beautiful designer things. Oh, that poor man.' Katie shook her head in dismay, but Eduardo laughed.

'The Count scorns sympathy, Miss Carter. And he would not recognise anything from this collection. Everything here is brand-new. Look—the ones that are not handmade still have their price tags in place. The Contessa rarely wore anything more than once, if at all. Ensembles were either sent back to their designer after use or thrown away. Very occasionally she would take a particular fancy to something. Then it would be cleaned and filed…' He pointed towards a smaller but still impressive range of closets on another wall.

Katie went on staring as Eduardo flicked through the clothes with the air of an expert. He pulled out a lilac sheath, held it up against her, frowned and put it back. This was repeated with several more beautiful dresses. Katie had never thought she would be reluctant to get her hands on the work of Ferragamo and the rest but her mind was filled with doubts. Any woman who could wear clothes like these must have been absolutely drop-dead gorgeous. How on earth could she possibly compete tonight? *Not that Count Giovanni Amato could ever be expected to look twice at a commoner like me,* she thought, and then stopped. Eduardo had reached a dress that made them both sigh. It was cut from sapphire silk taffeta, discreetly spangled with bugle beads. He lifted it out with reverence. They both nodded. Katie knew this was The One. He handed it to her and she gazed in admiration, then turned for the door, believing the search was over.

'Wait! You cannot try it on yet, Miss Carter—we haven't been through the green section. And what about your shoes and accessories?'

By the time Eduardo had run through the 'palest mint to laurel' cupboard, she was agonising as much as he was over the final choice.

'In the green strapless lamé you would look like a mermaid, Miss Carter. Especially if you wore your hair loose around your shoulders.' Eduardo admired the gloss on the auburn braid she wore while working.

'But I always keep my hair tied back. And on the other hand—the blue silk makes rather less of a statement…' Katie mused. She was still not at all sure which dress to go for. 'Remember, Eduardo, I am not a proper guest. I should be discreet. I am only attending to make up the numbers.'

He gave her another strange look. 'Yes…' he allowed, 'and as such jewellery will present a problem at the moment. It would not be right to ask Signor Amato if you could use something from the historic Amato collection. Hmm…' He tapped his teeth with the keypad. Then he had a brainwave. 'I know, while you prepare for the party, I shall ask around among the female staff. The Count pays good wages. I'm sure someone will be more than happy to lend you a few trinkets for such a good cause.'

'You mentioned that this was a charity event,' Katie said as Eduardo looked her out a pair of cream leather stilettos and a matching purse. 'Which one is the Count supporting tonight?'

'His own foundation, set up to study the causes of still-birth.' Quick as a flash, Eduardo threw a cashmere shawl across the gowns lying in Katie's arms. 'There. That will set off either ensemble most elegantly.'

It was a masterstroke. Katie was dazzled. She was halfway back to her suite before she realised that Eduardo must have filled her arms with luxury to stop her asking any more awkward questions.

CHAPTER FOUR

Two hours later, Giovanni strode down to the grand entrance hall of the Villa Antico. He was expecting a long wait, but as he checked his Rolex he heard a door closing on the upper floor. He had time to straighten his cuff-links and adjust his tie in the cheval-glass beside the front doors before anybody came into view behind his reflection. Then he stopped and turned. A complete stranger was walking along the landing and it was the most glamorous vision he had ever seen. Then with a jolt he realised it was Miss Katie Carter. For long moments he relished her approach, holding his breath. Then she reached the top of the stairs and realised he was watching her.

Seeing the look on his face was enough to make her hesitate at the top. He was gazing at her with rapt, unswerving attention and it was wonderful.

Giovanni took his time, appreciating her slender beauty. Framed against the faded splendour of his house, it was the ideal contrast between austerity and soft, pliant loveliness. That blue silk dress showed off her creamy skin and delicate collar-bones to perfection. At her slightest movement, a provocative slit in its side seam revealed that her legs really *did* go sky-high. He cleared his throat and stepped forward

Unprofessional arousal was haunting him again. The antidote was to break his own awestruck silence.

'Miss Carter—over the past centuries queens, contessas and courtesans have used that staircase. You inherit their tradition beautifully.'

'Thank you, Signor Amato.' Katie took it as a compliment, revelling in his smile. She had been nervous, but now his words gave her a rush of confidence. Suddenly she felt more like a princess than an interior designer. Surely anything was possible on a night like this. Taking a deep breath, she raised her head, put her shoulders back and tried to descend like a true consort. He watched her every heartbeat and it gave her more courage. In return, she could not take her eyes off him. He was perfectly groomed as always, but instead of the shirtsleeves in which he usually worked, he was dressed in a three-piece suit. Seeing him in such a formal outfit made Katie realise what a serious event this was going to be. Nerves threatened to overwhelm her again and she wondered if her palms were damp.

'Stop there for a moment,' he said as she reached the ground floor. For a few agonising seconds he was silent, studying her from every angle. His face never lost its expression of wonder and eventually he nodded. 'Yes…'

Everything was contained in the way he said that single word. Katie almost collapsed with relief.

'Oh, thank goodness! When I couldn't decide between this dress and the green one—'

That broke the spell. He put his hands on his hips and whistled. 'Miss Carter, you amaze me. I never imagined a sensible, working woman like you would pack more than one formal gown for a stay here.' His expression of amazement quickly became a wry smile. 'Nevertheless you certainly look the part tonight, Miss Carter.' He paused. 'I must warn you, however, that parties are not my first love. I *never* entertain formally at my properties, and only rarely on my yacht.' She caught his gaze and saw a twinkling in his eye. 'But when I do, Miss Carter, it is usually quite an evening.'

Katie felt a sudden return of spirit. Tonight she would be part of his world.

One of the Amato limousines was waiting for them outside. Katie automatically went towards the rear passenger door, but Giovanni placed a hand on her arm to stop her. She jumped at his touch and looked up at him in alarm. Their eyes met, but before either could speak the chauffeur had opened the car door and was waiting for her to step in. Katie moved forward again. Giovanni's fingers fell from her wrist, but their touch lingered like fire. It almost made her forget the promise she had made to the indoor staff.

'Oh—wait—I must just…' One foot inside the carpeted luxury of the car, she stopped and looked around at the façade of the grand old house. Dark shapes were moving behind the muslin curtains at several windows. Raising a hand, Katie waved. The crystal earrings and blue beaded choker she had been loaned were not the genuine article, but they glittered and sparkled in the evening sunlight like the real thing.

'I'm actually beginning to enjoy this,' Giovanni said, watching her settle herself inside his car. 'Now *there's* something I never thought would happen.'

The chauffeur shut the car door between them before Katie could reply. She had to wait until Giovanni got in beside her before answering.

'Why do you hold parties if you don't like them, Signor?' she enquired as they were wafted away from the villa.

Giovanni looked out of his window. If she saw him smile now, she might think he was smug, condescending, or both. That was not his intention.

'They are the price one should pay for living like this.' He indicated the limousine's interior. It was plush with upholstery and fragrant from a tiny flower arrangement set on the rear parcel shelf. 'I use my money to try and make others part with theirs. Sometimes it is business. Tonight it is in the interests of charity, which makes it doubly important. The more we can persuade them to pledge this evening, Miss Carter, the happier I shall be.' When he looked at her now, his face was touched with genuine warmth. Despite her nerves, Katie found it easy to respond.

'Then I shall need some information on your guest, Signor Balzone, if I am to play my part properly.'

'He is a media man, Miss Carter, and extremely wealthy. His goodwill means a great deal, so we need to charm him like he has never been charmed before.'

'I am surprised you are bothered by the fact he is rich,' Katie said as their car drove sedately towards the helipad. 'I would have thought a successful man like you could have funded any number of good causes single-handed, Signor Amato.'

'Financial success is not everything in life, Miss Carter.'

He might have donated a smile at this point, she thought. He did not.

'If Agosto Balzone enjoys himself this evening, he could become an important sponsor of my charity.' Giovanni stretched out his long legs and brushed an invisible speck from his suit. 'He may also give us free publicity and airtime, cheaper advertising rates, or all three.'

'So Signor Balzone has only been invited to this party because he can do you some good?' Katie enquired slowly. It sounded a horrible ploy.

'That is the only reason anyone is ever invited anywhere, Miss Carter. To be brutal, it is why you are sitting next to me now rather than stuck in your suite, poring over your plans for my house.'

In that moment her romantic dreams faltered and died. Her Cinderella fantasy must end here. Tonight was going to be 'business as usual' when it came to their relationship.

Fine—that's just the way I like it, Katie thought. Or at least, it was…

'It is an approach, I suppose,' she said warily. 'Well, I shall do my best to help your plans, Signor Amato.'

'Good.' There was real appreciation in his voice as he opened a flap in the limousine's interior. It revealed a glittering, fully stocked mini-bar. 'I appreciate it is asking a lot of you, Miss Carter, to hold your own in an assembly full of strangers. But please remember, I am extremely grateful for the way you have stepped in at the last moment. If you feel unhappy or uncertain about anything at all, you can always look to me for help.'

'Don't worry, I'm determined to enjoy myself,' Katie responded. 'Although I want to do more than just make up the numbers at your party.'

Giovanni looked at her acutely as he offered her a drink. 'You will be careful though, won't you, Miss Carter? What you get up to overnight is your own affair, of course, but as your host I feel responsible for you. If there is the slightest hint of a problem you must come straight to me. I don't want you to feel pressurised by anyone, in any way. Not even by me,' he added mischievously.

Katie accepted a glass of fresh orange juice, but with caution in her eyes. 'You've worried me now. Eduardo said this was a dinner,' she said with slow meaning. 'He never mentioned anything about "overnight".'

Giovanni looked perplexed. 'It would not have occurred to him that there was anything worth explaining. I can hardly expect guests to come from far and wide without offering them the chance of an overnight stay.' He made it sound like the most natural thing in the world.

Katie was troubled. '*I* won't be expected to stay though, will I?'

'Of course,' he said nonchalantly.

He clearly did not expect Katie to need things spelled out. In the face of his certainty she began to feel nervous again. 'I knew that you sometimes spent time on your yacht but I never expected to be included.'

'Didn't you?' At that point the corners of his mouth almost lifted, but his eyes remained wary. Katie remembered the office gossip about his love-life and realised that a lot of women probably tried to play the innocent with him.

'No, I didn't,' she said firmly. 'If I had, I would have made sure I brought more than this purse. Some perfume, lipstick and a handkerchief are hardly going to see me through a stay on a luxury yacht, are they?'

'An overnight case has been packed for you. It is stowed away in the back.' He tipped his head towards the rear of the car.

Katie was aghast. 'How on earth did you know what I might need?'

'I didn't.' Giovanni took a sip of chilled mineral water. 'That is Eduardo's job.'

Katie was not convinced. 'I'm not sure I like the idea of relying on someone else to pack my bag for me.'

'I think you may be pleasantly surprised, Miss Carter. Eduardo has never let me down yet.'

'Yes, but you're a man.'

'So you've noticed?' Giovanni leaned forward to check that

the intercom connecting them to the driver was switched off, a smile haunting his lips. 'My father always suspected that Eduardo was not interested in women. You should have no worries there.'

Katie thought of Eduardo's expertise in kitting her out for the evening. 'So—is Eduardo gay?'

'I neither know nor care.' Giovanni looked at her as though she had suggested he should move to Siena. 'Eduardo has been an excellent employee for many years. Before I inherited, he saved the house of Amato from many scandals. Discretion is everything, Miss Carter.' He took another drink and looked out of the window.

They were not in the car for long, driving only as far as the estate's airstrip where a pilot had the Amato helicopter ready for take-off. Their seats were deep, roomy and comfortable but Katie did not have much time to get used to her luxurious surroundings. The horizon soon became a glittering line. As they flew towards the coast, the usual perfume of hot herbs took on a seaside tang.

'Oh, look! The beach!' Katie said in excitement, before she could stop herself.

'Enjoy the view, I'm afraid we won't be able to stop and visit, Miss Carter.' Giovanni laughed. 'Some of my guests might want to venture ashore, but I doubt it. They visit me for a break from that kind of life. Viareggio is too busy for my liking. In the past, I have seen far too much damage done by the relentless pursuit of pleasure. I prefer to keep it at a distance, myself.'

Katie wondered what he meant. Her childhood had been spent listening to her mother hankering after things she could not have. Perhaps there had been some of that going on in his life, too.

'I just assumed your boat would be parked in a marina.' She looked puzzled.

'My *Viola* is hardly a boat, Miss Carter,' he said with quiet pride. 'She is moored offshore. That gives good views of the coastline, but it is a long way from the holidaymakers and paparazzi lenses.'

'I can understand why you like that,' she said with a sigh, 'but it would have been nice to feel the sand between my toes for once. I haven't been on a beach for ages.'

'Then you shall visit the seashore beside *Viola*'s pool, Miss Carter.'

She laughed, imagining a heap of grit beside a hot tub— and then she saw where the helicopter was going to land. It was spiralling down towards a vast ship. Katie stared out of the window as they landed on a dedicated flight deck that was large enough to house at least two other helicopters.

'This isn't a yacht—it's—it's an ocean liner!'

'Oh, hardly that, Miss Carter,' Giovanni said affably as a member of his crew helped them out on to the deck. 'Show Miss Carter to her allotted suite, Guido. How is life with little Pepito now? Are you and Maria managing to get any sleep yet?'

'Not a lot, Signor, but at least Maria has my company here, overnight.' The young man gave a rueful laugh. 'Thank you for letting her come with me this week—it would have been hard for her, looking after a new baby at home, alone.'

'Don't mention it, Guido. A father's first duty should always be towards his wife and child. Now, I haven't checked my emails since this morning so I am off to the office. As for Miss Carter, she has a desire to see the pool. Give her directions to it, would you?'

With that he was gone, absorbed by work again. Katie tried out an uncertain smile on Guido. 'I'm just an interior designer. I'm not with Signor Amato…in any meaningful sense,' she ventured.

'Of course not, Miss Carter.' Guido smiled.

As he led her to her room, Katie used the opportunity to try and find out a little more about Giovanni and his past. But, as she questioned Guido, she realised Amato staff members were beyond such tricks. Even though she found out nothing, the loyalty Giovanni obviously inspired in his staff impressed her.

Guido led her along yet another corridor, his footsteps muffled by thick carpet and efficient air conditioning. 'Here is your suite, Miss Carter. The pool is down the corridor to the left.' He unlocked the door and stood back, holding out the key. Katie took it, realising she was not going to find out any more. Thanking him, she went inside to explore her new surroundings.

Her suite was only slightly smaller than the one at the villa. Instead of plasterwork, the interior here was oak panelling, polished to a glassy shine. Soft upholstery and heavy velvet curtains made it feel like a luxury hotel rather than a ship. Katie's rooms looked out towards the shore, which was bright with all the colour and noise of early summer. She had wondered why Giovanni never looked genuinely happy, but perhaps now she had a hint of his reality. Although he had all the wealth, status and 'boy's toys' that any man could ever want, his past had injured him in some way. Katie realised now that money really could not buy happiness.

She checked over her luggage quickly, marvelling that Eduardo had put in everything she could possibly need, and more. Then she set off for a look round. Before Guido had left her, he had asked if she would like drinks served by the pool. Katie had been delighted by the idea. She was even more excited when she reached it. The *Viola* really was equipped with a beach of silvery sand as well as a deep blue pool, and waiting beneath the shade of an awning was Giovanni. As she approached he offered her a glass of chilled champagne. The sand rushed into her borrowed stilettos as she crossed the beach towards him, but she hardly noticed.

'Do we really have time for this, Signor?'

'There is *always* time for Taittinger '95. Force yourself, Miss Carter,' he teased. 'It is well worth the effort.'

She raised her glass to take a sip, but he stopped her. 'Wait. We should have a toast in anticipation of your triumph this evening. I have every confidence that this party will be an astounding success.' He touched his glass against hers. The pure crystal rang with quality and Katie took a first taste. He joined her and they both savoured the champagne's lemon and almond fireworks. Then he raised his glass again. 'And now to you, Miss Carter: for not only making up the numbers, but for doing so in such spectacular fashion.'

They drank, and he topped up her glass with another foaming meringue of bubbles.

Katie wondered why no other man had ever affected her as Giovanni Amato did. Her sympathy for his shadowy past was only a tiny part of it. One look from him, and it was all forgotten. His gaze made her feel as though she—a working-class nobody—was the only person in the universe. Common sense tried to tell her that he must look at all women in this way. That was the way good manners and charm worked—but sense didn't have much to do with the way Katie was feeling. Then the trill of Giovanni's phone alerted him.

'They're here,' he began, but before Katie's nerves could get the better of her he shot her a conspiratorial smile. 'You'll find that anticipation is the worst part. It'll be OK once we're up and running. Just remember—they've come here for a good time, not a long time. Sometimes that's the only thought that keeps me going. That, and the sparkling medicine out of these bottles, of course. Have another dose.' As Katie giggled, he filled her glass again.

As they left the spa area to stroll along to the observation deck, Katie realised something strange. It was the first time she had been alone with a man without feeling the urge to fill every pause in his conversation with nervous chatter. Today she was happy to stay silent and absorb the drift of Giovanni's clean, cool fragrance on the breeze.

The air and sea around the *Viola* became busy. So many helicopters and launches arriving within minutes of each other would have thrown anywhere else into chaos. It did not happen on Giovanni Amato's yacht. Everything was managed smoothly and without fuss. Katie was alight with nerves, but once all the guests had embarked there was no time to be shy. She swung into full personality mode. It was something that the naturally shy Katie had trained herself to do. To succeed in her line of business, she had to make herself sell ideas to rich people. The only difference between her work and this party was Giovanni Amato.

For Giovanni's part, he was encouraged by the way she tried to adapt to her unusual role. Although busy with his guests, he took every chance to glance over at her. At first he was relieved to see her laughing, or nodding in response to an anecdote. Then a faint unease began to creep over him. The audience gathered around her was mostly male. What had he done? She didn't deserve to be cornered. This was, after all, only Miss Katie Carter. She was a working woman, unused to the high life and the way it was lived. He frowned. She was his contractor, and an unusually retiring one at that. Tonight she was also his guest. Unlike the others, she was doing him a personal favour by being here, not a financial one. It all made him feel strangely protective towards her.

As long as she did not look at her host, Katie could sparkle like the sea. She concentrated on being pleasant but discreet. Then Signor Balzone was announced at the door. Giovanni was at her side in an instant.

'You're doing a great job,' he whispered as their guest of honour approached.

'Are you sure?'

'Believe me, the Princess Miadora herself couldn't do any better.'

This time, Katie did not have to make any effort to smile as Giovanni introduced her. His protective hand, nestling in the small of her back as he drew her forward, saw to that. Her warm glow increased as Agosto Balzone began talking to them. He had seen the work she had done for several other clients, and was delighted to meet her. Katie could hardly believe her luck. Keeping this man happy would be easy. He already liked her work and his interest was genuine.

Giovanni did not share her relief. As Katie began to relax, he found himself becoming strangely tense. Conversations about commodities and hedge funds held little interest for him now. His mind kept drifting over to where Katie was being monopolised by a fat, balding man who had more ex-wives than sense.

She was so beautiful, and Balzone was such a rogue.

Giovanni wondered if he ought to warn her of the man's reputation. It was only to stop her getting hurt, he told himself, and that made sense. He was beginning to realise that a girl like Katie could have her pick of any man in the room, despite her humble beginnings. He knew he should have felt pleased at giving her such an opportunity. Instead it irritated him. He put it down to his own dislike of being paired off.

The whole company progressed to the ballroom, where drinks and canapés were served. Katie was enjoying herself hugely, especially when Giovanni materialised at her side. Cupping her elbow with one hand, he drew her aside gently.

'I am concerned for you, Miss Carter. Balzone is to be charmed, but not at the expense of everyone else.' He pursed his lips. 'Take care you do not get out of your depth.'

'I can manage, thank you,' Katie said firmly, plunging back into the assembly. She had not expected to be patronised for doing as she was told. Giovanni's words burned, and her only remedy was to charm everyone. It was difficult to memorise all the names, but luckily a few of the faces were familiar from her work. One was a client, and several others had visited the Villa Adriatica while she had been working there. Katie managed to circulate, smile and delight them all. When a uniformed maid announced that dinner was about to be served, Agosto Balzone took her arm and escorted her into the dining room like a princess.

Katie expected to shuffle around, looking for her name on a place card. Instead, she was ushered straight to a seat at one end of an enormous dining table. Giovanni, she noticed, was positioned at exactly the opposite end. Signor Balzone was seated on Katie's right, while the young man on her left was introduced as one of Giovanni's distant cousins from Milan.

The seating plan had split couples up and scattered them around the table, to help conversation. Katie found Agosto Balzone great fun, but Cousin Severino Amato was a different matter. He was an archaeologist, and as nervous as only a scientist on a yacht full of money could be. As another outsider, Katie got on with him really well. Then she realised that Giovanni's eyes were haunting her all the way from his position at the head of the table.

* * *

Time sauntered by with no one taking any notice of the clock. Only when Signor Balzone showed signs of flagging did Giovanni call for more coffee. The guests who were not staying overnight used this as an excuse to leave. Katie slipped away to her suite as soon as it was polite to do so, but she could not stay there for long. Something about the salty breeze blowing through the open windows made her feel reckless. Instead of getting ready for bed, she decided to go for a walk around the deck. Coming out through the spa area, she found it lit by starlight. It was so idyllic she had a sudden urge to go and lie on a sun-lounger and look up into the velvety night sky. Stepping out on to the pool surround, she closed the door behind her with a loud click before realising she was not alone.

Giovanni Amato was leaning over the ship's rail. Glass in hand, he was gazing across the bay to where lights twinkled along the coast like a string of beads.

He turned at the sound of the door closing and saw her. There could be no escape.

'Good evening again, Miss Carter. So your admirers have finally let you go?'

Katie had been conscious of his watchful gaze all evening. It had been a support when her nerves flagged, but she did not like this hint that she might have been doing her job *too* well.

'Agosto is really nice. I'm going to the Uffizi Gallery with him next week. He knows how to get in without having to queue for hours.'

He raised an eyebrow mockingly. 'I could have told you that.'

'Oh. Then I'm sorry you didn't, Signor Amato.'

He took a sip of cognac and smiled. 'I'm amazed you can manage sightseeing, with your busy schedule.'

'I think it will be fun. Everyone is entitled to some time off,' Katie continued, unaware that she was being teased. She wondered whether to tell him it would not be a date with Balzone, but rather a foursome with good intentions. Like her, Agosto Balzone had felt sorry for their fellow dinner guest, Severino, the fish-out-of-water. Agosto was going to ask his bookish young niece along on the gallery trip, supposedly to make up the numbers.

Katie was beginning to think Giovanni Amato was the only member of the monied classes who wasn't obsessed by matchmaking.

'I suppose Balzone has offered to make you the star of his television company.'

She tilted her chin in defiance. 'No, he hasn't. And even if he had, Signor Amato, I wouldn't be interested.'

'I must admit to being relieved, Miss Carter. As I told you before: you are a guest in our country living under my roof, and you are an attractive young woman. I have to protect you.'

Katie seethed. Wine with dinner and the many compliments she had received from his guests had buoyed her up enough to challenge him. 'Don't you think that's a rather old-fashioned view, Signor Amato?'

'Good sense never goes out of fashion, Miss Carter.'

'You can call me Katie, you know. All your grand guests were quite happy to call me by my Christian name this evening, and vice versa,' she recalled with a touch of pride at having managed to blur the class divide.

'That is true,' he allowed. He took another sip of his drink and then looked at the remaining contents of the glass. There was so little left he downed the last drops in one go, then stood upright. 'Indeed, everyone remarked to me that you were the perfect hostess, Katie. Even finding time for that poor lad Severino.'

'There was a reason for that.' Katie shivered in the cool

night air. 'I've heard that you're full of scorn for people who try to set you up with single girls. Poor Severino couldn't imagine why he was attending your dinner, but I knew only too well. His fortune-seeking mother dragged him here. She brought her son in the hope of finding him a well-connected single girl—you could see it in her eyes.'

'Now before you go any further, Miss Carter, I should tell you that the "fortune-seeking mother" and I share a much loved great-uncle,' Giovanni interrupted her with a chuckle. 'May I take it, then, that you frown upon gold-diggers and all their works too?' Pushing himself away from the rail, he placed his empty glass on the nearest table.

Katie thought of her mother. Biology was the only thing she had in common with that woman, who had run away in pursuit of a bigger bank balance when things got tough. 'I certainly do, Signor Amato. I am afraid I have seen far too much chasing after money to have any respect for the people who do it.' She sighed.

'You don't know what a relief it is to find someone who thinks like that.' He smiled and, before Katie knew what was happening, his hands were on her shoulders, gently drawing her close.

'Thank you so much for making this evening a success, Katie. And for being so beautiful,' he breathed, brushing the lightest of kisses against her cheek.

Her heart stood still. This couldn't be happening—and yet it was. His fingers were still resting lightly on her silk-clad shoulders. She could not move. The slightest disturbance might cause him to release her and, with a pang, she realised she wanted to stay like this for ever.

They stood on deck, alone. Giovanni had intended the kiss as nothing more than a gesture of thanks, but something was happening deep within him. Tonight Miss Katie Carter had been transformed into a desirable young woman. He was seeing her with new eyes and it was drawing him across an invisible boundary. Now he was actually touching this different reality. It was novelty, delight and wonder all wrapped up in the warm mystery of a Mediterranean night

Until that moment, Giovanni had spent his entire life being sensible. Suddenly, sense was no longer enough. He needed this woman and drew her into his arms. At the exact moment her mouth opened in surprise, he covered it with his own.

Katie almost lost consciousness with the surging power of dreams come true. She had fantasised so often about sliding her hands over those powerful shoulders and being crushed against him like a possession. Now it was happening. For moments on end she revelled in the delicious feeling of having her own desire returned with interest. He was moulding her willing form to his body, caressing away her inhibitions. Any moment now, Katie knew he would break down the last of her reserve and possess her, bringing her to a state where she would give her all, willingly…

And then a terrible thought arrowed through her misty mind.

This was just the typical end to a typical dinner party for the world's most desirable man.

How many other girls had been here and done this?

Within seconds, Katie's dream tumbled into a nightmare. She had to stop him. Her principles as well as her morals were at stake. If she let him carry on like this, she would never be able to look him—or any other male client—in the eyes again. To jeopardise everything she had worked for in a moment of weakness would be fatal.

With almost superhuman strength, she forced herself from his arms.

The moment Giovanni felt her resistance he released her,

shocked. She had melted into him. She responded to his kiss in a way that had wiped all other thoughts and memories from his mind. And now she was pushing him away.

She stood before him now like a Cinderella of the high seas, wide-eyed, beautiful and as astonished as he was about what had happened.

Her initial reaction to his kiss had been adult and wanton. Now she looked like a little girl. This was not how it should be. He had spent the whole evening concerned about her vulnerability, but in the end *he* had been the bad guy. He had betrayed her trust.

Now it was up to him to rescue the situation. He brushed the back of his hand softly down her cheek, the tender action making her shiver. 'Good night, Katie Carter,' he said softly and then turned his back on fourteen generations of wanton Amato forebears and walked off to his stateroom.

CHAPTER FIVE

KATIE felt the magical touch of his lips all night. Her dreams fired by fantasies, she woke early, with a feverish ache that needed to be cooled. The ideal cure would be to spend some time in the on-board swimming pool, but she was nervous. Despite the fact that the *Viola* was a large ship, it was a small space in which to avoid anyone. Particularly when the person in question put in a hundred lengths or so each morning.

She spent ages weighing up the likelihood of Giovanni choosing exactly the same moment she did to take a swim. Then she thought of the more alarming prospect of Agosto Balzone seeing her in a bikini and decided against going to the pool at all. Their guest of honour had done nothing over dinner to suggest he was anything but a perfect gentleman, but Giovanni had warned her about him. On balance, Katie decided it was safer to keep out of everyone's way. She took breakfast in her room, but could hardly manage a mouthful. Her mind was full of Giovanni and he left no room for anything else.

Life on board the yacht was beyond anything she had ex-perienced before. One maid collected her laundry, while a second laid out her clothes for the day and ran her a deep bubbly bath. Katie lay in the water and tried out a thousand different ways of acting towards Giovanni when they sat next to each other for the flight home. She tried to tell herself she had done the right thing. A man like Giovanni could have any girl he wanted and probably did. He had respected her when she'd called a halt. All she needed to do was put it down to experience, as he would. When she next met him, she ought to act as though nothing had happened. It had been a mutual mistake, nothing more.

The trouble was, Katie could not convince herself of that. She now knew she would sacrifice everything for this man. There had been nothing wrong about his kiss—it had been perfect. Her only regret was that she had ended it.

While she fretted, everything that would not be required until her arrival back at the Villa Antico was packed away. By the time Katie emerged from the bathroom, her suite had been completely valeted. Fresh flower arrangements were in place and her suitcase stood beside the door. The whole operation had been carried out with the minimum fuss and the maximum efficiency.

Katie sat on a velvet chaise longue and flicked through the selection of glossy magazines supplied for her. It was hopeless. If there had been full colour photographs of Bigfoot riding an UFO she would not have noticed. The only pictures going through her mind involved Giovanni. Kissing him had been an unbelievable experience. Desperately, she tried to convince herself it had been a dream. That did not work. Then she told herself imagination had blown the whole event out of proportion. She did everything to rationalise her thoughts before her next meeting with Giovanni, but there was no cure.

Katie had tasted paradise and she was greedy for more.

The time came for her to set off for the flight deck. She checked her appearance in the mirror a dozen times. There was nothing left of the glamorous creature who had felt Giovanni's kiss the night before. Her hair was pulled back from her face and trapped in its usual plait. She was wearing her normal practical-but-dull working clothes of black trousers, matching jacket and plain white top. Her borrowed jewellery was carefully hidden away. Katie tried to pace herself on the long walk from her suite to the helicopter. In reality she was fizzing with anticipation. Would she be lucky enough to be greeted with another kiss? She blushed, knowing that this time she would not be able to resist. It was all she had been thinking of, night and morning. His lips on hers, and the warmth of his touch matching the heat of her newly discovered passion…

When she reached the helipad, Giovanni was already deep in conversation with the pilot. She looked around, hoping that conditions would mean they could not fly. Another day spent with Giovanni on the *Viola*, beside his pool…

She was to be disappointed in more ways than one. The weather was perfect for flying, and Giovanni acknowledged her with nothing more than a casual nod.

'Good morning, Katie.'

Her ready smile faded with this everyday greeting.

'*I* shall be flying us back to the Villa Antico. There seems little point in using Ugo again, when he has work to do here on board ship,' he announced, carefully helping Katie up into the body of the aircraft before she had time to say anything.

'…I am sorry about last night, Katie,' he murmured as soon as they were alone. Taking his place in the pilot's seat, he immersed himself in pre-flight checks. 'It was very wrong of me to take advantage of your good nature. It should never have happened.'

After that, they travelled in a communications blackout. He

was concentrating on getting them back to the Villa Antico. Katie could not trust herself to speak, so she used the time for reflection. Giovanni had sounded as though he regretted what he had done, and she was suffering for it. Screwing her handkerchief into a ball, she tried to transfer all her pain and rage into it. She had been right all along. People were trouble. The minute you let them affect you, it was the end.

She squeezed so hard that her nails bit right through the fabric and into the palms of her hands. In front of her, Giovanni adopted perfect pilot practice. He kept a lookout in all directions—except hers. He spoke to his radio—but not to Katie. His hands moved about the control panel with all the swift assurance she wanted him to use on her body.

It was too much. By the time the groves and avenues of the Villa Antico swung into view, Katie had worked herself up into indignant fury. How dared this man toy with her emotions and then act as though nothing had happened? She would show him!

No woman had ever turned Giovanni down before. It was uncharted territory for him. He had spent a sleepless night wondering what was wrong with her. Their silent journey home made him realise that the only way to find out for sure was to ask her directly.

He did not get the chance. As soon as they touched down, Katie jumped out of the helicopter and marched off towards the villa without a backward glance. He stood and watched her go.

All the doors in the villa were standing wide open. Katie felt a refreshing breeze cool her hot cheeks as she went towards Eduardo's office. A door banged somewhere, a distant telephone rang. She did not notice. All she wanted to do was hand in her borrowed jewellery and get back to her one true friend—work.

'Here she is—the belle of the ball.' Eduardo was sitting behind his desk, as smug as a cat.

'I was hardly that.' Katie made a face as she handed over the earrings and necklace for him to return.

'On the contrary, Miss Carter, incoming emails and calls have told me all I need to know about your triumph. You charmed them all. As well as playing your part, I have a feeling you have given Carter Interiors some good publicity.'

'It was *supposed* to be a fund-raising evening, Eduardo.'

'Don't worry—it was a success on every level. You were a star, and the Amato Foundation has received promises running into hundreds of thousands of euros. The only person who did not mention you at all was Mrs Dale-Carr. She said she was ringing up to thank Signor Amato for last night's little soirée, but *I* know she was calling on the off chance of speaking to him directly. That woman is intent on luring him over to her home in the USA for a holiday.'

'I guessed as much. It was impossible not to hear her telling Signor Amato how much he would enjoy the chance of a break on her ranch.'

'That goes to show how little she understands him.' Eduardo thrust out his lower lip in disapproval. 'Signor Amato does not know the meaning of the word "holiday."'

Katie frowned. 'Mrs Dale-Carr is a widow who runs a large stud farm. In which case, Signor Amato should fit in there perfectly.'

It was a mistake. Eduardo's ears pricked up at the reference.

'Oh, yes?' There was suspicion in his voice. His head was on one side and he quizzed her silently.

'I've heard that seduction has been a popular hobby with some of the Amato clan, that's all,' Katie improvised, trying to stop any rumour before it could begin. The way she was feeling now would make whispers too painful to bear. Despite her smile, she was falling apart. Giovanni's moonlight kiss had proved to be nothing but a meaningless gesture and he had written it off as a mistake. He was a cold, hard, calculating machine.

So why did the thought of Giovanni with that Dale-Carr woman—with any woman—twist such a knife in her heart?

Because I've been falling in love with him since the first moment I saw him, Katie admitted to herself. *And when he finally reached out and touched me, it made things a million times worse. This awful feeling only comes from wanting something I cannot possibly have.*

That was the rational explanation. The trouble was, this irresistible man made her feel anything but rational.

For the next few weeks Katie did everything in her power to avoid the temptation called Giovanni Amato. She tried to stay away from him. Complete isolation from a client was impossible, but Katie did her best. Each time he interrupted her, she was quick to turn back to her work. She had to: the tremors that shot through her body each time she saw him were too powerful to be denied. Keeping her eyes averted from that taut, handsome body took all her concentration. And the thought of those wickedly delicious, but now grimly serious lips touched all her dreams.

It built into a record-breaking summer. Giovanni had all the doors and windows in the White Office thrown open each day to take advantage of any breeze. Business always took precedence with him, but on this particular day something was working away at the back of his mind like grit in an oyster. Tomorrow marked the end of Katie's stay. At the moment, she was making a last circuit of the villa. He could hear the reel of her tape as she checked measurements, her voice as she chatted with his staff or the sound of her footsteps on the gravel terrace outside.

Giovanni had almost reconciled himself to the slip he had made that night on the *Viola*. The way he saw it, he had acted in the heat of the moment. Now he was busy, and she was busy, too. Neither of them had any time at all for the other. That was how it should be, between employer and employee, he kept telling himself.

He stopped congratulating himself as he became aware that it had gone quiet. For some weeks his bleak, empty house had been filled with chatter and laughter. He had put this down to the staff bedding in with his regime. This return to silence was unsettling. Strangely disturbed, Giovanni found he could no longer concentrate on his work. Then suddenly, when he least expected it, there was a loud knock at the main door to his office. He glanced up. It was Katie.

'May I come in and do one last quick tour of your office, Signor Amato?'

Her cool detachment was utterly professional. Giovanni had to hand it to her. No one would have guessed that for a split second she had turned to liquid fire beneath his hands. The image of serious dedication she displayed now was complete except for one thing. She was staring at the thread-bare Indian rugs as she made her request, not at him.

'Fine. Go right ahead.' He almost smiled as his words had the desired effect. She could not resist a quick glance at him. In that second, he saw the days fall away. Her lips parted and a blush coloured her usually pale skin. She was remembering. Knowing what was going through her mind pleased him strangely. He smiled at her. Heat rushed to her cheeks and, in her embarrassment, she did a clumsy, lightning circuit of his room. In her hurry to reach the furthest corner of his office, she managed to drop her box of tools. He bent to help her as she scrabbled to retrieve her things, but she had already hastily gathered them up. She thanked him quickly and left.

When she was gone, Giovanni stood up and went over to get himself a drink. As he poured the ice-cold water he noticed something white on the floor beneath his desk. It was a sheet of paper, which must have blown off his table in a draught between the open doors. He returned to his seat and picked it up. The top lolled heavily. He flipped it back and found that a weight of bills had been stapled to one corner. The word 'Unpaid' had been stamped across the top one. Concerned, Giovanni thumbed through the rest. They were all marked in the same way. Some were underlined in red, others added the words 'Final Demand.' Sitting down, he turned his attention to the letter accompanying these accusations. This must take top priority. Amato International had not received mail like this since his father's death, when Giovanni had been left to salvage the firm from approaching disaster.

The letter was scrawled in Biro. This was unusual for his business mail, but not unknown. Before reading it, he flicked through the receipts again. The first was from a garage. The rest were unpaid grocery, laundry and credit card slips. A horrible chill told him the letter must be intended for someone else. Turning back the tide of debt, he checked the final page. Instead of a signature, the single word 'Mummy' was underlined with a dozen kisses. Without reading anything else, he looked at the opening words of the letter. It was addressed to 'Dear Katie…'

He stood up. Katie's mother must be cast in the same mould as his own father. Life as an only son had taught Giovanni all he needed to know about spendthrifts. He had too much relevant experience to stand by and watch Katie suffer in the same way. His mind began to work. He had to say something to her, but what advice could he give? Every confrontation with his own father had piled on the pressure. Giovanni had heard every hard luck story, every promise and every threat. Fighting the same battles for years had hardened him until he'd developed a sob-proof shell. He thought of Katie's recent coldness towards him. Perhaps this explained it. Under constant threat from her mother's lifestyle, the same thing was already happening to her.

Giovanni knew he could not let it happen. Drumming the fingers of one hand on his desk, he stared down at the sheaf of demands. He had never managed to get his own father's wild living under control. What made him think he could advise Katie? Tomorrow was her final day here. Whatever he did, it would have to be quick. Without giving himself time to dwell on the rights and wrongs of his decision, Giovanni strode over and opened the door to his office. When he did, he was confronted by a vision.

Katie was looking out of one of the great windows that lined the upper hallway. Her hands were flat on the wide stone sill and she was frowning at something below in the grounds. A shaft of sunlight falling through the glass turned her hair into an amber halo. She turned and smiled at the sound of an approach, but the look vanished as she saw who it was.

'Signor Amato—what is it? What is wrong?'

For the first time in his life, Giovanni could not think what to say. He filled the void by holding up the letter, hoping she would rush forward and snatch the horrible thing from him. She did not. Instead she stayed where she was. The worry in her eyes was almost unbearable. Giovanni passed her the letter.

'I came out to give you this.' He paused, then chose to ease the tension by not dwelling on the letter's content right away. 'And to see what all the racket was about.'

She sighed gratefully. 'They've just finished putting up a marquee over by the helipad. Now there's some discussion about who's in charge of transporting all the tables and chairs over to it.'

'Ah, yes.' He joined her at the window. From here he could see Eduardo's small bald spot. He did not need to hear the conversation. Stefano was waving his arms about eloquently enough. 'That is for the staff party tonight. I am sure they will have told you about it already, Katie.'

'It's to celebrate the way your great-uncle returned to save the Antico estate in 1945, isn't it?'

'That's right.' Giovanni was gripped by a sudden impulse. 'Would you like to come?'

Her beautiful eyes became troubled. Giovanni cursed his reckless passion aboard the *Viola*. He had frightened her and lost her trust. Gazing at her now, he knew this chance to admire her might have to last him for the rest of his life. That thought forced him to play his trump card.

'I think perhaps you should, Katie. Think of it as a final opportunity to enjoy yourself before returning to real life.'

As he spoke, he glanced at the letter clutched in her hand.

'Does your mother expect you to bail her out by settling these bills?' he asked gently.

'Of course.'

'And will you?'

'It is called family loyalty,' Katie managed when she could force the words past the hard knot of indignation where her heart should be. 'What else can I do? Dad's health is not good, so I've told Mum she mustn't worry him. My mother has certain…problems when it comes to money. The result is that she looks to me to sort everything out for her.'

'I am no stranger to that type of person myself,' Giovanni said wearily. Once upon a time he had thought he was alone in working all the hours God sent for the benefit of someone else. It was horrible to discover he shared the experience—and with her, of all people.

'That is why my work is so important to me, Signor Amato. It allows me to fund the care my father needs—'

'—And your mother's spending,' he inserted grimly. 'Has she always been so reckless?' He gestured in the direction of the letter Katie was now running nervously through her fingers.

'I suppose so—she left home when I was young. Contact with her has been patchy for years. Still, I suppose she did me one favour. Growing up without her made me independent. My mother and I are totally unalike, Signor Amato. I don't need anyone in my life.'

A surge of pride gave him a sudden lift. 'That is not the message you sent out after my party on board the *Viola*. A cold-blooded woman would have shaken off my hands before I kissed her properly.'

She determinedly held back the tears that she could feel brewing. 'That was a lapse of professionalism, Signor. It will not happen again.'

With an awful finality, he nodded. 'I understand, but if you would still like to come to the party, my invitation stands. You can rest assured *I* will never add to your burden of worry again, Katie.'

Katie did not know which was the greater shock. The fact that Giovanni Amato now knew the grubby reality of her back-ground, or that she had effectively slammed the door in the face of the only man she would ever love. After their exchange he had turned and gone straight back to work. She knew that her only hope of seeing him again before she left for England would be at the party that evening. At least she had a good excuse to attend. He was, after all, her stellar client. The example her mother set meant that money was always a worry for Katie. She was careful with it, as she had seen what misery debt could bring. After her father's heart surgery, she had become doubly keen to provide financial security for him. As a result, she could never fully relax before any payments owing were safely lodged in the Carter Interiors bank account. Worries about cash flow haunted her, and increased with her mother's most recent plea for funds. Katie didn't want her father stressed by his ex-wife's bills. She tried to believe that it would be the last time, but things had fallen into a sadly predictable pattern. Katie would pay up, on the understanding that the amount would be returned in monthly instalments. These arrangements only ever lasted until her mother found a rich new lover. Then she would be too busy to worry about what she called 'minor details' like debt. Katie, and a growing list of Mrs Carter's innocent new contacts, would be left to wait for settlements that never happened.

The last thing Katie needed to do was upset a client like Giovanni Amato at a time when she was faced with the bills for her mother's latest spending sprees.

Later, Katie met Eduardo as she was on her way down the back stairs. When she mentioned her invitation to the party, he warned her it was another black-tie affair. The same thought struck them both at once. When he suggested in a whisper that she might make use of a second dress from the Contessa Lia's collection, they both knew which one it would be. The green lamé might have been too daring for a charity dinner, but its stunning colour would strike exactly the right note at a party to celebrate the Antico estate's rebirth. As she showered and slipped into the beautiful bias-cut gown, Katie primed herself. Since arriving at the Villa Antico, she had discovered a new, slightly daring side to her personality. Tonight at the party she would give it free rein. Giovanni had accepted her first refusal as final, so she had nothing to lose. This evening she would hide her broken heart and try to forget her miserable, lonely future without him.

Remembering how Giovanni had reacted when she had hesitated at the top of his grand staircase, too scared to descend, Katie decided her attitude would be different from the start. This time she breezed out of her suite, head already held high. Then she got her first surprise. The usually quiet entrance hall was cheerful with chatter. She looked over the balustrade and saw all the house staff gathered below. They fell silent. As one, they all turned and gaped at her. Katie stopped. They stared. Only one person continued speaking. Giovanni Amato was still working, busy with his mobile phone. Then the outbreak of peace filtered through to him and he realised something had caught his employees' attention. As his call ended, he snapped the phone shut and turned to see what it was.

He stopped, looked up and rewarded her with a slow, lazy smile.

'Well, well, Miss Carter, you have done it again. You have pulled off another spectacular transformation.'

It was a reaction that filled Katie with confidence. She felt herself casting off the pain and growing in stature. It was not only because she wanted to act as though worthy of her surroundings. There was something about Giovanni's expression that drew her. He knew her guilty secrets, yet he could still look at her like that. Common sense told Katie that a real man like Giovanni must gaze at every woman like this, but she didn't have to believe it—not tonight.

'Get a move on, everybody—don't stand there like statues. We have a party to attend. Anyone would think you had never seen an English princess before.' He laughed, ushering his staff out through the great front doors.

Giggling, Katie hurried downstairs to join them. The train of her dress rippled after her, trickling over the steps like sparkling green water. For someone more used to the comfort and practicality of trousers, it was a wonderfully glamorous feeling. She carried herself now as she had done on that other fateful night. Unconsciously, she displayed all the qualities she was normally too shy to reveal in her client's presence.

By the time she reached the ground floor, everyone else had filed out. The place was deserted, with the notable exception of Giovanni Amato. He had been chivvying staff and gathering up his notes from a side table, but eventually he could not avoid turning his attention to his last guest.

When he turned and looked at her, Katie realised something. His face was alight in a way that made her feel weak with longing. He gazed at her for a long time, taking in everything from her pink painted toenails to the coils of red gold hair dressed around her shoulders. It was obvious he had something to say, but there was a long pause. Katie could only wait as good breeding fought with his instincts. He tapped the furl of papers he held in one hand against the palm of the other. He drew his lips tight against those perfect white teeth. All the time he maintained a dignified silence, until Katie could not stand it any longer.

'Do you think there is something wrong with this dress, Signor Amato?' she ventured.

'No…no, not at all.' His smile warmed her all over. 'If I am lost for words it is because I am realising what a treasure has been hidden under my own roof. You are a revelation to me, Katie. You are intelligent, you work hard and then you transform yourself like this.'

Katie laughed with him, but self-consciously. She had wound herself up to attend this party, but nothing had prepared her for his penetrating gaze. If only he had not said he would never repeat his approach on the *Viola*. Open admiration for her was written all over his face, but she knew a proud man like Giovanni would never go back on his word. She could only hope he could not read her mind. Chastity was the last thing he would find there.

He cleared his throat softly and spoke again. 'Katie, although I promised to keep things strictly impersonal between us tonight, I feel I must say something. Should you not be wearing jewellery to set off that dress?'

'I don't have any, Signor.'

'There was nothing wrong with the trinkets you wore on the *Viola*.'

'I can think of two things.' She giggled. Every movement rippled the chestnut tide of her hair into soft waves lapping over her creamy shoulders, he noticed.

'For one thing, blue jewellery doesn't exactly go with a green dress and, for another, those things were only borrowed.'

This inspired him. 'Then, if you don't mind, I shall lend you the perfect finishing touch for your ensemble. Wait there,' he commanded and went over to raid Eduardo's office. A few minutes later he emerged with a jingling collection of keys. Their rattle echoed through the great hall as he disappeared into the cavernous under-stairs area. Katie listened to the piping of electronics as he disabled a security system. She heard a heavy door open and his footsteps receded. An age later, all the sound effects were repeated in reverse order. He reappeared in the hall holding a flat leather case. Once the bunch of keys was safely returned to Eduardo's office, he strode over to a side table, which stood next to the cheval glass.

'Come here, Katie.'

She did as she was told.

'Now…turn around…'

He was busy behind her with the click of a fastening. Then she felt him draw very close. At the corner of her vision she saw his raised hands, before a cold glitter of diamonds and emeralds was dropped around her neck. Katie's hands went straight to the glorious waterfall of sparkling silver and green that ran from her throat to her cleavage.

The excitement of wearing real jewels was one thing. The physical thrill of having him so near and feeling his hands work their way beneath her hair to secure the necklace outshone it.

'I can't possibly wear this, Signor Amato!'

'Why not?' He was taking his time over the clasp. 'No one else makes use of them, and you can hardly attend the estate party dressed simply like that. You may prefer to put the earrings on yourself.'

Katie turned and saw a pair of elegant droplets exactly matching her borrowed necklace. They lay in a bed of black velvet, waiting to be loved. In seconds she had removed her plain gold sleepers and fixed the precious antiques in their place. When she looked in the cheval-glass, she gasped.

A generous smile toyed with Giovanni's features. He was standing back, evidently admiring the Amato jewels. Katie waited for him to say something. All he did was look at her—but his eyes were so eloquent, that was all it took. Desire for what might happen was almost crushed by fear of the consequences, but that did not stop her. In one quick movement she rose on tiptoe and touched a kiss against his cheek. He sprang back as though burned, but the moment passed so fast Katie was already halfway to the front door.

'Come on, Signor Amato—or they will start the party without you.'

It was a mistake, Giovanni thought. Everybody is enjoying themselves too much tonight—and that was the problem. *His* body was no exception—but it was his mind that really tortured him. His staff had goggled at the sight of an interior designer coming down that grand staircase dressed very like his late Contessa. That was bad enough, but it was nothing to the way they'd reacted on seeing her draped in Amato diamonds.

Dr Vittorio had been warning Giovanni about the dangers of overwork and isolation for years. Now it felt as if all his demons were finally catching up with him. His mind was not on the evening's noisy entertainment. He circulated, exchanging words with everyone, and accepted a glass of the Bacchari family's latest *tavola vino*. Small talk gave him the excuse to keep his eyes fixed firmly on his farmers and growers, rather than casting about the assembly and seeing Katie in *that* dress.

It was so like the one Lia had provoked him with that night—

He crushed the hideous thought and accepted another glass of wine. It was a first outing for this particular batch, Grandad Bacchari was telling him, which was drinkable without being a classic.

Giovanni hardly heard. He was lost in memory. Lia had known he disliked the colour green. It reminded him of unripe lemons, the hard, sour apples that grew wild around the estate—and jealousy. They had argued.

So what? That had been nothing new. Giovanni's lip curled with thoughts of life with his late Contessa. He obliged his tenants by sampling some more of their wine…and then a glitter at the edge of his vision made him turn his head.

It was Katie.

Giovanni remembered how the argument with Lia had begun. Dr Vittorio had been telling her for months that she did not need to lose any more weight, but she must have gone on dieting. In between her final fitting and the delivery of a consignment of gowns, Lia's measurements must have changed again. Giovanni had caught her padding out her new green dress with tissue and challenged her.

Their fight had been spectacular. Then Lia left him, in the middle of the night, and went home to her over-indulgent parents.

That felt like the end of everything, but a month later Lia returned. Then, things got much, much worse.

Giovanni had been alone for five years now. He had been freed from his cold, dead marriage—but by a disaster drawn straight from Dante's circles of hell.

He tried to focus on the party.

It was impossible. Katie was inspiring a drift of more recent happy memories. She obviously did not need to resort to tissue paper. Her dress fitted like a second skin. The gentle swell of her breasts rose above the boned, strapless bodice, appealing to every red-blooded male in the place. The jealousy he now recognised from that party on board the *Viola* struck again. Giovanni took another drink. He had been as sober as an inquisitor that night with Lia and it had done him no good at all.

It began to occur to him that the crowd around the wine-tasting table was thinning. People were moving off towards long trestle tables that had been set up at the far end of the marquee. As host, Giovanni waited until they sorted themselves out. Searching out Katie, he saw that she had found herself a seat. The Bacchari family had absorbed her into their clan. Then he made his way to the place of honour at the top table.

Giovanni cleared his throat. 'This is a very important evening for the Villa Antico estate,' he began, and every face turned to look at him. He was conscious of only one. He delivered a faultless speech of welcome and appreciation. As usual, it was crammed full of everything his audience wanted to hear. First, there were the old stories about everyone pitching in and doing their bit for the greater glory of the Amato family. Then, more recent events were highlighted, family by family. Finally, Giovanni rounded off his speech by talking about the future. Once again he managed to fit everything into the shortest possible time. As he always pointed out at the end, his tenants came to feast, not listen. This was greeted with a cheer and the eating began.

Giovanni was more than happy to let the gathering attack the food without him.

'Mmm…these calzone are good,' Dr Vittorio said through a healthy mouthful. 'I'm not so sure about the pasta salad, though. There are too many seeds in it for my liking. Gimi's eldest girl made it. She's on holiday from university, although I don't think Gimi is going to let the rest of his mob follow her there if they're all going to come back from Urbino as vegans—Oh, for goodness' sake!' the doctor burst out suddenly. 'Where are you, Giovanni? You certainly aren't here, listening to me!'

Giovanni roused himself, but without much enthusiasm for conversation. 'I have decided I don't like having house guests. They disrupt the place too much.'

'Oh, I suppose you're talking about your interior designer,' the doctor grunted into his dinner. 'Still, she won't be here for much longer, will she? I've heard she'll be gone by the weekend.'

'She is leaving tomorrow afternoon. Eduardo has already supervised her packing.'

'There you are, then.' The doctor hailed another passing calzone. 'In twenty-four hours' time you will be back to business as usual. She will be gone.'

'Leaving a trail of devastation in her wake,' Giovanni added.

CHAPTER SIX

KATIE was one OF the first to leave the celebration. She was also one of the last to get home. The Bacchari family invited her back to their farm and she had been unable to resist. The family's sow was due to give birth and they wanted to make sure the animal was not alone for the big event. Six people, including Katie, piled into an unstable old Fiat and clattered three kilometres to their holding. Nature had beaten them to it. Rosella the pig was already busy with half a dozen little ones by the time her audience arranged themselves around the low walls of her sty. Katie was treated to some home-cured salami and a drink that tasted as if it had been brewed from apricots and iron filings.

Eventually, young Pino was given the task of getting her back to the villa. This he did in record time, while Katie hung on with her fingertips and tried to keep smiling. The Fiat finally skittered to a halt outside the ancient walls of the original Antico enclosure. Katie got out and saw that Pino had parked beside a wooden door almost as old as the wall. When they finally wrestled it open, Katie realised she was entering the villa grounds by way of the swimming pool terrace. Beyond the illuminated stretch of water, the Villa Antico rose like a fortress. Only one light showed on its craggy stone face.

With a tingle of excitement, Katie realised it must be coming from Giovanni's suite. What was he doing in there? Just ordinary things, she told herself, but that didn't stop her wishing she could see him doing them. She watched for a moment, but there was no movement from within the bright, but closed, French windows. After saying goodbye to Pino, she started to cross the grass, but her feet were on fire. Taking off her borrowed sandals, she padded over to the pool in bare feet. There was no one about. No one would see.

Hoisting the beautiful green lamé dress up above her ankles, Katie stepped delicately on to the first level of the spray pool. The relief was wonderful. With a sigh, she sat down on the edge and dangled her feet into a deeper section. Sounds of the countryside at night stole over the high grey walls and into her sanctuary. Nightingales in the olive grove sang lullabies to cicadas and crickets out in the scrub. A warm breeze brought the fragrance of roses from climbers clothing the walls. It would be such a wrench to leave this place. Everything about the Villa Antico was so special. The people were wonderful, too.

And one person in particular, she admitted to herself. It was no use denying it. Work had always been her refuge from real life. Now things had changed. One word, one glance, from Giovanni Amato and work was no longer enough to satisfy her.

She would be leaving tomorrow afternoon. All they had shared was a few moments in moonlight, and only one proper kiss. Katie sighed again, imagining how it might have felt to give in and lose herself in his arms. If only she had not stopped herself responding to his kiss they might have been enjoying this evening together.

She sat up straight, telling herself she was being ridiculous. Fantasising about Giovanni tonight did not help, any more than it had done over the past few weeks. Why he managed to cast such a spell over her was a mystery. The man was a total work-aholic. As a count, he probably took little notice of ordinary people like her, and he certainly didn't grant wishes. And yet…

Katie knew she had to be firm with herself. There was no point in wasting any time on affairs of the heart. People messed you around and let you down. Work never did that. You got out of it what you put in. Katie was a firm believer in the old saying that the more you gave, the better it got. And yet…

She could not bear to let herself think back to that single time aboard the *Viola*. It was torture enough remembering how it had felt to kiss his cheek in the entrance hall earlier. His skin had been smooth and warm. If she tried hard, she could still taste the cedary, spicy tang of his aftershave.

As she recalled the sensations, her lips burned with those memories from the yacht. It had started with such an innocent gesture. Then her emotions had been fired in a way she had never experienced before. When he had gone on to possess her lips with such urgency, she had been brought to fever pitch.

Katie closed her eyes, reliving the moment. On the other side of the wall a new nightingale began its recital. She lay back on the smooth, flat stones of the pool surround. They were still warm from the day's intense heat, but a chill ran through her as she heard an unexpected sound. The grating of a lock cut all the birdsong off in mid-flow. She sat up. Someone had opened the French windows of the illuminated suite above her. They were walking out on to its balcony. That someone could only be seen in silhouette, but Katie knew who it was. No one but Giovanni Amato had such an aura of silent power. Nothing moved. Beyond his garden wall, even nature fell silent.

Katie's hand flew to her neck.

'It is no use trying to hide, Katie.' His voice was low with amusement. 'You are twinkling like Venice across the lagoon.'

'I didn't want to keep the necklace and earrings on after the party, Signor Amato—I asked Eduardo to take them back before I went off with the Bacchari family. He said only you were allowed to take them.' She was gabbling, suddenly aware of the risk she had run with his heirlooms. 'I was very careful, and the Bacchari are all *very* honest.'

'Calm down—nothing has happened to them, has it? In any case, I was rather more concerned about you. If they take a liking to someone, the Bacchari can be overwhelming. I sent Raphael down to the farm in case you needed an excuse to escape from them.'

Katie scrambled to her feet. 'Then I'm afraid he's had a wasted journey.' Picking up her shoes, she began to head in the direction of the villa's front door. When she reached it a few minutes later, Giovanni opened it himself.

'Oh, no. I suppose you had to open the door because Raphael is out looking for me!' Her guilt increased by the second as she followed Giovanni into the house.

'Don't worry—it is nothing. I would have come down in any case, to relieve you of the jewellery.'

She went over to the side table where the battered leather case still lay open. The only things lying on its worn black velvet were her small gold ear studs. She laid the emerald and diamond droplets down in their tailor-made indentations and put her own earrings back in. Then she bundled the luxuriance of her hair up on to the top of her head so that he could unfasten the necklace.

It was no easier for Giovanni's hands the second time he attacked the problem. Despite that, he kept any contact between his fingers and her skin to a minimum. The nearness of him fanned the flame of desire that had been dancing deep inside Katie since their very first kiss. She tried leaning back towards him, but the treacherous necklace was already slipping away, drawn on to his palm for inspection. Katie let down her hair, ruffling it into position over her bare shoulders again.

'There's nothing wrong with it, is there?' she asked with concern as he continued to run the fine, warm gold through his fingers.

'No, nothing at all.' He moved to lay the precious antique back in its velvet bed. This he managed without fully turning his back on her. She moved her bare feet on the cold tiles of the hall. This provided wonderful relief for her sore toes, but it did not prompt Giovanni into giving her any clues about whether she should retreat to her room.

'Thank you for inviting me this evening, Signor Amato.'

'Think nothing of it.'

He was concentrating on closing the jewellery case. As he moved, she caught the warm aroma of him again. His after-shave was fainter now, and tinged with the ghostly essence of party. Katie knew time was running out for her.

'I really enjoyed myself, Signor.'

'Despite the fact that you spent half the evening in a farmyard?'

There was no hiding the amusement in his voice. With a heavy heart, Katie came to the conclusion she had been dreading. An aristocrat like Giovanni was not going to give her a second chance to snub him. She might as well give up all her romantic dreams now, before she made a complete fool of herself. With regret, she lifted the hem of her skirt and set off up the grand stair-case. It was only when she reached the top that she realised no sound of doors, keys or security systems was reaching her from down in the hall. Instinctively, she stopped and looked back.

Giovanni had not moved from his position beside the table, but something had changed. He was watching her. Katie pulled herself up to her full height and returned his gaze with equal openness. She was not going to let him think she was in any way disappointed about anything. Independence had got her this far in life. It would see her through the pain of crushed fantasies.

'Goodnight, Signor Amato.'

He gave a nod of acknowledgement. 'Goodnight, Katie.'

There was nothing that could possibly be read from his expression. With a hollow heart, Katie continued to her rooms.

She hardly had time to put down her sandals before there was a light tap on the main door of her suite. She jumped and, hurrying through from her dressing room, stopped a metre short of the door to listen. There was no sound from outside. Perhaps it had been her imagination. For ten heartbeats she waited. Then the silence was broken by another knock, louder this time. It took a few seconds for Katie to find her voice. All the time her mind was working frantically. *If it is Giovanni, he will not wait,* she thought. *He will go away, and I shall be saved from any more shame.*

The knock came again.

Katie tried to fool herself that it could not possibly be him. It could *not* be, after all this delay.

'Who is it?'

'Me.'

Her heart bounced so hard against her ribs that she could not catch her breath.

'What do you want?' she gasped, praying that she did not know the answer, but hoping that she did.

'I forgot to offer you coffee. Some was prepared for me, if you would like to take advantage of it.'

It was the chance of seeing him again, not coffee, that persuaded Katie to unlock her door. He had taken off his jacket
and waistcoat, but looked as magnificent as ever. Outlined by
soft light from the hallway, he held out a thimble-sized cup
of espresso. It sat on a bone china saucer, dwarfed by his hand.
His perfect, pale gold skin contrasted with the stark white of
his turned back shirtsleeves. Katie looked up at him. His expression was as enigmatic as ever. If there was any question
in his mind, he was going to make *her* put it into words.

She reached out to take the coffee from him.

'Thank you, Signor Amato.'

He inclined his head slightly. 'You are welcome, Katie.'

'Well, this should make sure neither of us sleeps tonight.'

She meant it innocently enough, but it had the effect of
making them look at each other warily. Katie took a step back
into her suite. Giovanni started to leave, then thought of something and turned back. 'That reminds me—I might have to go
into the office first thing, Katie. This may be the last time we
speak before you leave. I have no doubt your stay here will
have been successful, but I should like to wish you a good
journey home.' His mouth twitched in a formal smile. Katie
took it to mean that her audience was at an end. All she had
to do was bring things to a dignified close.

'Then I must thank you again, Signor Amato. As I mentioned before, I have really enjoyed my stay here.' Her smile
was equally brief, but genuine. Especially when she thought
of the touch of his lips against her own… 'I will be in touch
in due course. Goodnight.'

It took all Katie's will-power to close the door on him. She
stood, leaning back against it, until his footsteps faded away
along the hall outside. She should have known better than to
expect a man like that to wait for her to change her mind.

* * *

She had missed her last chance. Katie went over to her dining table and sat down. There was nothing else left for her to do but drink the coffee. She lifted the cup he had given her. Its contents were as thick and black as molasses, but not as sweet. The saucer held a spoon, but no sugar. She looked down into the depths of his favourite Napoli blend. Its oil-dark surface trembled with concentric rings, throbbing in time to her pulse.

Nobody could be expected to drink this without sugar. Grabbing the opportunity, Katie flung open her door and walked along the corridor to Giovanni's suite.

She heard the ancient floorboards creaking long before he eventually opened the door. Wall lights dimly illuminated his room and a soft resinous sigh of cedar wood and coffee drifted out to meet her.

'Katie?' he enquired as though it was the first time they had met that day. 'Can I do something more for you?'

'Yes! That is…I—I mean, may I have some sugar for my coffee, please?'

'I'm sorry, I don't use it.' His grey eyes had already lost their thoughtfulness. They were now questioning her closely. 'And neither do you.'

'I do when I drink espresso,' she improvised a shade defensively.

'There may be some milk in my fridge,' he said carefully. 'Eduardo keeps it well stocked, but I don't often drink *latte* in here.'

'In your fridge,' Katie repeated faintly. 'Right.'

They continued to look at each other for some time, until he stood back and gave her a prompt. 'Would you like to come in and get some?'

She looked up at him tentatively 'Yes. '

He took another step back to allow her in. Katie walked

forward and then jumped like a frog at the sound of a soft click. Looking over her shoulder, she saw that he had closed the door.

'Would you prefer me to leave it open, Katie?'

'No—no, not at all.'

He led the way, one hand placed protectively on the small of her back to guide her.

She took one last look around his drawing room as she went with him. In the course of her work she had been over every inch of it and the plans of his entire suite were safely stored in her luggage. But that was not real. There was no substitute for inhaling the rich masculinity of his natural surroundings, or feeling the hard-packed luxury of genuine Turkish rugs beneath her toes.

'I'm glad you called. Are your French windows open?' His rich, deep voice drifted over her and his soft touch made her shiver.

'No, I closed them before we left for the party.'

'That's a pity. I was going to suggest you take this last drink of the evening as I do, to the accompaniment of the nightingales outside. The noise of your doors being unlocked is sure to disturb them. They are in full flow now—can you hear?'

She nodded.

'Why don't you come and share my table and listen to them from there?'

Katie could not wait. This was her last night at the Villa Antico. Her one remaining chance to share some time alone with this man who dominated her every waking moment and her dreams as well.

As she nodded, he poured a thin stream of creamy milk into her cup, watching for her signal to stop.

'That's enough.' She sensed him putting the container back

and closing the door, but could not look. He did not offer her another direct invitation to join him. Instead he went to stand beside a small table in his salon. It was set up just inside his open French windows and, as she approached Katie enjoyed the liquid cadences of half a dozen nightingales rippling in from the night.

A single chair stood beside the table, which Giovanni pulled out. Swinging a matching antique seat over from its place beside the wall, he sat down beside her. The table was so small that beneath its surface she could sense the nearness of him. She would have loved to lose herself in the nightingales' song, but the distraction of having such a man within touching distance filled her mind. She had been finding it difficult to look at him directly, ever since that moment on the boat. Now her heart trembled each time she heard his coffee spoon rattle against its saucer or caught sight of his hand as he reached for one of the biscotti lying on a plate in the centre of the table. Her silence did nothing to disturb him. In fact, he seemed more at ease than when they had been downstairs in the hall together.

'I should tell you that I don't make a habit of visiting strange men after dark, Signor Amato,' she managed, whispering for the sake of the birdsong.

'I have never considered myself to be strange. In fact, for many years I was the only normal person I knew. Now *you* are unfathomable, Katie. For example, you dress like a duchess for a trip to a pigsty.'

She looked up at him quickly and saw that he was smiling. She smiled, too.

'That's better. You have had a haunted look about you for days, Katie.' He fell silent again, but she felt that the tension between them had eased slightly. As a result she relaxed and managed to take some pleasure in the natural cadences throbbing in through the window.

The sound of a distant engine grew closer and became the rattle of a farm vehicle. Their nightingales shivered into silence. The racket out in the lane bucked and kicked all the way along the other side of the terrace wall. As the vehicle passed by, its engine note changed. They heard it check, reverse and then stop altogether. After that performance, the only sound left was a far off owl, hunting along the river valley. Katie clicked her tongue in disappointment that there would be no more nightingales, at least for a while.

'That is Raphael, returning from his search for you.' Giovanni drained his coffee. Putting down the cup, he began going through the pockets of the jacket hanging from his chair.

Katie stood up. 'I must go. Raphael will need to come and tell you that I put him to a lot of trouble for nothing,' she began, but Giovanni motioned for her to stop while he used his mobile. Opening it, he pressed a few buttons, then smiled into the middle distance as it was answered.

'Raphael? *Si, so. Grazie e buona notte,* Raphael.'

He snapped the phone shut with a flourish. 'There. That has ensured we will not be disturbed again. Raphael will be halfway to Elena's arms by now.'

Any concern for her own safety vanished as Katie realised the staff might have more to worry about than she did.

'You aren't supposed to know about *that*!' she said desperately. Elena had told her about the romance in giggling confidence. The girl had been horrified at the thought her employer might find out. Giovanni's only reaction to the news was to twitch a shoulder dismissively.

'Relationships between unmarried servants was almost a

hanging offence in my great-uncle's day, but I take a more…liberal stance.'

Katie breathed again. 'Oh, Raphael and Elena will be so glad to hear that.'

He inhaled deeply. 'Actually, I'd be grateful if you kept my admission to yourself. I like to keep them on their toes.'

She smiled. 'Of course, Signor, which is why I must go now, to show them that you play by the same rules.'

'Ah.' He stood up, a lazy, teasing smile forming on his lips. 'That need not necessarily be true, Katie.'

She waited, hardly daring to breathe. He took two slow, measured steps towards her. 'You look exquisite tonight. And you know, as well as I do, what happened the last time I saw you looking so beautiful.'

'I haven't been able to forget it like you.' It was meant as a rebuke, but she realised as soon as she spoke that he read it quite differently. His bittersweet smile touched her through the shadows and from that moment on she was lost.

'Oh, Katie, if you can read my mind like that, why have you been so distant since that night on the *Viola*? If I frightened you then by going too fast, it was only because I found you so irresistible.'

She gasped, wondering how to tell him how tortured she had been. There was no need. He took her gently in his arms and sipped a single gentle kiss from her lips.

'Oh, Giovanni…' she breathed. All thoughts of his other women vanished with the realisation he was going to give her a second chance. Katie had spent every moment since the *Viola* regretting the way she had recoiled from him. Tonight was going to be different.

Dimly, far off, the sounds of nightingales began drifting in through the open windows again. Giovanni barely heard them.

His senses were full of the steady, insistent beat of life, rising with an intensity he had never enjoyed before. He moved one hand to her hair, caressing it away from the silken skin of her shoulders. Then he dipped his head to sample the taste of her. It was more delicious than he had imagined, and he had imagined it often. His hands slid to her waist, holding her protectively as he kissed her again and again. This was wonderful, and her gentle modesty was so refreshing. It had been a fact of life since Giovanni's teens that women threw themselves at him. They flirted, they cajoled, they stripped and jiggled. The only woman who had done nothing for him was Lia.

He pondered this thought as he stood in the half dark with Katie in his arms. Lia had been ice—except when wearing that green dress, so like this one—then she had become a spitting, vicious fury. In contrast, Katie was like orchid petals beneath his hands.

For once, he shut his mind to memory. This was so much more restful. Katie showed no signs of nagging him for anything, and holding her was giving him so much pleasure. Surely she deserved something in reward?

After some long and deliciously stress-free moments, she received what she had been yearning for.

CHAPTER SEVEN

GIOVANNI bent forward and rested his face against the side of hers, breathing in the perfume of clean hair and warm skin. He could afford to take his time. Usually, there were so many calls on him that an unspoken urgency to get on, to get busy, to get going drove him on. Tonight was different. There was no hurry, especially as the full-on approach had scared her away before. He nuzzled her neck, searching for the right spot. Every woman had one, and this alabaster figurine was no different. With a soft moan her head fell back, exposing her throat. Kissing and nibbling his way up to her lips, he cradled her close to his body. His hands strayed down to cup her bottom, gently kneading it, as he tasted her lips properly for the first time. She responded. This was infinitely better than his impulsive approach on the *Viola*. With a rush of satisfaction, he felt his kiss returned. His own response was increased a million times by knowing that he was fuelling a growing desire within her. She was eager for him this time. He relished the way her mouth accepted the first tentative touch of his tongue tip. When her arms wound around his neck as though she would never let him go, it told him everything he wanted to know. That realisation, coupled with his growing physical arousal, was a turning point. He seized the opportunity in both hands. This woman had fascinated him since the first moment she had arrived in his office. She had charmed his staff, his relations and his business associates. Now it was his turn.

Katie was beautiful; she was everything he could wish for in a woman and, best of all, she was foreign and a contractor. He could take her tonight without any of the society harpies who craved his body being any the wiser. Katie's discretion was legendary. Tonight's enjoyment would be theirs alone. It would be sex pure and simple, with no questions asked and no comeback.

The idea inflamed him. Working his hands inside her dress, he felt the delicacy of lace panties beneath his fingers. She trembled as he eased her out of her clothes, but she never protested. Her lips were too hungry for him.

'You want me.'

His low, urgent voice contained all the desire Katie recognised in herself. She thrilled with the vibration of it. His maleness was raw, total and so completely irresistible. When he kissed her now, his urgency was almost out of control. There could be no going back—and she did not want to. Passion powered her until she felt dizzy.

He took her mouth, his tongue thrusting demands that were answered by her faint mews of delight. That was all the encouragement he needed. It set his hands roaming over her body again, testing each curve and nuance of her nakedness. A long, low moan of pleasure escaped from Katie's lips as he crushed her body against his own. With a need born of instinct, she pushed her hips against him, mirroring his own movements.

'Bed is the only place for this,' he murmured and was not to be denied. She had tempted him for so long. It was time to do something about it. Burying his face against her shoulder, he lifted her off the ground and carried her into his shadowy room. Settling her gently on the bed, he lay down beside her, fully clothed. Supporting his head with one hand, he used the other to appreciate the smooth rise and fall of her body.

He breathed in the warm perfume of her hair again. Her fingers responded, tentatively at first, then with more certainty as they found buttons. With his encouragement she undid them, one by one. Dragging off his shirt, he pulled her closer still. The sensation of his crisp curls of chest hair pressed against her tender flesh squeezed out a ragged gasp of anticipation.

'You enjoy the touch of skin against skin?'

She could hear the smile in his voice as his hand circled her shoulder and then swooped down to cup her breast. Each finger moved independently, bringing her nipple to sharp arousal before going anywhere near it. When at last his thumb rolled over the dark bead, its pad raised her effortlessly to a peak of excitement. He kissed her again, his tongue exploring her willing depths as his fingers continued to tease her breast. Then, slowly but surely, he kissed his way down over her cheek, her neck and the delicate collar-bones he had so admired at the party. When she offered no resistance he moved lower, until his playful hand slipped away to her ribcage.

As taut as a violin string, Katie waited. She could feel his breath dancing over her skin. Then tiny kisses rained down on her, circling the proud summit of her nipple until she could stand it no more. Closing her hands around his head, she drew his mouth towards her breast. It had the desired effect. His body rose up, rolling her on to her back. His mouth enveloped her nipple while his chest pressed against her nakedness. The light pressure of his body on hers was maintained as the tip of his tongue teased spasm after spasm of excitement from her. All the while he was stroking the roughness of his chest

hair against the delicate skin of her belly. Rhythmic movements crushed his lower body against her legs. She could feel
the hardness of him, even though it was still contained within
his clothes.

Katie was beyond imagining. She wanted to unleash all his
power, to absorb it greedily and take everything from him that
she had so far denied herself. In his bed there could be no fear
of rejection, only a desperate need to accept everything he was
offering to her. Her body reacted to him instinctively, primitive urges driving her higher and higher. Her back arched, her
hair tangled against his white pillows and she became aware
of a strange song crying through the night. It took a while to
realise she was responsible for the sound. He was bringing a
whole new, wordless language to her lips. She was hardly conscious of anything but his delight as he revelled in her reactions.

Giovanni was still determined to make all the rules. Taking
his time like the connoisseur he was, he moved kiss by kiss
across her. The pleasure repeated was more than redoubled.
Once again, he savoured the feel of her beneath his fingers and
lips. She was so responsive. The more she enjoyed herself, the
more he wanted to prolong the satisfaction it gave him. Despite
that, the warm night and the extent of his physical arousal were
making clothes too restricting. He stopped caressing the sensitive skin beneath her arm for a moment and released the
buckle of his belt. She froze at the sound. He paused.

'What is the matter?'

'Nothing. Nothing at all.'

There was a certainty in her voice that made him wonder.
He rolled away from her and sat up. She did not move.

'There is enough trouble in the world already without an
unwilling partner in bed.' He looked across at her intently. 'Do
you want me to carry on?'

Katie held her breath and tried to catch her thoughts. She wanted this more than anything else in the world. It was so wrong and yet so right. All her life she had fought against letting anyone get too close. Now none of that seemed to matter. She was suspended in a dream, desperate for the simple human contact she had denied herself for so long. And what a way to indulge her desires. The sight of his naked body in the swimming pool had been electrifying enough. Now it was warm and available on the bed beside her. She wanted to touch, explore, enjoy…Was that such a crime?

Soundlessly she sat up and reached for him. Neither of them needed any more encouragement. His mouth searched hungrily for hers and possessed it. As they sank down on to the bed again, her hands roamed over his smooth back. Undulating beneath her hands, he eased his way out of the rest of his clothes until they were both free to explore through the anonymity of night.

Katie had never known such abandon. His body felt as good as it looked. Biceps toned and sleek from exercise and the smooth hard curves of his chest were all hers to fondle. As he kissed her, she searched for his nipples. They were as hard as hers. She tried to copy the movements he had used to kindle fire in her. Instead of enjoying it as she had anticipated, he convulsed, catching at her hands.

'That is too much of the wrong sort of pleasure,' he whispered, his laughter liquid in the shadows. Taking her hand, he returned it to the small of his back.

It had never occurred to her that men could be ticklish. She wondered what other parts of his body might be open to exploration. Bewitched by his kisses, she let her hands stray forward over the rise of his hip. He did not stop her this time. Instead he twisted his body so that her fingers could find what they were seeking. She gasped. The combination of sensitivity and thrusting maleness fascinated her. Encircling him with her touch, she felt his arousal kick with anticipation. Trying to catch a glimpse of him through the darkness, she leaned forward. As she did so, a lock of her hair coiled against his thighs.

He responded gruffly. 'I was concentrating on *you*.'

Rolling her over again, he moved his hands appreciatively until he reached the cap of curls that hid her sex. His palm covered it for a moment, the fingers resting lightly on her thighs. Katie could not help herself. When his fingertips asked a silent question, her body replied. He parted her petals and found nectar. By coaxing the tiny bud at the heart of her femininity, his expertise sent her into ecstasy overload.

Katie had not known such perfection was possible. It was incredible and almost too much to bear. He was sending fervent darts of excitement so deep into her that they began to cross the line between pleasure and pain. She writhed around to catch him again, grasping the shaft that pulsed so magnificently between her hands.

'This is supposed to be for your benefit, not mine.' His thick chuckle reached her through a miasma of need.

'It will be.' She sighed as her fingertips explored the beauty she had imagined so often. With delight, she recognised a sudden wicked urge to kiss and nibble all the places that were reacting so vividly beneath her touch. 'This is better than I could ever have imagined, Giovanni.'

He gave a wicked smile. 'And this is only a warm up to the main event.' Stretching out on the bed, he wondered why tonight should be so unusual. He felt strangely light-hearted for once. Whether it was the Baccharis' *vino*, the lateness of the hour or…something else, there was a subtle difference in this evening's pleasure. Katie had a distinctive way about her, that was for sure. Most women only wanted to take pleasure from his hands and mouth. She was different. She wanted to give as well, and continually whispered to him for instructions. She had a mischievous hesitancy—but surely no woman he bedded could be *that* innocent. It could have provoked him. It wouldn't have been the first time he unmasked a woman for acting a part, clamouring for his money and status. Instead, Katie aroused something more than lust in him—curiosity, for one thing. She had spent virtually her whole stay at the Villa Antico dressed in camouflage, with her head down and working busily. Only on two occasions had she emerged, like a butterfly from a chrysalis. Each time something had inspired him to act out of character. First, he had kissed her. And now he was going much, much further. What on earth was it about this woman that moved him to do such things?

There was no need to ask what was happening at the moment. Katie was using her beautiful mouth in most enjoyable ways. He smiled and shut his eyes, thinking of his latest harbour bill for the *Viola* in an attempt to quell the rising tide of his urgency. After a few moments he gave up. She was so good, so distracting that going all the way with her began to feel like the worst idea in the history of big mistakes. For five years, Giovanni had stubbornly refused to allow any woman to have influence over him. Katie could easily smash that rule. Making love to her once would not be enough. He knew he would need to repeat the experience with her, and her alone; over and over again…so he had to call a halt now, before things went too far.

He drew her up towards him. 'No more of that for the moment, Katie.'

'Oh, but I was enjoying it,' she breathed.

Kissing her deeply, he replied, 'This evening is about giving you pleasure.'

'But what about *you*?' she whispered.

'Tonight, Katie, all I'm interested in is *your* enjoyment.'

She looked up at him in puzzled innocence. 'That doesn't sound very satisfying for you.'

'It's fine,' he murmured, stroking her face.

But she drew away from him. 'So…don't you want me after all?'

Her voice was very small. She sounded so vulnerable, so innocent. He reached down and lifted her up until they were face to face. Then he began kissing the inquisitiveness out of her.

She responded by straddling his body and he could feel that glorious tumble of hair rippling over his own skin as he pressed his mouth against hers again. With senses heightened, he could feel the very personal imprint of her against his hard, flat belly. Wrapping his arms around her waist, he bundled her over on to her back He had intended to overwhelm her with pleasure again, without giving her the chance to raise questions in his own mind. Her reaction got the better of him. It was purely physical. Twining her limbs around him, she pleaded with her body.

He hovered between sense and desire. The fact that she was a temporary attraction spurred him on. After all—where would be the harm? Tomorrow she would be gone.

He sighed and in response she breathed his name softly into the night.

'Are you safe?' he questioned.

'Oh, yes…perfectly…please…take me…'

Her soft entreaty would have been hard enough to refuse. When her hands went up to cup his face in appeal, it broke the final link in the chain of his self-control. In a torment of ecstasy he plunged into her. At the exact moment when he realised why she was so different from all his other women she cried out.

'You were a virgin?' Heart pounding, he forced the words into the night.

She could not reply and he could not repeat the question. Giovanni cursed himself again for being overtaken by events. This should not be happening. Horror at the responsibility of being her first lover struggled inside him with primal male delight at being the only one to possess such purity. They lay perfectly still, their two hearts thundering as one. Then, in the same instant, both began to move. Ebb and flow, together and apart. Slow, perfectly synchronised movements drew them towards an experience that neither would ever forget. It felt as though no one in the history of the world had experienced such totally absorbing delight. For eternity and for no time at all they were locked in an embrace that could have only one conclusion. As she felt him begin to pulse with ecstasy, she kissed him as though with her dying breath. In one last unbearable pang of longing he exploded, driving his passion deep within her. He had found satisfaction. This was it. This was what he had been searching for, for so long…

Later, much later, night crowded in on them again. Giovanni's hold on her became a caress as he rolled on to his side, drawing her with him.

'You may not have come here to audition for the role of mistress, Katie, but believe me, it's yours. Any time you want it,' he murmured deep into her ear.

She listened to the steady rise and fall of his breathing, so different from her own ragged gasps. Her limbs were trembling from the powerful reactions he had fuelled in her, over and over again. It was not only physical feelings that tormented her now, but also realisation. Giovanni had made her his contessa for the evening, but he considered her to be nothing more than mistress material. He had just said as much. She had allowed herself one night of passion, but now knew that the experience could never be repeated. This was a man who had been unable to find love, although every rich and titled woman in the world had been paraded for his approval. There was only one reason why he had taken her to bed tonight, and it was not affection. Lust had driven her, too, but there was also a deeper undercurrent. Now, in darkness, she realised what it was. She loved him with a fervour that was painful. This had been her fairy tale, where the handsome prince transformed her with words that really meant something. But the truth was that there could be no happy ever after. The morning would divide them for ever. Giovanni would go back to his world and she must return to hers.

A single tear escaped from the corner of her eye. Tonight had been paradise. It was also everything she feared most in the entire world. She had let him into her mind and from there, into her body. For one brief, shining moment Katie had believed it could be for ever. Now, in the blank, sleepless hours before dawn all she could think of was her childhood. She had always tried to do everything right. Her mother had soaked up all her love, but had abandoned her when something better had come along. Katie knew that if she tried to stay with Giovanni, the same thing would happen. He would cast her off—if not today, then tomorrow or the next... History would repeat itself, magnifying her pain.

She had to get away now, before it was too late.

Giovanni's brow was pressed against her own as his arm encircled her. It was a weight she would have been only too happy to bear if it had come alone. Instead, it held all the horrors of the past. She loved him, so he would leave her. That was how loving had always worked in her life so far. Katie could not expect Giovanni to be any different.

He pulled her closer, fitting her snugly against his body.

It was not enough. She had to escape—she had to get away before he could trample on her heart.

CHAPTER EIGHT

A LOUD banging wakened Giovanni next morning. Gradually, he realised it was not only going on inside his head. Somebody was knocking at the door of his suite. He rolled into a sitting position and found that Katie was missing.

'Come in,' he called out, wincing. It was dazzlingly bright. Late mornings never did him any good. He reached for his watch, but it must have stopped the evening before. The display showed eight forty-five.

The door opened, but it was not Katie. It was Eduardo, carrying a tray and a sheaf of correspondence.

'Good morning, Signor. Here is your breakfast and I have printed out the emails received so far this morning.'

Giovanni checked his Rolex again. 'Then I really have overslept?'

'Indeed, Signor.'

Groaning, he rubbed his face. He needed a shave.

'Did everyone have a good time last night, Eduardo?' he began casually.

There was a significant pause. 'Yes, sir.'

'It was a good evening, although the Baccharis' latest *vino* ought to have a health warning on it.'

As he spoke he remembered his night tray and groaned

again. It was still standing on the table, complete with the telltale wreckage of two empty cups.

'Perhaps I should tell you at this point that Miss Carter has already left for Malpensa, Signor.'

'Katie has gone?' Giovanni gasped.

'Indeed, sir. In her eagerness to get away, the young lady apparently *carried her own cases downstairs*.' Eduardo was tight-lipped with disapproval at such a break with tradition. 'Nonna Bacchari was on her way to work in the kitchens and she saw the taxi arrive.'

Giovanni leaned forward and rubbed a weary hand through his hair. Of course she had gone. He had seduced her—a virgin. 'Mistress' was obviously not the word she wanted to hear. He groaned. Not even Katie could sleep with him without hearing wedding bells. Women really were all the same. Why had he expected anything else from her?

Eduardo swept around his employer's king-sized bed, but hesitated before actually picking up the abandoned coffee cups.

'Shall I close the windows, Signor?'

They had been left standing open all night. Giovanni stared into the cup of espresso he was holding. It stared back at him, as black as his thoughts.

'Do you know what went on in here last night, Eduardo?' he said slowly.

Eduardo looked at him directly for the first time that morning. The PA wore a particularly wintry expression as he cleared his throat to reply. 'I really have no idea, Signor. And neither do the rest of the staff. That is none of our business.'

Partly satisfied, Giovanni turned his attention to breakfast. He could rely on his staff to be discreet. His own conscience was more of a problem. Sex with Lia—it could never have been called 'making love'—had shown him what a dangerous activity it could be. At best it was nothing but a bargaining tool, at worst, a death sentence. And now he had risked everything with Katie. The girl whose uncomplicated loveliness promised everything had proved to be interested only in status, like all the rest.

Abandoning the breakfast, he realised there was only one way to wipe all this from the record. He would have to plunge into the day and get working.

Katie ran. She arrived at Milan Airport hours before her plane was due to leave for England. There would have been plenty of time to go right into the city, roam the Via Montenapoleone or call in to the Café Doney. Instead, she sat beside her cases on the concourse and waited. Her mobile rang constantly, but it was only work. A million people passed her by, but the million and first never arrived to carry her back to his villa.

There was no point in asking herself what she had done. That was only too apparent, from the dull ache, the vacancy, where she had held him so close for such a perfect time. It was obvious, too, from the way she was the only woman wearing a jacket on that hot day. Her fingers strayed beneath its fabric to the bruises made by Giovanni's teeth. She had thought she was alone in experiencing such ecstasy. Then she had felt all her own feelings mirrored in Giovanni's rapture, each time they had made love. It had been spectacular.

Now it was over. She could never see him again. Katie knew she was deluding herself by expecting him to rush to the airport and stop her flight. They were complete opposites in every way. He could never love her. He had said as much, in the way he had offered her the job of mistress. She doubted that Giovanni could love anyone. Aristocrats could afford to

turn their backs on their conquests. Katie had suffered aban-
donment once and was not about to let it happen again. So
she was going to make it simple for them both by leaving him
before he could dump her. She would slip back into real life.
From now on her staff could deal with the fantasy that was
the Villa Antico.

Katie's success at the charity party on board the *Viola* paid
dividends. Carter Interiors suddenly had more work than
any normal company of its size could handle, but they
managed magnificently. Katie worked eighteen-hour days,
but for all the wrong reasons. Once it would have been for
the love of it. Now it was to block out the pain that was
coming at her from all directions. It was not only Giovanni
who was breaking her heart. After exhausting the patience
of her current lover, Mrs Carter had moved back home permanently. Katie worried about her father all the time. He was
still unwell and she could not bear to see the hope in his eyes.
He was trying to convince himself that his ex-wife had
returned for good, but Katie knew better. Her mother would
be off again, as soon as there was more generosity on offer
elsewhere. Until that time, she expected to be waited on as
a guest. Katie had no problem in looking after her dad, but
her mother was entirely different. Nothing was ever right: the
TV was the wrong size, the kitchen was five years out of date
and the patterned carpets gave her a migraine. Katie coped
by practically living in her office, or out on jobs. Both she
and her father lost weight. Mrs Carter never cooked and, after
years of Katie's good home baking, Mr Carter found it hard
to tolerate ready meals and takeaway food.

Katie was often too busy to eat. Her tastes had changed
since returning from Italy as well. The smell of milk in her

tea now turned her stomach. Fried food of any sort made her long for the cooking of the Villa Antico. She was living mainly on pasta and fruit. It was a hollow attempt to relive those few unforgettable weeks.

She knew she should delegate the rest of the Villa Antico job. Each time she checked the wall chart of work in progress, the gold star signifying the date of a confirmation visit drew her eyes. *Someone* would have to go to Tuscany with the final plans and samples. Could she risk one of the girls? Or would Giovanni Amato ensnare her, too? Katie could not bear to think of anybody else sharing her sentence of checking emails hourly and snatching at ringing telephones.

She wondered about sending one of the guys—although that could be worse. He might come back with lurid tales of what Giovanni was getting up to and with whom. Katie did not want to find out things like that at second-hand. Her mind was full of suspicion already.

Finally the day came when a decision had to be made. Katie spent a sleepless night. She began by turning over in her mind the dangers of sending someone else. Then she added up the advantages of going herself. She already knew how plausible Giovanni Amato's charm was. This time she would be immune to it. She pushed her secret desire to see him again to the back of her mind, convincing herself that it was the best thing for the company if she went herself.

It was nearly two a.m. when Katie finally rolled over to try and settle down. As she did so, she winced. All the weight she was losing seemed to be migrating to her breasts. Making a sleepy note to buy some new bras for her trip to Tuscany, she closed her eyes and drifted off to sleep.

* * *

It had been warm during her first visit. Now it was intolerably hot. The sun hit with the force of a hammer, baking stones and pedestrians alike. Katie was relieved to see a Villa Antico chauffeur waiting for her at the airport as arranged. She almost forgot her nervousness as he swung her cases into the limousine that had been sent to collect her. All she had to do was sink into its air-conditioned luxury.

'Signor Amato sends his apologies but he will not be at the villa when you arrive, Miss Carter.' Her driver threw the information over his shoulder as he eased the big car out on to the busy road.

'Thank you, Sebastien.' Katie smiled but her thoughts were jumbled. She might just as well have sent someone from the office after all. It would have saved her all this tiresome travelling. She never seemed to get any restful sleep any more. Perhaps it was all the stress. Sometimes it took a real effort to stay awake, especially in the afternoons. Today the problem was particularly bad. She almost dropped off on the way to the villa. Her head kept nodding forward and she had to shake herself awake several times.

Perhaps it was time to buy a new bed.

Eduardo met her at the door, smiling broadly. 'There has been a change of plan, Miss Carter. Signor Amato decided it was not worth travelling to the city in this heat. He is in the length pool at the moment. If you would like to go to the terrace, I shall arrange some refreshments for you both.'

It was the last thing Katie wanted to hear. The temperature must be up in the thirties. She dragged herself around the side of the house. The pool was empty, but she saw Giovanni's mark in wet footprints leading towards the pool house. Walking around the water's edge, she remembered the last time she had been here. The night of the party had been momentous. Now she was about to put herself in the way of temptation all over again.

Inside the pool house, Giovanni had already showered and towelled dry. He congratulated himself on deciding to miss that meeting in Milan. His absence from the villa might have given Carter Interiors the wrong impression. He was pretty sure that Katie would not come out in person. Not after she had run from him with such certainty.

He interrogated his reflection as he shaved. The first time he'd kissed Katie had been a mistake. He admitted that. Their lovemaking had been mutual pleasure, but then the scales had tipped against him. She wanted more than he was willing to give. That was why he had resisted every impulse to contact her since that night. She had run out on him. That was her choice.

He heard footsteps outside. Wiping away the last of the shaving foam he checked his appearance and went out to put on a polite show for the contractor.

Katie's head was pounding. With the sun almost right overhead any shadows were slender. She blinked. The dark was growing darker, the light brighter.

'Katie!'

She shut her eyes and then opened them wide. Giovanni was coming towards her from the pool house. She had no time to decide how she felt. His expression had gone from amazement to worry within a second.

'Katie? What is it? Are you all right?'

She could not answer. Suddenly, a wave of unbearable weakness almost knocked her off her feet. She reached out for him—but he was already there, supporting her gently as she slipped into unconsciousness.

The moment Giovanni strode into his villa with the unconscious Katie in his arms, his staff swung into action. They opened up the small guest suite and rang for the doctor. Reaching Katie's old room, Giovanni laid her gently on the bed. Her eyes opened while he was still bending over her.

'Katie? What is the matter?'

It must be serious. She saw concern in his eyes and heard anxiety in his voice, then ran out of time. Her stomach was swimming. Diving off the bed, she just made it into the suite's bathroom, where she was very sick into the sink. When she eventually returned, Giovanni was sitting on the edge of her bed, deep in conversation with Dr Vittorio. She tried to smile, without much success.

'I'm so sorry you've been troubled, Doctor. It's nothing. I don't think this heat agrees with me, that's all.'

The two men exchanged glances.

'Are you sure, Miss Carter?'

She stared at the doctor blankly. 'What else could it be? I was perfectly fine until I reached here. There hasn't been time for it to be a reaction to the water or anything. I only flew into the country this morning.'

'Are you pregnant?' Giovanni cut through all the concerned looks and came straight to the point.

'Giovanni!' The doctor was horrified at his lapse in tact.

Katie laughed, but soon stopped. Now she came to think about it, pregnancy might explain several things…

'It may have been badly put, Doctor, but there is a lot at stake here. Answer me, Katie?' Giovanni demanded in a dangerously quiet voice.

She burned with embarrassment. Raking over the embers of their passion like this, and in front of a witness, made her skin crawl.

'I—I don't know,' she whispered.

Giovanni raised his hands and let them drop to his sides. For a few glorious hours he had deluded himself. He had been wrong all along. Hard-working, discreet Katie Carter had never needed him for himself. As usual, it had been the money, privilege and position he could provide. The more he thought about it, the worse it became. If she *was* pregnant, it had happened suspiciously close to receiving that begging letter from her mother. Ensnaring a man through pregnancy was bad enough. To do it on behalf of a third party showed her to be as weak and silly as every other woman he had tangled with.

Katie moved her hand protectively across her stomach. 'A baby?' she murmured, feeling everything click into place. 'Perhaps that explains why I've been feeling so strange.'

'A simple test ought to confirm it, Katie,' Dr Vittorio was saying softly.

She looked at Giovanni with a blaze of spirit. She had spent weeks mourning the loss of him, when all the time she might have been carrying something equally precious within her.

Giovanni looked away. Sensing the atmosphere between them, Dr Vittorio sent him down to the kitchens. If Katie needed an examination, Nonna Bacchari's company was required. An unwilling father was not.

Later, the doctor went to find Giovanni. He found him sitting in the shade of an isolated summer house. After giving him the news, he retreated. Vittorio had dealt with the Amato family for long enough to know that Giovanni would need some time on his own.

That was true, but not for the reasons Vittorio imagined. The pain Giovanni felt was the agony of betrayal. It was indescribable. Katie had come back, but only to present him with the emotional blackmail of pregnancy. His instincts had been right all along. Now he knew why his father had spent so recklessly and lived so fast. There was no point in waiting for that one special woman. She didn't exist. If even Katie—clever, delightful, lovely Katie—could pull a trick like this, then there was no hope.

Part of him wanted to have her thrown out and abandoned like the scheming slut she was. Glowing with disappointment, he stood up and started on the long walk back to the small guest suite—but something slowed his steps. It was the memory of an unhappy child—absent parents, arguments and a life lived on the edge.

Giovanni vowed then and there that he was never going to let that happen to his child. Whatever it cost him.

'That was quick. Dr Vittorio said he was going to tell you to take a walk while you got used to the idea.' Katie lay in her shadowy room, watching the tall figure silhouetted on the threshold. He was watching her.

'I did.'

Crossing the room with heavy strides, he took a chair and sat down beside her bed. He was out of reach, but waves of anger flowed from him like static electricity. They burned Katie's happiness to ashes.

'I expected better of you,' he said coldly. 'I don't know which will be worse—being trapped into becoming a father or being the child of a one-night stand. What arrangements did you make at work before you left to come here?'

'They are expecting me back on the last working day in

July,' Katie said miserably. She had expected him to react to the news in the same way she had—overwhelmed at first, but then excited at the thought of their baby. Instead he was angry, as though the whole thing was her fault and hers alone.

'I had some holiday due,' she went on, wondering why he was not as pleased as she was. 'When I finish here, I plan to take a break in Florence.' She did not add that the thought of returning home while her mother was still there had been the spur for her first proper holiday in years.

'Good. Then you will stay here instead. My growing child must be protected from city air at all costs. Dr Vittorio says that an ultrasound scan should be able to give us meaningful information about the foetus within a month. After that, we can make a decision about the future.'

Katie could hardly take in what he was saying. It sounded so at odds with his simmering fury that she looked up at him uncertainly.

'So…you *do* want this baby as much as I do?'

He looked as though her question was too stupid for words.

'I doubt that I could, since a baby must have been central to your plans,' he said tersely. 'No, Katie. I need a son. You are young, strong, intelligent and—' he paused '—beautiful.'

He knew he should have smiled at this point, but the pain of her treachery was too acute.

'You will make a far better mother than some anonymous surrogate, which was Eduardo's latest suggestion for continuing the Amato line.'

'To think of it… Me—having a baby,' she whispered, smiling to herself. She was determined to be happy, whatever Giovanni's reaction. Now she would always have a part of him to cherish. 'I can hardly believe it…'

'You will have to get used to the idea.'

Katie pursed her lips. His scorn was bad enough, but it was sowing seeds of doubt in her mind. 'I hope I can manage,' she said uncertainly. 'Being a good mother is going to be difficult.'

'You should have thought of that earlier. But don't worry,' he went on crisply. 'Instinct coupled with all your other talents will see you through.'

'I didn't exactly have the best teacher when it came to parenthood.' Thinking of her own mother began to germinate Katie's fears. 'What am I going to do?'

Giovanni sighed. 'You will stay in this house until a scan can confirm that you are carrying my son. He must be born in Italy, of course—'

'*He?* What if it is a girl?'

'I need an heir,' he announced and then stood up. Without another word, he walked straight out of her room.

It was the clearest indication Katie could have that bearing a daughter was not an option. She lay down again and stared at the drawn curtains. Leafy shadows were playing over their thin summer-weight material. A branch of climbing rose had broken away from its support and was lolling across her balcony. She watched it dance without seeing anything.

If she had a son, her life would be over. He would be taken away from her. Her baby would be sucked into the aristocratic lifestyle that had made his father such a hard man. Giovanni must have a core of steel. How else could he make demands like these, using her unborn child as a bargaining counter? Things would be bad enough if he got his heir, but if she was found to be carrying a girl…Katie could hardly bear to think what might happen. She would lose Giovanni. And then she would have to return home to face her father's pain and her mother's horror, while she was kept alive only by the idea of Giovanni's baby growing inside her. All she would have to sustain her for the rest of her life was this single keepsake, a living memory of their one wonderful night together.

Unfamiliar tears welled up and rolled down her face. Katie prided herself on being able to cope with anything, but this was different. She could not bear it. Alone in a foreign country, scorned by the man she loved and tortured with sickness, it all became too much. She cried and cried until exhaustion overtook her.

When she woke the shadows had moved around. For a second she wondered what she was doing in bed during the day. Then she remembered.

'Congratulations, Katie.' Eduardo's voice came from somewhere near the foot of the bed. She struggled to sit up, at once confused and angry.

'Then Signor Amato has told everyone?'

Eduardo held up his hands with a smile. 'No—I am the only person he has trusted with the information so far. Although…Nonna and the kitchen staff have been in such high spirits this morning I doubt that his news is the total secret Signor Amato intends it to be. He will only make a formal announcement if the result of your scan is favourable.'

'You mean if I am expecting a son.'

Eduardo's smile became brittle 'After such a bad start, it is important to the count that his family name has a second chance to continue.'

'What does *that* mean?'

'The Contessa Lia died in—' Eduardo's eyes slid around the room, looking everywhere but at Katie. 'The late Contessa was never strong and she died in…distressing circumstances,' he finished somewhat secretively.

It all came back to that. Katie did not need Eduardo to finish his sentence. Giovanni's glamorous wife must have died without giving him the son he craved. That was why his family tree had been altered, to remove a painful memory. Now Katie was giving Giovanni a second chance, but all she could ever be to him was a runner-up in his race for immortality.

Anger began to make her feel better. Besides, she had to get up. People died in bed. That was what her father always said, immediately before recommending work as a cure for all ills. Not that it had done his heart any favours, but Katie was certainly not ready to follow the shadowy Contessa just yet. Cautiously, she swung her legs over the edge of the bed and stood up. It did not feel so bad, so she began searching for her shoes.

'I came to summon you to the dining room, Katie. Lunch is about to be served.' Eduardo checked his watch. 'The Count wishes you to be present. Even if you cannot face any food,' he added with a kind smile.

'Actually, I've just realised I'm absolutely starving!' Katie said in wonder. An hour before, sickness had convinced her that food would never touch her lips again. Now things were looking brighter. She dismissed Eduardo with her thanks and then took a quick shower. That therapy worked so well she felt almost human as she walked down to the summer dining hall.

The enormous table was already laid. When Katie had been shown to a seat, Giovanni dismissed the butler and got up to pour her some orange juice himself.

'Thank you, but perhaps I'd better stick to mineral water.'

'You are carrying a child, Katie—my child. You must learn to look after yourself properly.' He filled her glass to the brim.

She turned to plead with him, catching hold of his sleeve. 'Please don't be so angry. I never planned this—honestly. If you aren't happy about it, then I'm sorry. Just tell me what I can do,' Katie implored him.

He moved away from her and sat down. Seeing her agitation, he spoke. '*You* do not have to do anything, Katie. Everything is in hand. Bookings have been made, my diary has been rearranged, your office has been informed—'

'What?' Katie leapt to her feet, but his expression pushed her back down into her chair.

'Please calm down, Katie. My office merely informed your people that I had certain reservations about your designs and samples. They have been told that you will need to return here after your break in Florence to reassess my exacting requirements. The whole business is expected to take some weeks. That is the official line. In reality, of course, I have every confidence that your existing plans for my house will be exactly what I want. You will never leave the Villa Antico.'

Startled, Katie was relieved to see no trace of threat in his eyes. They were as watchful as ever, but that changed with her next words.

'All the same, Signor, I shall have to go back home to make sure everything is all right.'

'No. There is no need, Katie. Nobody is irreplaceable— except, of course, the mother of my son. For the next few weeks, all you need to do is relax, unwind and produce some new designs for the West Wing. Then, if necessary, it can be transformed into a state-of-the-art nursery section.'

Katie missed one of the implications of his words. She was too amazed at the other.

'But your father's "entertainment suite" is in the West Wing,' she whispered.

He turned on an inscrutable smile. 'Indeed, Katie, but I have never needed it and never will. If I have a son, it will be his nursery.'

'And what happens if I don't? What happens if my baby is a girl?'

Giovanni tore off a piece of bread to accompany his lunch. 'There is a fifty per cent chance it will not be. In any case, what can you do to influence the baby's sex? Nothing. So why spend the weeks until your scan worrying?'

'I'm being realistic.' Katie seized on some dimly remembered fact she had picked up somewhere. 'What happens if I miscarry? It's very common. Or the baby might not survive—'

He dropped his fork with a clatter. 'No.'

Katie shrank back. She had clearly touched a nerve and regretted it instantly. Contessa Lia's fate and that charity dinner on board the *Viola* began to form a horrible jigsaw of ideas in her mind.

'You…have had a child in the past?' She eased the words into the sunlit silence that enveloped them.

He picked up his fork again as though nothing had happened, but gave a brief nod. Nothing else was forthcoming. Eventually, after an agonising pause, Katie ventured a few more words.

'Will you tell me what happened?'

'No.'

The moment passed. With a sigh of regret, Katie picked up her cutlery and began her own salad. It was only when her mobile rang that they made eye contact again.

'Is it work?'

'No. It's my mother.' She sighed.

'I expect she will be delighted to learn of your pregnancy,' Giovanni said with a tinge of sarcasm.

'There's no way I'm telling her!' Katie said with a return of her old spirit. It helped her make an effort and smile into the phone. 'Hello, Mum. What can I do for you today?'

Her face fell as she listened to her mother's latest tale of woe. The neighbours weren't speaking to her, she had no money, her ex-husband wasn't willing to go on subsiding her—it was typical. So like her mother, so petty, so *normal*—

Katie felt totally abandoned. Giovanni was treating the baby she already loved as nothing more than a commodity. She wanted and needed support, but as usual all she got was orders and moans from every side… Suddenly it was all too much. Katie had had enough and burst into tears. Great unstoppable sobs poured out of her, drowning out everything else. Mrs Carter was so staggered she stopped speaking long enough for Katie to blurt out, 'I'm pregnant, Mum. I'm going to have a baby…'

Her mother's reaction was instant. 'Get rid of it. Get rid of it like I should have got rid of you. Children ruin your life. Look what has happened to me—'

It was like being kicked. All the air rushed out of Katie's lungs and she thought she would die. Her entire early life had been wasted trying to please her mother. She had been hurt and confused when nothing she ever did was good enough. Now she knew why. Her mother had resented her from the start. Katie had never been anything more than a mistake. It was a horror too great to put into words. Would Giovanni's anger affect her own poor, innocent little baby in the same way? The thought was too much to bear. With a terrified cry, Katie dropped her mobile and made a break for her suite.

A few minutes later she heard a knock at the door of her room.

'Go away!' She pushed her face deeper into her pillow.

There was a rattle as somebody tried to come in anyway. Katie had locked herself in, but seconds later she felt a presence beside her bed.

Giovanni had used the connecting doors that gave access

between the pairs of suites. The door was still shivering with the force he had used to throw it open. They glared at each other. His rage was uncomplicated. Hers was magnified through tears and fear.

On their first meeting, Katie had imagined him to be master of his emotions, only allowing others to see the image he wanted to project. The past few hours had swept all that away. Seizing a delicate Louis XVI chair from its place beside her tea table, he flung it towards the bedside and sat down on it. Katie lay still. She could practically see the fury engulfing him.

'I have just spoken to your mother,' he managed eventually.

'W-what did she say?'

'That's not important,' he answered quickly. 'What is important, is that I have informed her that we will marry if you are carrying my son.'

Katie frowned, puzzled. 'We will?'

'Of course.'

'Do I have a say?'

He gave a mirthless laugh. 'Surely you must have factored that into your calculations. Any Amato heir must be legitimate. That means marriage—but only if you are carrying my son. If not, then you will remain close so that I have access to my child, and you will be compensated accordingly instead. But only on one condition.' The look he was giving her changed. She guessed he was calculating how best to broach an unspeakable subject.

'Did my mother say the same thing to you that she said to me?' she asked slowly. 'Does she expect me to have an abortion if we don't marry?'

His normally calm features worked with suppressed anger.

'If you try to harm my baby in any way, Katie Carter, you will be thrown straight out of this house. You will be hurled back on to the tender mercies of your mother,' he growled, without bothering to hide his disgust.

Katie closed her eyes, flooded with relief. 'You need have no worries there, Signor Amato. Whatever sex our baby is, nothing could persuade me to do such a thing,' she said quietly. 'I would protect this little one with my life.'

His fists unclenched and his features lost their taut, dangerous look. Only when he regained his usual composure did he stand up to go.

'It does not sound as though your mother will be offering you much support, after all,' he sighed.

'That's my mum.' Katie tried to smile. 'It is as I told you, Signor Amato. Whatever talents she has, good parenting skills aren't among them.'

He stared at her as though gauging how best to answer.

'Your past is not as unique as you may think,' he said eventually, 'so perhaps we should both look on this as our chance to shine, Katie. We will show everyone how it is done.'

CHAPTER NINE

OVER the next few weeks Giovanni pushed himself harder than ever. He felt cheated, and it hurt. For a while he had connected with something really special in a woman. That feeling had not outlived their night together. She had abandoned him, only returning when she could use the missing part of his life as a bribe. So Giovanni threw himself into making the best of a bad situation. He toiled to consolidate the Amato fortune and made sure it would continue to grow. He re-drafted his will. The one thing he did *not* do was lay a single finger on Katie. They took their meals together, but only so that he could watch what she was eating.

The best books on pregnancy and child-care took the place of Dante and Jack Canfield on his reading schedule. It amused him that every source agreed that making love gently and in a restrained fashion should be perfectly safe.

The trouble was, Giovanni did not feel gentle and restrained. All he wanted was to relive that wild, exciting night of passion when their bodies and souls had soared, but it was too much of a risk. Katie had deceived him once already. His previous experience of women told him that she would do it again. For one brief moment he had been able to forget all the pressure, all his commitments and everything that had gone before. He wanted to take her to paradise again and again, to a place where she was Katie and he was Giovanni. He wanted to make up for all the times she had to rush grey-faced from his dining table, but his own pain and pride stopped him from bridging the chasm between them.

He had never known time pass so slowly.

The day of the scan arrived. Katie woke that morning with a different sick feeling. The nausea she suffered was easing, as peppermint tea and fresh ginger appeared regularly on the Villa Antico menu. It was apprehension at the thought of what the day might bring that made her queasy now.

Her appointment had been made in strictest secrecy. The staff were told that Giovanni would be flying to Milan on business, and Katie's decision to check on some fabric outlets was supposed to be a spur-of-the-moment idea. In fact it had been meticulously planned. The moment Giovanni brought his board meeting at Amato International to a close, he left to meet her at the clinic.

There was no question of queues and waiting rooms. They were ushered straight into a side room by a smiling young sonographer.

Katie's tummy was coated with gel. The operator apologised that it might be cold, but Katie did not notice. Her mind was filled with dread. She simply wanted everything to be over.

The probe rolled over and around the gentle swell of her belly. No bump was visible when she was wearing clothes, and now the unaccustomed sight of her pale, smooth skin transfixed Giovanni. He only stopped staring when the sonographer began to make cheerful noises.

'Everything seems perfect—all four chambers of the heart are visible and baby looks perfect for your date of the twenty-second of February—oh, and see this, Mama—baby is waving to you.'

Katie watched the flickering shape, wishing that Giovanni could take some pleasure in their achievement. This should be such a happy time for them both, but he had become so detached and silent.

And then the operator gasped.

'Ah, Signor—look—you have a son.'

Katie waited. Giovanni bent closer to the screen. There was a moment of absolute stillness. Then she heard him murmur something under his breath.

'Thank you, madam,' he said aloud to the operator. Then he put a hand on Katie's shoulder and shook it gently. 'Come along, Katie. We have things to discuss.'

He sounded almost pleased. She would have gasped, had her happiness not been tainted. She knew the future would be perfect for their son, but she would never feel Giovanni's love.

He had changed in an instant. Linking arms with Katie for the short walk to their car, he shortened his stride to fall in with hers. 'We must get home straight away. Eduardo has to be given the go-ahead for the arrangements. A date has already been pencilled in for the ceremony. All it needs is my confirmation.'

'Then we really are getting married?'

'There is no need to look so surprised, Katie. I told you my son must be legitimate.'

Her mind was not working properly. Ideas, hopes and fears all jumbled together. It was impossible to get a proper grip on anything. 'It's a lot to take in. I always dreamed that if I ever met Mr Right, his proposal would be a bit more…romantic, I suppose.'

'Very well—then, if you like, you can look through the

Amato collection as soon as we get home. You can choose yourself an engagement ring. Is that romantic enough for you?'

Katie had to nod, although the thought of wearing a second-hand ring chilled her blood.

'But first, we must send for my solicitor. He has drawn up the pre-nuptial agreement.'

The words weighed heavily in the air, snatching away any hint of romance.

They hardly spoke on the journey home. Katie stared out of the window, wrapped up in thoughts of her new, great responsibility to the house of Amato. Giovanni was silent, too, but for a different reason. His every movement now had new purpose and when they reached the villa he was firing off instructions before the helicopter's rotors had stopped turning. The staff were to be summoned to a meeting in the great hall, and Eduardo was sent down to the cellar in search of some Bollinger '92 to toast the occasion. Katie was sent up to rest until the time of the announcement. A few weeks earlier, she might have resented his order. Now it came as a relief. Besides, a strange change was creeping over her. For once in her life she was glad not to have to make decisions all the time. It felt relaxing and somehow *right* to let Giovanni shoulder some responsibility.

Despite Katie's new position in his household, Giovanni was not about to let Carter Interiors off the hook. Dr Vittorio thought it would be a good idea for Katie to keep her mind busy. Over the next few weeks the planned restyling of the Villa Antico went ahead, with her in charge. She was glad to get back into the routine of dealing with builders, decorators and samples. It was not as though she had anything else to do.

The new Contessa-in-waiting was attended night and day. Nothing was too much trouble. Nourishing, healthy meals were served to her at regular intervals. A car was put at her disposal. She had a beautiful suite, an estate to wander in, a choice of swimming pools—as her fiancé kept repeating, she could do what she liked, as long as it did not endanger his growing heir.

Her new life should have been wonderful—but there was something missing.

That something was Giovanni.

The wedding was arranged around her. Katie sat in her private drawing room like a queen as couturiers, florists, caterers and photographers arrived to spread out examples of their finest work before her. It was amazing. All she needed to do was ask and her smallest wish was granted.

She had been fitted for her wedding dress in a calico mock-up so she did not see the final result until her last fitting. That was on the day before the ceremony. The designers carried in a large cardboard box as though it contained a priceless treasure. It did. Katie instantly thought her wedding gown was far more beautiful than the most expensive design among the Contessa Lia's clothes.

The dress was made from finest raw silk, in a shade of cream that perfectly complemented her colouring. To distract eyes away from her midriff, it was cleverly cut and there was a matching stole lined with liquid silver silk. The skirt was embroidered with roses, violas and vines in the palest water-colour shades of silver, lavender and green. It was breathtaking. Katie still could not believe anything could be so beautiful when she was helped into it on the morning of her wedding. She wanted to look elegant rather than spectacular, and this was the dress. Her fervent hope was that Giovanni would realise how seriously she was prepared to treat her new role. He had practically accused her of tricking him into marriage. Katie knew she had a lot of ground to make up to regain his trust. To be his perfect bride on their perfect wedding day would be a start.

Her veil was held in place by a wreath of tiny mauve orchids flown in overnight from Singapore. In accordance with tradition, her bouquet was delivered on behalf of Giovanni. The florist had designed a matching work of art for her to carry. Sprays of the same beautiful little orchids joined fresh vine tendrils, trailing from a shower of cream roses. The effect was staggering.

Her parents and the entire staff of Carter Interiors were flown over to Italy in Giovanni's private jet for the ceremony. Katie's father was passed fit enough to escort her the short distance to the Amato family chapel, but when he saw her he was speechless. For a few precious seconds Katie allowed excitement to get the better of her. Everything was going exactly to plan. Everyone was telling her how lucky Giovanni was and how beautiful she looked. Surely her fiancé would be swept away by the romance of the day, too, and forget all his suspicions about her?

One look at Giovanni's expression when she reached the church dropped iced water on all her hopes. When he moved out from his seat to stand in the centre of the aisle, he turned his back on the altar to watch every step she made. He said nothing. When he bent to kiss her, Katie's reaction was to raise her hands and put them on his shoulders. The heat pulsed between them as their lips touched, but Giovanni did not indulge her for long. As they broke apart Katie let her hands slide down his arms in a sad gesture that was missed by the enormous congregation. They cooed with appreciation, but

Katie was dying inside. It was almost as though he had only planted a kiss on her to keep them happy—because it was expected of a bridegroom.

The ceremony passed Katie by in a blur. Formal portrait photographs had been made of the principal guests the previous evening, so only a few pictures were taken outside the chapel to record the event. Katie managed to smile, but she dared not look in Giovanni's direction. She could not risk seeing his expression. Here was a man who hated fuss and commotion, and now he was set right in the heart of it. Dignified in their own respective silences and scattered with a hailstorm of rice, confetti and tiny bags of sugared almonds, they walked to the grand marquee that had been set up outside the front of the villa. Swagged and lined in lilac, with flower arrangements to match Katie's bouquet, it was perfumed by crushed grass and a dozen different designer colognes. Katie visited each table, accepting kisses from all the male guests and good wishes from everyone. She smiled all day until her face froze into a mask of politeness. *Giovanni does not love me,* she thought. *All this is nothing more than window-dressing to him. He wants to save the honour of his family, nothing more.*

'Smile, Katie, or people will think you are not enjoying yourself.'

She looked up sharply at the low music of his voice. He was smiling—but not at her. Eduardo had brought him a message, and the relief on Giovanni's face was obvious.

'The helicopter is ready, Katie. It is time for you to begin your new life as Contessa, and for us to become officially man and wife.'

Giovanni had specifically asked that Katie did not change out of her wedding dress before they left on honeymoon. He wanted the crew of the *Viola* to see her dressed as his Contessa. His words made Katie feel even more like a symbol than a living, breathing person. As soon as their helicopter set down on the flight deck, he helped her out and together they went over to the line of staff assembled to greet them. There were more smiles and good wishes. Giovanni hurried the moment along, checking his watch continually.

'The Contessa must be shown to her suite. It is time for her rest,' he announced, and a maid led Katie through hushed corridors below deck into a panelled suite set with gold fittings. With her flowers taken away to be preserved, Katie suddenly felt very glad that Giovanni imposed such a strict routine on her. Exhaustion had crept up unnoticed. As she undressed and showered, her movements became slower and more laboured. Despite half her mind being back at the reception, wondering how her father was coping, she could hardly keep her eyes open. The moment she slipped between the cool cotton sheets, she fell fast asleep.

A maid woke her in time for a light supper packed with goodness but sadly lacking in fat, sugar or salt. Katie thanked her and tried to think of the good each healthy mouthful was doing for her baby. When her tray was taken away, she was left alone in a brand-new king-sized bed in a room decked with flowers. The calm and luxury was beautiful. Everything she could possibly need was in reach. It consisted of a gold tasselled bell-pull and a bedside telephone complete with printed directory of on-board facilities and international dialling codes. Katie knew all she had to do was pull the cord or lift the receiver to summon anything her heart desired— with one exception. It looked as though her married life was going to be as lonely as her single existence had been.

There was no pleasure in lounging alone. There were books

and magazines on interior design and Tuscan history. There was a television set with any number of stations. Her rooms on this luxury yacht were the last word in indulgence. Everything was marble, glass or gold plated, and it came with a perfect view over azure water and the sunlit coastline. All in all, her honeymoon had everything any woman could desire—except a husband.

It was not good enough. Katie decided to get dressed and go and find him. If nothing else, she had to thank him for being such a perfect host in the face of her mother's gushing approval. Joyce Carter had raved about everything, from the villa's monogrammed silver cutlery to its grass.

The *Viola* was even bigger than Katie remembered. She searched through every one of its public rooms before she found him. None of the salons were named, but as soon as she pushed open one set of doors Katie immediately knew she had found the music room. A full-sized grand piano took pride of place on a polished beech wood platform. Giovanni sat at the opposite end of the salon, beside an extensive sound system. He was lounging back in a large easy chair. His jacket had been lost at some point and his white shirtsleeves were turned back to expose the pale gold of his forearms. A brandy glass hung from the fingers of his right hand with a centimetre of tawny liquid in the bottom. His eyes were closed, but she knew he was not asleep.

Now she had found him, Katie did not quite know what to do. She entered the room and closed the door quietly behind her. His eyes opened, but he did not move.

'I'm sorry, Giovanni. I've been looking for you, but I did not mean to interrupt anything.'

'You apologise too much, Katie.'

Still he did not move. She had to do something, so she

walked towards him. Each squeak of the floorboards, every rustle of her skirt was magnified into a disturbance of his peace.

'I like the music you are playing. Is it Mozart?'

He nodded. 'It is a piece that is not heard as often as some of the others.' Taking a final sip of his cognac, he put down the glass.

'Would you like a drink? I had them put some fresh fruit juices in the fridge over there.'

'It sounds as though you were expecting me.' Katie tried to keep her voice light as she went over to a discreet serving area in one corner of the room.

'I thought you might take the opportunity to wander around your new territory.'

Katie poured herself a drink of grapefruit juice and added plenty of ice.

'I wouldn't presume to do anything of the sort. I was waiting for you to give me a guided tour.'

'Does that mean now?' He raised an eyebrow questioningly.

'It might be a bit more pleasant for the staff if they knew we were spending some time together, Giovanni, rather than apart.'

'A solitary lifestyle doesn't bother me. I prefer this to the noise and jangle of today's carnival.'

'That sounds a bit harsh.' She frowned, unable to bear criticism of a party that everyone else had enjoyed so much. 'It was good to see people having fun, especially the secretaries from Amato International. Don't you ever get lonely, keeping everyone at such a distance?'

He shook his head.

'I do,' she said heavily, staring at one of the enormous colour co-ordinated floral arrangements that flanked the speaker system. She didn't expect him to reply. When he did, it was a shock.

'Then come over here.'

Giovanni was still lounging comfortably in his armchair, but his eyes were alert. He watched her reaction intently. 'It is our honeymoon, Katie, after all.'

'I thought you had forgotten.'

He raised an eyebrow at the remark, and she bit her tongue.

'And I thought you had some sort of hidden agenda, Katie. You have been extremely quiet—ever since your return from England, in fact.'

Katie took a drink of her juice. Its bitter chill sent a barb straight down to her heart.

'I'm worried,' she confessed. 'And it isn't only the baby that is doing it—although goodness only knows how the poor little thing will cope with me as his mother. Work is my thing—not…not whatever it is mothers are supposed to do…' Katie floundered with the realisation she had no idea what was expected of her.

'We have an army of staff. You won't need to "cope" with anything. You will be in charge.' Giovanni spoke with quiet authority. 'But you hint that you have more concerns. All new mothers must have worries, but there is something else. I have seen it.'

Katie shut her eyes. She was making small circling movements with her hand, causing the ice in her drink to clink against the glass.

'It's only the same problem I've had since I was old enough to realise what was going on at home. Goodness knows how much Mum has persuaded Dad to spend on her for their stay at the Villa Antico—half a dozen changes of clothes, for a start. Since his operation, Dad's lost all his drive and he's always been a soft touch where Mum's concerned. He's been left sitting in the shade all day, while Mum's been hot on the trail of your friend Signor Balzone.'

'I know. I kept your father company for a while, when you were waltzing with Severino and the others. We had a long chat. He and I both prefer to talk than to dance, it seems.'

Katie sank into a chair on the opposite side of the salon from her new husband.

'Oh, no—don't say history is repeating itself,' she muttered. 'We have a phrase back in England: "If you want to know the wife, look at the mother." Well, it must be true. And to think—I've tried so hard to make sure I am different in every way. The hours I suffered, listening to her moaning about the way Dad hated partying. Now I am inflicting the same thing on you.'

'You knew what I was like when you agreed to marry me.'

She exhaled softly. 'It wasn't exactly a proper proposal, was it? This is nothing more than a marriage of convenience. The best thing for you would be if I disappeared off the face of the earth the moment your precious son is born.'

He sat up. 'No, Katie—you must *never* say that.'

Her eyes flew open at his tone.

For a few seconds his features worked, as though he was struggling with some inner demon. Then he spoke in a low, clear voice. 'My first wife died giving birth to our son. He was stillborn,' he added before she could ask for details.

'I see,' she said softly.

'No, you don't. There is much more to it than that. You spoke of history repeating itself, Katie.' He passed a hand over his face and she knew things were going to get worse. 'The night I saw you walking down the grand staircase in that green dress…'

Katie gasped. Eduardo's hoard of clothes could not be as secret as he thought.

'Oh, no…don't tell me I looked like your Contessa Lia…' her breath escaped in a low moan '…I couldn't bear it!'

For a moment his troubled expression became more thoughtful. 'No. You certainly did not look like her. You, Katie, were altogether more…desirable. It is just that I remember the night that my wife wore green—it was the night of our worst and most vicious argument.'

His eyes had been fixed on hers but now his dark lashes drew down a barrier.

Katie's mind worked feverishly. The gown Eduardo had lent her must have been put straight back in the closet after their quarrel. Giovanni *had* seen that unworn item and the argument had impaled its image on his mind. That was why he had been so transfixed. The diamonds must have been something Lia had worn. Katie thought of his glamorous last Contessa with an awful feeling of inadequacy. This was their world, not hers. She was an intruder here.

'No. That gown was thrown away later on my express orders.'

Katie had been about to confess, but on hearing that she changed her mind. She would simply have to live with her guilty conscience. Nothing would persuade her to get Eduardo into trouble.

'I only saw Lia's dress for an instant, but I hated it immediately. It stood for everything that was bad about our marriage. It was flashy—all show and no substance. When you appeared at the head of my staircase on the night of the estate party, Katie, for a split second I was about to send you back to change. Yet you looked so spectacular, no man could have resisted you.'

Certainly not me. He roused with the memory of it. Seeing the molten copper of her hair flowing over the glittering green gown that night had wiped all thoughts of Lia from his mind. That was until this instant. Her ghost now stood between them. It had to be exorcised, once and for all. To his surprise and relief, Katie had accepted the responsibilities of her position as well as the benefits. He wanted that to continue, but there was one last great test. He stood up and went over to the serving area in the corner. Taking a bottle of mineral water from the fridge, he broke its seal and poured a measure into a fresh glass.

'I don't feel spectacular at the moment.' Katie sighed. Somewhere, a clock chimed the hour and she automatically checked her watch. 'Right now, my father should be taking his medication. What happens if he forgets? I usually ring him with a reminder, but he told me not to bother while we're on honeymoon. What if he's relying on Mum? She'll be too busy to think of it. She's probably still making a fool of herself with one of your grand guests. I hope she doesn't embarrass you too much, Giovanni.'

'Don't worry about me,' he said brusquely. 'Go on—what else concerns you?'

'Isn't that enough?' She looked up at him hopelessly. 'The certainty that Mum will be off any day now and this time Dad will have no one at home to help him through it?'

'What about money?'

Her expression became guarded. 'Well, I suppose we should have discussed this a long time ago, but with Dr Vittorio being so in favour of me continuing to work now, I sort of assumed you'd be only too glad to see me go back to Carter Interiors once the baby was born.' She edged each word out, watching his face for clues about how he was taking her suggestion. When he did not immediately shoot it down in flames, she gathered a bit more courage. 'I *have* to work, Giovanni. Dad's council tax bill is over a hundred pounds a month, then there's the carer who pops in when I'm away, and regular bills for water, heat and light. It all comes out of my bank account and, as a self-employed person, I can't rely on any help with the costs. I'll have to get back in harness as soon as possible to cover it all.'

'I knew about your mother's bills,' he said grimly, 'but why have you never mentioned that you are supporting your father, too?'

She looked at him blankly. 'What else could I do? He is too ill to work, so it's my responsibility. Not that I think of it as any sort of burden, you understand,' she added.

Giovanni had been watching her closely. For weeks now he had been waiting for the requests to start—pay this, cover that—but they had never happened. Perhaps his earlier conviction that she was only after his money had been wrong. Perhaps it was time to put them both out of their misery.

Slowly, he went over and crouched beside her seat. Catching her hand, he squeezed it and looked deep into her eyes. 'Don't worry, Katie. Everything will be all right. I have already arranged to take care of all your mother's bills. Call it a wedding present from me. She will be told that this is the one and only time—'

'But Dad will still be left to bail her out in future.'

'No, he won't. I have something in mind to prevent him from backsliding.' A real smile began to warm Giovanni for the first time in weeks. 'Your father and I got on well today. I would have no objection to him coming to live at the Villa Antico. He could have his own suite, or a cottage in the grounds if he preferred. That way, you can keep a close eye on his health and welfare while I shall fortify him against your mother, if necessary. I have no patience with gold-diggers. Although for the truly generous in heart and spirit I have all the time in the world.'

Placing a kiss on her forehead, he tried to fill it with all the relief he felt. Distantly he was aware that they both put down their drinks and that Katie was searching for his lips. They kissed, and for long, luxurious minutes were suspended in their own personal heaven of sensations. It was Giovanni who was the first to manage his thoughts into some sort of order.

'Stop—Katie, just for a moment. If this is going to be a new beginning for us, then there is something more I must tell you about the Contessa Lia,' he said, and then words deserted him again. He wanted to be honest with his new wife, but the prospect of losing himself in her arms again after his self-imposed exile wiped every other thought from his mind.

'Talking about her can wait,' Katie murmured, leaning against him with a sigh.

CHAPTER TEN

GIOVANNI drew her closer. He had denied himself for weeks, aching for this moment. Now she was surrendering to him of her own accord. It was time. He took control and pulled her into another kiss so passionate that all inhibitions flew away. He had longed for this moment ever since she'd escaped from his bed. There could be no going back after this. He lifted her into his arms and carried her through the private quarters to his state bedroom. The place was in darkness. Large windows along one side gave a view of twinkling harbour lights across the bay. Everywhere else was velvet-black. The ship was silent and still.

For the first time in ages, Katie was alone with Giovanni in a bedroom. He laid her down on the bed and she sighed in anticipation. Through the darkness, the stark white of his shirt shimmered as it was thrown aside. Katie closed her eyes as she heard the quick quiet sounds of him shedding the rest of his clothes. Within seconds he was beside her, warm and insistent in the expectant darkness.

When they kissed, nothing seemed to matter any more. 'This is what I have been waiting for.' His voice was an urgent growl of primitive desire.

Katie felt a thrill of sexual excitement run right through her.

He held her close and there was no resistance as he covered her body and feasted on her lips. She gave herself up to wanton need, swept along on the crest of his overwhelming ardour.

His tongue probed between her lips, testing her and finding no resistance. When his mouth left hers to cover her throat with hungry kisses, she let out a long, low moan of pleasure. In response his hands glided over her body, her flimsy silk dress falling away as his hands sought her breasts.

Katie gasped as he cupped their growing fullness, his thumbs rolling over the hard, darkening points of her nipples. Instinctively she began to move her body against his, reacting to the tingling expectancy his fingers were teasing from her. Her hands began roaming his body, searching for a way to please him as he drove her up towards the stratosphere.

'No,' he warned her, 'I intend to make the most of this.'

He had waited so long to taste her again; nothing was going to make him hurry over the moment.

'Please,' she begged, 'I want you so badly, Giovanni…' Her voice ebbed away as he moulded his body to fit the curve and flare of hers. His palms moved over her shoulders, warm and assured. With each heartbeat Katie felt herself growing closer to him. Deep within her, a slow-burning fire was growing. He drank kisses from her now, savouring the taste of her lips, her tongue and her skin. She clawed at him, desperate for his attentions to go further. Digging her fingers into his hair she pulled her willing body up to meet his mouth. That was too much. Giovanni took back control, scooping up the dark luxuriance of her hair and cradling her head as his body moved in liquid accord with hers. As they kissed she felt the slow, sure movement of his hands on her skin. Passing down over her ribcage, he circled her hip, as her murmurs of delight became the birdsong of longing. When he parted the lips of her sex she trembled in urgent anticipation. His caresses were irresistible, encouraging her writhing abandon as he caressed the whole length of her, teasing the nub of her clitoris into swollen arousal as he moved up, circled around and down, never lingering long enough to satisfy her, only heightening the sexual tension that sang through the warm, dark night.

She was the first woman to offer herself to him so simply and so wholeheartedly, he realised. His own arousal bucked against the pressure of her body and he wondered with a hot twist of pleasure how much longer he could resist total temptation.

She was ready: soft, warm and willing to bring him to heights that she was already enjoying beneath his fingertips. Pride and desire surged through him, fighting for supremacy. In a few months' time this woman was going to give him the greatest prize any man could wish for. He had proved that his magnificent body combined libido with potency—and she was the living proof of it. This moment deserved something special.

She released a gasp of protest as he left her, but it was only for a second. His hands were already moving over her body again as she opened her eyes to see what was happening. The darkness had been pushed back a little by the soft glow of dimmed lights. He drank in her naked beauty. Their first couplings had taken place under the dark veil of night. Now there was no hiding from him. She cried out and tried to cover herself with her hands. Then she saw the effect that her body was having on him. She looked up into his face, her eyes full of eloquence.

'I want to see the body that is going to give me my son,' he told her. 'I want to see what brought me such pleasure and fulfilment over those few wonderful hours.'

There was no denying him. Any objections were stroked away beneath his fingers. As he caressed the delicate folds of her femininity all thoughts of embarrassment or shame evaporated. He appreciated each petal before moving deftly up to the heart and soul of her arousal. When he reached the rosebud of her clitoris, it was already beaded with dew. It swelled and blossomed beneath the pressure of his fingertip, making her cry out in helpless need. The sound triggered a primal urge in him. He lowered his head to taste her arousal.

The tip of his tongue teased her into a ferment of excitement. His hands moved upwards in long sweeping strokes, reaching for her breasts. The nipples were hard peaks, irresistible summits for his questing fingers. A similar bittersweet ache of tenderness was inspiring her. Sliding her legs up to encircle him, she felt the soft, dense spring of his hair against her inner thighs. In response, her muscles clenched and she sensed him pushing his body down hard against the bed, holding back his own urgency.

He could feel blood surging through every single vein in his body at once. The desire to enter her would not be denied. Where his tongue eased the path, his finger followed—slowly, carefully, gentling its way into her. She seized him with spasms of excitement, clenching and releasing in a way that raised a fine mist of sweat all over his body. It was incredible, but he forced himself to take things slowly. With infinite enjoyment he let her body set the pace. Each time she relaxed he probed a little deeper, until he could be sure that she could accommodate his towering need.

She called his name, over and over again, begging for release. Her body synchronised itself with his, moving with rhythmic thrusts that would soon draw them both to the peak of satisfaction. She was desperate for him, and him alone, in a way that no other woman had ever been. It delighted him and he could not get enough of it.

He rolled on to his side and let her nestle against him. The urge to sink straight into her was almost overwhelming. Eager for his body, she accepted him with a delight that swept away all restraint. Dipping smoothly into the waves of her passion, he gained release in a way that knew no limits. When he felt her muscles rippling over him in orgasm he unleashed his own body in waves of shuddering climax that wrenched a cry from deep within his soul.

Slowly, slowly, they drifted back to earth together.

'This is better than I ever dreamed it could be,' Katie murmured from within the protective circle of his arms. 'I have so longed for this moment… Oh, Giovanni, I wish I could be as happy as this for ever…'

She smiled into the deepening darkness. Her body and soul had been aching for years and now she knew why. All her life had been leading towards this moment. Loving Giovanni had taken her to a different planet. She moved the palm of her hand idly over her belly, back and forth. There was not a centimetre of her that he had not kissed and loved with a desire that made her head spin just to think about it. Then, as she drifted between sleeping and waking, a new, unknown feeling fluttered beneath her fingers.

'Giovanni! It's the baby!'

'What!' He was half out of bed before she managed to stop him.

'Don't worry—there's nothing wrong—I just felt him kick!'

'Where?' He flicked on a central light. Squinting against its glare, he strode back to the bed. All his concentration was on her naked body, but it was a different passion that consumed him now. 'Let me feel. Show me where he is.'

Katie lay on her back and took his hand, placing it low down on the gentle rise.

Within seconds his face was transformed with a smile. 'My Donatello is a lively little boy and no mistake. He is every inch his father's son.'

'Donatello?' The name catapulted Katie out of her trance. 'Where did *that* come from?'

'My great-uncle saved the Villa Antico and its estate from ruin. He raised me as his son during the frequent times when my father was…indisposed. I promised him on his deathbed that my son would bear his name.'

Katie could hardly argue with that, but she could not let it pass. 'You didn't think to tell me.'

'There was no need.'

She sat up, reaching for the sheet that had fallen unnoticed from his bed an age before. Covering herself up to her chin, she looked at him acutely.

'Does this mean I am to have no say in my son's life at all?'

Giovanni turned an impassive look on her.

'Donatello is first and foremost the Amato heir. Everything must be done to ensure his safety, security and well-being. That is why I act as I do. For example, Dr Vittorio has already booked you into the very best private hospital for your confinement.'

'*What?*'

'You will be moved there one week before the expected date of Donatello's arrival, unless of course there are indications that the transfer should be made sooner—'

'No—stop right there, Giovanni! You might have Donatello's life planned down to the last minute, but you can't do the same to me. I want to have him at home. I won't go into hospital. I *can't*!'

'But you must. It is the safest place for him to be born. How can you dream of bringing my son into the world in a place like the Villa Antico, which is so far from medical help?'

Katie began to panic. Surely no one could force her to do such a thing? Not after what had happened to her on the one and only occasion she had been admitted to hospital in the past. Her mother had abandoned her there. What would she lose this time? Her baby? Giovanni?

'There will be your friend Dr Vittorio on hand, Giovanni. Women have been giving birth for thousands of years without the benefit of hospitals. It's a perfectly natural occurrence. It isn't an illness!'

He was looking at her as though she was mad.

'I have my reasons, but they should not be allowed to trouble you, Katie. This is not a night for memories. It is an occasion to plan for Donatello's future.'

'And I have my own reasons,' Katie announced stubbornly.

He lay down beside her and stared up at the ceiling. *This is not the time or the place for explanations,* he thought. *But if not now, when? And if not here, where?*

The big black cloud threatening to engulf Katie rolled in. It had been hovering around for weeks, but Giovanni's unexpected show of emotion had brought it billowing right over her now like a shroud. In an instant she was seven years old again, held down by nurses and screaming for her mother, who had never come back…

'I can't go into hospital, Giovanni. I can't! Couldn't you just think about the idea of me giving birth at home, in the Villa Antico?' She edged around the subject as though treading on broken glass.

'Certainly not,' he said firmly.

And that was that.

Katie led a strange double life for the rest of the summer. While Giovanni was away at work she supervised a wonderful transformation of the Villa Antico. When he was in residence at the house, she lived according to his timetable. He had cancelled as many foreign engagements as he could, relying instead on conference calls and video links. He would not let Katie travel long distances, but that did not worry her. Work filled her days, and one or other of the limousines was always on hand for any short expeditions she might want to make. On the rare occasions Giovanni was not at his desk, he supervised her exercises in the pool or they caught up on their respective paperwork beneath the bowers of roses and vines on the pool terrace.

Before meeting Giovanni, Katie had been afraid that a close relationship would rob her of her independence. Marriage to an irresistible man, coupled with the seething hormones of pregnancy soon taught her a different lesson. Giovanni was accustomed to dabbling with intimacy, as and when he chose. Once Katie sailed away from the choppy waters of morning sickness, she could indulge her newly discovered passion. Giovanni was delighted. He was always ready to sweep her up to heaven, whenever she wanted. Things should have been perfect, and in a way they were. Katie had all the luxury she could handle. She was married to the world's best-looking billionaire and living in a house that was being refurbished to her exact designs. Her mother and father had declared a truce, although there was a cottage waiting for Mr Carter on the Antico estate, ready for when the inevitable happened.

Money was no longer a worry for Katie and she had the joy of making love to Giovanni.

But there lay the problem. She knew deep down it wasn't love—it was just sex. Bed with Giovanni was mind-blowing and brilliant every time, but Katie always felt something was missing. It was a long time before she could pin down her last remaining need. Then one day, between her daily aromatherapy massage and her weekly shopping trip to Florence, she realised she would swap all the money and status and luxury for one simple thing.

More than all her other blessings put together, Katie wanted to be *loved*.

CHAPTER ELEVEN

As the year shrank away, Katie's baby grew. She watched Nonna Bacchari and her crew deal with the chestnut harvest, their old hands impervious to all the sea anemone spines. There was a bumper yield of grapes. Later, olives came in by the truckload. It was proving to be a fruitful year for the Antico estate.

And then, in late November, winter arrived. It was carried on alpine gales and they found every chink in clothing and houses. Little Donatello was the only one guaranteed never to feel it. Christmas came and Giovanni invited Katie's parents over for a month. Katie's mother complained about the cold, the isolation and the fact that she had to walk all the way through her dressing room to get to her marble *en suite* bathroom. The Carters returned to England after a single week. Katie could not help a sigh of relief.

The New Year roared in on a north-east wind. Glad of indoor work, the builders made good progress on the Villa Antico. With the nursery finished, they began stripping out the suite containing Lia's things.

'Are you quite sure of this, Giovanni?' Katie asked him a few weeks later over breakfast. The two dresses she'd borrowed had long ago been returned to their closets. They would now be auctioned along with everything else in the room, in aid of Giovanni's charity. It gave Katie a pang, but she had started discovering her own style rather than relying on Eduardo's secret supply of luxury. Besides, she never wanted to risk Giovanni recognising another gown again. 'You really do want to get rid of all Lia's clothes?'

'I have never been more certain of anything in my life.' He toyed with the silver spoon beside his coffee cup. 'And now, as my Contessa, Katie, you cannot possibly be expected to continue sleeping in the guest wing.'

At this, a tiny flicker of hope flared in Katie's heart.

'That is lovely, Giovanni. It will be a privilege to move into such a beautiful suite.' Her new rooms connected with his, but all she really wanted was the pleasure of sleeping with him every night, of being able to reach out and touch him whenever she wanted to…

'There isn't much urgency about that, of course. You will need time after Donatello's birth to regain your strength. I have discussed the matter with Dr Vittorio. Even if all goes well, it would be better to wait a few months before you conceive again.'

'We haven't had *this* baby yet!' She laughed, then realised that Giovanni was in deadly earnest.

'We won't be taking any chances.' His expression killed all the hopes she might have had of a happy-ever-after. 'Donatello cannot be an only child. That was part of my father's problem—he was never easy in his mind, knowing that all the family's hopes of succession rested on my survival. We will have to provide the house of Amato with at least one more son.'

He made them sound like machines for reproduction. In their short married life Katie had seen his mask of efficiency slip only once—when he had told her about Lia. All those years spent in offices full of job descriptions and timesheets had taken their toll on him. Katie put her hand to her stomach. At that moment Donatello gave a little wriggle and she felt her heart break all over again. This poor baby knew nothing about agendas or time-and-motion. She had a horrifying vision of Donatello's future. The fact that Giovanni had not bothered to tell her what was planned for the child growing inside her showed Katie where she came in the Amato pecking order. Right down at the bottom. She had no function here, other than to provide him with sons.

'And what if your next child happens to be a daughter?'

He motioned for another cappuccino. Stefano poured it out as his master gave a careless shrug. 'Then we will try again.'

Katie dropped her knife. Pushing back her plate with one hand and her chair with the other, she stood up.

'No. No, Giovanni, that cannot possibly be right.'

The butler rushed forward. 'Then shall I fetch you something else, Contessa?'

'No. My breakfast was fine, Stefano, thank you. It is my life that is all wrong.' Giovanni cleared his throat meaningfully. Katie did not care. 'Thank you again, Stefano. I think we can manage now.'

The butler bowed and reversed out of the room.

'Try not to lose your temper in front of the staff, Katie, it upsets them.' Giovanni took a sip of coffee.

'It needed to be said.'

'I don't see why. What is it about this life of yours that displeases you?' Giovanni looked genuinely puzzled. 'I provide you with the best of everything. All your plans for the villa are in place—now you have nothing to do but nourish my son and secure his future. By the way—I rang your consultant to request a viewing of the suite that has been set aside for you at the hospital. A visit in advance is bound to make you feel happier about going there for the birth.'

Katie's insides contracted with fear. A strangled cry escaped from her lips and she pushed her plate away. 'There you go again—forcing everything to fit your master plan. I can't even have my baby here at home, where I feel safe. You're going to have me bundled off, banished to hospital, where I can serve your purpose with no thought for my feelings at all!'

Throwing her chair aside, she stormed towards the door.

'Katie!' he called out but she did not stop.

'Come back.'

Katie took no notice. All he wanted to do was tie her down—to make her go into hospital—a place where only bad things happened. Her mother had not been there for her, and Giovanni would abandon her once he had his son, too.

She rushed out into the hall, reaching the front door and wrenching it open before anyone could do it for her. Her tears were burning fiercely, but now they froze in a blast of cold air.

Snow driven straight from the Apennines piled up in fluffy clouds of meringue against the north face of the villa. The staff had cleared a neat pathway out of the building, but it could not contain Katie's headlong dash. She blundered out on to the front doorstep, heading for the pure, clean snow of the forecourt. She wanted to stamp it, mark it, ruin its clean innocence in the same way her life had been trampled and spoiled by Giovanni Amato. In her blind rage she did not notice that freezing rain had glazed the snow with a surface as slippery as glass. Suddenly she was falling. Twisting to try and save herself, she crashed down heavily on to the hard, frozen gravel. There she lay, winded.

It was hard to catch her breath, accompanied by the sound of panicking staff and running footsteps. She began dragging herself up, her first thoughts for the baby. Then she sank down on to her knees. Just as Giovanni arrived to take control of the situation, a pain lodged itself in her spine.

'Stefano! Eduardo! One of you must ring for Dr Vittorio—quickly.' He stepped out of the villa and bent to help her to her feet.

'There's no need. It's just my back. The baby is fine. He's OK.' Katie pulled herself out of his grasp and tried to scramble up unaided. Her head was ringing and there was such an ache where she had wrenched herself.

'But how are *you*?'

She looked at him sharply. There was real concern in his eyes and it echoed through his voice.

'I'm fine, too.' Katie smiled, although she had a cold, terrifying feeling that she might not be. Something about the pain refused to die but, if she told him, he would send her away to hospital.

'Then we can manage by ourselves now. Thanks, everybody.' Giovanni nodded to the staff members who had followed them outside. 'Go and ask one of the girls to make sure the Contessa's room is ready, would you?'

Giovanni and Katie were left alone outside the great old house. She looked up at the north face of the villa. From here, it still looked bleak and bare, but inside she had transformed it into a home. This was the place where she wanted her baby to be born.

'You need not bother yourself on my account, Giovanni.'

'That was a nasty fall. I shall not be happy until you have been examined properly.'

She looked into his face and was shocked out of her anger. For once, she could believe him. His eyes had softened to dove-grey and were questioning her silently.

'I was trying to get away,' she said, shamefaced.

'There was no need, Katie.'

'There was every need. Giovanni, you dictate my every waking moment. You're going to take my son away and feed him into some hellish system that turns out aristocrats to order and, worst of all, you are going to make me go into hospital.'

Giovanni hesitated. He could see that her anger was a front. More than anything else, she was frightened. His mind still reeling from the effect of seeing her crumpled in the snow like a broken flower, he was taking some time to come to terms with his feelings. Seeing her reduced to this affected him deeply.

This entire situation was his fault. At the start, his body had wanted her too desperately to avoid those first fateful misunderstandings. Later, his mind had taken over, keen to salvage something from the situation. Their marriage of convenience had been the logical outcome. Now, when he least expected it, his heart was taking control.

'There are two good reasons why I must insist on a hospital confinement, Katie. You and Donatello.' He watched her face. She looked as shocked as he felt at his sudden compassion.

'People die there.'

'People sometimes die because they cannot get there in time.' He put his arm around her. She responded to his cautious gesture by leaning against him, gingerly at first, but then with more conviction. It felt good. He smoothed her hair. 'You will see when we visit next week—there is nothing to be afraid of. It will be the best place.'

'Not for me,' she said miserably. A tear dripped onto the snow, then another, harsh shards on his conscience. 'My mother took me there to have my tonsils out and while I was away she left home. It was an excuse to walk out of my life until I could be of some use to her. What am I going to lose this time? My baby?' *And you,* she added with a silent cry of yearning. *Although how can I lose you when I have never really had you?*

'Dr Vittorio is out on a call, Signor.' Eduardo appeared at the front door. 'He should be here within the hour.'

'Good. Then I will take the Contessa to her room. We are not to be disturbed under any circumstances, Eduardo, until the doctor arrives.'

He lifted Katie into his arms and started towards the house. 'There is something I must tell you, Katie,' he murmured as he made his way carefully up the stairs. 'I'm sorry, but it will not be an easy confession for me to make. Or for you to hear…'

CHAPTER TWELVE

SHE had to be told the truth, and it had to come from him. Giovanni took a deep breath and then another, but they reached her suite and still he had not managed to say anything. Then, because he sensed that she was about to start questioning his silence, he laid out his private nightmare as they reached her bedroom.

'Katie, the fact is that I killed my first wife It was my fault Lia died.'

He felt her body go rigid beneath his hands.

'You don't mean that.'

'How I wish I didn't,' he muttered, laying her gently down on the bed.

'But…how?' There was a nervous suspicion in her beautiful eyes and her voice could barely rise above a whisper. Giovanni could feel waves of apprehension flowing from her. There was no going back now. She would have to hear the whole sad story.

'Lia left me, only returning when she discovered I had made her pregnant. She lived a frivolous lifestyle and she didn't want the responsibility that came with being a contessa. Yet, when she realised that producing an Amato heir would provide better benefits, Lia decided to stick with the devil she knew. The problem was, she never looked after herself. She was too interested in fashion to put on enough weight. Her diet consisted mainly of probiotic drinks and cereal bars. Nothing the doctor or I could say would persuade her to eat properly. Lia and I were living in a flat at the top of the Amato building at the time. She wanted to be close to the shops and I was so overwhelmed with work it was easier to live at the office. Lia's parents didn't think it was a grand enough place to welcome our child. They wanted the baby to be born in their palazzo. My father was no help. He sided with them. He was in residence here at the time. The Villa Antico was the best place for him, away from all the temptations of town.'

His shoulders had been drooping, centimetre by centimetre. Katie watched, biting her lip. She said nothing, because there was nothing to say.

'In the end, I became so sick and tired of all the arguments I let them all get on with it. Everything was taken out of my hands. A team of specialist nursery designers flew in from California. They produced a suite at the palazzo that outshone anything in the glossy magazines. Lia had her portrait painted. The baby's name was put down for public school. A flock of Norland Nannies was ready to take care of him from the moment he was born. The only thing missing was a sense of reality.'

'And common sense, by the sound of it,' Katie said quietly.

Giovanni raked a hand through his hair—a movement of frustration and anguish. Katie put tentative fingers on his shoulder. He looked back at her. Now she understood the reason for the torment that clouded those grey eyes.

'I should have stood my ground and insisted that Lia's safety and the life of my child were the only things that mattered. My pride did not allow it. When complications set in, she was stranded at her parents' house, out in the middle of nowhere. Lia was never strong. She did not survive the journey to hospital—which was delayed because her parents could not decide whether she should be transported in a *public* ambulance,' he finished bitterly.

'And your baby was stillborn?' Katie asked gently.

It was a long time before he replied. The old wounds were obviously as raw as ever and he was looking straight into them. 'He could never have survived in that condition…' He sighed. 'The doctors told me that these things happen, but we all knew it was because Lia did not eat enough of the right food or look after herself properly.'

Katie vowed from that instant never to complain again about the way he policed her meals.

'That is why I must beg you to reconsider, Katie. I cannot bear to think of the same thing happening again.' He took both her hands in his, enclosing them in warmth. His voice became more urgent, speeding up as though time was running out for them both. 'Over the past few months something has changed between us—but I didn't allow myself to admit it until a moment ago. I have been totally blind. When I saw you looking so helpless and afraid just now I realised I had driven you too far. I can't lose you now, Katie, because the truth is that I—' He stopped. Words deserted him, and for long moments all he could do was look at her. Eventually, when he had not managed to say the one thing that would change everything between them for ever, he had to think of something to switch the focus back on to her.

'Why didn't you tell me about your fear of hospitals?' He levelled a serious gaze at her.

'I—I thought it might go away…and then—and then I realised that you had less reason than my mother did to be there for me… Once you had Donatello, you would both be out of the door and I would lose you…' She ran out of words, too. All she could do was stare at him, willing him to hurry up and say something more. Her pain had started to advance and she was beginning to feel very strange.

'I have been doing some thinking, too, Katie. Our marriage should not be like this. I admit responsibility for my own actions, but it must be said my father was not an ideal role model. All his life he loved unwisely, and too often. I have been so determined not to repeat his mistakes, I may have gone too far in the opposite direction. Yes, I need an heir. It is such a powerful desire within me that I almost lost sight of the blessing that was already within my reach…Katie, what is it?'

'N-nothing. Just one of those practice contractions you're always telling me to expect…' Her words ended with a groan. She curled forward, trying to make the pain small. It did not work.

Giovanni's arm tightened around her shoulders.

'Don't worry. It will be fine.'

He slid into control mode. Encircling her with one arm, he reached over to the bedside telephone. As he was ringing for help, Katie creased again. Abandoning the call, Giovanni laid her back against the pillows. He started telling her that help was on its way, but she could no longer register anything beyond the pain that would not let her go.

It went on and on. People came in and out of her room, bringing linen and newspapers and reports that Security had just admitted the doctor's car. Nonna Bacchari brought ice for her lips. Life whirled around her, but for Katie it was reduced to the circle of Giovanni's arms.

'Oh…Giovanni…this wasn't supposed to happen. I've done something terrible to Donatello, and you don't even love me…' she managed weakly.

He held her close to him, feeling that at last he could pour the words into her. 'Work and the past have stopped me admitting it to myself until now, Katie, but I *do* love you. Now I realise how wrong I have been, not revealing how I truly felt. Please forgive me, Katie… Let me love you. Let me keep you safe here, for ever…'

The doctor burst in on a ripple of cold air. Once his examination was complete, he took Giovanni aside. Katie was left in the care of Nonna Bacchari. The old lady sponged her face and gave her more ice to suck.

'Oh, but it is such a shame you will not be able to get to the hospital.' Nonna shook her head and sniffed in disappointment. 'You should not have to give birth at home. I thought my generation would be the last to have their kids like this.'

'What about all your grandchildren and great-grandchildren? Wouldn't you prefer them to be born on Antico land?' Katie was struggling to keep awake between pains, and wondered if this was a bad sign.

'No, no, no!' The old woman cackled with laughter. 'This is the twenty-first century, Contessa. Hospitals are palaces of leisure today. Everything is to hand, there is no washing up…any woman who has the chance of going there seizes it with both hands. It is the only place we can get any rest. Ah, but then things are different for you. We are here to do everything for our Contessa.'

Nonna stopped laughing so abruptly that Katie knew something was seriously wrong. She opened her eyes as Giovanni slipped his arms around her again. His expression was so tortured that in an instant Katie knew her own agony and fear no longer mattered. She would make any sacrifice now, just to stop his pain.

'I—I've changed my mind, Giovanni,' she said quickly

before he could get a word in. 'This feels as if it's going to be a lot tougher than I thought. I—I should really like to go to hospital, please,' she finished with a gasp.

'After what happened to you there the last time? After all you have said?'

She nodded. At that moment the look of total relief on Giovanni's face was worth everything to her. Going into hospital would be unbearable, but it would ease his torture and she had to think of little Donatello, too. He was being catapulted into life early, and kilometres away from any specialist help. Her future meant nothing, if anything happened to him.

'Are you sure, Katie?' Giovanni asked softly, but they both knew it was only a formality.

She nodded. 'You wanted Lia to go to hospital and she wouldn't, and you have been blaming yourself ever since. You aren't going to lose a second son, Giovanni. I won't let it happen. You *must* take me to hospital.'

He was silent until the next contraction rushed between them. Her grip tightened on his hand like a tourniquet. Covering her fingers with his own, he hung on. 'Don't worry, Katie. I am *never* going to run out on you. You won't have to suffer anything alone, ever again. I shall be here for you, every minute of every day.'

'Of course you will,' she said flatly, as another shot of pain smashed her into fragments. Giovanni gathered her up, pressing his face against hers as she gasped and tried to catch her breath.

'Believe it,' he murmured. 'Believe me, Katie. I will not leave you. I love you. I need you.'

The terror ebbed away. Katie came to her senses and realised she had been crushing his hand again. Releasing her death grip, she watched the blood flow back into his whitened fingers. It saved her having to look him in the face as she spoke again.

'I understand. And now—all that matters is Donatello. And you.' She put out a hand to touch his face. Then the pain rose up again like an instrument of torture. It dragged her back, crushing her like a rag doll. When it passed she took a long time to gather her strength again.

'Listen to me,' she whispered quickly, afraid that the pain might silence her forever next time. 'What happened before— it is not going to happen again. Donatello is well fed and strong. He takes after you. He will be all right.'

Giovanni bent down to rest his brow against hers. 'But what about you?'

His forehead felt ice-cold. She realised it must be because her own was burning-hot. She tried to smile. Giovanni could not even pretend to do the same. She was so pale that even her lips were losing their colour. Instinctively he reached out and grabbed her hand again. It was cold and grey. He brought it to his lips and kissed her fingers. The bitter taste of salt lingered.

'I can't bear to think of you going through the same thing all over again.' She tried to moisten her lips with her tongue, but now Nonna had taken the ice cubes away it was too much of an effort. 'Perhaps…perhaps we could make a start for the hospital?'

'I shall ring for an ambulance.' Dr Vittorio was fumbling for his mobile, but Giovanni was already on his feet and heading for the doorway to summon help.

'Eduardo! Go and tell the men to get the helicopter ready— right now. I shall fly you myself,' he called back to Katie before he was engulfed by a hubbub of preparations.

'Dr Vittorio?' Katie's voice rose weakly from the bed.

'Yes, Contessa?' He leaned close to catch her voice.

'Giovanni is under a lot of pressure.' She tried a smile, hoping that he would return it. 'Make sure he does not fly as fast as he drives, would you?'

Giovanni carried Katie out to the helicopter. Placing her gently inside, he could hardly bear to let her go, but time was slipping away. He kissed her longingly and then hauled himself into the pilot's seat.

'I want to go on holding you, my love, to keep some contact with you, but I need both hands. I have to concentrate on the controls. It's the weather—'

Sleet was driving horizontally into the windscreen.

'It doesn't matter, Giovanni. Talk to me. I shall hold on to your voice.'

'You're going to be all right,' he said, concentrating on the switches and blinking lights of the display before him.

'Yes—as long as you are more careful in the air than you are on the roads.' Katie managed another smile for Dr Vittorio, who was crouched beside her. He did not return it.

'If we are going to reach the hospital, we should leave immediately, Giovanni.'

Katie shut her eyes. The doctor must mean the weather was closing in.

Giovanni was not so sure.

Staying conscious was becoming more and more of a struggle. The pain was a rolling wave now. It dragged Katie back and forth in a cold dark sea, sometimes allowing her to come up for a gasp of air but more often submerging her in its depths. Suddenly her face was spattered with real drops of water. The air she was almost too weak to breathe was forced into her lungs by a tremendous down-draught. There was noise—

clatter, confusion and rattling as she was jostled and jolted out of the helicopter and onto a stretcher. She tried to open her eyes, but it was raining hard. And there were too many voices—loud, angry sounds…

'There. Didn't I say I would never leave you?' Giovanni was speaking quickly into her ear. 'I shall be with you for every second of the time. Don't leave me, Katie. I love you too much.'

'And I love you, too.' She tried to put her fingers out to touch the face she could no longer see. As she did so her hand was grabbed and stabbed, but there was no time to ask why. Everything—the cold, the pain—was already beginning to ebb away. Katie sighed. She did not care. The only thing that mattered was one voice and those three words.

'I love you!'

He said it again. He was saying it to her. The last thing Katie remembered before it all slid away was: *He means it. He really wants me. I am going to get over this, if it kills me…*

Things got very confusing after that. Katie drifted in and out of consciousness. There was so much noise—electronic pulses and alarms, the clatter of steel on steel, the sound of people moving about. They all hovered around the edge of her awareness, but nothing matched Giovanni's warm reassurances.

Whatever the medical team was doing continued in near silence. Then a waterfall of gurgling snuffles formed itself into a wail so tiny that it was drowned by congratulations. Giovanni was kissing her and saying all over again how much he loved her. Katie heaved a huge sigh of relief. Everything was going to be all right for Giovanni this time. He had his little Donatello, safe and sound. Her job was done.

She could let go and sleep.

* * *

Some time later, Dr Vittorio spotted Giovanni out in one of the hospital's floodlit quadrangles. He was leaning back against a wall, eyes closed, his face raised to the fine freezing drizzle. The doctor pushed open a door and called out from the warm security of the corridor. 'Giovanni? What on earth are you doing out there? You should be inside.'

'I came out for a few seconds to use my mobile while Katie was asleep. Everyone must be given the news.'

'I hope you aren't thinking of flying yourself home tonight?'

He shook his head. Pulling out his phone, he tapped in the villa's private number. 'I won't be parted from Katie now. I am going to ask Eduardo to arrange some transport home for you, Doctor. I was too distracted to think of it earlier.' He gave an exhausted sigh.

'Look, I'm sorry, Giovanni. Mistakes happen, but—' Vittorio looked away and clicked his tongue.

'I'm not bothered about all that now.' Giovanni's attention snapped back to more pressing matters as his call was answered.

'Eduardo? Yes, yes, I shall tell you everything in a moment, but right now I need you to bring my car…'

The first time Katie woke, it was still dark. A bird was singing not far away. She moved her head. The curtains of her room were closed, but harsh electric light was poking in through a gap. It must be either very early in the morning or late in the afternoon. Gradually, she came to realise that nothing was hurting any more. Revelling in the memory of Donatello's little cry, she relished the absence of pain for a minute. Then in the darkness she began trying things out—wiggling her toes, putting an experimental hand on her tummy…

Her small movements alerted the nurse on duty in her room. The woman rustled forward with a smile.

'Shall I call your husband? He is only just downstairs, with your daughter.'

Katie frowned. This must be a case of mistaken identity. 'My daughter? No, that can't be right—Giovanni has a son, Donatello. Where is he?'

'There, there.' The nurse expertly silenced Katie with a thermometer under her tongue. 'It's nothing to worry about, dear. Baby swallowed a bit of fluid, so they want to give her a thorough examination. Your husband was torn between staying with you and going with her, but I told him to go. You were supposed to sleep for hours yet,' she finished briskly, checking Katie's temperature and marking it on a chart.

Too weak to argue, Katie settled back into her pillows and closed her eyes. The nurse must have mixed her up with some other mother. Giovanni Amato had his son and heir, so nothing else should matter.

But something mattered very much. Her new family was nowhere to be seen. Aching with sadness, Katie came to a terrible conclusion. Everything was running true to form, after all. The aristocratic machine had absorbed her little Donatello. His proud father was probably already supervising the re-gilding of his family tree, back at the Villa Antico.

As Katie slipped into sleep again, her lashes thickened with tears.

'I told you we would be back before the Contessa woke,' Matron sang out, waking her.

Katie opened her eyes and gasped as Giovanni entered her room. He was drilling one of his killer looks into the nurses who accompanied him. A small white bundle was cradled in his arms.

'You should know better than to hand a baby over as though it is nothing more than a caterpillar in a cocoon, Matron,' he was saying. 'This is *my* child, after all!' He scowled as all the staff fluttered away.

Carrying the baby as though it was an unexploded bomb, Giovanni lowered himself carefully on to the chair beside Katie's bed.

'What *do* they think I pay them for?' he said in disgust.

Katie's voice cut quietly through his indignation. 'I thought you had gone.'

His beautiful eyes still contained all the power he had used to rally her during those long dark hours. She gazed back, breathless with the realisation that she had been wrong. He had not deserted her. His promises had all been true. It hadn't been a dream.

'I told you I would never leave you, and an Amato always keeps his word,' he said with quiet conviction. 'Now, Katie, we have things to do. We must choose a name.' He settled the little bundle in her arms and pulled a small book from the pocket of his jacket. Katie was too busy staring down in wonder at their new arrival to notice in detail what he was doing. The baby was so tiny, with perfect little features set in a face not much larger than a clementine. Only a little over nine months ago she had fallen for Giovanni so completely she had felt her heart would never have room for anyone else. Now she knew differently.

She looked up into the face of the only man she would ever love, as though waking from a dream.

'You chose Donatello and that is fine by me since you want to honour your great-uncle. Once you had explained the reason for your choice, I understood.'

He laughed and it was so natural and unforced that Katie reached out and touched him in delight.

'Giovanni, you are the last person in the world I would have imagined with stubble, designer or otherwise.'

He put up a hand to cover hers, pressing it to his cheek. 'And whose fault is that? It feels as though I have not been home for days.'

'Oh, I know the feeling,' Katie sighed.

Her eyes were drawn back to the little bundle in her arms. It was wrapped tightly in a white shawl. With nervous fingers, she pulled back a fold. A tiny mottled fist protested against the touch of fresh air. Catching hold of the identity tag attached to the baby's wrist, she read it out loud.

'"Baby Amato. Weight 2.41 kilograms. Female." Oh, my goodness—Giovanni?'

She looked at the baby even more carefully. Now she came to think about it, that tiny face certainly looked very feminine. Baby Amato had a mouth like a rosebud and the dark lashes fringing her tightly closed eyes were even longer than her father's.

Looking up, Katie gazed at him with growing wonder.

'You needed a boy so badly, but she's a girl. And yet you are still here?'

'I shall have that sonographer shot at dawn,' he said, laughing softly. 'Oh, Katie—how many times do I have to I promise I will never leave you?'

'Please keep saying it. I can't hear it enough. You have been saying a lot of other things, too.' She smiled at him, almost shyly. 'I seem to remember something about…love?'

He could not tear his gaze away from his wife and their new arrival. 'Throughout my entire adult life, Katie, I have told only one woman that I love her. And that is you, Signora Katie Amato.' Putting aside the book he leaned over and kissed her tenderly. The moment was only broken when the baby between them began to stir. Katie smiled dreamily into Giovanni's mist-grey eyes. He was looking at her with a new honesty and it was gentle. All her fantasies about a future in Giovanni's arms, surrounded by flocks of his children, swam back into her mind.

'Do you think,' she said carelessly, as she began investigating their precious bundle, 'that you might also consider saying it to a *Luisa* Amato, for example?'

He tried it out for himself a few times, then nodded. 'Luisa. Yes, I think that would be perfect for our beautiful baby. Who is almost as beautiful as you,' he finished in a murmur as he kissed her again.

THE ITALIAN'S
UNWILLING WIFE

BY
KATHRYN ROSS

Dear Reader,

The Italian's Unwilling Wife is my thirty-fourth novel for Mills & Boon. I got the idea for this story when I was horse-riding on a beach in St Lucia. It was such a beautiful setting, and my imagination took over. I conjured up a heroine who lived alone there with her secret baby, and an Italian hero who had ruthlessly pursued her to find his child.

My hero Damon is a passionate man. He wants his son to be brought up with all the traditions that he holds dear, and he also wants the heroine back—but this time on his terms. So he sweeps both away to his home on the warm shores of Sicily, where he is planning a wedding.

I invite you to that wedding now, and hope you enjoy their story.

Love,

Kathryn

Kathryn Ross was born in Zambia, where her parents happened to live at that time. Educated in Ireland and England, she now lives in a village near Blackpool, Lancashire. Kathryn is a professional beauty therapist, but writing is her first love. As a child she wrote adventure stories, and at thirteen was editor of her school magazine. Happily, ten writing years later, *Designed with Love* was accepted by Mills & Boon. A romantic Sagittarian, she loves travelling to exotic locations.

PROLOGUE

REVENGE was an ugly word. Damon Cyrenci preferred to think of his actions in more clinical terms. He had seen a business opportunity and had taken it.

The fact that he'd had his eye on the Newland Company for a while, and that this takeover gave him a greater sense of personal satisfaction than any other, was irrelevant. What was important was that John Newland's days of trampling his opponents into dust were almost at an end.

As his chauffeured limousine travelled along the Strip, Damon watched the sun setting in a pink glow over the Las Vegas skyline. This was the city where his father had lost everything. It was also the city where Damon had made the mistake of allowing a woman to get under his skin. It seemed fitting that it should be the place where he would put everything right, get back what he wanted.

They passed the MGM Grand, Caesar's Palace, New York New York and, as the pink of the sky turned to the darkness of night, the desert lit up with fiercely glittering light.

The limousine pulled up outside the impressive façade of the Newland building, and Damon allowed himself to savour the moment. His target was almost achieved. In a few moments he would meet John Newland face to face, and have him exactly where he wanted him.

For a second his thoughts drifted back to the last time they had met. How different that meeting had been.

Two and a half years ago it was John who had held the balance of power. He had faced Damon across a boardroom table and had calmly refused his request for a stay of execution on his father's business.

One week—that was all Damon had needed in order to release valuable assets that were in his name and save everything. But Newland had been coldly adamant. 'I am not a charity, Cyrenci; I'm in the business of making money. Your father must honour his commitments immediately and hand over the title deeds to all of his properties. However…' He'd paused for a moment's reflection. 'Your family home in Sicily is listed as one of the company's assets. I might allow you to keep that—on one condition.'

'And what's that?' Damon had asked coolly.

'You walk away from my daughter and never see her again.'

Damon could remember his incredulity and the hot fury in his stomach as he had looked across at the man. Somehow he had remained calm and impassive. 'I am not going to do that.'

And that was when John Newland had laughed at him. 'Abbie really fooled you, didn't she? Let me enlighten you, Cyrenci. My daughter has been brought up with a certain standard of living. She enjoys a luxurious lifestyle—a lifestyle you can't match now the family business has gone. I assure you, she won't be interested in you now.'

'That's a risk I'll take,' Damon had told him smoothly.

'Your choice.' John Newland had shrugged. 'But you lose all ways round. Abbie only dated you in the first place as a favour to me. I needed you out of my hair, and she was the perfect distraction. You think your weekend away together in Palm Springs was a wild impulse?'

John had asked the question scornfully and had shaken his head. 'It was planned—all set up by me. Abbie knew I needed some time to finish my business with your father, and she was happy to help me—but then, just as long as the money is flowing, Abbie will be there. Believe me, she won't hang around you now the game is over and your money is gone.'

The chauffeur opened up the passenger door for Damon, letting in the intense heat of the desert night, a heat almost as intense as the anger he had felt back then. It hadn't been hard to discover that for once John Newland was telling the truth. Abbie had known what her father had been up to, and had in fact assisted him.

Just like her father, she was nothing but a cold-blooded, money-grabbing trickster.

Snapping out of his reverie, Damon stepped out of the limousine.

It had been a lesson hard learnt. But Damon had picked himself up and with strong determination he had seen to it that their fortunes had been reversed.

Briskly he walked up the red-carpeted steps into the cool of the air-conditioned foyer. The entrance to the Newland hotel and casino was palatial; gold-leafed ceilings and stained-glass windows gave it the air of a cathedral, and only the rolling sound of nearby slot machines revealed the truth.

With just a cursory nod to the hotel staff, he headed for the lifts. He knew his way to the boardroom and he strode with confidence towards the door he wanted. This was the moment he had been waiting for.

John Newland was sitting alone at the far end of the long polished table. The lighting in the room was dimmed, his face in shadow. Behind him the picture windows gave a panoramic view of Vegas, glittering like a mirror-ball in the night. But Damon wasn't interested in the view.

'I believe you are expecting me.' He closed the door quietly behind him.

There was silence.

Damon advanced until he could see his nemesis clearly: grey-haired, thickset with glittering hooded eyes. The last time they had met, the man's features had been alight with triumphant disdain. Today, however, his expression was carefully schooled, but Damon could see the signs of strain in the pallor of his skin and the tight way he held his mouth.

It was hard to believe that this was Abigail's father. For a second a picture of her drifted into Damon's mind.

He remembered the day he had met her. She had been swimming here in the hotel pool, and he had watched as she'd pulled herself out. Water had dripped in silver beads over her toned skin. He remembered the sensational curves of her body in the scanty bikini, the perfection of her features, the wide blue eyes, the softness of her lips.

How he had wanted her.

The sudden memory of how badly he had wanted her made heat rise inside him.

'You're early, Cyrenci. The board isn't due to meet for another half an hour.'

John Newland's terse words focussed Damon's thoughts back to where they should be. He would have time to concentrate on Abbie later.

'We both know that the board meeting is just a formality, Newland.' Damon put his briefcase down on the table and opened it. 'You are on your way out.'

John Newland blanched. 'Look—Damon—we've had our differences in the past. But I hope we can put all that behind us and perhaps come to some mutually acceptable deal.' The brusque tone was gone now, replaced by pure desperation. 'I've spoken to a few members of the board—'

'It's over,' Damon said coolly. 'I think you would be advised to just accept that.'

'But you could help me if you wanted to.'

Was the man serious? Damon looked at him with incredulity. 'Why would I do that? To quote something you said to me years ago, John: I'm a businessman, not a charity.'

'I have a few bargaining chips left.' The man shrugged.

'Such as?' Damon was barely listening. He was taking papers out of his case and his eyes were running down a list of the company's assets—assets that now belonged to him. He knew John Newland held no aces, because they were all right here in his hand.

'Well—I recall you once wanted my daughter…'

The words trailed away as Damon fixed him with a cool, penetrating stare. He could hardly believe what he was hearing.

'In fact, you wanted her so badly you were willing to give up your family home for her,' John reminded him tentatively.

'We all make mistakes.' Damon's voice was icy.

'She had her twenty-first birthday last week, and I assure you she is even more beautiful now than she was,' John Newland continued swiftly. 'And her mother was Lady Annabel Redford, you know. Abbie has some influential connections in England that could open doors to a businessman like you.'

'I'm not interested.'

'I think you should be. And if I were to have a word with her…'

'Still at Daddy's bidding, is she?' Damon remarked scathingly.

'I have influence.'

'You have nothing.' Damon put his list of the company assets down on the table in front of the man.

'That's her, isn't it—the property that's marked a few lines underneath my old family home in Sicily?' Damon pointed to a line almost at the bottom of the page. 'Redford Stables, St Lucia.'

John Newland made no reply, just stared down at the list.

'Do you think Abbie will be happy to assist you, John, when she finds out her luxurious lifestyle and her home are lost as part of the company's assets?'

Still the man made no reply, but he started to drum his fingers with agitation against the table.

'No, I didn't think so. As we both know, Abbie's loyalty is to the highest bidder. So I don't believe you or indeed your daughter are in any position to negotiate,' Damon continued smoothly. 'But rest assured I will be looking over my new property with close attention to detail. In fact, I'm heading out to St Lucia tomorrow. Have you any message you would like me to pass on to your daughter?'

There was a moment's considered silence before John looked up. 'No, but I have one for your son—tell him his granddad says hello.'

John Newland watched the shock hit Damon Cyrenci and felt a gleam of satisfaction.

CHAPTER ONE

It was hurricane season in St Lucia and the warnings had gone out. 'Michael' was a category three, but was gathering pace at sea and heading for shore. The weathermen were predicating a direct hit sometime within the next twenty-four hours.

But for now the sun was setting in a perfect blaze of glory over the lush rainforests, and not a breath of air rustled the tall palms that encircled the stables.

Abbie, however, was not taken in by the deceptive calm. She had experienced the full force of a hurricane the previous year; it had taken the roof off her house and almost decimated the stables. It had taken a long time to put everything right, and financially she was still reeling from the disaster. She couldn't afford another direct hit.

So she had spent the afternoon trying to prepare. She had nailed down everything she could, and long after most of her hired help had gone home for the day she was still moving heavy equipment into the storerooms.

'Abbie, your father has been on the phone for you again,' Jess called across to her as she came out of the house. 'He's left another message on the answer machine.'

'OK, thanks.' Abbie brushed her blonde hair distractedly back from her face. She had nothing to say to her father, and she wasn't interested in his messages, but she couldn't help but wonder why he had started ringing her again.

Putting the last of her work tools away, she headed up to the veranda. Mario was in Jess's arms, and as he saw his mother walk towards them his eyes lit with excitement and he held out his arms to her.

With a smile, Abbie reached to take her baby. He snuggled in against her and she kissed him, breathing in the clean scent of his skin. Mario was twenty-one months now, and adorable. He was the one thing in Abbie's life that made everything worthwhile.

'Do you want to get off now, Jess? You've got a date tonight, haven't you?' she asked as she cuddled the child.

'Yes. If you are sure you can manage, that would be a great help.'

'Absolutely. You go and have a good time.'

For a moment Abbie stood and watched as the young woman strolled towards her four-wheel drive. At eighteen, Jess was the youngest member of her staff, and also the hardest working. Not only was she a qualified child-minder and a superb horse-woman but she helped out a lot around the stables. Sometimes Abbie wondered how she would manage without her.

She waved to Jess as she reversed and pulled away down the long driveway.

Darkness was closing in now. The stables were on a lonely track leading down to a deserted cove. Her nearest neighbours were miles away, and very few cars passed this way. Usually Abbie didn't mind being on her own; she enjoyed the solitude. But for once as Jess's car disappeared she was acutely conscious of her isolation.

It was probably the approaching storm that was making her feel so on edge, she told herself as she went back into the house. Plus all these phone calls from her father.

As she stepped inside, her eyes were immediately drawn towards the phone, where a flashing light proclaimed there were now ten messages.

Whatever her father wanted, she wasn't interested. She would put Mario to bed and delete the calls later, she told herself as she headed for the stairs.

The child went down into his cot easily. Abbie set the musical mobile playing above his head and watched over him until he fell asleep. Then, leaving the night light on, she crept from the nursery to her bedroom across the corridor to shower and change.

Abbie had just put on her silk dressing-gown and was about to go back downstairs to make herself a drink when the phone in her room rang again, and the answer machine clicked on.

'Abbie, where the hell are you?' Her father's irate tones seemed to fill the house. *'Have you received any of my messages? This is important.'*

It was strange how just hearing his voice made her nervous. She supposed it was all those years of conditioning—of being afraid to ignore his commands.

Wrapping her dressing gown more closely around her body, she reminded herself fiercely that her father no longer had a hold over her—he couldn't hurt her any more.

'Do you hear me, Abigail?'

He probably wanted to summon her back to Vegas to host one of his parties. She shuddered at the thought. She'd escaped from that life over two years ago—she would have thought he'd got the message by now. His bullying blackmail tactics no longer worked. She wasn't going back.

She was on her way across her bedroom to switch off the machine when she heard him mention a name—a name that made her freeze and the world start to zone out as darkness threatened to engulf her. *Damon Cyrenci.*

For so long she had tried to block that name out of her mind, pretend he had never existed. And the only way she had been able to do that was by filling her every waking hour and making herself so bone-tired that personal thoughts were a luxury. But, even so, sometimes in the silence of the night he would come to her as she slept and she would see his darkly handsome face again. Would imagine his hands touching her, his lips crushing against hers, and she would wake with tears on her cheeks.

'I've lost everything, Abigail—everything—to Damon Cyrenci, and that includes the stables because they are part of the company's assets.'

Through the turmoil of her thoughts, Abbie tried to concentrate on what her father was saying. The stables were hers, weren't they?

'And he's on his way out there now to look over his property.'

The words hit her like a hurricane at force five. Damon was on his way here! Her heart raced—her body felt weak. Damon—the love of her life, the father of her child, the one man she had given herself to completely. The memories that went along with all those facts twisted inside her like a serpent intent on squeezing her very soul. And along with the memories there was a fierce longing—a longing that had never really gone away, a longing that she had just learnt to live with.

She sat down on the bed behind her; it was either sit down or fall down. *Damon was coming here.* It was all she could focus on.

What would he look like now, what would he say to her? Would he still be angry with her? What would he say when he discovered he had a child?

Had he forgiven her? The wrench of yearning that idea brought with it was immense.

As the phone connection died, she buried her head in her hands.

She remembered the day she had first met Damon. She remembered that the blistering heat of the midday sun had come nowhere near matching the heat he had stirred within her. She remembered shading her eyes to look up at him as she'd climbed out of the pool. He was tall—well over six-foot-four and he had been wearing a lightweight suit that had sat perfectly on his athletic build.

'You must be Abbie Newland?' he had said quietly, and the attractive accent had added fuel to a fire that had quietly and instantly started to blaze inside her.

He was ten years older than Abbie, Sicilian, with thick dark hair and searing, intense dark eyes, and to say he was good-looking would be an understatement of vast proportions. He was quite simply gorgeous.

'I'm Damon Cyrenci. Your father said I would find you here.'

The disappointment inside Abbie was almost as intense as her attraction for him. Because this was the man her father had ordered her to date. The command had infuriated her, but she wasn't at liberty to refuse; her plan had been to snub him, then just walk away. Then she could honestly tell her father that he hadn't invited her out. But, as soon as her eyes met with the handsome Sicilian, her body didn't want to comply with that idea at all.

'Do you want to join me for a drink?' He nodded over towards a bar that was cocooned in the tropical shade of the gardens.

'Maybe just for ten minutes,' she found herself saying. 'I haven't got much time.'

'Why, what else have you got to do?' The question had been asked with a glint of humour, and it had been apparent right from the outset that he had judged her as little more than a social butterfly.

She didn't really blame him. To the outside world, that was probably exactly how her life appeared, but the remark still smarted. She wanted to tell him that appearances could be deceptive, that she was in fact trapped within her gilded cage, forced to dance attendance on a father whose every whim was her command. But of course she didn't—he wouldn't have been interested and anyway, if word got back to her father that she had said anything, the consequences would have been dire.

So somehow she just forced herself to shrug. 'Let's see. I'm the rich, spoilt daughter of a millionaire—what else could I be doing this afternoon?' She slanted him a sardonic look. 'Apart from lying in the sun, shopping and visiting the beauty salon, you mean?'

He smiled, unapologetic. 'Must be a tough life.'

'It is. But someone has to do it.' Although she tried to sound flippant, something of her annoyance or distress must have shown in her eyes, because suddenly his tone softened.

'Shall we start again?' he asked, and held out his hand. 'I'm Damon Cyrenci, and I'm in town to negotiate the sale of a chain of restaurants owned by my father.'

She looked at the hand he held out, and she hesitated a moment before taking it. What exactly was her father up to? she had wondered. What harm would following his orders do?

Then her eyes met with Damon Cyrenci's and she told herself that, no matter what her father was up to, this man was more than capable of looking out for himself.

'Abigail Newland.' The net was cast as she placed her hand in his. She liked the touch of his skin against hers, liked the feeling in the pit of her stomach when he smiled.

She remembered having dinner with him that night. She remembered him kissing her, a searing, intensely passionate kiss that had made her long for so much more.

She had dated him for five short weeks, but with each meeting her feelings for him had intensified. Her hands curled into tight fists just thinking about the way he'd made her feel. But because of the situation she had always forced herself to pull back.

Damon hadn't been used to a woman pulling away from him, and somehow it had made him all the more determined to pursue her.

Yes, the net had been cast—but she had been the one caught in its fine weave, because somewhere along the way in those few short weeks she had fallen in love with Damon Cyrenci.

The phone rang again, interrupting Abbie's thoughts, and she listened as once more the answer machine cut in.

'Abbie, please pick up the phone.'

Abbie just sat numbly, listening. She hadn't spoken to her father since her mother's death just over two years ago. And, no matter what was at stake, she still couldn't speak to him now.

'This is about revenge, Abigail—and you are next on Cyrenci's list. He knows what you did—knows you were perfectly complicit in his father's destruction.' Her father's voice was abrasive. *'But luckily I'm still thinking for both of us. I told him about Mario. He was shocked and angry, I could see it in his face. But the child gives us a bargaining chip—it means he doesn't hold all of the aces.'*

Abbie felt sick inside. She hated her father—hated the sordid, horrible way he even thought.

The line went dead again. Abbie didn't know how long she just sat there after that. Her father stopped phoning, but the silence of the house seemed to swirl around her with his words.

Then she heard the distant sound of a car engine.

He's on his way out there now to look over his property…

Certainly, whoever was in that car was heading for this house—there was nowhere else out here.

CHAPTER TWO

THE shrill ring of the doorbell cut through her. And for a few moments she was immobilised.

Was Damon really outside her door? There had been moments when she had dreamed of this, dreamed that he'd come to her when he found out about his child, and that he would forgive her.

But they were just dreams. She was sensible enough to realise that the reality was encapsulated in her father's phone messages.

Damon wasn't going to forgive her—she'd known that at their last meeting, when he had angrily confronted her about what she had done, and she had tried desperately to explain her actions. He hadn't wanted to listen; all he'd been able to think about was the fact that she had assisted in his father's downfall. Even when she had falteringly tried to tell him that she was as much a victim as his father he had cut across her contemptuously.

'You must consider me really naïve if you think I'm going to fall for any more of your lies. I know what you are. I have evidence to support exactly what a lying, conniving, deceitful—'

'Damon, please!' She had broken across him tremulously.

'Please believe me, I never wanted any of this to happen. The time I spent with you was special to me, and I—'

'Give the acting a rest, Abbie.' The scorn in his voice had cut through her like a sword. 'At least the one good thing about this whole sorry mess is the fact that, as far as I was concerned, our time together was all about sex—I felt nothing for you, other than the pleasure of taking your body. Nothing at all.'

There had been a harsh coldness in his words and in his eyes that she had never seen before. It was as if a mask had been ripped away at that moment and she had seen the true Damon for the first time. It had shocked her to the core, and it had hurt. God help her, it still hurt!

But it also made her very sure that if it was Damon outside he wasn't here for any sentimental reasons, and he certainly wouldn't be interested in the fact that she'd had his child.

The shrill ring of the doorbell sliced through the night again, and Abbie tried to focus on what she should do. There were a few heartbeats of silence whilst whoever it was gave her a moment to come to the door. When she didn't, he put his finger on the bell again and held it there.

It had to be Damon! If there was one thing she should have remembered about him, it was his determination to get what he wanted.

He was going to wake Mario up! Her son was a deep sleeper, but he had his limits.

Suddenly anger surged to Abbie's rescue. She wasn't going to hide up here, feeling guilty about the past, because the truth was that it hadn't been her fault. She had been forced to do what she did. And nobody had a right to roll up here and make such a racket at this time of night.

Drawing her dressing gown closely around her slender figure, she marched downstairs, and, taking a deep breath, she threw open the door.

Damon Cyrenci was standing on her porch, leaning against the door jamb with his finger on the bell. Even though she had been expecting to see him it was still a shock.

He stepped back as the door opened, and silence reigned.

For a second his eyes swept over her with audacious scrutiny, taking in everything about her from her bare feet to the wild tumble of blonde curls around her shoulders.

And the strange thing was that for a moment Abbie was transported back to their first meeting, when he had looked at her in exactly the same way. She felt a tug of sexual attraction rising from somewhere very deep inside her. His appearance had hardly altered. The business suit he wore emphasised his fabulously well-honed physique, and the dark thickness of his hair was unchanged. Maybe there were a few silver strands at the temples, but they just made him appear all the more distinguished.

As her eyes held with the dark, searing intensity of his, her heart lurched crazily. He was the same drop-dead-gorgeous man who had stolen her heart away—except that man had only ever been an illusion, she reminded herself fiercely. Despite the heat of the passion they had once shared, she had never meant anything to him. Behind the façade the real Damon had just been a seducer—a predator who'd enjoyed the thrill of the chase and nothing more.

Falling in love with him had been a mistake, and she had learnt her lesson.

The memory helped her to pull herself together and focus her senses.

'Hello, Abigail. It's been a long time.'

His voice was coolly sardonic, and yet the attractive accent still managed to lash against the fragility of her defences.

'What are you doing here, Damon?' Somehow she managed to sound calm and controlled.

'Is that all you can say after all this time?' Again there was the same mocking tone to his question. 'How about "nice to see you, Damon—why don't you come in?"'

The strange thing was that one part of her—the wild, illogical part—wanted to say those words, but his manner forbade it. Something in the cool tone and the glint of his eye told her very clearly that although he was here on her doorstep nothing had changed from their last meeting, and his opinion of her was as low as you could get.

'I haven't got time for games, Damon,' she grated unevenly.

'Really? Strange how you had plenty of time for games in the past.'

Her father's words reverberated through her consciousness. *This is about revenge, Abigail—and you are next on Cyrenci's list.* She swallowed hard and slanted her chin up. 'Obviously this isn't an impromptu social call, so just say whatever it is you've come to say, Damon, and then go. You'll forgive me if I don't invite you in.'

'No—I don't think I will forgive you, Abbie.'

Although he said the words matter-of-factly, there was an undercurrent that struck her and hurt—and that in turn made her angry. Why should he still have the power to hurt her like that? She tightened her hold on the door. 'Well, you are not coming in.'

He shook his head. 'I really don't think you are being very friendly, and I'm sure given the circumstances you can do better than that—in fact, your father assured me that you could.'

What had her father been saying to him? 'I don't know what's been going on between you and my father. I believe you now control the Newland empire—well…' she shrugged '…I don't care. It has nothing to do with me.'

'That's where you are wrong, Abbie. This has everything to do with you.'

The chill certainty in his voice flayed her.

'I just want you to go now.' To Abbie's distress, her voice faltered slightly.

'I'm not going anywhere.'

'Well, you are certainly not coming inside my house.' She started to try and close the door but she didn't move quickly enough, and he put his foot in the way, effectively stopping her.

'Let me spell things out for you a little more clearly.' His voice was suddenly very serious. 'We have unfinished business, and I'm coming in whether you like it or not.'

'Damon, it's late and you're scaring me.'

'Good.' He sounded cold and unyielding.

'I'll have to ring the police if you don't go now,' she threatened shakily.

'By all means, you do that.' For a second his eyes narrowed. 'At least that way we can speed things up.'

'Speed what things up?'

'The legal side of things.' He watched impassively as the colour drained from her face. 'As you have so rightly pointed out, I'm in control of the Newland assets now. And according to company records no rent has been paid on this place for— oh, quite some time.'

'That's because the place belongs to me!' she hissed furiously.

Damon shook his head. 'No, it belongs to me,' he corrected her quietly. 'And I'm here to take stock of my belongings.'

'Well, then, you'd better contact me through my solicitor.'

Damon smiled at that. 'Oh, don't worry, I will be doing that. Because I also want access to my son.'

The words dropped into the silence like a bombshell, and Abbie's limbs suddenly felt as if they didn't belong to her.

'So are we going to do things the easy way or the hard way?' he enquired silkily. 'It's up to you.'

She couldn't answer him. Her hands dropped from the door, and as she momentarily lost her hold on the situation he took his opportunity and walked past her into the house.

His eyes swept over the lounge area, taking in the brown leather sofas, the polished wood floors and the huge stone fireplace. The place was very stylish, but it wasn't what he had been expecting. The furniture, when you looked closely, was old, and everything had a slight air of faded opulence. But Damon wasn't interested in décor; he was searching for telltale signs of something that interested him far more. He found what he was looking for as his eyes lighted on a box of toys by the far end of the sofa, and a discarded teddy bear on a chair. At the sight of those toys his insides knotted with a fierce anger.

'So, where is he?'

As he rounded towards her again, Abbie sensed a seething fury that made her truly afraid. She could hardly think straight for a moment, never mind answer him.

'Where is my son, Abbie? You may as well tell me now, because I will find him even if I have to go through every room in this house—or every house on this island.'

The determination in those words stunned her, but they also brought an inner answering strength welling up inside her. 'You keep away from him, Damon. He is not a belonging listed under the company assets. He is a little person in his own right, and I won't have you marching in here upsetting him.'

'And what about his right to have a father—or doesn't that count in your twisted logic?'

The question smote Abbie's heart. It was something she had asked herself time and time again—something that had kept her awake long into the lonely nights when she had discovered she was pregnant. Yes, she wanted Mario to have a father—a loving father who would put his needs first. But

Damon had left before she'd realised she was pregnant, and she hadn't known where he had gone. She'd tried to track him down, but to no avail. She had consoled herself with the fact that he wouldn't have been interested in his child anyway. Damon didn't go in for commitment, he led a playboy lifestyle. He'd told her that when they'd first met.

But the strange thing was that when he'd held her in his arms she had imagined that his feelings for her were different, that what they had shared had meant something. But of course she had been fooling herself. That had been quite clear when he'd walked away from her.

The memory hurt so much that she wanted to tell Damon that the little boy upstairs was not his, and that he had a father in his life—a wonderful, loving father, a man who also loved her. She opened her mouth but the words refused to come.

When it came right down to it, she couldn't lie about something as important as that.

'Of course having a father counts,' she said shakily instead.

'Right—which, of course, is why you came to me and told me you were pregnant?' Damon's tone was scathing.

'And if I had would you have wanted to stay around and play happy families? I don't think so. We had had a few weeks together of wild sex—it meant nothing.' Even as she said the words, the memories that flared inside her made her hot, made her voice tremble with suppressed feeling. 'You said as much yourself—you said…' She shook her head and pulled herself together before the tears could gather in her voice. 'Anyway, all that is in the past and irrelevant. The truth is that I didn't find out I was pregnant until after you'd gone. I didn't know how to get in with you. You hadn't left your address or contact numbers. I didn't know where you were.'

'You are good at making excuses.' Damon shook his head. 'No, Abbie, you didn't tell me because your father held the purse strings and you thought I had nothing. That was a more important consideration for you at the time.'

'That's not true!'

'Like hell it's not. You forget, Abbie, that I know you exactly for what you are.' Damon's eyes raked contemptuously over her, but as they did so he couldn't help noticing the sensational curves of her figure beneath the silk of the dressing gown. How come her beauty could still blow his mind? he wondered hazily. How come when he looked at her now after all this time he could still remember exactly how she had felt when he touched her—how she had tasted, how she had moved beneath him?

Back then she had been firm and pert and he had wanted her like crazy—but he could excuse that because he hadn't known the truth about her then.

How come he could feel the same stirrings now?

'We're wasting time,' he grated, furious with himself for being sidetracked even momentarily like this. 'And I've already wasted enough of that.'

To Abbie's horror Damon started to head towards the stairs with a look of determination.

'You can't go up there.' She hurried to stand in his path, tried to grab hold of his arm, but he brushed her away as if she were an annoying fly and swept past her.

'Damon, you have no right!' Her voice caught on a sob as she raced after him, but he didn't break his stride.

'Actually, as the child's father, I think you will find I have lots of rights.'

The words brought a strange kind of helplessness washing over Abbie. It was the same feeling she used to get when dealing with her father. It was the knowledge that someone more powerful than you could dictate your life, and there wasn't anything you could do about it, because if you didn't comply the consequences would be more than you could bear.

She watched as he pushed doors open along the landing into deserted bedrooms.

'Stop it!' The anguished whisper made him halt in his tracks to look back at her.

'Don't bother to try and turn on the false tears, Abbie, because it's not going to work,' he told her acerbically. 'I don't care how you feel—in fact I couldn't give that—' he clicked his fingers softly '—for your emotions.'

'I know,' she said softly. 'I've always known that.'

Something about the way she said those words caught at him, and for a brief second he felt a tug of some long-forgotten emotion as he looked into the blue depths of her eyes. He remembered the first night that they had made love. He remembered the vulnerable way she had looked up at him as she'd allowed him to unfasten the buttons of her dress, almost as if she'd been afraid to trust her emotions to him.

The memory infuriated him. Abbie Newland was an actress—there had been nothing remotely vulnerable about her. She had been playing the part her father had set for her, and she had done it very well, and had enjoyed a little fun along the way.

His dark eyes hardened at the memory. 'Well, at least we understand each other.'

'Yes, at least there's that,' she whispered numbly. 'But you should also understand that my child is more important to me than anything and if you upset him in any way I will make you pay for it.'

She tried to draw herself up as she said the words. It was probably a bit like facing down a lion without any real weapons, but she wanted him to know that she would fight to the death if necessary for her child.

'Just because I don't care about your feelings doesn't mean I don't care about him.'

The answer should have reassured her slightly, but it just stung at raw nerves. Still she held his gaze with determination. 'He's in the room at the far end of the corridor,' she said quietly. 'Let me go into the room first, just in case he's awake. You are a stranger to him. I don't want you scaring him.'

Damon considered her words for a second, and then stepped back to allow her to lead the way.

Her whole body felt as if it were shivering with reaction as she walked past him. She guessed she was in shock.

Why did Damon want to see his son? She couldn't believe it was out of any paternal interest. Those sentiments didn't fit with the man she knew him to be. Maybe this was just curiosity. Maybe he would take one look at his child, make a token pretence of being interested, before getting back into his car to get on with the real things in life that mattered to him, such as revenge and money and power... And, of course, womanizing.

Yes, that was probably what would happen, she told herself as she opened the door to Mario's room.

She was relieved to see that the child was still sleeping. He was lying on his back, his face turned sideways against the pillow. He looked the perfect picture of peaceful innocence, his cherub mouth slightly parted, his long dark lashes resting against the satin-smooth skin.

She glanced back at Damon. 'You can come in, but only for five minutes.'

'I think your days of being in charge of this situation are over, Abbie,' he said quietly as he stepped past her.

The words hit Abbie like a punch to the solar plexus. But the feeling was nothing compared to the reaction she felt, witnessing the powerful intensity on Damon's features as he looked down at his sleeping child.

She felt her heart racing against her chest as the realization hit her that this was about far more than just idle curiosity, and to try and dismiss what was happening in such a way would be to vastly underestimate the situation.

For a long moment Damon just looked at his son. Then abruptly he turned and left the room.

For a second Abbie couldn't move. Her mind was reeling with confusion—she couldn't get a handle on this situation at all. What were Damon's intentions? Why was he really here? Hastily Abbie followed him back out onto the landing.

He was already at the other end of the corridor. 'So, now you've seen him,' she said breathlessly. 'Where do we go from here?'

He made no reply; he didn't even look around at her, just headed down the stairs. The front door was still lying wide open, and he marched through it without closing it behind him.

'Damon, where do we go from here?' she asked again, a note of desperation in her voice. She needed to make some sense of tonight, needed to understand what Damon was thinking—and she couldn't let him walk away without giving her some clue as to what was to happen next.

'Damon?' She followed him downstairs and out onto the porch. 'Damon, *please*!'

His footsteps slowed and then he looked around. 'That's better.' There was a gleam in his eyes as he looked over at her. 'If you keep that tone in your voice, we just might get somewhere.'

The cold churning in the pit of her stomach intensified.

'I agree that we need to talk rationally about this situation.'

He made no reply, and she thought he was going to climb into his car and drive away, but then to her surprise he went to the back of the vehicle and took out a small bag.

With the flick of a switch the car was locked again, and then he was heading back towards her with resolute strides.

Although there was a part of her that was glad he wasn't just going to drive away, leaving her wondering what was going to happen next, she didn't like the look of this latest development at all. Her heart thumped nervously against her ribs. 'Where do you think you are going with that bag?'

'I'm bringing it inside my house,' he said curtly. 'And then I'm going to have a drink and get into bed, because it has been a very long day and I'm tired.'

'You can't stay here!'

'Why not?'

'Because…I don't want you here.'

He stepped past her and into the house. 'Tough.'

The door slammed closed behind him.

CHAPTER THREE

FOR one horrible moment she thought he was going to turn the key in the lock, leaving her stranded outside in the dark in her dressing gown. But to her relief the door opened easily as she turned the handle.

With a mixture of trepidation and fury, she glanced around. His bag was at the base of the stairs and she could hear him opening and closing cupboard doors in the kitchen.

She followed the sounds and watched from the doorway as he found a bottle of vodka and poured himself a drink. 'What are you playing at?'

'I think I just told you.' He lifted the glass in a mocking salute.

With difficulty she reined in her temper. This situation was not going to be resolved by losing her cool.

'Damon, you can't stay here. It's not appropriate.'

He laughed at that. 'As if you'd know anything about appropriate behaviour! I have to say, all those years mixing with the aristocracy at those English boarding schools weren't wasted, were they? You've certainly learnt the art of pretending to be genteel.'

With difficulty she ignored the insult. 'This isn't solving anything. Why don't you go and check into a hotel for tonight and then come back tomorrow? We can talk properly when we have both calmed down and are thinking rationally.'

'I am calm.' He took a sip of his drink and regarded her levelly over the rim of the crystal glass. 'And I'm thinking very rationally. It's one in the morning, there's a storm coming in, and I have no intention of going to a hotel now—especially as I own a perfectly good house here.'

'Damon this is ridiculous!' Her voice rose in panic. 'You are not being at all reasonable.'

One dark eyebrow rose. 'Really? I think given the circumstances I'm being extremely reasonable. Let's look at the facts, shall we? You don't actually own this property. In fact, you are heavily in debt and behind with rent—'

'I am no such thing!'

'Plus you've hidden my child away from me, depriving me of precious time with him,' Damon continued as if she hadn't spoken. 'I don't think any court is going to look too kindly on you at all. In fact, I think you will be the one who is judged unreasonable.'

'You're twisting the facts!' She pushed a distraught hand through her blonde hair. 'I didn't know I was pregnant until after you'd gone. I didn't hide anything. And will you stop pretending that you give a damn about having a child? We both know that you would still have walked away from him even if I'd told you I was pregnant.'

'Do we?' Damon's voice grated with sarcasm. 'You don't know the first thing about what I would have done, because you don't really know the first thing about me.'

'I know that you are a playboy who likes to roam the pleasure fields.'

'Certainly.' He inclined his head. 'And I never planned on having children of my own. But you've changed that.'

Damon looked at her pointedly. 'Enlighten me, Abbie.

What were you planning on telling my son when he gets older? That his father is dead? Or that his father didn't want to know him?'

Abbie hesitated. 'I wouldn't have lied to him. I'd have handled it.'

'Believe me, no matter how you handled it, it still wouldn't have been right.' Damon's voice was heavy. He remembered all too well what it was like growing up without a parent. His mother had walked out of the family home when he was eight. It was so easy to screw up a child's life. Maybe that was why he had avoided settling down and having children. The responsibility was awesome, and he believed implacably that a child deserved two parents and a stable home.

'You had no right to keep Mario a secret from me.' Damon's eyes burnt into hers. 'Any court will tell you that.'

'He wasn't a secret. And will you stop talking about courts and judgements!'

He shrugged and took another sip of his drink. 'Courts and judgements are very much the reality; you better get used to it.'

'Why are you being like this?' The question sprang from her lips with anguish.

'Like what?'

'So…brutal…as if you want to punish me.'

He looked at her then, and gave a short, mirthless laugh. 'Why do you think?'

The sardonic question tore at her. 'My father was right— this is all about revenge, isn't it?' She made herself say the words, her voice trembling with emotion.

He took another sip of his drink, and then threw the remaining contents of the glass down the sink.

'You're angry about what my father did, and I understand that.' Abbie tried very hard to remain calm. 'And I'm sorry for my part in it. But as I tried to explain long ago, it wasn't my fault I—'

'Of course not. But then shallow, spoilt socialites like you don't believe in taking responsibility for your actions, do you? You think you can do what you want, and sorry is just a word.' His voice grated with sarcasm. 'But let me assure you that angry is a bit of an understatement for how I'm feeling right now.'

Abbie glared at him furiously. 'I am none of the things you have accused me of being.'

'And Father Christmas really does slide down chimneys on Christmas Eve.'

The scorn in his voice made Abbie's temper soar. But, as much as she would have loved him to know the truth about the past, she knew she could never tell him about her mother now. She had tried to explain her actions to him at their last meeting. She had braved the contempt in his eyes, and had haltingly started to open up to him, only to have him laugh scornfully in her face and cut her off. She couldn't go through that again. The pain of trying to tell him something so raw, so deeply personal, was beyond endurance. And why should she put herself through that when it was clear his opinion of her hadn't changed? He thought she was a liar, and he wouldn't listen to any explanation—wouldn't believe her, anyway. It all hurt far too much.

Some things were best left in the past, she told herself firmly. What mattered now was her child's welfare.

That fact made her swallow her fury and keep her cool. 'So you want to punish me,' she forced herself to continue. 'I can handle that. But going to a court to get access to a child you don't want—that isn't going to make this right. Please don't take this out on Mario.'

'How do you know I don't want him? You're making sweeping assumptions.' Damon's voice was cool. 'What did you think was going to happen when your father told me I had a child? Did you think I'd just throw money at you and disappear? If that's what you want, then you are dreaming. Because, believe it or not, I'm thinking about what is best for my son now. Something you seem incapable of.'

'I have always put my son first,' Abbie told him fiercely. 'And I don't want anything from you.'

He fixed her with a look that told her in no uncertain terms that he didn't believe her.

She swept an unsteady hand through her hair. Obviously he was never going to believe that she was anything other than a scheming witch. 'So what are you going to do?' she asked quietly. 'What do you consider *best* for Mario?'

Damon didn't answer her immediately. He appeared to be thinking about his options. Abbie could feel her nerves twisting and stretching. Was he deliberately trying to torment her? Was this part of his revenge? Maybe she should be flinging herself on his mercy instead of being confrontational.

But on the other hand maybe that was what he wanted. Her father used to enjoy controlling her through fear. When she'd tried to rebel, he'd reminded her of what he could do, and she would be yanked quickly back into line.

The memory made her angle her chin up defiantly to meet Damon's cool gaze. She had sworn that no one would ever have that power over her again. 'If you go for custody, I'll fight you every step of the way.'

'That's your prerogative.' He shook his head. 'I admire your spirit—but of course I will break it.'

He watched the bright glitter of fury in her eyes. She was so very beautiful—more so than she had been at eighteen; her father had been right about that. The thought stole, unwelcome, into his mind and he found his gaze drifting down once more over her body. He could see the firm curves of her breasts through the thin silk of the gown, and because the bright lights of the lounge were behind her he could also see the long, shapely outline of her legs.

She had always been attractive, but she had matured into a stunningly desirable package. Pity about her cold, mercenary heart, he thought dryly.

Abbie noticed the way he looked at her—noticed, and bizarrely felt her body throb, as if his eyes were actually touching her. She tried to ignore the feeling, tried to pretend it wasn't happening. How could she feel like this when her mind was racing with fear—when she hated him? 'Maybe you just have rage issues that need to be readdressed, Damon,' she said evenly.

He laughed. 'Maybe you are right.' He put his glass down on the draining board with a thud.

'So what are you going to do?'

'Right now, I'm going to bed,' he said calmly.

'You can't!'

'Why not?'

'Because you can't make statements like that and just leave things! I need to know what your intentions are regarding Mario. You are not really thinking of fighting me for custody, are you?'

Damon stared at her for a moment. When John Newland had told him he was a father, he had been shocked—then he had been furious. All kinds of emotions had been racing through him ever since. Some of the feelings had come as a complete surprise to him—such as the feeling of protectiveness when he had looked down at his sleeping child.

Yes, he'd decided a long time ago that he wasn't going to settle down and have children. But the fact was he had a child, and abandoning him wasn't an option. He couldn't walk away from that responsibility; he strongly believed in doing the right thing.

But what *was* the right thing in this situation? His eyes flicked over towards Abbie, and for a second he found himself thinking about her father's words to him in the boardroom.

Abbie could be of use to him.

The words sizzled provocatively through his consciousness. Abruptly he tried to dismiss them. 'I'll sleep on the problem, and we'll discuss terms in the morning,' he grated tersely.

He was so arrogant! So infuriating! She watched as he walked past her towards the lounge.

'I don't want to discuss terms in the morning. I want to discuss terms now! And it may have escaped your notice but there are no spare beds in the house. All the rooms you looked into tonight are empty. The only other bed in the house is mine.'

He turned slowly and looked at her. 'Is that an invitation?'

He watched the flare of heat under the creaminess of her skin with detachment.

'You know it's not.'

'Do I?' He shrugged. 'Nothing you would stoop to would surprise me. In fact, when I faced your father in the boardroom at Newland he made me a very bizarre offer.'

'What kind of an offer?'

'The deal was that I help him retain his place on the board, and in return I get you.'

'What do you mean, you *get* me?' Her voice was stiff.

'Just what I said. In return for my help getting him back on the board of directors, he said he could arrange for you to… Well, accommodate me in whatever way I saw fit, really. I'm not sure if he was selling you as a trophy wife who would have very useful business connections, or the convenient mistress there to entertain me in bed, plus play hostess when required—

that kind of thing. Of course, the second option caught my interest more at first. As you know, I'm not the settling-down type. But then, I didn't know I had a child at that point.'

He watched the colour flooding back into her cheeks. 'Don't worry, I turned him down. My motto has always been to cut out the middleman. Dealing direct is a much more satisfactory solution, don't you think?'

'What I think is that you are just as vile as my father.' Her voice trembled alarmingly. Just when she thought her father couldn't get any lower in her estimation, he sank to new depths. She felt degraded and humiliated by him—soiled by association.

'Dear me, have you had a fall-out with darling Daddy?' Damon walked back towards her and reached out to trail a finger down over the smoothness of her skin. 'What's the matter, are you annoyed because he can't bankroll you anymore?'

She flinched at the touch of his hand. She didn't know what hurt more, her father's disgusting business proposition or Damon's glib acceptance that she would be in any way amenable towards it!

His eyes held with her glittering gaze. 'Never mind. Although I've cut your father out of the equation, I'm still weighing all the possibilities up, I assure you. Trophy wife versus convenient mistress...' He shrugged. 'Or should I just take custody of Mario and walk away... The choices are endless.'

'You wouldn't get custody of Mario,' Abbie told him heatedly. 'And I wouldn't marry you if you were...if you were the last man left on the planet and lived in a gold-plated palace.' She angled her head up proudly.

Damon laughed at that. 'Oh, but we both know that you would.'

'You always did have an inflated opinion of yourself.'

'I just know how Ms Abigail Newland's gold-digging mind works.'

'You know nothing about me. I would rather die than go along with the idea.'

Damon smiled 'You didn't pass away with righteous indignation when you got involved with your father's deals last time.'

He watched her lips part noiselessly, watched the shadows flicker across the beauty of her eyes. 'That was different.'

Damon shook his head. She was a good actress, he'd give her that. 'You go where the money is—your father told me that about you over two years ago.'

He watched as her hands clenched and unclenched at her sides. She had such slender hands. Everything about her was so feminine; even her rage was simmering, contained—ladylike. Although, he remembered that in bed she hadn't been quite so restrained—not once he'd taught her what he liked and how he liked it.

He wished he could stop thinking about that. But the fact was he couldn't.

From the moment she had opened the front door to him tonight, he'd known that sexually he still wanted her.

He wanted her now. The strength of that need totally infuriated him. How could he feel like this when he knew her for what she was—disliked her, even?

He hated that. But it was a fact, and no matter how he kept telling himself to ignore it he couldn't. So what the hell was he going to do about it?

His eyes moved up over her body slowly, appraisingly. He had no doubt in his mind that she had known about her father's offer to him and had been hoping to play it for all it was worth.

Maybe the best thing to do here was to take control and play her at her own game. The more he thought about that idea, the more he liked it.

'So…' His tone was measured, his mind ticking over his options. 'You want to talk terms? Let's talk terms.'

The way he was looking at her was anything but clinical, yet the tone of his voice was detached, objective. What the hell was running through his mind now? Abbie wondered nervously. She moved her hands to draw her gown more tightly around her body, unaware that the instinctively protective gesture only showed her figure to clearer advantage.

She wanted to tell him to get out, that she wouldn't talk to him after the things he had said to her—the things he had insinuated. But she forced herself to calm down and think about what was important. And that was Mario. 'My terms are that my child stays where he belongs, and that's with me. Let's face it, Damon, you are a businessman who jets off around the world at a moment's notice. You sit in meetings that run on until the small hours. That doesn't fit with looking after a twenty-one-month-old baby. He's a full-time commitment.'

'Yes, he is. And that's the one reason I'm prepared to offer you a good deal.'

'What kind of a good deal?' The words were out before she could consider them, and she instantly regretted them as she saw the way his lips curved in a cool smile.

'You see? The Abigail Newland I know is never far away, is she?' he hissed. His eyes swept over her body again with a hard gleam of male appraisal. 'In a nutshell?' He shrugged. 'I guess your father's idea isn't completely off the wall. I suppose you would be a convenient package. You are the mother of my child and we understand each other. And, I have to admit, the whole idea of having a lady in the lounge and a whore in the bedroom does appeal.'

Fury swept through her at those mocking words. 'Well, maybe you'd better put an advert in the paper, because I sure as hell am not interested.' Her eyes flashed fire at him. 'The thought of you laying one finger on me makes me nauseous.'

She would have marched past him and out of the room at that point, but he caught hold of her arm and pulled her back.

'We both know that's not true.' Although his hand was holding her firmly, the touch of his skin against hers was like an electric shock sending weird little darts through her body, intruding on her rational mind—making her tremble deep-down inside.

He was right—it wasn't true. It was a long time since they had made love, but she remembered how much she had liked it—remembered how blissful it was to lose herself to the masterful dominance of his caresses, his kisses.

Why was she thinking like this? She hated him, she reminded herself fiercely. He had just insulted her beyond belief—hurt her beyond belief. Had she no self-respect?

'Let me go.' Her voice was harsh with reaction.

'You haven't heard the terms of the deal yet.'

'I don't want to hear the terms of the deal. I'm not interested.'

'Of course you are.' Damon smiled, but his eyes were singularly lacking in amusement. 'Your father has lost everything, and that means you have lost the goose that lays the golden eggs—you've even lost this place. But I can make everything better again.'

'All I have to do is prostitute myself to you—is that it?' Her voice was raw.

'Actually, as the mother of my child I'm prepared to offer you a better deal than that.' Damon spoke calmly, but his eyes seemed to bore down through hers. 'All you have to do is come back to Sicily with me and play at being the perfect wife and mother. Of course, you will have to share my bed. But in return I'll keep you in the style and comfort that you are used to.'

Abbie stared at him, her heart thundering against her chest. She just couldn't believe what she was hearing, or the fact that he was saying these things to her in such a clinical and calculating fashion.

'You'll have to sign a prenuptial agreement, of course. But as long as you abide by my terms and stay in the marriage you will have everything you want.'

'That's supposed to be a good deal, is it?' Abbie suddenly found her voice, but she was almost spluttering with rage. 'You really think I'd marry you? You've got a high opinion of yourself, haven't you? I don't even *like* you.'

'It's the best deal you are going to get, Abbie. The prenuptial agreement is non-negotiable.'

The harsh tone took her breath away.

'Your arrogance is incredible. You think I'd tie myself into a loveless marriage for…for—?'

'For wealth, security and all the baubles and trappings of luxury you could possibly want?' Damon cut across her dryly. 'Yes, I do. So let's just cut the pretence, shall we?'

'Yes, let's.' Her voice trembled. 'Because the truth is that even for all the money in the world I wouldn't want to share a house with you, never mind a bed. The very thought leaves me cold.'

Damon laughed.

'What is so funny?' She glared at him.

'You are. We both know that there's nothing cold about you. Maybe we don't like each other very much.' He shrugged. 'But we have a certain thing called chemistry. When I touch you, you come alive. Sex was always good between us.'

'As I said, you are the most conceited, arrogant man I have ever—' She broke off as he started to pull her closer.

'What are you doing?' She tried to wrench away from him, but he wouldn't let her go.

'I'm going to kiss you and prove a point.'

'Don't you dare!' Her eyes blazed up into his.

He smiled at her. 'The sooner you accept the fact that I'm calling the shots now, the easier it's going to be all around.'

'I will accept no such thing!'

Her breathing was coming in short, uneven gasps from anger and from the effort of struggling against him.

'You are just making life difficult for yourself.'

'No, you are making my life difficult! But that's what you want, isn't it?'

'No, Abbie, right now that's not what I want.'

There was something husky about those words, something strangely inviting. His gaze moved to her mouth.

And suddenly, as his head moved lower, she stopped struggling. She wanted him to kiss her. It was as if a tidal wave of desire suddenly hit her out of nowhere, flooding her entire body, pulling her under into very dangerous currents.

His lips touched against hers, gentle at first, and then as they tasted her acquiescence they became hard, demanding and brutal. She found herself kissing him back with equal strength, as if she couldn't get enough of him, as if she were intoxicated by his strength, by his passion.

Then suddenly, as she reached up to touch him, he pulled back from her.

She looked up at him, dazed by what had just happened. His gaze moved from her lips, down to the plunging neckline of her robe.

She noticed the look, and was suddenly very aware of the fact that if he reached out with his other hand he could pull her robe down from her shoulders, leaving her naked to his gaze.

For a shocking moment she wanted him to do that! She wanted him to touch her intimately, wanted to melt in against the powerful contours of his body. The feeling of longing overwhelmed her, rendered her helpless.

His dark eyes returned to hold hers, and there was a gleam of satisfaction there. 'You see, Abbie? You don't need to like me to make this *arrangement* work. All you need is to be your hot-blooded self and, of course, the perfect mother for Mario.'

Shame washed through her in waves. Why the hell had she kissed him back like that? *Why?*

She angled her chin up and forced herself to glare at him defiantly. 'I kissed you.' She shrugged. 'So what? Maybe I just wanted to give you a taste of what you are missing when I walk away from…from your offer.'

'Well, well,' he drawled softly. 'You really are—how is it you English say?—a chip off the old block, aren't you? Trouble is that, like your father, you have very little ground for negotiation. I'm not going to up my offer, Abbie. The prenuptial agreement is non-negotiable. You take what's on the table or you walk away.'

Her lips parted in a gasp as she realised he thought she was trying to make him increase his offer to her.

'You really are insufferable.' She grated the words unevenly, furious that he should make such an assumption. 'I'm not remotely interested in your offer, or in you.'

The sensual line of his mouth curved into a smile as his eyes once more moved down over her body, to where her breasts were straining against the satin material. She knew he could see the hardness of her nipples through the thin material, shamefully giving away the fact that even though his hands hadn't touched her she had been totally aroused.

'But you are interested, Abbie, because power and money are powerful aphrodisiacs for you. You want me more than you can say.'

She shook her head. 'I hate you!'

For one wild moment she thought he was going to pull her back into his arms to prove otherwise.

His lips stretched into even more of a mockingly amused smile. 'Of course you do, and you hate my money even more.'

To her relief, he stepped back from her. 'Well, why don't you run along to that bed of yours? That's if you really do want to go up there on your own.'

She didn't need telling twice; she almost fell over herself in her haste to get away. 'And why don't you get out of my house?'

He ignored that, merely smiled. 'Nice talking terms with you,' he called to her as she moved through the lounge towards the stairs. 'Think about my offer, because I'm only going to leave it open until tomorrow. After that, you will be doing all your negotiating with my lawyer. And, believe me, he won't be nearly as accommodating.'

CHAPTER FOUR

ABBIE lay on top of her bed, staring up at the ceiling. Outside the weather was deteriorating; she could hear the wind starting to whistle around the house with an eerie intensity. Strange how she had been so concerned about that this morning. But now even the threat of a hurricane outside wasn't as disturbing as the presence within.

Why had she kissed him like that? The question kept pounding through her senses along with the memory of his offer.

All she had to do was go back to Sicily with him and play at being the perfect wife and mother.

He could go to hell. She turned over and thumped her pillow. How she had ever once believed that he was a decent human being, she didn't know! And as for imagining that she had been in love with him! Well, she must have been out of her mind.

He'd made no attempt whatsoever to leave the house. A little while ago she had heard his footsteps coming up the stairs, and she had stiffened, her heart thundering against her chest. There was no lock on her bedroom door, and if he'd come in…

But he had merely gone into the bathroom next door, and the next moment she had heard the forceful jet of the shower being turned on.

She wasn't sure what would have happened if he'd come into her room. Yes, she hated him, but something really strange happened to her whenever he touched her. He made her lose control of her emotions so easily, turned her into somebody she didn't even recognise. And it had nothing to do with his damn money! Just what it was about him that affected her like that she didn't know. All she knew was that it scared her.

She heard him come out onto the landing again and she sat up straight, listening intently. But he turned away from her room and she heard him opening the linen cupboard at the top of the stairs.

He was obviously going to sleep on the sofa and was helping himself to some sheets and a pillow, making himself at home. But then the house did belong to him now. Every time she thought about that her anger soared.

The stables had been her refuge from the world, her place to run to. They had belonged to her mother, and it had always been understood that upon her death they were to revert to Abbie.

Obviously her father had got there first, and had taken the deeds as security.

Abigail's hands curled into tight fists as she thought about her father and his latest trick. Offering her to Damon as if she were a piece of property that could be traded! It hurt so much.

She took a deep, shuddering breath and told herself that it wasn't exactly out of character. John Newland excelled at using people.

Her parents' marriage had been a sham. Her father had married her mother because she'd been a member of the aristocracy and it had suited his purposes to play on that fact. As for her mother, although she had been a member of the upper classes she had been practically penniless when she'd met John Newland. Death duties had forced her to the brink of bankruptcy; she had been contemplating selling the house in Surrey that had been in the family for generations, and the riding stables in St Lucia, when John Newland had appeared in her life and offered to rescue her.

Her mother should have known better than to accept his proposal of marriage, but at the time she had believed that she loved him. It hadn't taken long, however, before she'd realised that far from being rescued she had been trapped in a loveless marriage, and her house had been lost, sold off to the highest bidder.

John Newland had been a controlling man, a bully and a womaniser. He had used his wife's connections and her name unashamedly, and at the same time he had despised her weakness in tolerating his behaviour.

As the years had gone by the relationship had deteriorated; even the birth of their only child, Abigail, had not softened John Newland. In fact he had grown worse, parading his women in front of his wife, and heaping scorn on her if she dared to complain.

Abbie had been six and they had been living in America when she'd first witnessed the full extent of her father's rage— a rage that could come upon him from nowhere and for no reason.

She had been packed off to boarding school in England afterwards, but she hadn't forgotten the scene that night.

Why her mother had put up with such a controlling husband for so long, she didn't know. It was Abigail who'd persuaded her to leave. On her sixteenth birthday, she had helped her mum pack a few belongings and had fled with her to St Lucia.

They had told John Newland that they were just having a few days' break to celebrate her birthday, but they hadn't gone back. And from there her mother had filed for divorce.

John Newland's rage had been fierce. Nobody crossed him.

Nobody walked away unless he said they could go. But Abigail had stood firm by her mother, and when her mother had started to get sick she had given up her chance of a university education to help her build up the stables so that they weren't in any way financially reliant on her father.

Things might have worked out. The stables had started to pick up. They had been selling rides to tourists and doing quite well. They might finally have been free of John Newland if her mother's illness hadn't been serious. The type of treatment she had needed hadn't come cheap, and they hadn't been able to afford it.

Nothing short of a life-and-death situation would have forced Abigail to go back cap-in-hand to her father. She had hated doing it, but she'd had no choice.

And of course John Newland had loved it. He had agreed to help his ex-wife by flying her back to the States and making sure she had the best medical help, but as usual the price of his rescue had been high. He'd blamed Abigail for the fact that his wife had ever felt strong enough to leave him, and he had set about making her pay for that betrayal over and over again. He had even threatened to withhold the medical care for her mother if Abbie didn't comply with his wishes.

Abbie had been forced to return to him in Vegas—to dance attendance and play along in his deals.

The worst of which had been the deal with Damon Cyrenci.

When her father had found out that she had fallen in love with Damon he'd seemed to take even greater delight in making sure, when it was all over, that Damon knew she had been complicit in his schemes.

Abbie lay back down against the pillow and stared into the darkness of the bedroom.

To be torn between doing the right thing for a dying parent and the man you thought you loved was a situation she would never forget. It had been pure torture, and of course there had been the guilt that if she walked away her mother might die. The guilt for the fact that Abigail had encouraged her mother to leave her father in the first place and, if she hadn't, John Newland would have paid whatever it had taken to get her better. Money had never been the issue.

So she'd been trapped in a situation that had felt strangely as if it was all her fault. However, when she had sat next to her mother's bedside and tried to say this, her mother wouldn't have it. 'I had more happiness in the few years of freedom we had in St Lucia than in my entire married life,' she had said firmly. 'I'm glad I left him.'

But then her mum hadn't known that behind the scenes Abbie was being torn apart.

At first her dates with Damon were chaste. With difficulty she drew back from his kisses, and deliberately kept him at arm's length, not because she didn't want him but because she wanted him too much and it scared her.

And she was right to be scared. Anything that involved her father always had a dangerous price attached. He'd drop little lines over to her: 'make sure you see Damon tonight,' 'make sure he's not back till late'. At first she did as she was told without question—the consequences of defying her father were too bleak to do otherwise.

But as she fell further under Damon's spell she was torn more and more inside. She desperately wanted their relationship to be untainted by the association with her father and his requests. She tried to reason with her father, but he didn't want to listen—in fact he was angry that she dared to question him. He told her that there was a weekend coming up when he wanted Damon out of town with his mind off business. 'Take him to my ranch in Palm Springs,' he ordered lazily. 'Entertain him until I tell you it is OK to come back.'

She knew her father was trying to pull a shady deal on Damon's father, also that he would only get away with it if Damon wasn't around to spot what he was doing. So for the first time ever she refused a direct command. But with just one cancelled cheque, her father reminded her that it wasn't her life that was held in the balance.

She wanted so much to fling herself on Damon's mercy at that point and tell him what was going on. She knew he would have been horrified, but at least he wouldn't have blamed her.

But then what would happen? She couldn't expect him to foot the bills for her mother.

Nor could she expect him to go away with her to Palm Springs. Maybe he would even confront her father. Either of those things meant her mother would suffer.

So she decided it was safer to say nothing, and she did as her father requested, and invited Damon away for the weekend. But Damon wasn't the walkover that her father was expecting. He was a shrewd operator, and brought in a lawyer to help oversee the dealings with her father.

She remembered Damon casually imparting this information as they sat alone, dining at the ranch. She remembered her relief; she felt as if someone had removed a death sentence from her. Everything would be OK, she told herself reassuringly. Damon hadn't allowed himself to be duped, and her father wasn't going to win this time. That knowledge made going into his arms so much sweeter.

She remembered undressing for Damon, and the strong, sure touch of his hands on her body. She remembered the wild passion that took them over. She remembered lying cradled in his arms afterwards, believing that she was deeply in love with him…

What an idiot! She couldn't believe now that she had been so stupid. Damon had only been interested in sex, not in love.

He'd enjoyed the thrill of the conquest—taking her over and over again. There had been no soft words, no promises.

And, as Damon enjoyed taking her that weekend, her father was busy buying off his lawyer.

Everyone, it seemed, could be used and bought. Everyone had a price. That was what men like her father seemed to thrive on, but she hadn't realised Damon was like that.

She wiped fiercely at some tears that dared to spill down her cheeks.

She had made a mistake falling in love with Damon, but the one good thing to come out of it was Mario. And no matter what it took she wasn't going to let Damon take him away from her. She was going to fight him.

She had been three months pregnant when her mother had died. It had been her lowest ebb. But she had proved then that she was made of strong stuff. She had picked herself up and she had fled back to St Lucia.

With her mother's death her father hadn't had the same hold over her, and she had shut him out of her life completely. She had started to build up the business in the riding stables again.

It hadn't been easy. Being a single mum with a struggling business had been tough—but she had managed.

No matter what Damon Cyrenci thought about her, she could look him in the eye and know that she was a hard working, decent person, not the money-grabbing gold-digger that he believed her to be.

But hard work and decency didn't help when you had lost your home to the devil.

The truth was that although she had managed to be self-sufficient she didn't have enough money for lawyers if Damon chose to play rough.

A violent roar of thunder tore through the night, and it seemed to echo the anger that tore through her.

He was probably bluffing, she told herself soothingly. He wouldn't want a baby cramping his style. And as for all that talk of offering her marriage—that was probably a bluff as well. Maybe he was just winding her up.

Maybe she would get up in the morning and find him gone.

Abbie buried her head into the pillow and tried to sleep, but it was impossible.

As the first light of dawn crept into the room it was a relief to get up, throw on a pair of jeans and a T-shirt and go across the corridor to see to Mario.

He was awake, and he smiled at her as she walked in.

'Hello, darling.' She bent to pick him up and he gurgled with delight.

Everything was going to be all right, Abbie told herself as she cuddled her son close. The storm outside seemed to be abating; the sun was starting to come out. As she busied herself with her usual morning routine of dressing Mario, the night before started to feel like a bad dream.

Maybe Damon would be gone this morning.

Holding on to that thought, she crept quietly downstairs, carrying Mario tightly in her arms.

The house was silent. The only sign of Damon was a neatly folded sheet and a pillow at the end of the sofa.

He'd gone. Her heart started to soar with relief until she walked into the kitchen. The back door was open, and Damon's tall, powerful body was silhouetted in the frame as he nonchalantly looked out at the morning.

He turned as he heard her. 'Good morning.' His eyes swept over her slender frame and the child in her arms. 'How did you sleep?'

How did he think she had slept? Anybody would think that this was a normal everyday situation, she thought angrily. Anybody would think that he hadn't issued her with an absurd ultimatum last night that threatened to upturn her whole life.

'I slept just fine, thank you,' she lied. She wasn't going to let him know she had spent the night tossing and turning and worrying. 'I thought you would be gone by now.'

'I don't know what made you think that. I made my intentions pretty clear last night.'

Abbie swallowed hard. She really didn't want to think about his intentions. If last night had been some kind of bizarre wind-up, he was taking it a bit far.

She settled Mario in his high chair, and then moved to organise his breakfast and switch on the kettle. Pointedly she tried to ignore Damon, but it was hard because she was aware that he was watching her every move.

Like her, he was wearing jeans and a T-shirt this morning. The casual look suited him, made him look younger than his thirty-one years.

She wished she didn't find him so attractive...but she did. She wished she could stop herself from darting a glance over at him as she walked past...but she couldn't. And as their eyes connected she found herself thinking about the way he had kissed her last night, the way he had made her want him. Abruptly she looked away from him again.

How could you hate someone yet find yourself drawn to him at the same time? It was a mystery. A mystery she could do without, she told herself angrily as she heated some milk for Mario and opened a packet of coffee. Maybe a strong shot of caffeine would help unscramble her brain.

'It looks like we missed the worst of that storm last night.' Damon shut the kitchen door. 'The weather seems to have settled again.'

She couldn't believe that he was talking about the weather now. 'Great,' she said dryly.

'Yes, it is.' He walked across and hooked a chair with his foot to sit down at the kitchen table. Mario smiled at him, one of his big, beaming smiles that made dimples appear in his cheeks. Damon smiled back and reached across to ruffle his son's dark hair.

'I've phoned the airport, and my private plane will be on standby this afternoon.' He glanced over at Abbie again. 'All restrictions on travel have been lifted.'

Abbie had been trying to spoon ground coffee into a pot, but her hand shook alarmingly at those words and most of it ended up on the counter-top. 'You're leaving!' She swung around to look at him.

'Yes. This afternoon at four o clock.'

So everything he had said to her last night *had* been just a wind-up. Relief surged through her. 'Look, Damon, I know it must have been a shock finding out about Mario the way you did. And a lot of things were said last night in the heat of the moment—'

'Were they?' Damon held her eyes steadily. 'I never say anything I don't mean.'

She frowned. She'd been going to tell him that maybe they could put the past behind them, and that he could see Mario when he wanted, because after all he was his father. But she left the words hanging in the air as she sought clarification. 'But you *are* leaving?'

'Yes, I'm returning home to Sicily, with or without you.'

'With?' There was a horrible silence for a moment as she digested this. 'You mean, you meant all that stuff about— about marrying me and the prenuptial agreement… Every-thing?'

'Everything.'

Abbie felt her heart bounce crazily against her chest at the look of cool determination in Damon's eyes.

She swallowed hard and turned away from him.

'I'll have a coffee while you're there,' Damon instructed calmly.

She wanted to say 'make your own coffee', but she didn't dare. She just poured the boiling water into the pot and got down some cups.

'You accept my offer and come with me to Sicily today, or I leave on my own and put things into the hands of my legal team. It's up to you.'

The decisive tone stirred up a sizzling kind of fear inside Abbie. She had never felt more out of her depth in all her life, and she just didn't know how to play this. So she kept her back to Damon and pretended to be engrossed in making Mario's breakfast.

Damon watched her as she moved around the kitchen. He'd thought long and hard about this situation last night, and the more he mulled it over the more sense his offer seemed to make. He wanted his son—wanted him with a strength and certainty that had taken him completely by surprise. But he knew he couldn't tear him away from his mother. No matter how much he threatened, that just didn't feel right. A child needed his mother. But he needed a father too.

So what should he do?

Offering Abbie marriage had been truly inspirational.

Mario would have his mother, plus he would have Abbie exactly where he wanted her.

She stretched up to an overhead cupboard, and his eyes drifted over the narrow hand-span of her waist to her bottom, noting its sexy curve in the tight jeans. *And he knew exactly how he wanted her.*

It was lust, of course—but there was an easy remedy for lust. He was going to make Abbie Newland pay in his bed for her gold-digging, deceiving ways, and at the same time he was going to rid himself of this thirst for her by taking her over and over again at his leisure.

'So, what's it to be?' he grated harshly. Now he had made up his mind about what he wanted, he wasn't going to wait around.

'I'll have to consider my options.' She tried to school her voice, rid it of all emotion, but there was a tremor there that she knew he would pick up on.

'You haven't got any options.' Damon smiled calmly. 'I've been looking through your accounts. They make dismal reading.'

'You've done what?' Her glance flew towards the small office that led off the kitchen. She noticed now that the light was on, and her papers were spread out across the desk.

'How dare you look through my private papers?' She swung around to face him.

'There's nothing private from me regarding the business here, Abbie. I own it. The sooner you accept that, the sooner we can move on.'

'I'll accept nothing of the sort.' From somewhere she found a flare of her old fighting spirit. 'I shall be seeking legal advice.'

'And what are you going to pay your legal team with?' he enquired with amusement. 'Washers?'

'I have some rainy-day money,' she told him shakily.

Damon laughed. 'Abbie, it's pouring down so hard that you have been washed away, and you know it.'

Abbie swallowed down on the knot of fear that told her he was right. The little money she had would be no match what-soever against Damon's might.

'I've offered you a way out. Holding out in the hope that I'm going to increase the terms isn't going to work,' he continued smoothly. 'In fact, if you don't accept today, I will pursue a custody claim for Mario—because let's face it, Abbie, you can't even put a roof over our son's head now. He will be better off in Sicily. I can give him everything you can't—a wonderful education, a comfortable home, a good future.'

'And what about love?' The question broke from her lips in anguish.

Damon regarded her steadily. 'I'll be a good father. You have my word on that.'

'That's so reassuring,' she ground out sarcastically.

'Well, if you are worried come with us. You know my terms.'

'I can't just leave—especially at such short notice! I have the horses to sort out, and responsibilities.'

Damon smiled. Things were turning in his favour; he sensed she was starting to crack. 'I'll employ more staff and a manager, and review the situation at a later date. Believe me, this place can be sorted out in a few hours—money has the advantage of making any situation run smoothly.'

'Don't I know it?' Abbie's voice croaked bitterly. Pitted against Damon's wealth and power, she could possibly lose a custody battle…lose Mario for ever. But the alternative was letting him buy her like an extra member of staff. Her mind whirled around and around, searching for an escape route, but she couldn't find one. Instead his words were playing mockingly through her mind. *You can't even put a roof over our son's head.*

He was right. She'd lost the house and the stables, and there was no way she could fight that. What would she do? Where would she and Mario end up?

Was giving in to Damon now her only option? An over-whelming feeling of powerlessness descended on her as she thought about walking away from the home and the animals she loved. And what about her staff here? What would happen to their jobs? Then there was her beloved horse, Benjo, a three-year-old gelding that she'd rescued from a life of grim abuse. He had stolen her heart away with his trusting eyes and his gentle ways. 'I can't…' Her voice broke with anguish.

Damon's eyes narrowed. She seemed so vulnerable, so fragile. He remembered, when they had first been dating, he had sometimes caught that haunted expression deep in the beauty of her blue eyes. He'd seen it that first day when they'd met by the pool. He'd made some joke about her being a social butterfly, and she had looked at him strangely—almost nervously—a million shadows chasing across the beauty of her expression. It had brought out a feeling in him that he couldn't explain, it had made him want to reel her in and hold her tight. No woman had ever made him feel like that before. What a fool he had been. She'd been the one reeling *him* in. She *had* been just a social butterfly—a devious one at that!

Remembering just how devious brought him firmly to his senses. She had played him for a fool once. He wasn't going to be taken in by her ever again. 'Abbie, I haven't got time for your fake emotional outbursts. I don't know whom you think you are fooling. I can see right through you.'

Abbie slanted her chin up and tried to pull herself together. He was so cold—so ruthless—and she was damned if she was going to give him the pleasure of knowing that he was hurting her.

'Coming back to Sicily with me will be the best thing for our son. He will have both his parents, and all the advantages in life that you wouldn't be able to give him. Plus, I shall put a ring on your finger.' Damon shrugged. 'It's a good deal. I'm prepared to be more than generous to you.'

'And I'm supposed to be grateful?' Abbie's voice trembled with anger. 'The ring you want to put on my finger will mean nothing more than a band of possession.'

Damon conceded the point with a curt nod of his head. 'But a band of possession that will entitle you to certain privileges.'

'In return for certain favours.'

'Favours?' Damon looked amused at the term. 'Oh no, Abbie, that's not how our arrangement will work at all.' He stood up from the table to walk towards her. 'The fact is that you like what I can do for you.'

He stood close to her and reached out a hand to trail it down the side of her face. The caress sent a tremor racing through her entire body—but it was a tremor of desire, not repulsion. A tremor that said he was right, she did like what he could do. And that fact disturbed her deeply.

'We're good together, and what's more now we understand each other.' Damon's tone was matter-of-fact, but his eyes were burning over her body. 'You'll just be my good-time girl, but on a regular basis and on a more honest basis than in the past. I hope we are clear on that?'

'Oh, I think you've made yourself more than crystal clear. But there's nothing *honest* about this,' she said huskily.

'It'll be more honest than what happened between us last time.' Damon tipped her chin up so that he could look into her eyes.

The words hurt her so much. She'd loved him in the past—or *thought* she'd loved him. 'Damon, I didn't have a choice, I—'

'There are always choices in life,' he cut across her firmly.

'Like my choice now, you mean?'

For a second the tremble in her voice stole under his defences. He noticed the shadows in the beauty of her eyes, noticed how they changed from deepest indigo to violet-blue.

'Damon, what happened between us was—'

'What—a regrettable mistake?' Reality swirled in around him. It was amazing how for just a moment she could still get to him. Obviously it was because he still wanted her sexually and that clouded his judgement—that had always been his weakness where she was concerned. His lips twisted wryly. 'I suppose from your point of view you could look at it like that. You made the wrong choice, you backed the wrong horse, Abbie—your father can't bankroll you now. But I can.'

It was strange how his voice was so brutal, yet the touch of his hand as he trailed it down her cheek was so seductively gentle. It sent conflicting signals racing through Abbie's body.

'You forget that I know you. I know how your mind works.' His eyes were on her lips.

She felt a lick of heat stirring through her body, the kind of heat that made her long for him to move closer.

How could she feel like this when she was so appalled by his words? She tried desperately to make herself move away from him—but she couldn't.

'This pretence of yours has gone far enough. Let's just cut to the chase shall we? Have we got a deal?' As he asked the question he grazed his thumb over the softness of her lips. The caress made the longing inside her grow stronger. She wanted him to kiss her, to hold her…

She couldn't understand it. How was he able to turn her on like this? How could he make her ache inside with this deep, burning anguish? Of all the men in the world, why *him*?

'Abbie, have we got a deal?' His voice was insistent, and as he spoke he moved his other hand to her waist, pulling her a little closer. She could feel the heat of his body only centimetres away from hers, and the touch of his hand at her waist was like a sharp brand of ownership.

She imagined being owned by him, sleeping with him in the deep comfort of a double bed every night. Her eyes closed on a wave of weakness as she imagined his hands on her body, his lips crushing against hers.

Sex had been so wonderful with him. He was right, there was chemistry between them. And she did like what he could do to her, liked it so much. That fact made her ashamed of herself. But, as much as she despised herself, she wanted him.

'Abbie?'

Weakness was flooding her body; she felt trapped by her circumstances—but also by her own emotions.

'Abbie, have we got a deal, yes or no?'

She shook her head against the deluge of longing that threatened to overwhelm her. She couldn't tie herself to a man who didn't love her.

But what choice did she have?

The question brought back some semblance of sanity. Her eyes flickered open. All she could do now was some damage limitation. 'What about the staff here?'

Damon frowned That wasn't the kind of question he'd expected from her. 'Their jobs will be safe.'

'And I need to read the contract you want me to sign before I can agree to anything.'

She was like a fish emerging from the water, wriggling on the end of a line. Damon's lips curved. 'Ah, at last, the real Abigail Newland!'

'Don't be smart with me, Damon.'

'The contract will state that financially the world is your oyster, just as long as you stay with me and abide by my terms.' Their eyes met and held. 'And you already know my terms.' He enunciated the words clearly. 'So, I'll ask the question for the last time: have we got a deal?'

Her heart was thundering against her chest so hard that it felt as if it were filling the room with sound. There was nothing she could do. He had her exactly where he wanted her, and he knew it. 'Ok…' She shrugged wearily. 'Yes, we've got a deal.'

She saw the flicker of triumph in his dark eyes. 'At last, an end to the pretence.'

CHAPTER FIVE

THE door of the aircraft slammed shut with all the finality of a cell door closing behind her.

Abbie shut her eyes and told herself that she was being fanciful. If she was going to prison, it would be a very luxurious one. It would be a place where her son would be given a good education and a wonderful life.

She was doing the right thing for Mario. She couldn't have fought against all of Damon's might and power. The one thing she had learnt from the years with her father was that if you had a plentiful supply of money it bought you anything you wanted…even people.

And now she had allowed Damon to purchase her.

But what else could she have done?

She still felt a bit dazed from the speed everything had moved at. One moment she had been standing close to him in the kitchen, the next she had been sent upstairs to pack her things.

'Just bring what you can fit in a small suitcase,' he had ordered. 'Essentials to tide you and Mario over. Everything else can be replaced by new things when we get home.'

Home?

Would she ever feel that Damon's house was her home?

Somehow she didn't think so. And she didn't want new belongings. She wanted her old things. She wanted to feel safe. She wanted to feel like she had her integrity back.

But she had the horrible feeling that her integrity had been left behind in her house along with all the belongings she had once cherished.

She could try to make herself feel better by remembering that she had no choice but to accept Damon's terms—which she hadn't. *But that didn't excuse the fact that she had liked the way he'd touched her—had wanted him to draw her closer—kiss her, caress her.*

The aircraft engines roared and Mario wriggled on her lap. She held him close. 'It's OK, baby, there's nothing to worry about,' she whispered soothingly against his ear.

Liar. There is everything to worry about, she mocked herself.

As the aircraft thundered down the runway she could think of a million worries. And number one on the list was how she was going to give herself in marriage to a man who was going to use her purely for sex.

She remembered how he had sought her out when he had discovered her deception in Vegas. How he'd refused to listen to anything she'd had to say. And then, as his rage had died, the coldness and the clarity in his voice as he'd told her the truth of how he had really felt about her all along. *'As far as I was concerned, our time together was all about sex—I felt nothing for you, other than the pleasure of taking your body. Nothing at all.'*

Those words had never left her. She wished they still didn't hurt. She wished she could forget them—*especially now.*

What future happiness could there be for her with a man who just wanted to possess her body and cared nothing for her?

Had she made the worst mistake of her life in accepting his terms now and getting on this plane?

The aircraft left the ground and soared away from the island of St Lucia. If she looked down she might be able to see her house nestled by the palm-fringed bay. She might be able to see her horse galloping out in the paddock, or Jess taking a group of holidaymakers down to the beach for a long ride across the sands.

Life would go on there without her. Whether she had made a mistake or not, she was on the path to a new life now.

She opened her eyes, and her gaze connected with Damon's.

He was watching her with a cool detachment that made her heart start to beat unevenly. Hastily she looked away from him again.

Where would she be sleeping when they arrived at his house? Would he expect her to just move straight into his bedroom?

The question tormented her.

It was two and a half years since their weeks of wild, abandoned passion. But she could still remember it like yesterday. Could remember the way he had made her feel—as if she'd come alive for the first time. And afterwards being held by him had been the most wonderful sensation. She had felt cherished and protected, and he'd made the loneliness deep inside her melt away.

Of course those feelings had just been an illusion, she reminded herself angrily. But, even so, in the intervening years she had failed to find them again. In fact, dates with other men had failed to stir any spark of excitement inside her. She had wondered if perhaps that side of her was dead. If it had been extinguished by the pain and the fear that if she got too close to someone she might be hurt all over again.

And then Damon Cyrenci had walked in through her front

door and had blown all those theories to smithereens. He could turn her on with just a glance.

It was a cruel twist of irony that the man who had smashed her heart, the man who cared nothing for her feelings—who despised her, even—was the one man who could turn her on.

She couldn't sleep with him tonight, she just couldn't. Fear shot through her in violent waves. She didn't know what frightened her most: the fact that she wanted him so much, or the fact that once he took her to bed she would reveal just how vulnerable she was where he was concerned. He already had such a powerful hold on her; giving him the satisfaction of knowing he was right, and she was his for the taking any time he pleased, was more than her pride could bear.

The aircraft levelled out and the seat-belt sign was switched off.

'Do you want a drink?' Damon stood up and headed to the back of the plane.

'No, I'm all right, thank you.'

She watched as he poured himself a coffee in the galley kitchen, and she tried to direct her thoughts away from what was going to happen between them. This was a lengthy overnight flight. They wouldn't be landing in Sicily until the early hours of the morning. The sleeping arrangements were a long way off.

She glanced away from him around the interior of the plane. She had never been in a private jet before. The last flight she had taken had been a scheduled one from Vegas when she had fled from her father. That flight had been full, and the seats had been jammed close together.

By contrast they were alone on this flight. The deep leather seats were soft and luxurious and placed far apart. There were personal TV screens that could be pulled down from the ceiling above her, and phones concealed in the armrests. There was also a recline button that would fully adjust and transform the chair into a bed.

Damon returned to sit opposite her. 'Do you want to put Mario down on the seat next to you?' he asked. 'Now that we are airborne it might be more comfortable. There is a booster seat, and you can put a blanket and the safety belt around him.'

'Thank you, Damon, but we're fine,' she assured him stiffly. Somehow she didn't want to relinquish the warm little body close to hers.

'Please yourself.' Damon shrugged and reached for some papers in the central armrest. 'I have some work to do,' he murmured.

Abbie looked out the window. How could he be so relaxed about this situation? How could he study his sheets of figures and concentrate on high finance when he had ridden rough-shod over her, made her homeless, torn her away from everything she knew?

Because he didn't care, she thought tiredly. Retribution was all he cared about.

Abbie leaned her head back and closed her eyes. Somehow she would get through this, she told herself fiercely. She had to, for Mario's sake.

Silence fell between them, filled only by the drone of the aircraft and the rustle of his papers.

Damon didn't look up from his work until a few hours later, when Mario made it known that he was hungry.

He watched as she soothed the child and moved him into the seat beside her.

She was good with him, he thought, as he watched Mario smile at her suddenly.

But then Abbie could charm the birds off the trees.

His eyes moved down over her figure. She was wearing the jeans she'd had on this morning, but she'd changed her T-shirt for a clinging black top with spaghetti straps. It kept riding up at her waist as she bent to secure Mario in his seat. Her skin was firm, and tanned a golden honey. Her hair swung silkily around her shoulders as she moved.

How he itched to take her; the need for her was burning him up inside. When he'd pulled her close to him in the kitchen this morning he'd wanted to unfasten those jeans and pull off her T-shirt to reveal the soft swell of her curves. And it would have been so easy to have her there and then. He'd seen the flame of desire in her eyes—a flame she had desperately tried to hide behind the pretence of being hurt by the crudeness of his offer.

'OK, sweetheart, dinner is coming.' She bent close and kissed the child. Then she glanced over at Damon. 'Watch him for me, will you, while I heat him something up?'

'Sure.' He inclined his head. Oh yes, she was sweetness personified—nobody would ever guess that her only qualm about selling herself to him had been how good a deal she would get from him.

Well, as soon as she signed his prenuptial agreement her game would be over and his would just have begun.

He put his papers to one side and reached to pick up one of Mario's toys that had fallen on the floor. He smiled at the child as he handed it back. Mario smiled back at him.

Pleasure intensified inside Damon. Oh yes, things couldn't be better. He had his son, and this was all working out very well.

Abbie returned a few moments later, and knelt down beside the little boy to help him with his dinner. Darkness fell outside the windows. Damon returned his attention to his work. He had a backlog to deal with, and he wanted to be sufficiently up to date when he returned to Sicily to be able to take some time off—time that he intended to spend making up for lost time with his son, and enjoying himself with his newly acquired wife…over and over again.

The sun was rising slowly in the east when Damon finally put his work away and the private jet started to make its final descent. Abbie leaned forward and watched as they skimmed in low over the Mediterranean. She noticed the golden glitter of sun on the water beneath them, and the dark shapes of fishing boats. As they approached the land she could see cypress trees and steep mountains silhouetted against the pink of the morning sky.

The touch-down was smooth, and within a few moments they had taxied to a halt and the seat-belt sign was switched off.

They were on the island of Sicily. Abbie wondered if she would suddenly wake up and find herself back in her own bed, find the last twenty-four hours had all been a wild figment of her imagination.

But as she turned her attention back inside the plane and her eyes met with Damon's she knew that this was real. There was no peace of mind to be found. Her future started here.

'Home sweet home.' His lips curved in a slightly mocking smile, as if he could read her consternation.

'If you say so.'

His smile merely widened at that. 'At least we are off to a good start.'

She looked at him enquiringly.

'You realise that what I say goes.'

'Very funny, Damon.'

'Who's joking?' He flicked her a wry look before standing up to gather their belongings from the overhead locker.

She angled her chin up and forced herself not to give him the pleasure of knowing that she could feel every nerve-ending inside her stretching and shaking under the tension.

The door of the aircraft slid open, and Abbie picked up her bag and gathered Mario up into her arms. It was a pleasure to step outside. The morning air was fresh with the promise of a hot day to come, and as Abbie followed Damon down the steps towards the tarmac she took deep breaths as if she were emerging for the last time into freedom.

There was a group of authorities waiting for them by the base of the steps, and behind them a uniformed chauffeur stood patiently next to a stretch limousine, the passenger doors open, ready for them.

'I need both your passports, Abbie.' Damon held out his hand and she scrabbled in her bag to find them and hand them over.

As the formalities of customs and immigration were observed smoothly and within minutes, it suddenly struck Abbie that this was a way of life for Damon Cyrenci.

He was used to people treating him with respect—used to his path being eased, to getting everything he wanted. She noticed their luggage being efficiently loaded straight into the boot of the waiting limousine.

She had to admit it was impressive, as were the warm tones of his accent as he spoke in his native tongue. It was the first time she had heard him speak in his own language, and she liked it. It gave her a strange, liquid feeling in her bones. The trouble was that it was a feeling that annoyed her intensely.

She didn't want him to have that effect on her, because that was giving him power over her, and Damon had enough power. He was arrogant and insufferable, and she wasn't going to be a walkover for him—no matter how attractive she found him. Maybe everyone else bowed and scraped to him, but she wasn't going to. Pride was the only thing she had left now, and she was going to hold on to it at all costs.

Trying to keep that thought firmly to the forefront of her mind, she walked across towards the waiting car.

A few minutes later they were speeding away across the tarmac, out of the terminal and onto the main road.

Damon talked to the driver in Italian for a few moments before closing the glass partition. 'Won't be long, and we'll be home.'

Abbie turned away from him and tried to pretend that she was interested in the scenery. 'You've still got our passports,' she reminded him curtly.

'They are with the rest of the documentation.' He stretched his long legs out. 'I don't know about you, but I could do with a shower and a lie down.'

His words prickled against her senses. Would he expect her to 'lie down' with *him*? 'They say the best cure for jet lag is to stay awake as long as possible, and try to sleep at the normal time,' she told him stiffly.

'Do they?' She could hear the underlying amusement in his tone. 'We'll have to try and think of a way to keep awake, then.'

Abbie bit down on the softness of her lower lip and kept her gaze averted from him. She watched as the Sicilian countryside flashed by in a whirl of colours. She noticed the baked, hard terracotta soil, the silver green of olive trees and the fierce blue of the sky. But all she could think about was the sleeping arrangements at the end of their journey.

The driver turned the car up through the winding, mountainous roads before dropping them back down towards dazzling views out across the coastline.

Then they slowed down and turned into a hidden entrance. Electric gates wound back to allow access to a long driveway that wound its way through lush Mediterranean gardens. As it curved around, Abbie had her first glimpse of the place that was to be her new home.

Her lips parted in a gasp of admiration, for it was more beautiful than she had ever imagined. It had the size and grandeur of a mansion, but it also had a character that stole her heart away.

Vines tangled across the warmth of the red bricks, jasmine and bougainvillea vying for position over the elegant arch of the front door.

'This is a beautiful house, Damon.' Despite the fact that she had been determined to make no comment about her surroundings, her enthusiasm would not be curbed, and it broke from her lips before she could check it.

'I'm glad you approve.' By contrast, Damon's voice was dry. It was as if he had expected her admiration, which of course she supposed he had. After all, his home had all the trappings associated with the residence of a multimillionaire: an infinity swimming-pool sparkled and merged into the deep, hazy blue of the Mediterranean, tennis courts were towards the other side and vast lawns sprawled out at the front.

As the car pulled to a halt by the front door a slim, smartly dressed woman in her late fifties stepped out of the house to greet them. She had dark hair swept into a chignon, and high cheekbones that gave her a regal air.

'This is my housekeeper, Elise,' Damon informed her as he climbed out into the heat of the day. 'Elise speaks good English, is a great cook and runs the house very efficiently. So there will be no problems for you to deal with.'

Abbie frowned. In St Lucia her days had been packed—she had worked long hours, and sometimes it had been difficult juggling motherhood and running the business. There had been days when she had longed for some time and space just to be able to spend time with Mario. But she had also enjoyed the challenge.

How would she fill her days here? she wondered.

Elise welcomed her with a friendly smile, and then cooed and fussed over Mario in Italian.

They stepped into the entrance hall where a grand, curving staircase led up to a galleried landing.

'I have a few business calls to make, Abbie,' Damon informed her curtly as the chauffeur carried in their bags. 'Elise will show you up to the bedroom. Go and make yourself at home. I'll be up presently.'

Abbie's heart was starting to thud so hard against her chest that it hurt. It sounded like he was ordering her to go upstairs and prepare for him!

Maybe he imagined, because she'd agreed to his terms, that all he had to do now was snap his fingers and do as he pleased with her. Well, he could think again. She had far too much self-respect to allow him to use her like that.

Oh no, Damon Cyrenci, you are not getting everything your own way, she told herself fiercely as she followed Elise up the staircase. She may have agreed to his obnoxious terms, but it didn't mean she was going to be a complete pushover.

The room Elise showed her into was palatial. Two arched windows allowed sunlight to flood in. One looked out towards the glitter of the pool and the sea, the other looked over the side gardens. But it was the bed that took her attention. It was a massive king-sized four-poster swathed in white, and it totally dominated the centre of the room.

'There is a dressing room through here.' Elise opened another door. 'I have placed Mario's cot in here, as Signor Cyrenci instructed.'

Abbie followed the woman and glanced into the room. Sure enough, a large cot was placed next to some walk-in wardrobes. Damon had been busy. All those phone calls before they'd left St Lucia had obviously paid off.

But then, as Damon had said, when you had money the way was smoothed very easily.

She felt suddenly exhausted.

'And there is an *en-suite* bathroom through here.' Elise opened the door next to the dressing room. 'Now, is there anything else I can get for you, Ms Newland?'

Abbie shook her head. 'No, everything is fine, thank you.'

With a nod, the woman took her leave. Abbie sank down onto the side of the bed and put Mario down beside her.

The little boy was delighted to be free, and he pulled himself up and toddled off to explore. She allowed him to run unhindered across the soft white carpet; there was nowhere for him to go, nothing for him to harm himself on, and the freedom was probably just what he needed after being confined for so long.

But what freedom was she going to have now? Obviously Damon didn't expect her to do any housework, which meant she would have no say in the running of the house. Was her only role to be that of mother and bedmate?

She noticed the long bank of wardrobes against the far wall. If she opened them up, would she find Damon's clothes hanging inside? Was this his bedroom? It was hard to tell from just glancing around; there were no personal items on the dressing table or on the bedside tables, not even a book or a clock.

Mario toddled back towards her, and she swept him up into her arms. She didn't have the energy to investigate or even think about this situation any longer. She would bath Mario, have a shower herself and deal with everything else a step at a time.

It took Damon a while to sort out the paperwork in his office. He read through the prenuptial agreement that he had asked his lawyer to draw up. He'd done a good job. Satisfied that everything was in order, he pushed his chair back from his desk and went in search of his quarry.

But when Damon stepped into the bedroom he found Abbie lying on top of the bed, fast asleep. He glanced through into the adjoining room and saw that Mario was also sleeping in his cot.

So much for getting her to sign his contract straight away! He crossed the room and sat down beside her on the edge of the bed. She didn't stir. She was lying on her side, her long, blonde hair slightly obscuring her face in a silky curtain. His eyes travelled down over her body, noting the fact that she'd changed into a white pencil-skirt, a white short-sleeved top and that her long legs were bare.

She looked achingly beautiful. He reached out a hand and stroked a strand of her hair back from her face. She moved a little at his touch but she didn't wake.

It was hard to believe that someone who looked like her had such a cold, mercenary heart. Hard to believe that the only thing that really turned her on was money.

He felt a dull ache of something swirling inside him. She looked so innocent in sleep, almost virginal, her lips parted softly, and her long, dark eyelashes thick and sooty against the soft perfection of her skin.

He remembered how he had felt when he had discovered that she was complicit in his father's destruction. She had played the game so perfectly—luring him in, drawing back from his kisses as if scared by the intensity of passion that had sprung between them, teasing him with her tremulous smile and her innocent, big blue eyes. But all the time she had known exactly what she was doing.

There was nothing innocent about Abbie. The knowledge stabbed through him fiercely as his eyes travelled lower over the soft curves of her body. She knew exactly how to use that beautiful body of hers to maximum effect. Knew exactly what she wanted.

Well, so be it—she could use her beautiful body to full effect, she could even have everything she wanted…but at a price. Their roles had been reversed. The huntress was now the prey. He was in control this time.

'Abbie.' He stroked a hand down over her face. 'Abbie, wake up.'

Her eyes flickered open. She looked disorientated for a moment, as if she didn't know where she was. And as she looked up at him the intensity of her kitten-blue eyes seemed to mock his determination to be cool and ruthlessly in control.

'So much for staying awake,' he said softly.

'I only meant to rest my eyes for a moment.' She stretched sleepily and his eyes followed the lissome movement. He noticed how she was very clever at showing her body to full advantage. The round-necked top was in a silky material that emphasised the curve of her breasts in a tantalizingly provocative way, especially when she put her hands over her head like that. The skirt showed how tiny her waist was, and how curvy her hips.

'Good job I've come to your rescue and woken you up,' he grated sardonically. 'We don't want jet lag interfering with our fun, do we?'

As sleep faded from Abbie's mind, the realization of her situation flooded back in. How long had Damon been in the room? How long had he been sitting beside her, watching her sleep?

She drew herself up. 'Damon, what are you doing in my room?'

'Your room?' His lips twisted with amusement. 'This is *our* room, Abigail. This is our marital bed.'

'Well, we are not married yet!'

Although her eyes flared with fire, she sounded flustered—almost nervous—and he laughed at that. 'Such old-fashioned virtue from such a modern—shall we say to be kind, less than virtuous—woman.'

'When were you last kind where I'm concerned?' she croaked huskily.

'Dear me, are you panicking already about how generous I intend to be?' He looked at her with a raised eyebrow. 'Now I understand the reason for the display of innocent virtuosity.'

He watched as the pallor of her skin flooded with colour. He had to hand it to her, she was a superb actress. 'Don't worry, I will be kind, you will get everything your heart desires.'

He reached out a hand to trail one finger down over her cheek. She flinched away from his touch. 'I don't want anything from you, Damon.' She was smarting from his words, from the touch of his hand. She knew his opinion of her, and it shouldn't hurt so much—but strangely it did.

'Drop the pretence, Abbie—we're past that now.'

The mocking tones lashed across her. She swallowed hard.

There was the sound of a car pulling up outside, and Damon stood up from the bed to go over towards the window. 'Ah, right on schedule. Put your shoes on, Abbie, and come downstairs. We may as well get business out of the way now.'

'I can't leave Mario. He might wake up and need me.' Abbie swung her legs off the bed. She didn't want to go anywhere with him—in fact all she wanted right now was to run away.

'Mario will be fine. There is a child-monitor installed. Switch it on and we'll hear him in my study if he cries.'

'You've thought of everything, haven't you?'

'I hope so.' He moved towards the door decisively. 'Don't be long. I'll be waiting for you downstairs.'

There was no alternative but to do as she was told, so she slipped on her high heels and went to check on Mario.

She tried to tell herself that dealing with Damon in the study was preferable to dealing with Damon in the bedroom. But somehow it wasn't much of a reassurance, and her feelings of vulnerability only intensified as she went down to join him. If it hadn't been for Mario, she might have been tempted to keep on going, out through the front door. But, even with Mario in her arms, where would she go? She had no money and no passport.

The knowledge made her heart thump unevenly as she found Damon's study.

'You've still got our passports,' she reminded him as soon as she entered the room.

'Have I?' He was sitting behind a large desk, flicking through papers, and he barely glanced up.

'You know you do.'

Damon shrugged. 'Well, they are not going to be a lot of use to you now anyway. Why do you want them?'

The calm question disconcerted her. 'Because I just do! You can't keep me prisoner here!'

He laughed at that. 'I've no intention of keeping you prisoner here, Abbie.' He sat back in his chair and opened up a drawer to take out some keys. 'In fact, these are for you.'

'What are they for?'

'One is the front-door key to this house and the other is the key for the brand-new silver-blue sportscar waiting outside on the drive for you. It's just been delivered.'

'Oh!' She was taken aback by the gift.

'Oh indeed.' He smiled. 'You see, I do intend to be generous, and you can come and go as you please. As long as you're here for me when I need you.'

The words were said in a certain, seductive way that made

her heart start to hammer even more fiercely against her chest. She noticed the way his eyes slipped down over her figure— assessing, warm.

'Have a look out the window if you want. You'll be able to see the car from here.' He leaned back further in his chair and watched her lazily. He was curious to see her reaction.

Her hands curled into tight fists at her sides. He was treating her like the mercenary little gold-digger he thought she was, and she wasn't going to play. 'I don't want your damn car,' she told him tightly.

'Abbie, don't be coy, it doesn't suit you and it doesn't fool me.'

'I want the passports back.'

He shrugged. 'And you can have them. But they will be utterly useless. They are out of date.'

'No, they're not!' She stared at him mutinously. 'They have years left on them—'

'Abbie,' he cut across her crisply. 'Mario's passport says that he is Mario Newland. That is not his name. His name is Mario Cyrenci. The error will be made right as soon as possible.'

Damon watched impassively as shadows flickered across Abbie's eyes. 'And, as for you...' He smiled coolly. 'I've arranged for a special licence. We will be married tomorrow afternoon.'

'Tomorrow!' Her eyes widened, and the panic inside her intensified. She felt as if she was backed into a corner with no way out. 'Isn't this all a little rushed?'

'Why wait around?' He leaned forward in his chair. 'All you have to do is sign this.' He tapped the papers that were lying on the desk. 'And then you can have these.' He picked up the keys and dangled them.

'Is this the carrot-and-stick approach?' She tried to make a joke, but her voice rasped huskily.

He smiled. 'You could call it that. And, speaking of carrots…' He picked up a small box from beside the papers. 'I suppose you should also have this.'

He opened the lid, and a magnificent diamond-solitaire ring blazed fiercely as the light caught it.

'You don't need to worry—despite the fact that it's an antique, it's worth a lot of money. It's flawless, and it's set in platinum.'

Abbie swallowed down on the shaft of pain inside her 'Why do you want to think the absolute worst of me?' The trembling question broke from her lips involuntarily.

'You know why.'

She wished he knew the truth—wished she could make him believe that what had happened wasn't her fault. 'Damon, I am not a mercenary person. I had no choice but to go along with my father…' Her voice was full of emotion as she tried to reach him. It was so painful even thinking about the past and her mother. 'I—'

'Save it Abbie,' he cut across her ruthlessly. 'I don't want to hear your excuses. Because only a fool doesn't learn by their mistakes, and I'm no fool.'

She stared at him wordlessly. You couldn't make someone believe you when they were just determined to think the worst.

'Now, are you going to sign these so we can move on?' He picked up a pen and tapped the documents in front of him.

What would happen if she said no? Abbie wondered suddenly. Would she be put back on a plane—without Mario? And a plane to where? She had nowhere to go, and nothing except for the one small suitcase she had brought with her.

'I never sign anything without reading it.' She tilted her chin up proudly. She was damned if she was going to make this easy for him. She wouldn't let him see she was beaten. 'You'll have to leave it with me for a few hours.'

'Fine.' He drummed his fingers on the desk impatiently. Then he picked the ring up out of the box. 'In the meantime, in an act of good faith, should I slip this onto your finger?'

She hesitated, and then shrugged. 'I suppose you could. I can always take it off again.'

Damon's dark eyes gleamed with a moment's annoyance. Every time he thought he had her just where he wanted her, she managed to do some kind of sidestep. 'I've really had enough of your games, Abbie.' He stood up and walked around towards her with a purposeful look in his eye, a look that made her heart race. Then he reached to take her hand in his and slip the ring firmly into place.

It fitted perfectly.

'There.' Instead of letting go of her hand, he sat down on the desk behind him and drew her closer.

'Now, you've had some tokens of my intentions. I think it's time I had some token from you.' He said the words roughly, but bizarrely there was nothing rough about the way his fingers stroked over her hand.

'What kind of a token?' She pretended not to know what he meant—but she understood all too well. She could hear what he wanted in the deep rasp of his voice, see it in the dark flame of his eyes.

'I think you should undress for me, Abbie, and show me exactly what *you* can offer *me*...'

CHAPTER SIX

THE command sent a strange pang of emotion shooting through her. There was a part of her that was horrified by his words, and another part... Well, the other part was weakened by the fact that he had pulled her very close and one hand had moved to her waist. He was so close to her and she could feel the heat of his body, smell the familiar scent of his cologne.

His eyes were dark and commanding as they held hers. Then they moved down towards her lips, and she felt something inside her turn over.

This was the father of her child—the man she had loved so passionately once, the man who had made her cry with pleasure when he'd brought her to climax. The man who had chased away the loneliness inside her and held her so tightly against him that she'd thought she would die from happiness.

The memories swamped her, just as they did every time he came too close.

She didn't want to feel like this. But somehow she just couldn't help herself.

'Don't, Damon.' She whispered the words unsteadily.

'Don't what?' He reached up to stroke a stray strand of hair away from her face.

The strangely gentle caress was like pure torture. 'Don't torment me!'

His eyes gleamed with a moment's dark humour. 'Darling Abbie,' he grated sarcastically. 'Why should I listen to that plea when you torment me so well?'

'Do I?' She looked into his eyes, startled by the remark, and he laughed.

'You know, if they were handing out Oscars for this performance you'd get one. You play innocent so damn well.' His words rasped with a slightly uneven edge.

'Now you're mocking me!' Her eyes clouded.

'Now you're going for the "best actress" award as well as "best newcomer".'

'Leave me alone, Damon. I'm not going to allow you to insult me like this—I deserve better!'

'Really?' His tone was sardonic. 'Well, show me what you think you deserve, then.' He let go of her suddenly.

The challenge riled her—riled her almost as much as the fact that he wasn't holding her now. She wanted to feel his arms around her.

She frowned as the realization struck. She wanted him to treat her the way he had when they were lovers; even if it was just an illusion of love, it was better than nothing.

She shut her eyes and leaned closer, and before she could think better of her actions she kissed him. It was gentle at first, almost tentative, but as she felt the warmth of his lips moving against hers she deepened the kiss. For a while she was in control, and she liked it—liked the feel of his body against hers, liked the way he responded to her.

Memories licked through her body, heating her up, making her ache. There had been this tenderness between them in the past, this tentative yet highly inflaming spark. She could feel it now, burning against her lips, sizzling through her consciousness.

His hands were on her waist again, drawing her closer. She could feel his arousal pressing against her.

She wanted him...wanted him so much.

His hands swept upwards and over her breast, caressing her gently, finding the hard peaks of her nipples and stroking them, teasing them into tight, throbbing buds that strained against the satin of her clothing.

'Now, this is better...' His words cut through the warmth inside her.

She closed her eyes and strove to cut the cynical tones from her mind. 'Damon, we were so good together once.' She whispered the words huskily. 'Maybe we could be like that again.'

When he didn't answer, she pulled away from him a little so that she could look into his eyes. 'Maybe we could put the clock back to the way we were together that weekend in Palm Springs?'

'When I didn't know the truth about you?' His eyes held hers steadily. 'I don't think so, Abbie.'

The sudden coldness in his tone struck her uncomfortably.

'I just thought... We have a child together, and if we are going to make this...situation work, then maybe we should try to forget the past.'

'Nice thought.'

Still the coldness was there in his tone.

'At least we could meet each other half way?' She looked up at him with beseeching blue eyes.

'And after we've met half way—then what?'

'Well, I told you, we could put the clock back, start again.'

'Just like that?' He snapped his fingers.

'We could, if it was what we both wanted.' Her heart was thundering against her chest. 'And it would be better for Mario if there wasn't this tension between us, if we could trust each other.'

He didn't answer her immediately, but his hands dropped completely away from her, leaving her aching for him.

'Well go on, then, show me how much you mean all this, hmm? Prove your undying devotion.'

She frowned, unsure of what he wanted from her. 'Well, we would have to take it a day at a time, but we could try.'

'Well, let's take it a minute at a time now. Do as I ask and undress for me.'

She took a step back from him. 'You're serious, aren't you?' Her voice trembled slightly. She wanted his tenderness so much, but he kept bringing it back to this.

'Why—aren't *you*?'

He sounded so cold, so ruthless, and yet when he'd kissed her, when he'd touched her, she had imagined she'd glimpsed the man she had thought she loved once.

It was as if a veil was down between them now, and it didn't matter what she did, she kept getting tangled up in it. Maybe she always would. Maybe no matter what she did or said he would always think of her as the mercenary gold-digger who had deceived him.

And then, before she could analyse what she was doing, or why, she started to take off the white silk top.

Her blonde hair fell in disarray around her shoulders as she pulled the top over her head. She was wearing a plain white bra, not overtly sexy, just plain white cotton trimmed with satin. Yet its plainness made it the sexiest piece of underwear Damon had seen in a long time, due in no small way to the pert voluptuousness of her curves.

Her eyes held with his as she unfastened her skirt and let it fall to the floor.

His gaze travelled slowly down over her body, taking in

every detail. She was wearing a pair of white satin pants that curved prettily over her hips. Her figure was as toned and sensational as he'd remembered, her legs long and shapely.

'You still look as good as you did back then,' he told her gruffly. 'You always were an incredibly sexy woman.'

He watched the flare of colour in her skin. She looked embarrassed and shy, yet she stood straight and met his gaze with guileless, clear eyes. 'But I'm not the same,' she told him softly.

'No?' He felt his insides tighten and his need for her scream out as her hands went around to unfasten the bra.

'No. I've had a baby since then. It changed my body.'

The bra fell to the floor.

Her breasts were fantastic—large, yet so perfectly shaped and firm, her nipples still hard and erect from his touch.

'It changed you in a good way,' he told her softly. 'A very good way.'

Her hand played with the thin satin of her pants, and she cast him a look that shot molten heat through him. She looked so vulnerable, so nervous. He couldn't stand her looking at him like, that it ate him away.

'Come here.' Before she could take the underwear off, he reached and caught her arm and pulled her closer.

'I thought you wanted me to take all my clothes off?' The soft yet tremulous question tore at him. Was she close to tears? He felt like someone had struck him. He pulled her closer and into his arms, and allowed her to bury her head against his shoulder.

'No, it's OK.' His hand stroked down over the softness of her blonde hair and then the smooth, naked skin of her back. She felt good in his arms, too damned good. 'I know it's as you English like to say: collar and cuffs all match.'

He just held her for a moment, his mind racing. What the

hell was the matter with him? Why did he feel so bad? She was a teasing, tormenting witch! She deserved a bit of humiliation.

She turned her head slightly and cuddled in against him. His thumb brushed gently over the side of her face. Was it wet with tears?

'Abbie?'

The rasp of his voice aroused her so much. She turned her head, and suddenly they were kissing with a heat and a need that tore her apart. It was as if the spark had ignited, and everything around them had caught fire.

His hands caressed her naked body, finding her breasts, grazing over her nipples, his fingers teasing them, squeezing them until she gasped for pleasure. She found herself turned around, so that she was the one against the desk, and the next moment she was lying over it and she could feel the cold leather against her back.

His mouth moved to kiss her neck and then trail a blaze down to her breasts, finding her nipples, sucking on them, licking them.

She wound her arms around his neck. All she could think was that she wanted him urgently, wanted him now!

His hands stroked down over the satin material of her pants, stroking her through the material.

'Damon, have you got anything?'

'Hmm?' He lifted his head to look at her.

'Have you got any protection?'

He smiled. 'Yes…somewhere.' As he moved away from her slightly, the contracts on the desk slithered to the floor.

'Maybe that's an omen.' She looked up at him through the darkness of her lashes, her eyes sparkling and seductive. 'Maybe we don't need those contracts now.'

He stilled.

'I mean, we don't need to rush into getting married,' she

explained softly. She reached up to run her hands through the darkness of his hair. 'We can take our time, recapture the past, get to know each other again and—'

'Stop it, Abbie,' he cut across her roughly. 'We don't need to get to know each other again. And I certainly don't want to recapture the past. I know you well enough.'

The brutal words cut through the illusion of their tender love-making. Nothing had changed, she realised dully. She had been fooling herself to think that Damon could ever forget what she had done.

She watched as he zipped up his jeans, and then bent to pick up the contracts from the floor.

'You are not going to get round me—you will sign the contracts, Abbie. Otherwise there is no deal.'

His voice was perfectly controlled, and it was all a million miles away from the passion of just a few moments ago.

She shouldn't have mentioned the contracts. Why had she said anything? 'I wasn't trying to get round you,' she said softly.

'Of course not.' By contrast his voice was almost contemptuous, and her skin burned as his eyes flicked over her naked body.

'I did as you asked,' she reminded him, putting her arms over her breasts to shield them.

'And now you can do as I ask again.' He put the contracts down beside her and picked up a pen. 'Sign on the dotted line.'

Her breathing felt constricted. She had been so turned on…and his cold, merciless manner hurt so much.

'Fine!' She snapped the pen out of his hand and stood up from the desk. 'Show me where you want me to sign and let's just get it over with.'

'Very wise.' He turned the pages over for her and pointed to the last line. 'And don't forget to date it.'

He was unbelievable! Abbie's heart thumped fiercely against her chest as she scribbled her name and the date.

Damon watched her detachedly, and then he couldn't help but let his eyes wander over her figure.

She looked so good, her blonde hair swinging around her shoulders, brushing against her breasts. She still had on her high heels.

The erection that had been straining against his jeans earlier suddenly intensified.

'There.' She slammed the pen down and turned to look at him, her eyes filled with vehemence. 'Satisfied?'

'No, not yet.'

The tone of his voice had changed; his eyes were like liquid fire.

To her consternation, the look turned her on. She was furious with herself. Couldn't she just learn her lesson where he was concerned? She tried to move away from him but he caught her arm.

'Now we can consummate the deal,' he said softly.

She shook her head. 'Oh no, you don't get everything your own way, Damon.' To her horror her voice trembled with feeling. 'You want the *deal*—as you like to call it—done correctly. You marry me first.'

'You're such a spitfire when you want to be.' He paid no attention to her words, just pulled her closer. 'But at least now we've cut through all that rubbish about turning back the clock. If you think I'm going to forget what you really are, then you are mistaken.'

'Fine, have it your way.'

'Oh, don't worry—I will.' His eyes drifted down over her body, and to her dismay she found the way he looked at her made her breasts instantly harden and throb with need.

'I'll have it my way over and over again.' He smiled, but he let go of her. 'And I'll look forward to that tomorrow.'

She glared at him with a mixture of fury and regret. She

didn't want things to be like this between them. She didn't want to yearn for him...but she did.

Rather than bend to pick up her clothes, she left them on the floor and fled from the room. She would rather take her chances bumping into Elise than give Damon the pleasure of watching her gathering up her clothing wearing just her pants.

Luckily she made it to her bedroom without bumping into the housekeeper.

Mario was still fast asleep. The room was tranquil and silent, but there was no solace to be found for Abbie. In fact that very tranquility seemed to mock the tempestuous emotions swirling around inside her.

How could she have allowed herself to think for one moment that they could turn back time? Damon would never forget what she had done, and he would never, ever even consider the fact that he might be wrong about her.

He was so damned smug and superior! She kicked off her shoes and took off her pants, then went to stand under the cool, forceful jet of the shower.

Well, he could go to hell—she hated him!

But as her face turned upwards to the jet of water she remembered how he had so easily turned her on. And she knew that she didn't hate him at all. One moment she had been lost and desolate...the next he had stoked up a fierce longing inside her that had allowed her to return his kisses without reserve, had allowed her to speak without thinking.

She should never have mentioned those contracts. She was such an idiot. But she really had thought that maybe they could start to put things right. She kept remembering how good it could be between them.

Wrapping herself in a towel, she returned to the bedroom to get dressed. She found a black linen skirt in her bag, and a white T-shirt, and hurriedly put them on.

She needed to forget the way Damon made her feel and concentrate on reality, she told herself crossly. But as she reached to pick up a brush to tidy her hair the diamond ring on her finger flashed fire, reminding her that the reality for her was, from tomorrow onwards, she would be Damon's possession.

Mario woke up and started to cry. 'It's OK, honey. I'm coming.' Glad of the distraction, she put the brush down and hurried in to pick him up.

Mario was hungry, which meant going downstairs and facing Damon again. Her stomach tied into knots as she carried the child out into the hallway and down the stairs.

She peeped her head around the door of the study, but there was no sign of Damon. Her clothes, she noted, had been placed on a chair. Part of her wanted to go in and get them, then run back upstairs with them, but Mario was fidgeting in her arms. He needed something to eat, and he was starting to grizzle about the delay.

So, ignoring her discarded clothing, she carried on down the corridor in search of the kitchen. She found it without too much effort. It was at the back of the house, next door to a dining room that looked as if it was big enough to be used as a banqueting suite.

The kitchen was also massive. It had a black-and-white tiled floor and black counter-tops against pale-beech units. Elise was standing at the far end of the room, peeling and chopping vegetables, before throwing them into a pan on the black range cooker. She looked around with a smile. 'Ah, the little one is refreshed now?' Leaving her work, she came over to fuss over Mario. 'He is adorable, and he is so like his father!'

'Yes…' Abbie felt her heart contract at those words. 'But he's a bit crotchety because he's hungry.'

'Put him down.' Elise drew out a high chair from beside the kitchen table. 'I'll make him some lunch.'

Cots and now high chairs, Abbie noted dryly. *Damon has got himself organised.*

'Thank you, Elise, but I can manage. You continue with your work. I don't want to disturb you.' As Abbie put the child into the chair, she spotted the bag she had brought with her that contained all the paraphernalia Mario needed for meal times. Their driver must have brought it in—or maybe Damon. 'Have you seen Damon, by the way?'

She tried to sound nonchalant as she asked the question, but inside she felt taut with tension.

'He came in a few moments ago to tell me he's going over to his apartment in town to sort a few things out.' Elise glanced over at her with a smile. 'Congratulations on your engagement, by the way.'

'Thank you.' Abbie wondered if Elise found this situation as strange as she did. A whirlwind wedding and an un-expected child all catered for in the space of forty-eight hours—it was a lot for anyone to get his or her head around. And, in fairness to Damon, he must still be in shock himself from learning he was a father. 'Did Damon say when he'd be back?' She wanted to see him, to try and make things better again.

'I rather assumed he wouldn't be,' Elise answered with a frown. 'He said he would be sleeping there tonight as it might be bad luck to see his bride on the eve of the wedding.' She must have seen the look of surprise on Abbie's face because she immediately looked concerned. 'He didn't tell you?'

Abbie shook her head.

'Maybe you both have a touch of pre-wedding nerves, hmm?' Elise looked over at her with sudden sympathy.

She thinks we've had a lovers' tiff and Damon has marched

off, Abbie realised. She wished suddenly that it were that simple. 'Perhaps.' She shrugged evasively. She couldn't possibly begin to tell the woman what was really going on; it was far too embarrassing.

'Damon has been a bachelor who has enjoyed his freedom—this is a big step,' Elise said soothingly. 'He's bound to be a bit apprehensive…'

'Yes, I'm sure.' Abbie's tone was dry. She knew exactly what Elise meant when she said Damon was a bachelor who enjoyed his freedom—no doubt he'd enjoyed more women than there were days in the year. She'd seen the way women looked at him. He was like a magnet for them. As for feeling apprehensive now—she didn't think Damon was in the slightest bit worried. As far as he was concerned, he would be gaining a legalised mistress tomorrow, nothing more.

'And it is difficult for you too,' Elise was continuing smoothly. 'You have come to a new country, given up everything you know. It's exciting, but also scary. There is bound to be tension.'

'Yes.' Elise had definitely got the last bit of that statement right. 'I don't even know him that well,' she found herself admitting softly.

'Signor Cyrenci is a very honourable and decent man. He's had a lot of sadness, with the death of his father. Watching someone you love die…' Elise shook her head. 'Well, it was terrible for him. His father was such a good man, and so strong and vital until illness struck.'

'When was that?' Abbie asked softly.

'Must be over two years ago now.'

'Around the time he lost his business?' Abbie felt an ice-like chill start to seep through her.

Elise nodded. 'It was some time after that, yes.'

'I didn't know!' Abbie felt distraught. Had the stress of losing his business made Damon's father ill?

Elise shrugged. 'Well, it's in the past—Signor Cyrenci probably doesn't want to remember it. Things are happier now, and you are getting married tomorrow.' Elise smiled. 'I'm so pleased for you both. Signor Cyrenci deserves this chance of happiness.'

But the reassuring words didn't help at all; Abbie felt sick inside.

'Are you OK?' Elise was looking at her strangely now.

'Yes.' Abbie tried to pull herself together, but she wasn't OK—she was anything but OK.

No wonder Damon wanted to punish her. Maybe he blamed her for not only helping to ruin his father financially but also for contributing towards his death.

'Do you want to sit down? I'll look after Mario.'

The housekeeper's kindness made her want to cry. She didn't deserve any kindness. She was guilty. Guilty by association…guilty of having a father who wrecked lives. 'I don't want to put you to any trouble.'

'Nonsense, it is no trouble. I told Signor Cyrenci I will be glad to help with Mario. I have had three children of my own; two boys and a girl. They are all grown up now.'

Abbie was grateful for the cheerfully efficient tones soothing over her, and grateful when the woman took over from her to heat Mario's lunch. She really didn't feel capable of anything right now.

'Thank you, Elise.' She smiled tremulously at the woman. 'If you are sure, maybe I'll go into the garden for a few moments and get some fresh air.'

It was a relief to step outside the back door, a relief not to have to pretend that everything was all right. It sounded as if Damon's father had died as a result of her father's actions. She walked around the side of the house, the gravel crunching beneath her feet whilst her mind crunched over and over the past.

There was sweet warmth to the summer morning, but Abbie felt cold inside. Her father had ruined so many lives.

She remembered the emotions that had swamped her as she'd watched her mother's life ebbing away. The helplessness of the situation, merged with the anger—then the guilt. If she hadn't helped her mother to escape from her marriage, she would have got treatment sooner and then maybe she could have got better.

Did Damon feel like that when he looked at her? Did he think if he hadn't gone away with her to Palm Springs that his father might be alive today?

If so then he would never forgive her, because he could never forgive himself. Those kinds of feelings could eat you away inside.

She paused as she reached the front of the house and saw the silver-blue sports car that Damon had given her the keys to that morning. She didn't want his gifts. She didn't want his money. All she wanted was to make things better between them again. But that hope seemed further away than ever now.

'Come out to admire your new acquisition, I see.'

Damon's mocking tones made her whirl around in surprise. He was standing a few yards away from her on the front doorstep, watching her. She noticed he'd changed into a pair of black jeans teamed with a black T-shirt. He looked heart-wrenchingly handsome, every inch the haughty Sicilian, master of all he surveyed.

Tomorrow he would be her husband. The knowledge drummed inside her with insistent force.

And then what would happen between them?

'Actually, I was just getting some fresh air.' She hastily tried to pull herself together. 'Elise told me you'd gone to your apartment in town.'

'I have one or two loose ends to tie up here first.'

She nodded and looked away from him. 'At least you've got the business side of things taken care of for our wedding tomorrow.' She tried to sound nonchalant.

Damon watched her through narrowed eyes. There was something poignant about the way she said that. She looked so innocent, so…

He swore under his breath. What the hell was the matter with him? She looked sad because he'd forced her to sign his contract, and she knew now that she wouldn't be able to have a quickie divorce in a few months' time and walk away with his fortune.

That was the type of person she was, and he couldn't allow her big blue eyes and gorgeous figure to cloud that reality in his mind.

He couldn't believe that in the office this morning he'd been filled with remorse for what he was doing to her—filled with shame for making her undress. And all the time she had been the one trying to seduce him into throwing away the prenuptial contract!

And now here she was, out surveying her car—weighing up how much it was worth, no doubt.

She was treacherous!

'Yes, the business side of things is in place,' he replied coolly. 'All we need now is the piece of paper from the registrar.'

She nodded and moved to push her blonde hair out of her face as a soft breeze caught it. The silky tumble of her hair around her shoulders made him think about how she had looked when she'd pulled her top off this morning.

He'd wanted her so much. He'd never desired any woman as much as her. How he had managed to regain his control and pull back from her, he didn't know. All he did know was that tomorrow he would make up for lost time; he would take her again and again until he'd purged some of this need for her out of his body.

'So it's to be a civil ceremony?' She maintained eye contact with him, and tried not to flinch from the fire in his eyes as he watched her.

'Of course it is. Were you hoping for a big high-society wedding? A white dress, your father giving you away perhaps?'

The derisive tone hurt. 'I wasn't hoping for anything.' She tried to angle her chin up a little further. 'I tried to tell you that this morning, that we could just live together…' She struggled for the right words, but she couldn't find them.

As she looked up into his eyes she wanted to tell him that she was sorry about his father—that she was desperately sorry for the part she had played, that she would try to make things up to him…in any way he wanted. But she couldn't say any of it; the words were stuck amidst a well of tears lodged deep inside.

Damon shook his head and came closer to her. 'No, darling Abbie, I think it's best that our arrangement is written down in black and white. You will marry me tomorrow and become a dutiful wife and mother.'

The scorn was sizzling, but she didn't rise to it. 'I'll do whatever you want, Damon,' she said softly instead.

Damon felt a flare of exhilaration as he realised he'd finally brought her to heel.

CHAPTER SEVEN

IT WAS her wedding day.

As Abbie stood in her bedroom and surveyed her reflection in the cheval mirror, she still couldn't quite believe that it was happening—that she was going to marry Damon Cyrenci.

As a little girl she had always maintained quite staunchly that when she grew up she would never get married. She supposed her parents' marriage had put her off; John and Elizabeth Newland had certainly not been a glowing advertisement for the institution.

She remembered telling her mother once when she'd been about ten that she didn't even want a boyfriend let alone a husband. Her mother had laughed. 'Abbie, when you grow up and find someone you truly love then you will change your mind. And I hope when you do that you find the kind of man who is protective and tender and strong—someone who lets you find your wings and soar. With that kind of love, you can conquer the world.'

Why was she thinking about that now? Abbie blinked back the tears. She couldn't think about her mother today—this was already hard enough.

Her eyes drifted down over her suit. She was wearing an ivory silk pencil-skirt that finished just under the knee, teamed with a matching nipped-in jacket that showed off her tiny waist and the swell of her breast.

On Damon's insistence she had allowed his chauffeur to drop her into town yesterday afternoon so that she could buy something to wear.

'Buy some new lingerie as well,' Damon had instructed as he'd peeled some notes out of his wallet.

She'd turned away from him before he'd been able to press the money into her hand. 'I can afford my own dress and underwear, Damon,' she had told him forcefully.

'But we both know that what you really want is to spend this…don't we?' He'd pulled her back and tucked the notes down into her bra.

Just thinking about that now made her upset and furious all over again.

He really thought that she was just interested in money. She bit down on her lip. She understood why he thought that. From his point of view she had lived off her father's ill-gotten profits without shame or remorse. She was calculating and mercenary. There was nothing she could say that would change the past. She had done what she had done and Damon's father had died a broken man. She could only hope that once they were married he would get to know the real her, would realise she had never meant to hurt him, and that deep down she wasn't a bad person.

Damon hadn't been there when she'd returned from her shopping trip. He'd spent the night at his apartment in town. Elise had told her that he would meet her today at the town hall, where they would be married.

She wondered how he had spent his last night as a bachelor, and how he was feeling this morning. What was he thinking? Had he spent the night with another woman?

That thought brought a punch with it that really hurt.

There was a knock on the door. 'The car is ready and waiting whenever you are,' Elise called out cheerfully.

But would Damon be ready and waiting for her? Maybe he'd decided that a marriage without love wasn't worth having, and maybe he was right except the thought of him walking away from her now hurt so much she could hardly breathe.

'Abbie?' Elise knocked on the door again. 'You're running a little late.'

With difficulty Abbie pulled herself together and went to open the door.

'Oh, you look so beautiful.' Elise smiled with delight as she saw her.

'Thank you.' Abbie reached to take her son from the woman. 'Has he been good for you?'

'A little angel,' Elise said quickly. 'Now, you mustn't worry about him this afternoon. I'll take good care of him.'

Abbie nodded. She'd wanted to bring Mario with her to the ceremony, but Damon had insisted that he stay behind with Elise.

'A few minutes and it will all be over,' he'd told her firmly. 'Why disrupt his routine? He has an afternoon nap, is that not so?'

'Yes, but—'

'Then we will leave him to his sleep. He is a baby, Abbie. He won't know what is going on. What happens between us tomorrow is between consenting adults. The only thing that will be important to Mario is that he has both his parents with him as he grows up.'

Abbie hugged the child close now, and he wriggled in her arms. He tired; she could see his eyes starting to close.

'I'll put him down in a few minutes,' Elise told her soothingly. 'Then I'll turn on the baby monitor and listen out for him.'

'Come up and check on him as well,' Abbie said. 'Just in case…'

'Yes. Please don't worry. I know all about taking care of babies. I'm not just a mother, I'm also a grandmother.'

With a smile Abbie handed her baby back over to the woman. She knew Mario would be fine with Elise. She was capable and kind, and Mario seemed to like her. Her real worry was what lay ahead of her.

Elise accompanied her back down the stairs, and stood framed in the doorway with Mario in her arms as she watched Abbie getting into the limousine.

The white-hot heat of the afternoon made the atmosphere strangely silent, as if everything was lulled into sleep. The scent of lavender and jasmine was heavy in the air. The chauffeur closed the door and climbed behind the wheel. Abbie waved at Elise and Mario, then settled back into the empty silence of the car.

She watched the scenery pass by. For a while there was an arid landscape of cacti, then dazzling mountain villages surrounded by lemon-and-orange groves against the backdrop of a cerulean blue sky.

The limousine pulled into a village square and ground to a halt under the shade of a large tree. Abbie thought that they would be getting married in the city where she had shopped for her outfit yesterday, but this town was quaintly charming, and had almost a surreal, romantic feel about it.

She smiled sadly at the thought. She was sure Damon hadn't chosen this location for any reasons of the heart.

She looked around. The buildings were painted a dazzling white and the narrow streets were cobbled. Somewhere a bell was chiming. But there wasn't a soul about. Abbie wondered where Damon was. Maybe he had stood her up. Maybe she'd been right about last night.

A black cat asleep under the shade of the tree uncurled to watch with curious green eyes as the chauffeur opened the car door for her.

Then as she stepped into the heat of the afternoon she looked up, and her glance met with Damon's.

Abbie felt her heart dart with a burst of pure pleasure.

He was standing at the top of some steps leading into an impressive-looking building. He looked so handsome in the formal suit, his dark hair glinting in the sun, that she found herself rooted to the spot just drinking him in, committing this moment to memory.

The car door slammed closed behind her, bringing her back to reality, and she walked slowly across to where he was waiting.

Although he was leaning nonchalantly against the pillar of the doorway, there was nothing casual about the way he was watching her. She noticed his dark Sicilian eyes held that blatantly bold look—a look that took in everything about her from her high heels to the way she had secured her hair up. A look that practically undressed her and made her sizzle inside with tension, but also with an answering need, a need that she didn't even want to try and acknowledge right at this moment.

'Hello.' As she reached his side, she smiled up at him uncertainly. What did one say in this situation? 'Am I late?' She cringed—that sounded absurd given the circumstances.

But he smiled back, his lips tugging in a crooked line. 'As a matter of fact, you are. But you were worth the wait.'

The husky undertone made her warm inside. 'That's all right, then.' She tried to sound nonchalant.

'I suppose it is.' He held out a hand. 'So, shall we go get this over with?'

She hesitated for just a moment before putting her hand in his and allowing him to lead her inside.

The possessive touch of his skin against hers made her even more nervous. It was dark inside the building, dark and cool. Her high heels echoed on the marble floors as he led her towards another door and opened it.

The room they walked into had a high ceiling and an ornate upper gallery. A large stained-glass window filtered sunshine in shafts of red and blue across the large wooden table at the top. Behind it there was a throne-like chair and a stand that held both the Sicilian and the Italian flags.

Wooden seating was arranged in the auditorium, probably enough for fifty people. But only a group of three waited for them at the top of the room, a woman and two men. All were dressed smartly. The men wore grey suits and the woman, who was an attractive brunette of perhaps forty, was wearing a blue business-like trouser suit.

'Signor Cyrenci.' The woman reached to shake his hand, and Damon let go of Abbie to greet her. For a moment the conversation was in rapid Italian and then the woman smiled at Abbie. 'My apologies, Ms Newland, I didn't realise you didn't speak Italian. The ceremony today will be conducted in English. We have two witnesses for you, Luigi Messini and Alfredi Grissillini, both clerks who work here.' The woman smoothly introduced the men to her, and they nodded their heads in acknowledgement. 'Now, shall we proceed?'

As Abbie and Damon moved to take two chairs placed before the table, the woman took the throne-like seat behind.

This all felt unreal, Abbie thought as she listened to the woman talking about the institution of marriage whilst at the same time taking out some documentation from a drawer.

She glanced over at Damon, who was listening intently. Her eyes moved over his rugged features, taking in the firm, square jaw, the sensual curve of his lips, the aristocratic nose. His thick hair gleamed an almost blue-black streaked with just a few strands of silver at the temple; it was brushed back from his face in an almost careless manner. She loved his hair, loved running her fingers through it when he kissed her.

The thought of him kissing her made her stomach do a weird flip of desire.

She glanced away from him hurriedly as the woman asked them both to stand.

'Abigail Newland, do you take this man, Damon Allessio Cyrenci, as your lawfully wedded husband? Do you promise to love, honour and obey him and for all time stay true only to him?'

Abbie looked over at Damon. He was watching her with an unfathomable expression in his dark eyes. She felt her heart speed up, hitting against her ribcage with a fierce intensity that was almost painful.

'I do.'

He smiled, and she tried to pull her thoughts together as they jumbled together inside her in the craziest of emotions.

'Damon Allessio Cyrenci, do you take this woman, Abigail, as your lawfully wedded wife, to have and to hold from this day forward?'

It wasn't lost on Abbie that the vows he took were different from hers. He'd written what he wanted. He'd made her promise to obey him—whilst he'd promised only to have and to hold. Damon did what he wanted, and was asserting that this was the way it would be from now on.

She felt a surge of pure anger. But as he took her hand in his, and slipped the plain gold band into place, he smiled at her and this time there was something in his eyes that stilled her anger.

'I now pronounce you man and wife.' The woman smiled at them. 'May I be the first to congratulate you on your new life together.'

'Thank you.' Damon didn't break eye contact with Abbie as he answered, and for a moment it was almost as if he were saying thank you to her.

'I suppose we should seal the deal with a kiss…hmm?' he asked her softly. He didn't wait for a reply. He leaned down, and his lips grazed tenderly over hers.

The sensual feeling sent shivers of desire racing through her entire body. She kissed him back tentatively, yet she desperately wanted more, wanted this place and these strangers to melt away and leave them alone to finish what they had started such a long time ago.

Damon pulled back from her, and then it was time for them to sign the register.

Abbie watched the coloured shafts of light slant over the papers, the light turning them to rose pink then to gold as they were moved for her signature. A few minutes later they were outside again in the fierce sun.

Had that really happened? Was she really married? Abbie looked up at the handsome Sicilian beside her. He was a stranger to her in so many ways, and yet so achingly familiar.

Damon glanced down at her and smiled. 'So, how are you feeling, Mrs Cyrenci?'

Abbie didn't know how she was feeling. 'Shell-shocked, I think,' she admitted softly.

Their chauffeur opened the doors of the limousine for them, and it was a relief to slip into the air-conditioned cool.

A bottle of champagne waited for them on ice, and Damon sat opposite her to uncork it as the vehicle glided smoothly out of the square.

He handed a glass across to her, and then sat back to give her his undivided attention.

How was it that he only had to look at her like that and the adrenalin started pumping wildly through her body? Was it something about his eyes? He did have the sexiest eyes of any man she'd ever met. Or was it his aura? He did radiate a powerful magnetism. Whatever it was, it really got to Abbie, made her temperature soar so much that she wanted to melt, made her heart race, made her body tingle with pleasure, made her think about the pleasure he could give her…

Hurriedly she looked away from him. Silence stretched between them. She felt awkward. She felt like she needed to say something to break the tension rising inside her.

'I can't believe that we actually got married,' she managed at last.

His lips curved in a smile. 'Well, we did. And you made a very sexy bride. I like the outfit.'

'Thank you.'

'Your hair also looks good like that.'

His eyes moved over her face, noticing the velvety softness of her skin, the blush of her cheeks and the peach-satin sheen of her lips.

She'd taken his breath away when she'd stepped out of the car. He'd never wanted anyone as much as he'd wanted her at that moment. The suit was perfect: sexy yet sophisticated. And her hair was also perfect—also sophisticated, but the tendrils that had escaped to curl around the beauty of her face gave her softness and a fragile vulnerability that tore him up inside.

She raised her blue eyes towards him now and he felt the same wrenching feeling inside. He wished he could rid himself of this sensation. He wanted to feel lust for her, nothing more…

'I told Frederic to drive us back to my apartment in town. The staff there will have laid us out a late lunch. And then I'm taking you to bed for the afternoon.' He said the words in a low, commanding tone and watched as her skin flared with colour. 'Are you hungry?'

Abbie hurriedly glanced away from him. Her heart was racing. She didn't want to eat. She didn't know what she wanted…

The thought of spending the afternoon in bed with Damon was infinitely exciting, yet terrifying, all at the same time.

'Not really.' She didn't dare look over at him. She felt foolish and unsure of everything. 'And don't you think we should go back to the house, not to your apartment? I want to check on Mario.'

'Mario will still be asleep.' Damon reached across and topped up her glass of champagne. 'And Elise is very trustworthy.'

She couldn't argue with that.

Would he ask her to undress the way he had yesterday… Would he be gentle? In the past Damon had always been a passionate yet sensitive lover. She remembered the tenderness in his kiss yesterday, and a floodgate of feelings for him opened up that truly terrified her.

She took a few hurried sips of her champagne and then put the glass down in the holder next to her.

Damon watched as she nervously fiddled with a couple of buttons on her jacket.

'You should take that off now,' he instructed.

Something about the instruction made her nerves stretch even more. 'Damon, I know you got me to promise that I would obey you, but I have to inform you right now that it is not a promise I intend to keep.' She suddenly angled her chin up and sent him a look of fierce defiance from her flashing eyes.

To her disconcertment he merely looked amused at her outburst. 'Breaking your vows already?' He mocked her with dark eyes. 'Dear me, Abbie…' He shook his head. 'That simply just won't do.'

'No, it won't!' She lowered her tone but her voice trembled alarmingly. 'I may be your wife, but I have my own mind, Damon. There are certain things that I will not be told about.'

'And what are they?' Damon sounded like he was enjoying himself—as if she were the most entertaining of women.

'What to wear, what to do—and on the subject of Mario—'

'On the subject of Mario we will confer and decide things together,' he cut across her firmly and smiled. 'You are his mother, and I respect that.'

The words took her aback, took the fire out of her argument.

'But as for what you wear and what you do especially in the bedroom…on that you will defer to me.'

His arrogance inflamed her senses, yet the melting eyes that held with hers made the warm darts of desire increase inside her.

She looked away from him, annoyed with herself.

'And by the way when I told you to take your jacket off it was because I thought you looked uncomfortable,' he added. 'I wasn't going to tell you to take everything else off as well.' He glanced at her. 'Well, not yet, anyway.'

'Very amusing.' Abbie fought down the flood of heat inside her. He thought he was so clever. 'And I can't believe you made me promise to obey you.' She shook her head.

Damon laughed. 'Well, you were late. I thought I'd fill the time waiting for you in a productive manner.'

The limousine pulled up by a marina. Luxury yachts bobbed on tranquil clear water, and there were some upmarket boutiques and restaurants. The place had a very sophisticated feel. It was obviously a playground for the moneyed, yet it still retained a charm and character from the past. Fisherman sat mending their nets by the harbour wall, and the new buildings along the quay merged seamlessly with old.

'My apartment is just here.' Damon pointed to a modern building.

It was all very swish, Abbie thought as she followed him into the foyer. A security guard greeted him by name, and then they stepped into a lift.

Damon's apartment was at the top of the building. By contrast with his house, it was ultra-modern to the point of minimalist. A bachelor's playground, Abbie thought as she glanced around, all tubular steel and appliances of science. Wall-mounted TV's, remote-control gadgets for everything, probably even the cooker. And the bed... Her eyes skimmed past the room that held the enormous king-sized bed.

Damon opened doors that led out to a large terrace. They were high up, and the view was spectacular across the harbour and the alluring blue glitter of the sea.

Someone had gone to a lot of trouble, and had set a table outside for lunch. The table was covered with a crisp white-linen cloth, and was laid with silver and crystal ware. An ice bucket held a bottle of champagne, and there were balloons everywhere across the wooden decking.

Damon shook his head as he surveyed the scene. 'I made the mistake of telling the staff that it was my wedding day—they must have thought balloons were a nice touch.'

'They are.' The fact that someone had gone to that trouble somehow touched Abbie. She met Damon's steady gaze and shrugged. 'Well, I like them...it's lovely.'

His lips twisted in an amused smile. 'There's something you'll probably like a little better waiting for you on the table.'

She saw the jewellery box sitting on the white place-setting, but didn't go to pick it up. 'What is it?' she asked him huskily.

'A little bauble to mark our wedding day. Go and have a look.'

Before she could answer, the ring of Damon's mobile phone interrupted them. He glanced at the dial before answering, then disappeared inside for a few moments.

Abbie could hear him talking in Italian, but she was barely listening. Why couldn't he get it through his head that she didn't want his gifts? She opened the box and glanced inside. Nestling on velvet was an exquisite necklace, a single diamond teardrop on a gold chain. It was probably worth a fortune.

For a moment her mind ran back to their conversation when he'd first suggested they get married, and she had rounded on him in outrage. *'You think I'd tie myself into a loveless marriage...?'*

'For wealth, security and all the baubles and trappings of luxury you could possibly want? Yes I do.'

She snapped the lid closed and put the box down as if it had burnt her. Then she moved towards the balustrade to look down at the harbour, but tears blinded her eyes.

'So, do you like the necklace?' Damon appeared behind her again.

She didn't answer him, couldn't answer him.

'It is real,' he told her dryly.

She closed her eyes. She understood why he thought of her the way he did—she just wished it didn't hurt.

His phone rang again, and after a moment's hesitation he took the call. 'Sorry about that,' he murmured a moment later. 'I've got an important deal going through soon.'

Abbie had been glad of the interruption; at least it had given her a moment to pull herself together. 'That's all right, you've got to get your priorities in order.'

'Well, today *you* are my priority—so I've switched the phone off now.'

She wished he meant that. She stared pensively out across the expanse of sea.

'So, shall we have something to eat?'

'I told you, I'm not really hungry.' She felt too tense to eat, too tense to even look around at him. 'I don't know what we are doing here. We should really have just gone back to the house.'

'You know what we are doing here, Abbie,' he told her softly.

She closed her eyes. 'Mario will be waking up soon.'

'Mario will be fast asleep.'

Abbie didn't say anything. She knew he was right, she knew she had no need to worry about Mario. She just wished that Damon hadn't bought her that necklace; she just wished that things between them were different. That the silly balloons meant something to him! What on earth was the matter with her? How stupid was that? she mocked herself fiercely.

She pulled herself together and blinked the tears away. Then, steeling herself, she turned to look at him.

'Elise told me about your father,' she said suddenly.

'What did she tell you?' he asked coolly.

'About his death—you know, soon after him losing the business, and…I just wanted to tell you how sorry I am. And I never wanted any of that to happen.'

The sincerity in her voice and in her eyes perplexed him.

'Well, I suggest we forget about the past and about the outside world for now, and relax.'

'But you can't forget about the past, can you?' she asked softly. 'And your father died because of it!'

'My father died because he smoked heavily all of his life,' Damon said with a frown.

'Oh! I thought… I thought it was the stress of losing the business.'

Damon watched the emotions flicker through her eyes. She looked like she had been genuinely distressed by the notion—but he only had to remember how cold-blooded she had been in the past to know that it was another of her little acting ploys. A woman who cared about hurting people didn't go around deceiving them, lying to them, didn't deliberately use her body to hurt others and get what she wanted.

'Abbie, you didn't contribute to his death, but you are right about one thing—I can't forget about the past or what you are. Because I'd be a fool to forget it.' His eyes swept over her suddenly and the contempt in them lashed at her.

'Feeling like that, I'm surprised you went through with the wedding,' she whispered rawly.

'On the contrary, when you stepped out of the car today and into the square I knew positively that I was doing the right thing.'

'Did you?' Her eyes lifted to his. 'Why?'

He looked at her for a long, considered moment and she could feel her heart racing against her chest.

'Because we have a child to look after. Mario has to come first now.'

Given the circumstances she knew she should be content with that, but the coldness of his response added to the ache inside her.

She watched as he turned away from her and lifted the bottle of champagne.

'Let's have a drink.'

He was so cavalier and nonchalant, and it made Abbie's temper rise. 'It's very noble of you, putting your needs to one side for your child's security,' she grated sardonically.

'Who said anything about putting my needs to one side?' He flashed her an amused look and she felt herself blush. 'I have absolutely no intention of doing that.'

He passed her the glass of champagne, and she was annoyed to find that her hand wasn't quite steady as she accepted it.

'But I want things to be right for Mario,' he continued smoothly. 'I know what it's like to grow up without a parent, Abbie. My mother walked out when I was eight, and… Well, I always vowed that I'd never put a child through that. A child

needs stability. Bringing up a family is the ultimate commitment.'

'Is that why you decided to just play the field for all these
years?'

He looked over at her wryly. 'Being a bachelor was something I was good at,' he said, his mouth curved with amusement.

Abbie remembered her suspicions earlier that morning,
that Damon had been out last night enjoying himself, had
brought someone back here to bed.

'And, now that we are married, do you *still* intend to play
around?' She forced herself to ask the question even though
she wasn't sure she wanted to hear the answer.

Damon watched the way her chin slanted up. What was she
thinking? he wondered. Despite the valiant angle of her chin,
there was a husky tone to her voice, and that look in her eyes…

He frowned and dragged his thoughts away from the absurd
wayward direction they wanted to go in. Abbie's greatest
concern was probably only the fact that, if he found someone
else, she might lose her golden ticket to riches.

'I thought I made my intentions clear—I want a stable
home for Mario.' He held her gaze steadily. 'So I intend to
amuse myself playing around with *you* from now on.'

She flushed a little and he smiled. 'I think you will manage
to keep me satisfied. You are very attractive, very beautiful,
Abbie—but then of course you know that don't you.'

The compliment sat painfully with her.

Damon watched the shadowy, dark glints of sapphire in her
eyes. She was so desirable, he felt his stomach tie up with the
thought of having her now…felt himself harden. He just
wished she didn't stir up these other emotions inside him.

Like now, for example; something in her expression made
him long to forget what she was and reach out to hold her
tenderly. It had been the same today when she'd stepped out

of the car into the square, and also when she'd looked up at him whilst taking her vows.

She wasn't going to get under his skin ever again, Damon reminded himself fiercely. When he touched her, when he held her, it would be to take her, possess her, use her the way she had once used him.

He picked up his own glass of champagne. 'So what shall we drink to—the future, hmm? Our new arrangement?'

'How about your new acquisition?' she supplied, her eyes sparkling with that mixture of defiance and rawness that he was starting to know so well.

'Or to Mario?' he suggested. 'The one thing we got absolutely right?'

She smiled at him suddenly, and it was like the sun had come out from behind the clouds.

His eyes moved over her slowly. 'So, here we are, Mrs Cyrenci…alone at last.' His voice was teasingly sexy.

'Are we?' She tried not to sound apprehensive. 'Where are the staff?'

'All gone. We have a very good arrangement that gives me maximum privacy.'

'Everyone around you is very cooperative.'

'Apart from one…' His eyes moved down over her body with a possessiveness that made her pulses race. 'My wife. The woman who has already informed me today that she intends to break her wedding vows.'

She tried not be affected by the way he was looking at her, but she was. And his teasing tone brought her skin out in strange little goosebumps. She liked the way he referred to her as his wife in that warm way, as if it did mean something to him.

But it doesn't, she tried to remind herself fiercely. He'd already made that clear. She didn't mean anything to him.

Even so when he reached out and trailed one finger along

the side of her face she felt herself melt inside. 'You belong to me now, Abbie,' he said huskily. 'And that means keeping the promises you made today.'

Her heart hammered fiercely against her chest as she looked up at him. 'I'll keep the ones that are most important,' she whispered.

Something about the way she said that, the way she looked at him seared him to the bone. He watched as she put down her glass, reached to unfasten the buttons on her jacket and then slipped it off.

Underneath she wore a peach satin camisole with spaghetti straps. It emphasised the firm upward tilt of her breasts.

Abbie looked up at him and saw the flare of desire in the darkness of his eyes. She liked the way he looked at her. But she knew he didn't love her. She knew what he thought of her.

Still, he did want her. And she needed him to want her. Needed him to fill the aching void inside her. He was the one man she had never really got out of her system. She didn't understand why, and she didn't want to dwell too deeply on the questions. All she knew was how he could make her feel. And she wanted to feel like that again.

'How private are we out here?' She looked up at him from under dark eyelashes.

'About as private as you can get. Why don't you put on the gift I bought for you and take off everything else?'

The seductive comment inflamed her senses. 'I don't want your gift, Damon.' She continued to looked up at him through cloudy blue eyes.

He reached out a hand and stroked it softly down the side of her neck. The caress made her tingle inside. 'Well, I want your gift to me…and I want it right now.'

His fingers moved lower, teasingly stroking her along the edge of the camisole top.

The touch of his fingers brushing against her skin felt so good. She knew what he was talking about, and she didn't try to misunderstand him. There was no point in pretending, not when the gravelly command had made her body burn with a need to comply.

'So…what do you want to do?'

Damon liked the question—liked the way she matched it with a shy, almost faltering look in her big eyes.

'Should I do this…?' He watched as she unfastened her skirt and let it drop to the floor. She was wearing hold-up stockings, and she looked so sexy that he felt he wanted to burst with the intensity of his need for her.

'You should definitely do that,' he told her quietly.

'And how far do you want to go?'

'You know how far I want to go, Abbie,' he instructed. 'All the way.'

CHAPTER EIGHT

HER top followed her skirt onto the floor.

His eyes moved over her body. Her underwear, unlike yesterday, was deliberately provocative. The bra pushed her up, showing the round peaks of her breasts to perfection, her lace pants were hipsters but see-through and as for the lace-top stockings… Well, they were just too sexy for words.

Hell, he wanted her, wanted to fill her completely…possess her completely.

The way he was looking at her made Abbie feel taut with need. She wanted him to take her into his arms, wanted desperately just to be held. 'So…shall I help you out of your jacket?' It was an excuse for her to move closer to him. 'Perhaps unfasten your tie for you?' Her hands slid up over his chest to smooth the jacket away from the breadth of his shoulders. It fell to the floor with her clothes.

She looked up into his eyes as she reached to unfasten his tie.

Before he could think about how or where he wanted her, he was picking her up and turning her so that her back was against the wall. 'You know exactly what you do to me, don't you, with those big blue oh-so-innocent eyes…?'

Her eyes locked with his as she looked up at him breathlessly, and then she trembled as he slowly and deliberately ran his hands over her body, stroking over the curves of her breasts, his fingers finding her nipples through the lace of her bra and squeezing them. The caress shot exquisite darts of pleasure through her body, and like shots of an addictive drug the feelings made her long for so much more.

He smiled as he heard her gasp with need. Then his mouth moved to possess her lips. The kiss was like nothing she had ever experienced before, masterful, fierce; it sent a feeling of passion so strong, so fierce, racing through her that she felt dizzy…possessed, almost. She opened her mouth and let him plunder the softness inside. All the time she could feel the hard warmth of his body pressing against the aching need of hers.

Just when she thought she was going to die with the desire to be closer, to be possessed totally, he pulled back.

'Don't stop!' Her eyes were wild with tumultuous feelings of desire. 'Please, Damon…' She didn't have to go on because suddenly she felt his fingers stroking her through her knickers.

She was wet and ready for him, and as he stroked her some more she shuddered.

'You like that, don't you?' He whispered the words against her ear.

She closed her eyes. Her breasts felt so tight, so hard; they were throbbing with the demand to be touched. Her body was telling her that she had to have him…it was telling her with such insistent force that she couldn't think straight.

Then suddenly she felt him pushing her knickers down and moving her legs further apart, touching her in a way that took her breath away.

She moaned with pleasure when at the same time he pulled her bra down and bent his head to suck on her nipples.

Her body convulsed with enjoyment, and she raked her

fingers through the darkness of his hair, giving herself up to him with a total lack of control.

Just as she thought she was going to die of sheer pleasure, he left her.

'Damon?' The momentary uncertainty in her eyes was almost his undoing.

'We'll continue this inside.'

He took hold of her hand to lead her through to the bedroom.

It was taking every inch of his willpower not to lose control. He wanted her. Just watching her in those high heels, the stockings lovingly curving around her slender thighs... He needed to contain himself, he reminded himself fiercely. But as she sat down on the bed he could hardly wait to get rid of his clothes.

She noticed that he tore his shirt whilst unbuttoning it... She'd made him do that. The knowledge gave her a flip of exhilaration, but it was nothing to the way she felt as her eyes moved over the sheer perfection of his physique.

His body was toned and strong, tapering down to the perfect six-pack. Abbie remembered his body very well, remembered having been in awe of him when she had first seen him naked. Those feelings hadn't changed.

He joined her down on the bed and she made to take off her stockings, but he lifted her up and moved her back against the satin pillows. 'Stay as you are.' He growled the words against her skin as his mouth moved to capture hers again.

His kiss was ragged with need, his fingers insistent as once more they found her nipples, rubbing over them, pushing her bra down further so that they were forced upwards for his mouth to take possession of them again.

He straddled her, and then reached for some contraception before his body captured hers with fervent, demanding thrusts.

She writhed and gasped with pleasure, and then he pulled back from her a little, stroking her tenderly, finding her lips and kissing her with such sweetness, his hands stroking her hair.

He murmured her name almost incoherently as his body dominated hers, taking her with almost ruthless determination and yet at the same time with an exquisite care, possessing her with ardent warmth that made answering warmth flood her body.

He looked down into her eyes and murmured something to her in Italian.

'I like the sound of your voice when you speak in your own language,' she murmured breathlessly. She moaned and arched her back, and ran her fingers down over the powerful muscles of his back.

He said something else that she didn't understand…then took her lips with his, before grazing down her neck to her nipples to suck on them, lick them, and rock her towards a climax that was so forceful and shattering in its intensity that she cried out. Only then did he join her, releasing himself as wave after wave of sheer joy racked through both of their bodies, fusing them together as one.

For a long time they just lay there holding each other. Abbie felt like crying, not with sadness but with sheer joy, because making love with him had been as incredible as she'd remembered. Once again he had conjured up all the crazy feelings of belonging, and had strangely given the power of his lovemaking a sense of such sweet tenderness.

But this wasn't love, it was just sex, she tried to remind herself fiercely before she got too carried away on flights of fantasy. But the trouble was it didn't feel like it was just sex. She frowned and cuddled a bit closer to him. When he held her, especially like this, the feeling was blissful. It was like the real thing…like she never needed to be lonely again because he was her soul mate.

She closed her eyes and tried to stop analyzing things. It was enough to be in his arms.

He stroked his fingers through her hair almost absentmindedly, and then kissed the top of her head.

It was such a tender gesture that she let her breath out in a sigh. 'Making love with you is so…so good.'

'Yes, the chemistry is as powerful as ever between us. I knew it would be.'

She rolled over a little so that she was looking down at him. 'It is powerful, isn't it?' she breathed huskily. 'You turn me on so much.'

'I noticed.' He smiled at her suddenly, his eyes teasing.

'I kind of noticed that I had a similar effect on you.' She snuggled against him. 'Apart from the obvious—I think you ruined a perfectly good shirt.'

He laughed. 'So how are you with a darning needle, Mrs Cyrenci?'

She smiled. The connection between them felt so strong, the outside world had ceased to exist. Surely he couldn't have made love to her with such searing passion if he felt nothing for her? She wondered, if she took the risk of telling him a little of how she felt right now, would he meet her half way? 'No one's ever made me feel the way you make me feel,' she admitted.

Their eyes locked together, and for a heart-stopping moment she thought he was going to say something similar back to her. She felt so close to him, not just physically but emotionally.

Damon hesitated. She sounded as if she'd really meant that, and there was no doubt that her responses to him had been wildly passionate—she really had wanted him. Making love with her always had been incredible, and it had been better now than he'd even remembered. He felt like he couldn't get enough of holding her, teasing her to arousal, caressing her, kissing her... He frowned. But of course this wasn't making love—there was no emotion involved, he reminded himself fiercely. He had to remember exactly what Abbie was.

Yes, she enjoyed sex, but even the most mercenary of creatures did. Probably what aroused Abbie so much was the thought of all his money.

He ran a tender hand down over the side of her face. That knowledge was difficult to accept when she was looking at him with such sultry blue eyes. But he had to accept it. And at least she did enjoy sex with him—because if she didn't, well, he'd never forced a woman in his life and he certainly wasn't going to start now. 'And that's why our arrangement is going to work so well.' He growled the words against her ear.

Pain spiralled inside her from nowhere. She hadn't expected a declaration of undying love—but she hadn't thought he would remind her quite so dismissively that this was just an arrangement. She could be so stupid sometimes where he was concerned. She pulled away from him abruptly.

'Yes, I suppose you are right.' She tried to match his flippancy so that she could hang on to at least a small shred of pride. She should have known better than to risk lowering any barriers.

Damon watched as she moved away from him, and he was aware of a sudden sharp feeling of regret, as if a precious moment had been lost.

What the hell was the matter with him? He was supposed to be using her for his own pleasure—not making passionate declarations! But for one wild moment he wanted to pull her back, wanted to tell her that she had the same effect on him. That no other woman could make him feel the way she could.

He was losing it, Damon told himself furiously. It had been the same when they were making love: one moment he had been totally enjoying himself with her, and the next she had sighed and cuddled into him and the feelings inside him had completely changed with a swiftness and a power that he'd had no control over. He'd wanted her so much…wanted to hold her close and pleasure her.

He watched as she sat up from him. Her hair had escaped from the pins that had held it up, and it was tousled and sexily dishevelled around her shoulders and her naked breasts, her nipples slightly pink and engorged from the heat of his caresses.

He wanted her again. She was like some kind of nymph who could put a spell on him with just a glance, lure him so easily away from rational thoughts. Well, he wasn't going to allow her to control him with her perfectly staged words and her come-hither looks—he'd fallen for that the first time around.

Abbie was aware that the silence between them was stretching tautly. 'We should be getting back to the house now.'

'You're not going anywhere, Abigail…' He pulled her back towards him suddenly and kissed her again. It was a kiss that sent tingles flooding through her entire body.

It was strange how his lips told her one thing, with their seductive, possessive kisses, and his words told her something completely different with their commanding, slightly mocking edge.

The mix set wildly conflicting thought patterns racing through her. Part of her wanted to pull away from him with a toss of her head—part of her wanted to melt into him. She swallowed hard. She didn't want to stop making love with him. The adrenalin was charging through her veins, changing her into somebody she hardly recognised. She hated herself for being so weak.

'Damon, I need to get myself a drink of water.' She pulled away from him abruptly and he let her go, and watched how she pulled her bra up to cover her swollen nipples, before picking up his shirt from the floor and pulling it on to cover her nakedness.

It swamped her, but it also looked incredibly sexy with her stockings and high heels.

He watched her walk away from him towards the kitchen. How was it that just when he thought he had her tamed and submissive she could so easily turn the tables on him? Damon wondered edgily. He got out of bed and threw on a towelling robe that was hanging on the back of the door.

She was pouring herself a glass of water from a bottle she had found in the fridge.

'I'll have one of those while you are there,' he directed softly.

'OK.' She didn't look round at him but reached to get a glass.

'You look good in my shirt, by the way,' he remarked as his eyes moved down over the long length of her legs. 'Even the way it's ripped is strategically enhancing.' He noticed as she turned that he could see the top of her thighs.

She flicked him a slightly nervous glance. She was good at looking at him with just that mixture of uncertainty and desire. It drove him crazy.

'All you need now is the necklace that I bought for you,' he murmured suddenly.

'I told you, Damon, I don't want your gifts.' Her voice trembled slightly.

'Of course you do.' He disappeared for a moment to pick up the jewellery from outside on the patio. Maybe if she wore this hunk of expensive, beautiful stone around her neck it would remind him of what she was, he thought forcefully. Because every time she looked at him in that raw, almost vulnerable way of hers he was in very real danger of forgetting.

'I don't want that necklace, Damon,' she told him softly

when he came back into the kitchen. 'I don't want you to put it anywhere near me.'

'What's the matter, isn't the diamond big enough to satisfy you?' he rasped.

'Don't, Damon!' The look she shot him was so beseeching that it cut.

It would be so easy to forget what she was. She was so gorgeously desirable, all kitten-warmth and come-to-bed eyes.

But he couldn't allow himself to forget…he just couldn't.

'Abbie, I bought this for you as a wedding present, so the least you can do is damn well wear it on our wedding day.'

'Sorry, but I'm not going to.'

'You are so stubborn!'

'So are you!' She glared at him as she walked across towards him with his glass of water. 'You don't listen to me. I don't want your money or your gifts!'

Who the hell did she think she was fooling? he wondered angrily.

'Come here.' He caught hold of her hand as she approached and pulled her towards him. Then, putting down the water on the kitchen bar, he pulled her towards one of the comfortable chairs in the lounge area and brought her down so that she was straddling his knee.

'Now, hold your hair up out of the way.'

She held his gaze with a mutinous stare.

'Do as I ask, Abbie—it's just a necklace.'

'But it's not, is it?' she asked softly. 'It's *not* just a necklace, it's a symbol of what you really think of me.'

He ignored that and opened up the box to take out the necklace. It flashed fire in the sunlight. 'Lift up your hair,' he ordered again.

When she still didn't comply, he placed it around her neck and fastened it over her hair. Then he reached and pulled her hair up, letting it trail through his fingers like liquid gold as he released it.

The chain fell around her neck, the diamond heavy and cold against her skin. He sat back to look at her. 'There… It looks good.'

She hated it, but she left it where it was and just held his gaze defiantly.

'Abbie, don't look at me like that.' There was rawness in his voice for just a second, a note that was at odds with the arrogant dominance of his actions. 'I'll buy you another necklace tomorrow, one that you can choose for yourself, all right?' As he spoke he trailed a hand over her chin, down the line of her neck.

It wasn't all right, but she couldn't speak, her throat felt too choked. She trembled at his touch; she felt so cold inside, yet just the slightest stroke of his hand made her warm again, stirred up a heat she didn't want, couldn't handle, couldn't control.

'Now, where were we?' He started to unfasten the buttons on the shirt, and then as it fell apart he pulled her bra down, exposing her breasts to the darkness of his eyes.

Her heart was thundering painfully against her chest. She wanted him too, so much it hurt.

His fingers played with her nipples, squeezing them, stroking them until they were hard peaks of need. Her hands moved to rest on his thighs, and his fingers became rougher yet inflamed her all the more.

Then suddenly he was inside her, bouncing her on his knee, watching how her breasts moved with each of his thrusts. He put his hands on her slender hips, controlling her, watching how she writhed, how her hair swung silkily around her shoulders, how the diamond sparkled as it nestled between her cleavage.

As she climaxed she called out his name, and he leaned forward and took one breast into his mouth, sucking on her, until he also reached his own climax.

She wrapped her arms around him and buried her face in the dark softness of his hair, holding him tight against her. Her body was convulsed with pleasure, throbbing from the aftermath of a sensation so pleasurable it had exhausted her totally.

They were wrapped so tightly in each other's arms and he was still inside her, still a part of her, so that it was almost as if they had become one.

He stroked her hair back from her face, and as she pulled away from him a little he captured her lips in a dominant, yet tremendously sensual kiss. She wanted it to go on and on, but he pulled away from her after a few moments.

Spent and exhausted, she cuddled in against him.

She tried to remind herself that part of her should still be angry about the necklace—about his dominant, insensitive ways. But try as she might she couldn't rekindle that anger. It felt too good being held by him.

He doesn't trust me—he doesn't love me—but when he's with me like this he is mine...totally mine, she told herself firmly. And for now that was enough, because she loved him so much.

The thought made fear and shock race through her so violently that she shivered.

'Are you OK?'

The concern in his voice caused even greater emotional waves to smash through her body. 'No, not really.' She buried her head into his neck. She couldn't allow herself to be in love with him—he'd never return the feelings, and it hurt too much. And yet she knew now that she was in love with him. Maybe she had never really stopped loving him, and had just tried to persuade herself that she had because it was the only way she'd been able to cope with losing him.

'I didn't hurt you, did I?' He sounded mortified. 'Abbie, I never intended to hurt you.' He gathered her closer, stroking her hair.

She squeezed her eyes tightly closed against the tears that wanted to flow. 'You didn't hurt me. I just had a momentary pang of...something.'

'Of what?' He held her away from him and looked at the bright glitter in her blue eyes. His heart turned over as a tear spilled down over the pallor of her skin.

She shrugged. 'I don't know, I'm being stupid.' She brushed the tears from her eyes harshly and pulled away from him to stand up. She was going to have to pull herself together. She couldn't possibly tell him that she loved him. She remembered his earlier response to her unguarded comment, and she couldn't risk seeing contempt in his eyes now—couldn't risk losing the little pride she had left. 'Maybe I'm just tired. I didn't sleep well last night and, well, it's quite an emotional business getting married, isn't it?'

He frowned. 'I guess it is. Abbie, I—'

'Are you hungry?' She cut across him firmly and smiled. It was the kind of smile that made his heart drum wildly against his chest. The kind of smile that made him question everything he'd done—everything he'd said to her in the last couple of days.

'Because I am,' she continued swiftly. 'I haven't eaten anything all day. I was too tense this morning for breakfast.'

'Were you?' He watched as she pulled his shirt over her curves.

'Of course. Marriage is a big step and, like you, it's something I said I'd never do.'

She moved away from him. In truth she wasn't in the slightest bit hungry, but she needed to do something—needed to change the direction of her thoughts to pull them away from the dangerous edge where they were poised precariously.

She opened the fridge door and looked in. 'There are all sorts of goodies in here—do you want something?'

Damon belted his dressing gown and stood up. Was it his imagination, or was her voice too bright? 'I'll have whatever you are having.'

Abbie brought out some smoked salmon and some salad and put it on the breakfast bar.

'Shall we sit here to eat? I know the table is laid outside, but I just want a snack, and somehow this seems more relaxed.'

'Yes, that's fine.' Damon pulled out one of the breakfast bar-stools and sat opposite her.

The glasses of water from earlier were beside them. 'I'll top these up with ice,' he said as he leaned over to the ice dispenser. 'They might be warm now.'

'Thanks.'

He noticed that she avoided his eyes as he put the glass down beside her again.

Why had she cried? The question burnt through him. Now he thought carefully back over their love-making, he didn't think he'd been rough. She'd seemed to enjoy it, had moaned, with pleasure not pain. Had called out his name with a little husky moan.

Just thinking about it made him want her all over again. How was it that even now, after a wildly passionate afternoon, he still needed her?

He forced himself not to think about that now.

'So you were nervous this morning?' he asked quietly.

'A bit.' She reached for the water and took a long swallow. 'Weren't you?'

There was a moment's silence, and she shook her head. 'Sorry, silly question.'

'It's not a silly question. I had a few last-minute qualms.'

'Really?' She looked at him then.

'I've been a bachelor a long time. Of course I thought deeply about what I was doing this morning.'

She nodded. 'Did you go out last night?' She tried to sound casual, as if she didn't really care what he'd done. But she did care, she cared way, *way* too much about everything.

He shook his head. 'I worked. I had a lot to sort out so I could have a few days off with you now.'

'Oh!' She smiled at him and felt some of the tension inside her easing as he smiled back. He had such a gorgeously sexy smile…

She reached for her glass of water again.

'Thirsty?'

'Yes. I know it's air-conditioned in here, but I feel a bit hot.'

'Again?' He looked at her with a mixture of warmth and humour, and she blushed prettily.

'Well, let me eat something and get my strength back first,' he murmured softly.

She liked the look he slanted across at her, liked the provocatively teasing tone in his voice. It made her sizzle inside.

It was nice sitting here with him like this. If she didn't think too deeply about things, she could pretend that they were just a regular couple—just married and too much in love to keep their hands off each other.

'You know what's missing in here?' he asked suddenly.

'Some music?'

'No, but that could be arranged.' He smiled. 'No, I was talking about the view.'

'You have a spectacular view.' She turned her head to look out the window across the dazzle of the blue sea.

'But it could be better.' He leaned across and unbuttoned the shirt she wore so that he could see the full curves of her body in the lacy bra.

The touch of his hands against her skin made her flare with a deep longing for him.

'And maybe we should get rid of this.'

To her surprise, he reached and unfastened the necklace from around her neck and set it down to one side.

Their eyes held across the table.

Her heart was thundering wildly against her chest as he smiled at her.

'Is that better?' he asked huskily.

She nodded. 'Infinitely better.'

CHAPTER NINE

ABBIE was pretending to read a book as she lay next to the pool, but really she was watching Damon. He was playing in the water with Mario. They'd got some water wings for the child, and he loved being in the pool with his father. He was laughing with delight now as Damon allowed him to kick his legs and make a splash whilst he supported him carefully in strong arms.

She smiled as she watched him raise the child into the air then dip his toes down again in the water, and she loved hearing Mario laugh. She loved watching the muscles ripple powerfully in her husband's arms as he moved. He really had a dreamily wonderful body, she thought distractedly as her eyes moved over his bronzed torso, noticing how his skin gleamed in the bright sunshine.

He looked like he worked out every day. There was a gym down in the basement of the house, but Abbie had never seen him use it. She'd asked him last night as they'd lain together in the deep comfort of their double bed if he ever used it, and he had laughed. 'Not enough hours in the day—anyway, I'm saving all my energy to work out with you.'

They certainly had 'worked out' a lot together this week. Just thinking about it made Abbie's heart race. Since Damon had taken that necklace from around her neck, it was as if they had turned some kind of a corner in their relationship.

She knew nothing had fundamentally changed—deep down he still distrusted her. But it was as if some sort of unspoken truce had occurred, as if a line had been drawn under the past. And Abbie was glad of it, because this had been the most wonderful week of her life. She loved the way Damon could make her feel.

She loved the way he couldn't seem to get enough of her, because she felt exactly the same. Even now, watching him in the pool playing with their son, she wanted him. Yet just a few hours ago he'd taken her back to bed for a siesta. Just thinking about that 'siesta' now made her melt with longing all over again.

She also loved the way he was with Mario, protective and gentle, yet fun. She'd noticed how over the week the little boy had fast grown attached to him, his dark eyes lighting up whenever his father walked into the room.

Damon looked up now and caught her watching him. 'Why don't you come in and join us?'

'No, it's OK, you carry on.' She smiled at him. In truth she didn't want to get too close to him, because she was feeling extremely aroused just watching him. And she didn't want him to know just how much she wanted him *again*.

'Come on, the water is lovely.' He splashed some of it in her direction and the cold hit the heat of her skin, making her jump.

'Ow! It's freezing! I'm definitely not coming in!'

'Don't be such a chicken.' Damon lifted Mario out of the water.

The little boy chuckled as Damon splashed Abbie again.

'Damon, stop!' She swung her long legs over the edge of the sun lounger and put her book down.

Damon's eyes swept over her body with bold approval. She was wearing a very skimpy black-and-white bikini and it looked sensational on her. 'Come into the pool with us,' he said firmly. 'We need you.'

'No, you don't.'

'Yes, *I* do.' He smiled with that half tug of his lips that made her go hot inside.

She watched as he hoisted himself out of the water, his muscles rippling powerfully as they flexed, water gleaming on his broad chest. He slicked his dark wet hair back from his face and grinned at her. 'So are you coming in of your own accord, or do I have to carry you?'

'Don't you dare!'

'Is that a challenge?' He laughed, and before she could say another word he had swept her off her feet and up into his arms. His body was cold against the heat of hers, but he felt so good. She wrapped her arms around his neck.

'Put me down.'

'Amazing how words can say one thing and the body another,' he teased.

'Yes, I often think that about you.'

'Do you? And what is my body saying now, hmm?'

'It's saying, *I adore you, Abigail Cyrenci.*' She whispered the words against his ear. *'And I wouldn't dream of putting you in that cold water…'*

The rest of her words were drowned out as he jumped with her into the pool. Water swished over her head, and the world was a blur as she surfaced, gasping with the shock of the cold.

She glared at him furiously, and he laughed.

'A good cooling-off is just what you needed.'

'That's not what you were saying to me earlier.' She slanted him a provocative look, and he smiled.

'True.'

She pushed her wet hair back off her face, and as she raised her arms it emphasised the firm tilt of her breasts. 'Maybe I'm the one who needs cooling off,' he added gently.

She saw the fire in his eyes, and it lit an answering one deep inside her.

Damon glanced over at Mario, who was happily sitting by the side of the pool playing with some toys. He caught hold of Abbie and turned her until her back was towards the child and pressed against the side of the pool.

'Now, where did we leave off this afternoon, hmm?' He bent his head and kissed her very slowly, very deliberately, on the lips. The sensation was blissful, and she curved her arms around his shoulders and gave herself up to the pleasure.

She could feel his body pressing against hers in the water, could feel the heat of his desire warming her.

One hand moved to pull her bikini top down.

'Damon, someone might see!' Her protest was half-hearted; she was facing the ocean, and she knew there was no one around—besides, she loved the feel of his fingers running over the cool of her skin in the water.

'Who's going to see us?' he murmured with a grin. 'A passing seagull would have difficulty in seeing anything. It's Frederic's day off, Elise is in town, Mario…' Damon's eyes flicked over her shoulder to where the child was busy making a tower out of some plastic bricks '…is otherwise occupied.'

'Even so.' She shivered with need and with pleasure as his fingers found the hard peaks of her nipples.

'Even so, we need to enjoy every moment we can…' He lowered his head and licked at her breast. His tongue was warm against the coldness of her skin and it inflamed her senses wildly.

She leaned her head back against the pool and looked up into the dazzling blue sky, luxuriating in his caresses.

'Because tomorrow I'm back at work.'

'Really?' Her head jerked upwards.

'Yes, really…'

He looked at her with a gleam of amusement in his dark eyes. 'As much as I enjoy taking you to bed morning, noon and night, I've got to get back to reality some time.'

'I suppose.' The words brought a coldness swirling inside to meet the warmth of her desire. She wished he'd said 'making love' and not referred to it as just taking her to bed. She supposed the truth was she really didn't want reality; she liked the dreamy world of desire she had inhabited this last week. What did getting back to reality mean? Was it a return to his cynical manner? Would he be travelling away on business? What would she do all day while she waited for him to come home to her?

'I want you so much…' She whispered the words softly. Her fingers moved tenderly over the strength of his back.

His mouth moved to capture hers, catching her shuddering sighs. His tongue probed her mouth as he pressed against her, invading her senses on every level.

The water swished softly around her body, stroking against it with satin warmth as the sun beat powerfully down.

'You were just getting out of a pool the first time I met you—do you remember?' Damon asked softly as he nuzzled in against her neck.

'Of course I remember.' She closed her eyes as his lips moved upwards towards her ears, the sweet kisses making her shiver with pleasure.

'You looked so beautiful.' He breathed the words against her. 'It was as if you cast some kind of a spell on me that day as you rose out of the water, and I just couldn't get you out of my mind after that—all I could think about was wanting you.'

'I felt the same, Damon,' she whispered tremulously.

He pulled away from her suddenly, his hands leaving her body.

'Damon?' Her eyes met with his. 'I wanted you too…'

Her heart crashed painfully as she noticed that the mocking light was back in the darkness of his eyes. 'And was that before or after your father told you how much money was riding on *wanting* me? Hmm?'

'It wasn't like that.' Her voice shook slightly.

But he wasn't listening, he was moving away from her, swimming with hard, powerful strokes down to the far end of the pool.

Abbie adjusted her swimming costume. She shouldn't have said anything. They couldn't talk about the past—she should know that. But she wished desperately that they could, and that he would know the truth about her feelings and about what had really happened in the past. But trying to cut through his scorn and derision was too hurtful.

She felt pain spiralling through her as she watched him get out of the pool and walk along towards Mario.

With a deep breath, she hoisted herself out of the water and reached for a towel.

'Elise is having a night off tonight.' She tried to keep her voice normal, as if nothing had happened, as if everything was fine and her heart wasn't splintering. She just wanted to put things back to the way they had been earlier.

'Yes, she usually has Sunday off.' Damon reached to take off Mario's armbands. He didn't look up at her. 'We can go into town to eat, if you want—there is a very trendy new bistro you would probably like, and if we go early enough we can bring Mario.'

'Actually, I thought I'd cook dinner for us.'

He glanced up then, and his lips twisted in that cynical way that tormented her so much. 'Can you cook?'

'Yes, actually, I'm a very good cook.' She slanted her chin up defiantly.

He shrugged. 'Well, if you want to make dinner that's fine.'

'Good.' She smiled at him. 'Because I do.'

Mario reached out with a red building-block and handed it to Damon. 'Dada,' he said with a smile.

'Hey, Mario—that's right—Dada.' Abbie crouched down beside the child and smiled at him. She'd been saying 'Daddy' to him a few times this week as she'd handed things over to Damon, but this was the first time he'd said the word himself. 'Clever boy.' She kissed the top of his head, and as she straightened her eyes connected with Damon's. This time there was no hint of mockery in his eyes, just warmth.

Mario's tower toppled over as he tried to put another two bricks on top at the same time.

'Oh dear.' Damon turned to help him pick them up. 'You've got to work at things slowly, Mario. One brick at a time.'

Maybe it was the same with their relationship, Abbie told herself firmly. If she tried really hard and took one minute at a time, one day at a time, then maybe one day there would be a framework for Damon to trust her. She couldn't give up on that hope—she just couldn't.

Damon put some paperwork to one side and glanced at his watch. Abbie had told him that dinner would be at eight, so he'd taken the opportunity to catch up with some work in the study. It was the first he'd done for a week and he really needed to get back into it. He definitely needed to go into his offices in town every day next week, probably some evenings as well.

Trouble was that for the first time in his life he didn't feel driven by work. The overwhelming desire in his heart these days seemed to be spending time with Abbie and Mario.

It was good to feel like that about his son—but his feelings for Abbie were troubling him. She only had to look at him in a certain way—touch him in a certain way—and he was in danger of forgetting the lessons of the past. It was dangerous territory.

But he wasn't a fool, he reminded himself sharply. He knew what she was. And today when she'd tried to pretend that she'd had feelings for him back when they met... Well, he couldn't allow her to think he was falling for that.

He was going to have to watch his emotions carefully. It was probably just as well that work was beckoning. Distance was probably what he needed to think things through.

Damon glanced at his watch again and put away the papers. For now work could wait. He was a bit early for dinner, but he was curious to see how Abbie was getting on. Domesticity wasn't her style. Why she wanted to cook dinner, he didn't know. He could have got someone else in to cater for them, or he could have taken her out and wined and dined her in style. He'd offered both before retiring to his study but she had been adamant.

The clock in the hallway said seven forty-five. He went quietly down towards the kitchen and then stopped by the door through to the dining room. She was standing by the table, lighting some candles. The place looked lovely. She'd lit a fire in the big open-cast fireplace, and laid the table with the best china and silver. Candlelight reflected softly over the polished surface of the table.

As he watched she smoothed a hand almost nervously over her black dress and checked her appearance quickly in one of the large gilt mirrors. She looked stunning, Damon thought as he leaned against the door and watched her with leisurely approval. She was wearing very provocative high heels, and her black dress hugged her slender figure. The square neckline plus the fact that she had put her hair up showed her long neck and her soft curves to full advantage. Her handbag was sitting on the sideboard, and she reached into it and took out a lipstick to apply a red gloss to her lips.

Damon wanted her so much that he ached. He watched as she put the lipstick back into her bag, and he was just about to step into the room to tell her just how much he wanted her when she took out a mobile phone and opened it.

He watched with a frown as she hurriedly started to key in some numbers.

Who was she ringing? he wondered. A part of him wanted to step forward and let her know that he was there, but he didn't. Curiosity rooted him to the spot.

Abbie pulled out a chair and sat down. She had two missed calls on her mobile—both were from the stables. All she could think was that something had happened to her horse. She knew all the business dealings with the stables had to go through Damon now, but Jess knew how much Benjo meant to her and if there was something wrong she would want to tell her personally.

It seemed to take for ever before someone picked up the phone. It was Jess and she sounded out of breath as if she'd just dashed in from outside.

'Hi, it's Abbie here. Have you been trying to ring me?'

'Yes… Oh, Abbie, I'm so sorry!'

The genuine distress in the other woman's voice struck horror into her. There *was* something wrong with her horse!

'It's your father.'

The words stilled Abbie's mind.

'He's been here, and he's been insisting I give him your mobile phone number—he wouldn't go away. I know you don't want to talk to him, Abbie, but in the end I had to give it to him, and I had to tell him where you were. He was—bullish.'

'I can imagine,' Abbie said dryly. She closed her eyes. At least it wasn't as bad as she had thought. She'd rather deal with a few phone calls from her father than hear that something had happened to her horse. 'Don't worry about it. I'll sort it out. How's Benjo?'

'He's in good form. We all miss you here, Abbie. But the stables are fine; you don't need to worry about them. How's Mario?'

'He's well—fast asleep, tucked up in his cot. We miss you too.'

The clock out in the hallway struck eight and Abbie remembered about dinner. 'Listen, I've got to go.'

'OK—and I am sorry, Abbie. I feel like I've let you down, giving your father that information, but honestly I had no choice. Oh, and after I told him where you were he rang someone called Lawrence.'

'Lawrence Woods,' Abbie murmured uncomfortably. She had hoped she'd never have to hear that name again. He was her father's very dodgy accountant.

'That's right, and he told him where you were and talked about some business deal.'

Abbie pushed a hand tiredly through her hair and wondered what her father was up to. Why couldn't he just leave her alone? 'Did he say what the deal was?'

'No, just that he was sure it would be in the bag now.'

'Don't worry about it.' Abbie tried to lighten her tone to make Jess feel better. 'I'll sort it out. No problem.'

'I hope so. That man is a bully.'

'I know. But I also know how to handle him. You take care, and keep in touch.'

As the connection was cut, Abbie's false bravado also died. The last thing she wanted was to deal with her father.

She sat quietly for a few moments, trying to pull herself

together, then she got quietly up from the table and pushed the chair back in. John Newland couldn't hurt her any more, she told herself fiercely. He was miles away, and she'd do what she had done in St Lucia and just ignore his calls.

'So…how is dinner going, Abbie?'

The voice from the doorway made her whirl around. Damon was standing there watching her.

'Fine.' She smiled at him, but he didn't smile back; he was watching her with deep, unfathomable eyes. 'I didn't hear your footsteps,' she said nervously. 'How long have you been standing there?'

'Not long.' One dark eyebrow lifted quizzically. 'Have you been on the phone?'

She hesitated for just a moment, wondering if he'd heard her. Then she realised he'd asked her because she was still holding her mobile in her hand. Even so, for a split second she debated telling the truth—and then she panicked. Her father was such an explosive subject between them, and things were shaky enough without any reminders of the past casting even more shadows. Besides, why let John Newland ruin a perfectly nice evening?

'I was just…checking my messages.'

Damon watched with a frown as she went to drop her phone back into her bag. And he knew exactly why she was lying.

At first he'd thought her conversation had sounded banal enough. He'd presumed, because she'd asked about a horse, that she was just talking to someone at the stables.

But then she had mentioned a name that had brought a red-hot wave of fury sweeping over him: *Lawrence Woods*. Damon remembered that name very well. Lawrence Woods was the accountant John Newland had used to help rip off his father in Vegas. He was her father's right-hand henchman.

And then she had asked what the deal was.

John Newland didn't do a deal without his crooked accountant. *She'd been talking to her father.*

The very thought turned his stomach. But the more Damon thought about it the more likely it was. Things had moved pretty fast since he had last seen Newland, and he'd probably been out to the stables looking for his daughter.

And he was probably very impatient to learn what kind of financial deal she had cut. He was probably looking for some money to invest in one of his shady deals.

Damon advanced further into the room. 'And were there any messages?'

She turned, and for a second he glimpsed a decidedly uneasy light in her blue eyes. 'No, nothing. Now I really had better get back into the kitchen.' She smiled up at him. 'Why don't you sit down, make yourself comfortable?'

But Damon didn't sit down, and as she walked over towards the door he was blocking her way, looking at her with those dark eyes in a way that made her very apprehensive.

She looked up at him questioningly. 'Is everything OK?'

'You tell me, Abbie.'

The grating, sardonic tone disconcerted her completely. 'Yes. I just need to turn the oven off…'

Still he didn't move out of her way.

On impulse she reached up and touched his face softly, then stood on tiptoe to kiss his cheek. He made no attempt to touch her, and that took her aback. Usually if she kissed him he would kiss her back, touch her. 'I want us to just relax and enjoy tonight.' Did she sound as tense as she suddenly felt?

Of course, he should have realised immediately that she was up to something when she'd offered to cook for him, Damon thought wryly. After all, he'd already heard via the grapevine that John Newland was searching around for money, trying to set up a shady business deal with an old associate of his. Abbie probably wanted to invest—she'd probably been re-assuring her father that she would be able to siphon money away from her new rich husband to send to him.

The more he thought about it, the more obvious it was. There had to be something in it for her. That was why she'd been suddenly so keen to cook him dinner. That was why she was looking up at him so seductively. Abbie wasn't the domestic type, but she was the seductive, temptress type who knew how to use every feminine wile in the book to get what she wanted. She'd proved that long ago.

Rage started to pound through him.

'Damon?' Her hands moved to rest on his chest, and she looked up at him, perplexed by the fact that he still hadn't made any attempt to either move out of her way or pull her closer and kiss her.

'So tell me, Abbie, what's this really all about?' he asked quietly.

'Sorry?' She frowned. 'I don't know what you mean.'

'I mean this.' He nodded towards the beautifully laid table. 'What was really running through that pretty head of yours as you lit those candles and played at being Ms Domesticated, hmm?'

The mocking tone made colour flare in her cheeks, and her hands dropped from his chest. 'I wasn't playing at anything. I told you, I want us to have a nice relaxing evening—after all, we are still officially on our honeymoon.'

His heart drummed ferociously against his chest. Her acting abilities were too good. But then of course that shouldn't come as any surprise to him; he'd experienced her acting skills before. He remembered how easily she had convinced him that she was vulnerable and shy as she'd given herself to him that first time in Palm Springs. Would he never learn where she was concerned? He didn't know whom he was angrier with—

himself for ever questioning the truth about her when he had held her in his arms, or her for being the gold-digging hussy that she undoubtedly was.

'You know, Abbie, if you want something you don't need to go to these great lengths. I've told you, you can have anything you wish for. All I ask is that you follow the terms of our agreement. And it goes without saying that I want you to have no contact with your father, and certainly no involvement in his shady deals.'

The sudden blunt statement took her very much by surprise, and it hurt. 'I've told you, Damon, I don't want anything from you!' She tried to pull away from him, but he put his hands on her waist suddenly and held her firm.

Her eyes burned as she looked up at him. 'Damon, I can assure you that I've had no contact with my father.'

'Just like you assured me that you were just checking the messages on your phone a few moments ago?' he demanded tersely. 'I know you were lying to me, Abbie. I heard you talking.'

He watched as her face drained of colour.

'So, are you going to tell me what it's all about?' he asked lazily.

'There's nothing to tell.' She was furious that he had tried to catch her out like this.

'Really?' Damon's tone was scathing. 'So, if it was such an innocuous phone call, why lie about it?'

'Because I didn't want to ruin our evening together!' She looked up at him, and for a moment her eyes shimmered with feeling. 'You always like to think the worst of me, don't you?'

His gaze held with hers steadily. 'I'd just prefer it if you didn't try to pretend, Abbie.'

'I wasn't pretending about anything.' She bit down on her lip. 'The phone call wasn't worth mentioning.'

'But worth lying about.'

'Because you never trust me!' The cry broke from her lips. 'Why can't you just trust me?'

Damon watched her, his eyes dark, cold and uncompromising. He wasn't going to be drawn in by her plea, or by the beauty of her eyes. He'd been stupid to ever doubt himself where she was concerned. She could lie her way out of anything. 'Why should I trust you?' he asked coldly. 'I only married you because you are the mother of my son—and also for your body, of course. "To have and to hold" I think was the deal…nothing more.'

The words shouldn't have come as any great surprise. She knew what the deal was, she knew how he felt. Yet after their week of glorious love-making they struck her as painfully as if he'd physically hit her. She had dared to hope that he was softening towards her, that if she was patient he would perhaps start to see her in a different light, but she knew now how stupid those dreams had been.

'So, let's drop the pretence, hmm?' he suggested now.

She shrugged. 'If that's how you want things.' Her voice was numb.

'It is.' He dropped his hands from her waist. 'Now, run along and see to whatever it was you were doing in the kitchen before you burn the house down.'

Anger shot to her own defence. 'If the house burns down it will be your fault, not mine.' How dared he talk to her like this? Who did he think he was?

She marched past him, glad to escape into the kitchen, but to her consternation Damon followed her and lounged against the door, watching as she moved towards the oven to turn it off.

'So, tell me about the phone call,' he demanded. 'And I don't want to hear any more lies.'

'Go to hell, Damon.'

'I want to know exactly what you were planning, Abbie.'

'I wasn't planning anything. And I certainly wasn't speaking to my father! We haven't spoken in over two years!' Almost before she could finish what she was saying, she heard her mobile phone ringing again in the next room.

'Well, well, I wonder who that could be?' Damon asked sarcastically, and watched as her skin once more flooded with colour. 'What's the betting, if I go and answer that, it will be Newland again with some instruction he forgot to give you?'

Abbie shook her head, but she couldn't find her voice to answer, because she was terrified that it could very well be her father, and Damon would never believe that she hadn't solicited the call. 'I don't take instructions from my father,' she managed shakily instead.

'Of course not.' Damon's tone was cynical. 'But it could be him?'

She shrugged helplessly.

'So, shall I answer it for you?' He made as if to turn away, and her eyes widened anxiously.

'No! Don't, Damon—please!'

He turned back slowly. 'So now we are getting to the truth.'

To Abbie's relief the phone suddenly stopped ringing. 'I suppose he wants money for some deal,' Damon said tensely into the ensuing silence. 'I had heard he was up to his old tricks.'

'I don't know what he is up to. I don't want anything to do with him.' She raised her chin and met his eyes steadily. 'And that is the truth.'

'You really are a great actress, Abbie.' Damon's lips twisted with bitter amusement.

He was never going to believe anything she said, Abbie realised dully. And could she blame him after what had happened in the past? She turned away from him, and tried to busy herself taking the dinner from the oven, but she felt like she was just running on some kind of automatic pilot. She didn't care about dinner now, and there was a knot of pain inside her that just wouldn't go away, no matter how she tried to swallow it down.

Damon watched as she bent over and took out the last of the dishes. He was furious with her, yet at the same time through the mist of his fury he couldn't help noticing how her skirt rode up as she crouched down to pick something up. Then she smoothed a hand over her dress as she straightened, and he found his attention wandering down over the soft curves of her figure.

She was an enticing witch, he thought, raking a hand through the thick darkness of his hair. But he'd known that from day one this time around, he reminded himself fiercely. Any weakness that he had felt for her as she had looked up at him with those kitten eyes had been entirely his own stupidity.

Of course she would be conniving with her father if she got the chance—that was what she did. *He knew that.*

All he could do was watch her carefully, and stick to his original plan—use her the way she had once used him.

'So what is on the menu tonight?' he asked suddenly as she straightened up and put the trays out on the racks to cool.

She shot him a look of uncertainty. 'I decided I would try some Sicilian recipes,' she told him tremulously. 'And I asked Elise what you liked.'

'Really?' Damon shook his head. 'I have to say that, even though I know it's just one of your little ploys, I like the idea, and you do suit the guise of the domestic goddess.'

She closed her eyes and tried to cut out the mocking scorn of his voice. 'It wasn't a ploy. I wanted tonight to be special.'

'You can still do something special for me.' His voice held a commanding, sensual edge that wasn't lost on her.

She bit down on her lip and shook her head. If he touched her she felt sure she would break down.

'Come here.'

'Damon, I—'

'Come here, Abbie,' he cut across her firmly, and after a moment's hesitation she did as he asked, stopping at arm's length from him.

'Don't ever lie to me again.' His voice rasped harshly as he reached out and pulled her closer. He put a hand under her chin, tipping her face so that she was forced to look up at him.

'You belong to me now, Abbie, body and soul. Don't forget that.'

How could she forget it when even the lightest touch of his hand against her face was like a burning brand of possession making her whole body tremble with longing?

He leaned closer and kissed her. There was anger in his kiss, but it was also searing, and achingly passionate. Before she could stop herself she was moving closer and responding. How could he give her so much pleasure and at the same time stir up so much pain inside her? she wondered hazily.

She hated the things he said to her, yet she still wanted him, she still loved him. She hated herself for her weakness.

She felt his hand hitching up her dress.

'Do you want to go upstairs?' She whispered the words breathlessly as need overtook all other emotions.

'No.' He found the lace of her knickers and pulled them down, then turned her around towards the kitchen counter. 'I want you here.'

CHAPTER TEN

DAMON stared up into the darkness of the bedroom. He hadn't been able to get enough of Abbie last night. He'd taken her ruthlessly, and she had responded totally to him, her fire matching his ardour.

And once upstairs the same thing had happened all over again. He'd taken her with a cold-blooded determination, as if trying to purge the need he felt for her. Yet the strange thing was that, no matter how many times he took her, that need was still alive.

He thought about the way she had given herself to him— that shy look in her eyes, and then the fiery, wild, uncontrolled way she had responded to him as he'd kissed her.

Afterwards she had taken a shower in the *en-suite* bathroom and had returned wearing a white satin nightdress. She'd looked so pure in it, her face fresh and scrubbed of make-up, and her blond hair lying in loose, glossy curls around her shoulders. Oh yes, she'd been the picture of beautiful innocence, which went to show how deceptive looks could be, he thought with a wry twist of his lips.

'Take the nightgown off,' he had murmured as she had reached the side of the bed.

'Damon, do you have to be so cold with me?'

She had sat down at the edge of the bed and looked at him with an underlying sadness in her eyes that had torn him up inside. Just thinking about it now made his stomach clench. He didn't know what bothered him more—the anger he felt for still allowing the way she looked at him to affect him, or her for playing her games so damn well.

When he'd made no reply she had taken the nightdress off, her eyes holding with his gaze, her chin tipped up so that there'd been a hint of defiance about her acquiescence. Then, as she'd slipped into the bed beside him, she had been the one to reach for him.

She'd rolled over on top of him and had looked into his eyes before kissing him deeply, opening her mouth and allowing him inside. 'I wasn't lying to you earlier, Damon. But you've proved your point,' she had whispered softly. 'I'm yours totally.'

She rolled over in the bed now, and he felt the warmth of her body against him. The soft sincerity of those words had plagued him all night. A part of him hated himself for taking her body the way he had. If she'd tried to pull back from him he would have stopped, but she had given herself so freely…so lovingly. He frowned.

She had given herself freely and lovingly in Palm Springs too, he reminded himself angrily. She was a con artist.

Dawn was breaking outside now, and the first rays of sunshine started to slant across the room. He turned on his side and looked down at Abbie, and impulsively he stroked a stray strand of hair away from her face so that he could see her more clearly.

Her skin was perfect; her lashes were long and dark, and her lips infinitely kissable. There was almost an ethereal loveliness about her, a delicate-rose vulnerability.

But of course all roses had very sharp thorns, he reminded himself tersely. But she was achingly beautiful…

Her eyes flickered open suddenly and connected with his. 'What time is it?' she murmured sleepily.

'Almost six.'

'You're awake early.' As she slowly focussed, memories from the night before came flooding back: Damon taking her again and again, his attitude demanding and ruthless. Yet just now as their eyes had met there had been something else. She frowned as she tried to place the expression in the darkness of his eyes. Regret?

'I've got to go into the office early.' He rolled away from her onto his back.

She didn't want him to go. More than anything she just wanted him to reach out to her and put an arm around her, wanted to close out the harsh memories of last night and the demanding way he had taken her body. Maybe he wanted that too. Maybe he regretted his coldness.

'Do you have to go?' she ventured softly. 'We could spend the day together, and—'

'I don't think so,' he cut across her firmly. 'I need to make sure my businesses are ticking along smoothly. And, anyway, I'm sure you'd rather I got my priorities straight—you don't want the money to dwindle, do you, Abbie? You wouldn't like that.'

She closed her eyes against the pain stirred up by those sizzling, scornful words. So much for him regretting anything! 'Don't, Damon,' she whispered huskily.

'I'm just being practical.' That was the way he had to be around her, he told himself forcefully. 'Why don't you go shopping today? Your credit card has arrived. You just need to sign it.'

'There's nothing I need.'

'I'm sure you'll think of something.'

The hard edge to his tone hurt. She took a deep breath and

tried to pull herself together, tried to face up to the reality of her life. She needed to stop lying to herself and recognise the truth: Damon would never love her; their marriage was purely a convenience for him. He'd made that abundantly clear even in the way he had taken her body last night.

He had pleasured himself callously with her and yet, through all of that, she had imagined she had tasted something in his kiss—something more than just raw sexual need.

It was known as 'grasping at straws', she told herself now scornfully. Or maybe she had just been trying to excuse the way she had responded to him.

'What time will you be home tonight?' she asked softly.

'I don't know, Abbie. I'll be late.'

'Fine.' She frowned and swallowed hard.

Something in the tone of her voice made him look over at her again. 'Go and have some fun spending money on yourself, Abbie. The credit limit on your card is high, and—'

'I don't want to spend your money, Damon!' she cut across him furiously. 'Why won't you ever listen to me? I want to spend time getting to know you, I want…' She trailed off as she realised that it didn't matter what she wanted. She was just grasping at more straws.

'You want to spend time getting to know me?' He leaned up on his elbow to look at her better. He sounded very amused now, and that annoyed her. 'What exactly do you want to know?'

'I don't know…everything.' She shrugged. 'You could take me on a tour of the island. Show me where you grew up.' She threw the suggestion at him wildly.

He laughed. 'And you'd be disappointed.'

'Why?'

'Well, my old family home would probably tick all your

boxes, I suppose, although it needs a lot of work doing to it as it's been empty a long time. But I only actually lived there until the age of eight.' He rolled over onto his back again. 'My father lost everything at that point and we had to move. I don't think you would be in the slightest bit interested to see where I lived for the next ten years. It was a bit of a slum area, to be honest.'

'So your father had lost everything once before?' She looked at him in surprise.

'Yes, and then made it all back. Bought back his old house. Only to lose it all again in Vegas. Bizarre, isn't it?' Damon stared up at the ceiling. 'He was a bit of a gambler. Not in the cards-and-horses sense, but in an entrepreneurial way. He liked to take risks in business. You'd think he'd have learnt first time around, that when something seems too good to be true it generally is.'

'So your mum left him when he lost all his money first time around?'

'Yes. I don't suppose he was easy to live with, and my mother—well, my mother likes luxury.'

'Likes? Is she still alive?' For some reason Abbie had assumed his mother was dead.

'Oh yes, she's in the south of France now, I believe. Hooked herself another millionaire and got married again about three years ago.' There was silence for a moment. 'I can understand her leaving my father. Living with someone who takes risks all the time can be hard. But he was a good man in other ways.'

Abbie sat up a little to look at him, and saw the shadows of pain for just a fleeting second in the darkness of his eyes. His childhood must have been tough, she thought with sympathy. She could understand a woman leaving her husband, but not her child. And she guessed Damon had had trouble accepting that too. No wonder he was so determined to give Mario a secure upbringing. Damon saw the expression of concern in her eyes. 'You don't need to worry,' he grated sardonically. 'I don't take wild gambles in business.'

'I wasn't worried.'

'No?' One dark eyebrow lifted in disbelief. 'Well, you can rest assured, the risks I take are all very well calculated.'

'I know that already, Damon. Your risks are calculated in marriage as well as in business.'

He didn't say anything to that.

She wondered if she had inadvertently struck Damon's Achilles' heel. Maybe, because of his mother, he thought most women were more interested in money than love, and his theory had been compounded by what had happened between them in Vegas.

Mario was waking up in the next room. Abbie could hear him happily talking to himself, but she didn't move immediately to go to see to him. It was the first time that Damon had ever opened up to her about his past and she didn't want to lose the moment. 'I would be interested to see where you lived, Damon, both before and after things went wrong in your parents' marriage.'

For a second he looked at her with an odd expression in his eyes. Then he shook his head. 'Maybe another day.'

He pulled away from her and pushed back the duvet. 'I've got to shower and get to work. And it sounds like our son needs his breakfast.'

She watched as he disappeared into the bathroom. Then with a sigh she reached for her dressing gown. The precious shared intimacies had been nothing more than illusion. The reality was that Damon probably regretted telling her anything.

Damon left for the office half an hour later, and Abbie, bathed and dressed in a skimpy pair of shorts and a T-shirt, carried Mario to the front door to wave him goodbye.

Although it was early, the air was already shimmering with heat. It promised to be another scorching day, and Damon felt a frisson of reluctance as he got into his limo and glanced back at the perfect tableaux of his wife and son framed in the doorway.

Abbie looked so beautiful and so young. He forgot sometimes that she was only twenty-one, because in some ways she was so mature for her years. But everything about her was deceptive, he reminded himself forcefully—she knew how to play innocent so well.

As Frederic drove along the twisting, mountainous roads, Damon took out some files and his mobile phone to try and get ahead with some work. He had several intense meetings lined up for this afternoon, and needed to get a handle on things well before then.

But somehow the columns of figures he was supposed to be studying seemed to blur as he read them, and his mind seemed to wander. He was remembering the way Abbie had curled in beside him this morning.

I would be interested to see where you lived, Damon, both before and after things went wrong in your parents' marriage.

The words teased him provocatively. Of course, it was all part of her act. She would be horrified to see where he had grown up. After his father had divorced, he had ploughed all the money he could back into starting again in business. Corners had been cut—and living accommodation had been one of those corners.

However, experiencing that poverty had strengthened Damon's character. Everything he had achieved in life, he'd worked for. Abbie wouldn't understand that—wouldn't be interested, even.

So why had she seemed so interested?

He frowned and tried to return his concentration to his papers.

Women like Abbie lived for shopping and luxury; they didn't want to delve too deeply into anything else.

So why hadn't she just grabbed her credit card and headed happily into town this morning?

Her words played through his mind over and over… *I don't want to spend your money, Damon! Why won't you ever listen to me? I want to spend time getting to know you…*

Damon frowned and closed the words out. She was just clever, that was all. She believed in playing the bigger game—she wanted cash to invest in her father's schemes, not a credit card that could be checked on.

The traffic increased as they approached the outskirts of town.

But she hadn't actually asked him for any cash, he reminded himself suddenly. Well, not *yet*.

And she had looked at him with such feeling in her eyes when she had come to his bed last night. He found himself remembering how he had taken her again. He remembered how pale her skin had looked against the dark-granite worktops in the kitchen. Then he found himself remembering again how she had looked in the white-satin nightdress.

I wasn't lying to you… Her tremulous whisper replayed in his mind.

Why the hell was he thinking about that? Of course she was lying—and why should he take any kind of risk on her? A marriage of convenience just suited him fine. She was good in bed and she was a good mother to Mario. That was all that mattered to him.

Your risks are calculated in marriage as well as in business.

He frowned as he remembered those words. She had a point.

The feelings Abbie had generated in him the first time around in Vegas had troubled him even before he'd found out

exactly what she was up to. Because he didn't trust easily—
he never had. Marrying Abbie on his terms, cutting away the
emotion and just making it a practical arrangement, had suited
him. She was right about that.

The truth of that sat uncomfortably with him.

They were gridlocked in traffic now. It looked as if there
had been an accident up ahead.

Damon leaned forward and opened up the partition between
him and his driver. 'It looks like we are going to be stuck here
for a while, Frederic. Turn the car around.'

'You want to find a way around this?'

'No. Just take me back to the house.' Damon frowned. He
needed to find his way around the thoughts plaguing him
before anything else.

Abbie felt lost when Damon left. She stood on the doorstep
for a few moments and watched as the car disappeared from
sight.

Then she returned to the kitchen to give Mario his breakfast. Elise was already there, and the two women chatted as
Abbie sat down to spoon-feed Mario his cereal. The little boy
seemed more interested in playing with the food rather than
eating it, and he wasn't happy when she took the spoon away
from him.

The shrill ring of the doorbell took them both by surprise.

'I'll go and see who it is. Won't be a moment.' Elise put the
bread she had been making into the oven and hurried out. She
returned a few moments later, and Abbie could hear her talking
to someone in English.

She frowned, wondering who it could be. Then she heard
a familiar male voice that made her heart freeze.

'Yes, I've just flown in this morning. I have some business
here, so I thought I'd drop by and say hello.'

The kitchen door swung open. 'Abbie, it's your father.' Elise led the man in with a smile. 'That's a nice surprise, isn't it…?' Her cheerful words trailed away as she saw the shock on Abbie's face.

'Hello, sweetheart.' The drawled words held a veiled sarcasm that wasn't lost on his daughter.

She hadn't seen John Newland since she had fled from Vegas a few months before Mario had been born. But he hadn't changed much. He'd never been what you would term attractive. Due to his love of excessive living he was a portly man, and he looked older than his fifty years, with greying hair and sharp eyes. He was dressed for business in a grey suit and looked like he'd just stepped out of his office.

'Shall I make a pot of tea?' Elise ventured gently into the silence.

'No thank you, Elise, my father won't be staying.' From somewhere Abbie managed to find the strength to get to her feet.

'Of course I'm staying—I want to see my grandson. Don't worry, I have plenty of time,' John contradicted her firmly, and then turned to Elise with a charming smile. 'But perhaps you'd give us a few moments alone? I haven't seen my daughter for a while and we parted on, well, unfortunate terms.'

'Unfortunate terms?' Abbie was incensed, and her voice was sharp with disgust. 'It was a lot more than that!'

'You obviously have things to talk about and need some privacy,' Elise said quickly. And before Abbie could say anything to the contrary she left them.

'Nice place you've got yourself here.' John walked further into the room. 'You've done well.'

It spoke volumes that all her father was concerned about was the wealth of her surroundings. He had hardly even glanced at his grandchild.

'You've got a nerve, coming here.'

'I think I've got every right to come here,' he replied calmly. 'And, well, frankly I expected a bit more gratitude than that.'

'Gratitude?' Abbie's voice rose slightly. 'Why on earth would I be grateful to you? All you've ever tried to do is ruin my life, like you ruined my mother's.'

'Not that tired old refrain.' John shook his head. 'Change the record, Abbie. If it wasn't for me you wouldn't have any of this.' He spread his hands out to indicate the house. 'I was the one who prompted Damon into doing the right thing by you. I suspected he'd take the bait. He always did like to think he was the honourable type—they are always quite easy to sucker.'

'He *is* the honourable type. You haven't suckered anybody!' Abbie moved to the back door and opened it. 'I want you to go. You are not welcome here.'

'Now now, Abbie, that's not very respectful!' Instead of moving to the door, he sat down in the chair she had vacated and looked at Mario. 'So this is the heir apparent. He looks like his father.'

'Just get away from him.'

Mario reached out a hand and smiled at his granddad, and Abbie watched with a stab of horror as her father took the little hand in his. 'Hello, little fellow.'

'Get away from him!' She stepped back into the room to pick him up, but her father stopped her by standing up and placing himself in front of the child.

'I'm just saying hello to my grandson. There is no need for these hysterics.'

'You haven't come to say hello. You haven't been interested enough to even bother enquiring after him until now.'

'Well, I tried to ring you just before you left St Lucia, Abbie, and you didn't take my calls.'

'You wonder why?' Her eyes glared stonily into his.

'Come on, Abbie, things don't have to be like this between us.'

He put a conciliatory hand on her arm, and she shook it away angrily. 'What do you want?'

'Well, like I said, I think a little gratitude is in order for setting you up here so well. You know I've always had your best interests at heart.'

Abbie stared at him, nonplussed. 'Best interests at heart? You blackmailed me into going along with your vicious deal in Vegas—told me that you wouldn't pay for Mum's treatment in hospital unless I did what you asked. You got me implicated in something that ruined Damon's father financially, a ploy that tore our relationship apart, and you think I should show you gratitude?'

'Well, you're happy now, aren't you? It all worked out for the best.'

'No, it did not work out for the best!' Abbie blazed with fury. 'I can't believe you are saying this! I knew you were evil, but I didn't think you were mad. You tried to ruin my life!'

'You know what? You sound just like your mother,' her father spat contemptuously.

'Good, because I loved my mother.'

'Don't I just know it—you made a laughing stock of me when you encouraged her to leave!'

'And you never forgave me, did you? But she needed to get out from under your thumb. You made her deeply unhappy with your womanizing, and—'

'Let's just cut to the bottom line, shall we?' John Newland sliced across her in a bored tone. 'I'm currently in the middle of some business negotiations that are doing well—but as you know, thanks to your husband, I am a little bit strapped for cash.'

'You've come here for money?'

'Yes. I've been talking to Lawrence, and he thinks a nice, round five-figure sum should get the deal in the bag…' John mused for a moment before naming his sum exactly.

Abbie stared at him in shock. 'I haven't got any money, and even if I had I wouldn't give you a single penny.'

'I think your attitude is a little unreasonable, Abbie. After all, we are partners in this…marriage arrangement. I suggested it—I told you how to play it. I set the ball rolling by sending Damon to you. I think the least you can do is settle your account.'

'I'm not partners with you in anything. I never have been and I never will be. And I haven't spoken to you since my mother died over two years ago!'

'I was hoping you were going to take a more realistic line than this.' John shook his head. 'I could make your life very uncomfortable here, Abbie. I could stir things up with a lot of force. Damon believed me once before, when I told him you were my willing partner in that deal involving his father. He swallowed it hook, line and sinker when I told him you are nothing but a little gold-digger. I could throw a few more curve-balls into his mind. A few telephone conversations—a few well-placed remarks.'

Abbie knew he was right. One well-worded sentence was all it would take to ruin her fragile marriage. That much had been more than obvious last night.

'All I need is that money then I'll be out of your hair.' Her father's tone was wheedling now. 'You won't see me again.'

'Until the next time there's some big deal and you need some more money,' Abbie answered quietly. She loved Damon, and she didn't want her marriage to fail, but she couldn't do this. 'As I told you, I don't have any money, but even if I had I wouldn't pay you a penny. You've blackmailed me once and I won't let you do it again.'

John Newland looked genuinely taken aback.

'Go—do your worst, dad. I'll take my chances with Damon.'

'You're not thinking this through.'

'On the contrary, my thinking has never been clearer.' A noise from behind them both made Abbie turn, and she froze with shock as she saw Damon standing in the open doorway. His features were grim as his eyes moved from her towards her father, and he looked truly menacing.

'Well,' he drawled. 'Look what's crawled out from under a stone.'

John Newland turned to face him. 'Nice to see you too,' he said in a falsely bright tone. But Abbie could see that, although he tried to sound as if he wasn't intimidated, he shrank a little as Damon took a step forward.

'Damon, this…this isn't what it looks like!' Abbie's voice was distraught. How much had Damon heard? He looked so angry—maybe he thought she had invited her father here. If that was the case, her marriage really was over.

'Get out of my house, Newland.'

'You can't throw me out. I have a right to be here.' John tried to pull himself up to his full height and face Damon down, but his voice wasn't steady. 'This is my daughter and my grandson.'

'No, this is *my* wife and *my* son. Now get out of here, before I call the police and have you arrested for trespassing.'

'Don't be ridiculous! You are making a big mistake…' For just a moment her father blustered. 'Abbie invited me here—'

'No, *you've* made the big mistake,' Damon grated, and as he took another purposeful step closer her father turned and ran for the door.

As soon as he'd gone, Abbie sank down onto the chair in shocked reaction. Her legs were shaking and she felt sick.

'I didn't invite him, Damon, I didn't!'

Damon didn't reply. He just stood by the door. She noticed his hands clenching and unclenching at his sides as if he was trying to get a grip on his emotions.

'You don't believe me, do you?' She covered her face with her hands. After last night and the phone call, he probably assumed she was indeed back in business with her father.

Mario started to cry suddenly, long, wailing sobs that brought Abbie instantly back to her feet. 'It's OK, darling.' She bent to look at the child and then, as she picked him up to comfort him, Damon walked past her and out of the room.

'Damon, we need to talk—' she called after him, but he'd gone, and a few minutes later she heard the front door closing.

CHAPTER ELEVEN

ABBIE had wanted to run after Damon, grab hold of him and beg him to listen. But instead she had stood immobilised until she had heard him driving away.

It was now nearly three in the afternoon and he hadn't come back. He was either still furiously angry with her or else he didn't care and was just carrying on with his work. Either way, any hope she had of making this marriage work was now effectively over, she realised with a heavy heart.

Even if he had stayed and talked to her, it wouldn't have made any difference. Damon would never believe that she hadn't invited her father to this house. He probably thought that the moment he'd left for work this morning she had been on the phone to him again, and that she was hatching some plot with him.

Mario was crying again. He'd been fractious all day, and hadn't settled at all to have his afternoon nap. She went to see him now and lifted him out of the cot.

'It's OK, darling,' she whispered softly to him, and buried her face against his. She felt like crying the way he was crying, giving in to loud, noisy sobs. But that wasn't going to solve anything.

He was very hot, she noticed. Maybe he was teething. She

reached for his soother and put it to his lips to see if it would help, but he pushed it away.

'You are out of sorts, aren't you, Mario?' Abbie pressed a kiss to his cheek. 'Come on, let's give up on sleep and go downstairs and sit quietly, see if we can settle you.'

But, down in the lounge, Mario seemed even more restless.

Elise came into the room as she heard his wails. 'This isn't like Mario,' she said with concern.

'No. I don't know what's wrong with him. I thought he was teething, but I think it's more than that now.' She put a hand to his forehead. 'He's running a bit of a temperature. I think I should make an appointment with the doctor for him. Just have him checked over to be on the safe side.'

'Yes, it might be best.' Elise nodded. 'Do you want me to ring up and make the appointment? Signor Cyrenci's doctor's number is on the diary in the study.'

Abbie nodded. 'If you don't mind, Elise, just in case I have any difficulties with the language.'

'No problem.' Elise bustled away and was back a few moments later. 'All fixed for half-past four this afternoon. Is that OK with you?'

'Yes, great, thank you.' Abbie was trying to put a cooling cloth to Mario's face but he kept pushing it away.

'Do you think we should ring Signor Cyrenci?' Elise asked suddenly. 'Tell him that Mario isn't well?'

'He's probably dealing with important business,' Abbie responded rawly, then thought better of the reply. She was angry and hurt with Damon for just walking out on her, for not caring enough to even talk to her about what had happened— for not loving her.

But he did love his son. And there would be nothing more important to him than Mario's welfare. 'But maybe you'd better ring him,' she added softly. 'I'd probably get his secretary who can't speak English or something…'

'Not if you phoned him direct on his mobile.' Elise picked up Abbie's phone, which was sitting next to her on the table, and passed it over.

She hesitated for a moment before taking it. It wasn't that she didn't want to speak to Damon—it was more a case of being afraid of speaking to him, afraid of losing the last shreds of her dignity and breaking down whilst he remained unmoved and uncaring. She didn't think she could bear that.

But this wasn't about them, this was about Mario, she reminded herself staunchly as she took the phone.

Elise smiled at her, and then reached to take Mario from her. 'I'll look after him for you while you do that.'

Even though she was left alone and in silence, it took Abbie several minutes to gather up the courage to make the call.

Damon answered almost immediately, and before he could say anything she took a deep breath and launched straight in.

'I wouldn't have rung you at work, only there's a problem with Mario and I thought I'd better let you know.' She heard the cold note in her voice, but she couldn't take it out. And why should she, anyway? He didn't care about her.

'What kind of a problem?' Immediately Damon sounded concerned.

'He's been crying all day and he's running a temperature. I've had to get an appointment for him with your GP.'

'What time is his appointment for?'

'Four-thirty.'

'Right, I'm on my way. I'll pick you both up at four.'

'There's no need, Damon. I can manage on my own.' Even as she said the words she ached for him. But she had stopped hoping for any kind of miracle in their relationship. If it wasn't for his concern over Mario, he wouldn't even have bothered talking to her now, never mind rush home.

'I know you can. But I'm still coming.'

He'd hung up before she could argue further.

However when Abbie went through and joined Elise in the kitchen she didn't have time to think again about Damon, because it was very obvious that Mario's condition was suddenly deteriorating fast. He was very lethargic, as if he was passing in and out of consciousness between bouts of crying.

'You know what? I don't think I can wait for that doctor's appointment, Elise,' Abbie said in panic as she took the child back into her arms. 'There's something really wrong with him.'

'Maybe you should take him to the hospital,' Elise agreed instantly. 'Shall I get Frederic to bring the car around?'

'Yes…and tell him to be quick.' Mario looked so weak, so unlike his usual robust self, that her heart squeezed with fear just watching him struggle to keep his eyes open. This wasn't good.

Damon arrived at the hospital ten minutes after the doctors had swept Mario away from her. She saw him striding down the corridor, his face gaunt with anxiety, and her heart welled up with emotion. Nothing from the past mattered at that moment, all that counted was the fact that she was so fiercely glad that he was here, as if somehow his very presence was going make their son better.

He looked up and saw her, and for just a moment there was a powerful expression of pain in his eyes. 'How is he?'

'The doctors have taken him away to do tests.' Abbie's voice caught with fear. 'Damon, he looks so ill I'm so afraid…'

She didn't get to finish her sentence, because the next

moment Damon had pulled her in close to his chest to hold her.

She melted against him, so glad to be in his arms again, and trying to draw strength from his presence. 'Do you think he'll be all right?' she whispered, desperate for reassurance. 'It all happened so quickly. I didn't know what to do.'

'You've done the best thing, getting him here so quickly, and he's going to be fine—he *has* to be fine.'

They stood for a while, just holding each other and holding on to that thought.

One of the doctors came through to the waiting room and looked around for her, and they broke apart. 'Is there any news?' Abbie asked anxiously.

The doctor didn't answer her immediately, but looked over at Damon. 'This is my husband, Damon Cyrenci.' Abbie introduced him quickly. 'How is our son? Is he going to be OK?'

'We are doing—more tests.' The doctor's English was halting, and Damon spoke to him in Italian.

It was deeply frustrating not to know what was being said. They were speaking so quickly that there was no way Abbie could even pick up on a few words, so she kept watching Damon's face nervously to try and figure out if this was good or bad.

It was hard to work out. Damon looked tense, but seemed like he was very much in control of the situation.

'So what is he telling you, Damon?' she asked as the doctor broke off to consult a chart in his hand.

'They are running a few more tests. Nothing is conclusive yet.'

'What are they testing him for?'

'Come on, let's sit down.' Damon nodded at the doctor and thanked him.

'But I want to see him, Damon. I need to be with him.'

'Not just yet. Come on, let's sit down.'

'Oh God, this is bad, isn't it?' She was suddenly terrified, and sank down into the chair that Damon had brought her towards.

'They suspect that he might have meningitis.' Damon sat down next to her and reached for her hand.

As he looked into her eyes, he saw the way her pupils dilated in fear at the word. 'Mario is really strong, he'll fight this.' Damon squeezed her hand. 'And the good thing is that you've got him here quickly.'

Although he was being positive, Abbie could see a muscle ticking along the side of his jaw. She looked down at the hand that held hers.

'I don't know what I'm going to do if I lose him, Damon, I can't bear it.' Her eyes misted with tears.

'We are not going to lose him.' Damon squeezed her hand tightly. 'He is receiving expert care, and the results of the tests aren't even back yet, so let's not cross bridges until we have to, hmm?'

She bit down on her lips and nodded. She knew he was right, but it was so hard not to let her imagination start running ahead.

They seemed to sit there for ages like that, just holding hands.

A nurse came by and asked if they would like a coffee, but they both refused.

'It's going to be all right, Abbie,' Damon said softly. He stroked a thumb over the back of her hand. 'He's a survivor, like his mother.'

She tried to smile, but couldn't. The touch of his hand against hers was so wonderful, so deeply comforting and reassuring, and yet so painful. Because if it hadn't been for their mutual love of Mario he wouldn't be holding her like this.

Damon looked down at the fragile hand in his and felt more helpless than he had ever felt in his life. He wanted to take away her pain, make this better, and have his son back in his arms.

The last few hours had been hell. Finding John Newland in his house like that had been a shock. Hearing their conversation had been even more shocking.

At first he hadn't been able to take it in. Part of him wondered angrily if it had all been staged, if somehow Abbie had known that he would come back to the house. But how could she have known?

And she had looked so scared. His heart had wrenched when he'd seen that look on her face, that anguish in her eyes. He'd had to get out of the house, had to take stock and think about things deeply. He didn't want to make any more mistakes, because he'd already made enough to last a lifetime.

A few doctors walked towards the door, and Damon and Abbie both looked up anxiously, but the doctors didn't come in. They were talking to the receptionist outside.

'This is hell,' Abbie grated, and he squeezed her hand even tighter.

The doctor who had spoken to them earlier suddenly appeared in the doorway and they both got to their feet.

This time the doctor smiled at Abbie. 'It is—how do you say?—good news.'

'Thank God.' Relief flooded through Abbie, and she leaned weakly against Damon as she listened to him questioning the doctor more closely in his native language.

'He has a viral infection, Abbie, but it is not meningitis and it can be treated,' he translated for her swiftly. 'They say he'll be fine in a few days.'

'Thank you.' Abbie smiled at the doctor, her eyes shimmering with gratitude.

Then impulsively she turned and went into Damon's arms.

It was so wonderful to be close to him, and the feelings of happiness and relief mingled with the sharp pain of knowing that this bond they shared was only one of mutual love for their son—nothing else.

'Can we see him?' Hastily she pulled away from him. Now that the worst was over and Mario was on the road to recovery, she knew that she couldn't allow herself the luxury of being in his arms.

CHAPTER TWELVE

ABBIE stepped outside the hospital front door and took a deep breath of the early-morning air. She and Damon had sat next to Mario's bed throughout the night, neither of them wanting to leave until their son's fever had broken.

Finally, at six o'clock that morning, Mario had smiled at her and she had seen the healthy colour returning to his skin. Then he had settled down into a peaceful and exhausted sleep. That was when she had allowed Damon to persuade her to go home.

She felt worn out as she waited for Frederic to bring the car around. The emotional turmoil of the last few days, added to her fears for Mario, had taken its toll. She knew she probably looked washed out, and she felt wretched. But she didn't intend to be away from Mario for long. She would just have a shower and freshen up and then go straight back. For one thing, Damon deserved a break as well. Sitting across the hospital bed from him, she had realised that the worry over Mario plus losing a night's sleep had also affected him—he'd also looked shattered and drawn.

The car arrived, and as Abbie settled into the comfortable seats she closed her eyes. It had been such a strange night. She and Damon had been at pains to be polite with each other after the worst had passed. It had been as if they had never held each other moments earlier or sat holding hands.

He probably was still furious with her for allowing her father into his house. They couldn't go on like this, she realised sadly. It was tearing her apart and it was probably tearing him apart, too. He didn't trust her—*couldn't* trust her. The situation was no good for either of them.

But what was the alternative—a divorce? For the first time she allowed herself to admit that might be where they were headed. She raked a hand in anguish through her hair as she imagined that situation—a polite distance from each other maintained at all times, except in periods of emergency.

At least she knew he would be there for his son no matter what. But living in close proximity to him like that and yet not being with him would be torture.

But what choice did she have? If they divorced she couldn't go back to St Lucia. She'd lost everything there, and anyway it wouldn't be fair to deny Mario regular access to his father. And it was obvious how deeply Damon felt about his son. Even after the doctor had told them everything was going to be all right, the bleak expression hadn't completely left his eyes.

No, her only option if they decided on a divorce would be to try and get a flat and a job somewhere nearby. She didn't want it to end like this, she really didn't. The pain in her heart felt overwhelming. But to love someone and know that there was no hope of them ever loving you back was also too painful to bear.

The car pulled up outside the house, and she went inside. Everything was quiet and the kitchen was deserted.

'Elise?' she called to the housekeeper as she went through to the hallway, but there was no reply. Maybe she'd gone for a lie down, Abbie reflected. She knew she had been very worried about Mario, and although Damon had rung her as soon as they had known he was going to be OK she had probably had little sleep.

Going upstairs, Abbie stripped off in the bedroom and went for a shower. It was bliss to stand under the hot, pounding water.

She was just pulling on her dressing gown when she heard a noise from downstairs.

'Elise?' She opened the bedroom door and looked out. 'Elise, is that you?'

'No, it's me.' To her surprise Damon appeared at the top of the stairs. 'Elise arrived at the hospital a few moments after you left, so I decided to take the opportunity for a quick break.'

'I see.' He did look like he needed a break—in fact, he looked terrible. 'But everything is all right with Mario, isn't it?' she asked anxiously.

'Yes. I saw the doctor again before I left, and he told me they might discharge him later today.'

'Thank God for that.' Abbie smiled at him tremulously.

'Yes.'

For a moment there was an odd silence between them. His eyes moved down over her figure. 'You were wearing that dressing gown when I arrived at your door in St Lucia,' he recalled suddenly. 'Seems like a lifetime ago.'

She nodded. 'Well, a lot has happened since then. Marriage, and now...' She trailed off brokenly. 'Now it's all such a mess.'

'You want a divorce, don't you?' He asked the question bluntly, and there was a very sombre look in his eyes now.

She yearned to tell him that a divorce was the last thing she wanted—that what she wanted was for them to make things work, and for him to trust her. But pride kept her silent. What was the point in telling him that? He wouldn't believe her anyway. When he'd found her father in his home, he had probably come to the conclusion that he couldn't continue with this charade.

So she shrugged helplessly. 'I think we both know deep down that we can't continue like this—' she whispered brokenly.

'Abbie, I can't bear it,' he cut across her suddenly. 'I know I have absolutely no right to ask you this—but I really can't bear for you to leave.'

Abbie frowned. She'd never heard that raw note in his voice before. He'd always been so much in control of the situation, and of her. 'Well, you know I can't go anywhere unless you allow me to leave. I have nowhere to go, Damon…' Her voice broke for a moment.

Damon raked a hand through his hair. He couldn't believe that he had done this to her—trapped her here against her will—used her.

Yesterday when he'd left the house he'd needed to put space and time between them, had needed to be alone when the blinkers had finally lifted from his eyes—because the guilt had been so damn overwhelming that he just couldn't bear it.

Overhearing the conversation between Abbie and her father yesterday had made him sick to his stomach. Hearing the truth had opened a pit of guilt and despair inside him that he didn't think he would ever be able to close. Now he knew the reason for the sadness in her eyes when she looked at him: she was innocent of all the charges he had laid before her. She was as much a victim of what had happened in Vegas as his father had been.

The conversation had confirmed what he'd wanted to believe. She didn't have a bad, selfish or mercenary bone in her body.

But the revelation had come too late.

He'd hurt her so much, trapped her in a marriage she didn't want, in a place she didn't want to be.

She had tried valiantly to make the best of the situation, and to make things work, but she didn't want to be here.

He remembered the way he'd tried to punish her—the way he'd talked to her, the way he had taken her body so ruthlessly. And he hated himself.

'Damon?' The soft, questioning note in her voice tore into him. 'Damon, I need you to believe me when I tell you I didn't invite my father to this house—'

'I know you didn't invite him. I heard every word.' His voice cracked for a moment under the weight of emotion that was tearing him up inside.

'You heard?' Her voice was stiff with disbelief. 'But you blamed me—you walked away.'

'I couldn't bear to look at you.' His voice was husky with a strange note that she couldn't place. 'I hated myself too much for what I'd done to you. And when I looked at you and saw the distress in your eyes... Oh, Abbie, I couldn't bear it— couldn't bear the knowledge of what I'd put you through—of what you'd been through before I met you.'

For a moment she stood silently, hardly daring to believe what she was hearing. 'So you believe I didn't lie to you? You believe I would never have done anything deliberately to hurt you? That my father forced me into a situation that I didn't want?'

As he listened to the pain in her voice, Damon's heart smote him once more with the horrific guilt of what he had put her through, what he had accused her of. 'Yes, I believe it,' he whispered. 'And I'm so sorry, Abbie. I've behaved so badly towards you. I believed the worst—I wanted revenge... And all the time you were an innocent victim of your father as well.' He shook his head, and she could hear the self-disgust in his voice. 'Abbie, why didn't you tell me about your mother?'

'I tried…' Tears sparkled in her eyes. The relief that he knew the truth was so tremendous, as if a weight of a hundred boulders had lifted from her. 'But you didn't want to listen or believe anything I said about the past. And it hurt so much, Damon, to try and talk about something so deeply personal and painful and have everything I said twisted and scornfully dismissed…'

'I should have listened and believed you, but I was so sure that you were lying—'

'Damon, it's OK.' She cut across him, hating to hear his voice crack like that. 'I understand why you couldn't believe me.' She took a step closer. 'All the evidence was against me. And I know you had trust issues, as well, from your past.'

Even now, after the way he had hurt her, she could still find it in her heart to excuse him. Somehow the fact that she was so gently forgiving made him feel worse. He'd got it wrong so badly—had ignored all the voices of caution and believed the worst of her. He didn't know if he would ever forgive himself, let alone expect her forgiveness. Hearing her tell her father how this situation had ruined her life had been gutwrenching.

'I don't deserve your forgiveness, Abbie. But I'm going to put everything right, I promise. I'll tear up the prenuptial agreement for a start. You can have whatever you want.'

'You don't have to do that. I don't want anything.'

'I know you don't want anything! But I need to do that—don't you understand? I couldn't live with myself knowing…' He trailed off. 'And I'll move out of the house, if that is what you really want, while we decide how best to proceed.'

'Move out?' Her voice was cold suddenly, and the feeling of relief inside her quickly started to turn to fear. 'Why would you do that?'

'Because I want to do the right thing by you and make amends.' He broke off and spoke in Italian for a moment.

'Damon, I don't understand.' She shook her head.

'I'm saying I always thought of myself as an honourable man, and I've treated you so badly that I'm ashamed. I've forced you into a marriage that you don't want.'

'Damon, I...'

'There's no excuse for what I've done. Yes, I wanted to give Mario the best and most secure of family lives, but instead I've just brought misery and acted selfishly.'

Abbie stared up at him, her heart thundering painfully. 'So you want a divorce?'

'No! That's the last thing I want, Abbie!' His voice grated harshly and there was such torment in his eyes as he looked at her that she wanted to reach out to him. 'I'm a proud man, Abbie—possibly too proud.' His lips twisted cynically. 'But I'm not too proud to beg you now. Please don't end our marriage.'

'Damon, don't!' She took a step closer to him. She hated to see him like this. 'You didn't need to beg. I know how much you love Mario. I won't take him away from you. I couldn't live with myself, knowing how much he means to you—'

'Yes, he means a lot to me.' Damon reached out and touched her face. 'But so do you, Abbie.'

'Do I?' The heart-wrenching question made Damon's insides turn over with regret. He murmured something in Sicilian, before shaking his head. 'I've been such a fool where you are concerned. I believed what John Newland told me about you, when he was an obvious charlatan.'

'Well, he could be very convincing,' Abbie murmured. 'When my mother got sick and I had to ring him for help, I believed for one crazy moment that he felt some compassion for her circumstances.' She shook her head. 'But that man doesn't appear to have an ounce of compassion in his soul.'

'Unlike his daughter—who has too much, who has forgiven me against all the odds.'

'You were hurt by him too.'

'Abbie, can we try again?'

The sudden question made her heart almost stop beating.

'I've been such an idiot,' he rasped. 'I've never deserved you. And I know I've made a mess of things. But we are married now…and we are good together, aren't we?'

The question tore her up.

'You mean the chemistry is still good between us,' she corrected him huskily.

'Yes.' For a second his eyes moved towards her lips. 'There is no denying that. Is there?'

She shook her head; there was no way she could deny that.

'And we've got the most wonderful son in the world who we both adore.'

She smiled at that. 'Yes.'

'So let me try and make amends by being the best husband you could wish for.'

For a second Abbie's eyes shimmered with tears. She wanted to say yes, she wanted to go back into his arms so badly. But she knew she couldn't. She just couldn't give herself to him again, knowing that the love between them wasn't there. That he would only be doing this for his son. It was too painful, and she loved him too much to be able to bear it.

'Damon, we were good together, and the chemistry between us is strong.' Her voice shook alarmingly. 'But it's not enough.'

'Don't say that, Abbie, please!' His eyes held hers steadily. 'I'm nothing without you. Please say you will be my wife for ever this time. For richer or poorer, in sickness and in health, all the days of our lives I want to cherish you and love you and be with you.'

'You want to love me?' Her heart skipped a few beats.

He nodded. 'Abbie, I love you more than you could ever know. I've just been too proud, and…' His lips twisted in a rueful way. 'Maybe too frightened by my feelings for you to admit it—even to myself.'

Abbie couldn't find her voice to say anything for a moment; she was too overwhelmed by what he had just told her. 'You really love me?' she managed at last. 'Really?'

'With all my heart.'

A tear trickled down her pale face. 'Damon, I don't know what to say, I…'

'Just say that we can stay together and give our marriage a chance. That's all I'm asking for, Abbie. I know you don't love me—in fact I know you've downright disliked me sometimes, and I've deserved it. I've said some terrible things, done some terrible things, and I'm deeply sorry. But let me try and make things up to you, please.'

'I've never disliked you,' she murmured. 'It's just something I said to cover my real feelings. To lie to myself.'

He frowned. 'But I've made you so very sad sometimes.' He wiped her tears away with a tender hand. 'On our wedding day, for instance, I made you cry.' His voice cracked with fierce emotion. 'I hated myself for that.'

'I didn't cry because you made me sad, Damon,' she whispered softly. 'I cried because I realised how much I loved you. I've always loved you. Right from that first moment we met in Las Vegas and I looked into your eyes out by the swimming pool.'

'You loved me?' His voice sounded strange as if he hardly dared to believe what she had said. 'But I heard you tell your father that what he had done had ruined your life. That everything hadn't turned out for the best.'

'I was talking about the fact that he'd turned you against me—that we had wasted precious years apart, that even now you didn't trust me. And I loved you so much.'

'Oh my darling.' He pulled her close and held her. 'My darling Abigail. I'm so sorry…for putting you through that torment. I misunderstood, and all I could think was that I had ruined your life by bringing you here. I felt so wretchedly guilty that I had to get out of the house—I didn't know what to do, where to put myself.'

She leaned against him and wound her arms around his neck. 'Damon, I love you, and I want to make this marriage work more than anything in this world.'

'I want that too, more than you will ever know.' He pulled away from her for a moment and then kissed her, a long, sensual, burning kiss that made her heart turn over with longing. He murmured something to her in Italian.

'I don't understand what you are saying,' she whispered.

'I'm saying that I love you so much,' he whispered hungrily. 'Need you so much.'

'Me too.'

He kissed her again and then, sweeping her up into his arms, carried her back into the bedroom.

Abbie laughed tremulously. 'We haven't got time for this, Damon, we need to get back to the hospital.'

'Yes, but first we have some more making-up to do.'

'And secondly?' She looked up at him playfully as he put her down on the bed.

'Secondly there are a few Sicilian phrases I need to run by you. Phrases like "I love you" and "I adore you" and "I will always be here for you"…'

'I'd love to learn those words, Damon.' She reached up to kiss him, knowing that for the first time in her life she was truly home, truly happy.

Special Offers

Every month we put together collections and longer reads written by your favourite authors.

Here are some of next month's highlights— and don't miss our fabulous discount online!

On sale 20th April

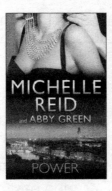

On sale 20th April

On sale 20th April

Save 20% *on all Special Releases*

The World of Mills & Boon®

There's a Mills & Boon® series that's perfect for you. We publish ten series and with new titles every month, you never have to wait long for your favourite to come along.

Blaze® Scorching hot, sexy reads

By Request Relive the romance with the best of the best

Cherish™ Romance to melt the heart every time

Desire™ Passionate and dramatic love stories